GRAFFITI PALACE

GRAFFITI PALACE

A.G. LOMBARDO

A complete catalogue record for this book can be obtained from the British Library on request

The right of A. G. Lombardo to be identified as the author of this work has been asserted by him in accordance with the Copyright, Designs and Patents Act 1988

First published in 2018 by Farrar, Straus and Giroux, New York

First published in the UK in 2018 by Serpent's Tail,
an imprint of Profile Books Ltd
3 Holford Yard
Bevin Way
London
WC1X 9HD
www.serpentstail.com

ISBN 978 1 78125 857 6
eISBN 978 1 78283 360 4

Designed by Jonathan D. Lippincott

Printed and bound by Clays Ltd, St Ives plc

10 9 8 7 6 5 4 3 2 1

For Echo

Again and again we must rise to the majestic heights of meeting physical force with soul force.

—Dr. Martin Luther King, Jr.

Blackbird singing in the dead of night
Take these broken wings and learn to fly.

—Lennon and McCartney

If ever America undergoes great revolutions, they will be brought about by the presence of the black race on the soil of the United States; that is to say, they will owe their origin, not to the equality, but to the inequality of condition.

—de Tocqueville, 1831

1

The sky is burning. A vast plain of scintillation. But it is only sunset, another rehearsal for some future promised holocaust. The dying light silhouettes towers of iron in rust's glow: great stacks, ziggurats of steel cubes, shipping containers wedged and balanced on pier's edge above the crimson diamonding of the Pacific.

Karmann Ghia turns away from the copper light drowning into the ocean, each lapping wave a sputtering flame that sparkles, dies. The world is a funeral pyre without him—when will he return? She walks along this upper Matson observation deck, her fingertips caressing, tracing a rail of rebar Monk welded last year. White plastic chairs and a table shift in sunset shadows. Below, some of the old cargo containers still advertise faded logos glinting from networks of rust, salt, and desiccated barnacles: SEA-LAND, PACIFIC, MATSON, WESTCON, YANG MING, RAM-JAC, EVERGREEN, PAN-IC (INTERNATIONAL CARRIERS). A city of iron cubicles latticed along the harbor, piled like a giant's stairway in gravity-suspended steps rising toward the burnished sunset, or skewed in angles and intersecting layers; some pitched, half toppled by long-ago-extracted cranes and ship's booms. The steel hulks loom like a metallic warren on the precipice of Slip Thirteen, an abandoned cargo depot jutting out into the smoggy dusk of

Los Angeles Harbor. The shuttered facade of the Crescent Ware-house Company along the East Channel obscures most of the old containers; beyond the protection of these warehouse buildings and the toxic, oiled patina of the channel waters is the city: only scattered buildings and glimpses of knotted freeways shift beneath the haze.

She descends the iron steps welded diagonally down the rusted side of the container, gripping the handrail of old, thin pipeline that Monk looped and welded around the crude stair-case. Dim corridors snake through the labyrinth of the steel boxes, created by confluences of gaps amid the containers, or shipping doors ajar, or crawl spaces through torched holes or peeling iron sides. There are ropes, ladders, stacked crates, purloined boat ramps, illegally welded rebar rungs and handholds, ingress and egress, but these signs of human habitation have been care-fully hidden from the city to the northwest.

Karmann disappears through an open cargo door, down a lad-der through a blowtorched portal, into the darkened nexus of the iron chambers. Electric bulbs strung on wires hanging from freight hooks and eyelets wash her black skin in dark rainbows of blue, yellow, green; she's changed some of these lights with col-ored bulbs, hoping for a festive aura here, but lately it seems to her the effect is garish, carnival; maybe that's just her soul of late.

In the main rooms now, a series of chambers extended by gap-ing cargo doors, containers torn open and welded together at dis-concerting angles. Windows torched through iron reveal views into other containers or sometimes the smoggy blue continuum of the channel waters and sky. An old sofa, tables, dusky lamps. Black-and-white shadows flicker from the Philco TV—Elizabeth Montgomery twitching her nose in *Bewitched*—hung with baling wire from a ceiling hook high in the corner, silent, volume down, its jangled antennas looped with wire snaking up corrugated iron walls for patchy reception. Some of Monk's friends mill about, drinking Brew 102 or Pabst or some of Karmann's Electric Purple lemonade from a glass bowl on the dining table, smoking cigarettes—although Slim-Bone over by the old fish-crate shelves splayed with crumbling paperbacks has just lit up a joint—the babble of conversations echoes, reverberating inside the steel walls, everyone's voices metamorphosing into a kind of amplified clang that has seeped into her head, one of those migraines that will take a day and a bottle and a pack of cigarettes to muffle away. Atop a converted old crab trap is the hi-fi, the turntable playing a scratchy Miles Davis riffing on "Boplicity." Cheap portable fans waft smoke up through vent flaps sheared open in the ribbed walls or through welded windows and opened hatchways. More guests appear now, like pirates storming a besieged vessel, men and women swaying up or down from planks and ladders, twisting down knotted ropes, appearing at the bases of staircase crates, laughing, talking, bearing bottles of wine and plates of chicken and ribs and corncobs. Always a rent party somewhere in the 'hood, and tonight it's Karmann and Monk's turn, sharing food and drink, even stuffing a few Washingtons—if you can spare them—in a fishbowl on the table next to the pile of green-for-money rent-party invitation cards, just enough to get a soul through another month, though Monk doesn't pay any rent, since no landlord knows about Box Town, but the money bought food and gas and wine and cigarettes and records and bail, maybe a few bills stashed in the reserve for any needy soul's emergencies.

"Hey, Slim-Bone," a new arrival, a young man in a purple silk shirt, calls out as he tosses another green rent card on the table's pile:

> **Don't move to the outskirts of town**
> **Drop around to meet a Hep Brown**
> **A social party by Monk and Karmann**
> **Saturday. Latest on Wax. Refreshments.**

The rent party ebbs and flows through several levels of iron lozenges: couples caress on backseat divans torn from gutted cars, dance to Motown blaring from radios, rise toward observation containers to toast the sunset or descend into sublevels where old mattresses and piled pillows and hammocks tucked away in shadowy metal corners wait like silent confidants for the new scents, pressings, and stains their lovers will bring. The electric bulbs blink and sputter with voltage stolen from surrounding harbor grids, feeding into shipyard transformers and underground vaults and through portals and under gangplanks of dry-docked, decommissioned navy ships: a discotheque effect, strobes of rainbow lights flashing, illuminates faces beaded with sweat, clear plastic cups sloshing dark wine, glistening black Afros, silvery strata of cigarette smoke, purple eyeliner, silver and gold chains webbed in moist chest hair glinting from open silk shirts.

"Hey, Karmann." She frowns: Felonius, one of Monk's more disreputable friends, swaggers up to her; Lamar, already stoned, hangs on to Felonius and stares down at her, his lips—always mumbling in some kind of incomprehensible drugged soliloquy—twisting into a demented grin. The reflected lights seem to sparkle in Lamar's black sunglasses and greasy, slicked-back hair.

"You like a widow, ol' Monk's never home." Felonius's gold tooth seems to always siphon off her eyes and then all her thoughts, unweaving, until Felonius dissolves, leaving only the glimmering nugget of gold twinkling out of existence whenever his upper lip obscures the precious metal.

"A black widow?" Karmann smiles. Behind her, President Johnson speaks in muted silence, staring down at the party from the Philco TV, then a storm of static reveals grainy footage of Huey helicopters hovering over rice paddies.

"Girl, ya all could do better'n ol' Monk." He pulls the ring tab from a can of Pabst, foam bubbling up as he pours beer into a plastic cup. "Ol' Felonius, for example, I'm a community activist—"

Lamar nods, then retreats into a mumbling conversation with himself.

"Is that what they're callin' unemployed now?" Karmann laughs, sipping her wine.

"Oooh, tha's col', baby." Felonius grins, gold tooth winking. "I'd shower you with rings and treasure, baby," slipping the beer can's pull ring on her small finger.

"Shower yourself first. With water." Karmann smiles, drops the pull tab into his plastic cup, and threads her way back to the phonograph to change the record. She sets the needle to a new album one of the girls has brought, and Sam Cooke's "Little Red Rooster" reverberates through the iron rooms. Marcus and his girlfriend Dalynne materialize through cigarette smoke with a bottle of wine. "When's Monk comin', honey?" Dalynne fills Karmann's cup.

"When he gets here, I guess." Dalynne and Marcus are already stoned, their black eyes shriveled like those famous raisins in the sun.

"Chasin' graffiti, huh?" Marcus shakes his head. His woolly beard drapes to his belly, flecked with gray. "What's he studyin', he say? Signology?"

"Semiotics. The study of signs." Her Monkey, Monk and key, an initiate searching for keys to unlock each signpost, an anchorite lost in a profane world.

"Signs? You mean like stop signs and shit?" Dalynne laughs, her straightened, chopped hair bobbing on her shoulders. "Girl, how he gonna get out of the ghetto lookin' at signs?"

"It don't matter nohow, because we're in the fourth generation." Karmann sighs. Marcus is going to pontificate again. "You see, it's only been four generations since Lincoln freed the slaves, not enough time. Gonna take ten generations, according to my calculations. Our future's still a slave's future. We throw these parties 'cause we never been taught to keep money, the plantation store always kept our money, ya see? We leave our wives, girlfriends, 'n' babies, 'cause back in the old days the boss man'd

break us families up and sell us down the river. Monk's still fightin'
it is all."

"You better talk sense or this girlfriend's gonna leave *you*."
Dalynne scowls at Marcus.

"Tha's why a brother's got to have sisters and babies all over
town. It's that ol' slave reflex of makin' lots of babies 'cause the
mastah gon' take 'em from ya—"

"Bullshit!" Dalynne, spilling wine. "Black man just like any
man, can't keep his dick in his pants!" She grabs the bottle from
Marcus but instead of hitting him over the head stalks away into
the smoky haze.

"Hey, man." Lil' Davey—six foot six—nods down to Marcus,
slinking toward the radio.

"See? It's all around us." Marcus frowns, edging closer to Karmann. "Brothers call each other *man* 'cause back in the slave days
whitey called us *boy* . . . now the hippies say *man* this *man* that,
always ripping off the nigger, just like with our music . . . ten generations, Monk'll see, ain't no use fightin' it." Karmann's cataloged
some of the debris in Marcus's beard: caked mustard, tobacco ash,
wine drops, flecks of avocado dip, cracker crumbs. "You know,
Karmann," Marcus says, swaying to the Four Tops, "when I'm 'round
you I can't help myself neither. Onion ring?" Waving a greasy onion
ring in her face. "Maybe we could, ah, dance," Marcus running a
yellow fingernail down her forearm, pressing close to her, the wild
beard blotting out the world.

"Excuse me." She pushes away, weaving urgently past dancers
and smoke. She finally catches up to Dalynne, who's staring out
through a patch of window blowtorched in the iron wall. Dalynne's
arms are crossed protectively across her breasts. "Honey, don't feel
bad." Karmann slips a hand on her shoulder.

Dalynne turns, eyes red with tears. "He's such a pig." Karmann nods, sips her wine. "I need to find a good man, like
Monk."

"He's always gone," Karmann says. "Maybe he's thinking about not coming home."

"Don't say that! He love you more than ever, you both blessed." Dalynne wipes a tear away. "Look at you . . . you hardly even showin'."

Karmann smiles, lights a cigarette, taps one out for Dalynne.

"How you feelin'?" Dalynne lights up and Karmann blows on the match, tossing it through the window, into the harbor darkness.

"Okay, just a little sick in the morning's all."

"You smoking and drinkin' too much, girl?"

"The doctor said wine and a few cigarettes are good, keep down the stress."

"He a white doctor?" They both laugh. "You feel him kick yet?" Dalynne lightly presses her palm into the almost imperceptible swell of Karmann's stomach, then moves it away quickly, a pang of embarrassment or envy in her eyes as she sips her wine.

"Not yet. How do you know it's a him?"

Dalynne laughs. "Well, I guess I don't. You feel the kicks soon. How along are you? Three months?"

"Three weeks more than that."

"Shit, you feel him anytime now. My mama says if you eat a banana every day it'll be a boy."

They laugh and drink wine. "I'm serious." Dalynne grins. "Eat bananas for a boy, lemons for a girl." Karmann laughs, drinks wine, starts to feel better. "You know what? Later we'll go on up to your room. Now listen, I'm serious. Mama told me this too. You lay down and expose your belly. We get a pencil and tie it to a string, and I'll hold it over your stomach. Now if the pencil wobbles around, it's gonna be a girl . . . but if that pencil stays straight 'n' true, it gonna be a boy." More laughter. "I'm gonna find Marcus." She hugs Karmann and wanders through the party.

Karmann sighs and passes through a welded-open hatchway,

toward the kitchen. Down a staircase of crates into a double-wide Sea-Land container where a knot of guests crowd around a Zenith TV precariously balanced atop a six-foot crab cage leaning against a wall, talking, drinking, smoking, eating chicken from greasy paper plates. On the flickering tube, Amos 'n' Andy mug and ham it up, but their lips move in silence, the volume's turned down: Amos's face looks black and bloated beneath the white sweat-stained fedora as Andy, distracted, scoops up a pair of dice next to the bowl of mints, chomping, grimaces, chokes, eyeballs popping out of his black face like white eggs.

"I'm tellin' you, those are cracker actors," someone says behind her, "they put shoe polish on their faces."

"No way," another voice says, "them's black and that's that."

"They was white on the radio, my mama said."

"Yo' mama tol' me last night, 'Oooh, that feels nice.'" Laughter, cursing. Someone dances by, transistor radio half buried in his Afro, Little Anthony and the Imperials blaring "Take Me Back." Amos 'n' Andy fade away and it's that Walter Cronkite at the news desk, the black-and-white cyclopean eye of CBS behind him. CBS NEWS LIVE crawls over and over along the bottom of the screen, half buried in flurries of snowy static. "Hey, turn it up." . . . *bat in Vietnam. Once again, the Pentagon today at three o'clock Eastern Standard Time has acknowledged for the first time publicly that U.S. troops are engaged in active combat in Vietnam . . .* Tendrils of smoke from Cronkite's pipe curl around the network's Cyclops eye, which seems to glare down at the revelers. *Now we take you to our Washington correspondent—*

"Say, Karmann, you lookin' fine tonight." Cooky, swaying in the smoke-hazy nimbus of colored lightbulbs, tall and skinny, like a tree topped with the black manicured canopy of an Afro big as a beach ball. Cooky, for the legendary amount of cookies he consumed daily, hundreds, a superhuman addiction to sugar, a side effect of his darker addiction, heroin. "You better snap me up 'fore I go off to that Vietnam War." Chain-smoking a Lucky Strike.

"Cooky, you're just a stick, bones made out of milk, anyway."
Karmann laughs. Is everyone stoned? Why is every fool here
hitting on her? Felonius, Marcus, Cooky, just a little innocent
flirting here, the wine's getting to that headache of hers. "You're
not going to fight in any white man's war, one look at you they
going to say there's a four-F."

"That mean four fucks? What girl tol' you about my man powers?" Cooky, grinning, takes a pull from a tequila bottle—that
other sweet sister when he's out of smack—he's liberated from
Monk's liquor cabinet. "Well now, I'd fight if I was an American
citizen but I ain't because us niggers been denied our citizen
rights," exhaling smoke. "I can't see the system because it can't see
the black man. Only draft this nigger's gonna feel is if they open
the window down at Willie's Pool Hall." Laughs, snorting, gulps
another amber shot of tequila from the bottle, wiping his wet lips
on a paisley-print sleeve. He holds the bottle up to her lips, an
impenetrable light in his eye that makes her feel off-balance as he
exhales a perfect blue smoke ring that hovers between them.

"No thanks." Now they're stealing Monk's liquor. "Excuse me,
Cooky, I have to serve up some chicken." Karmann moves past
more people, through thunderheads of marijuana smoke, which
now masks the cigarette smoke in bands of thick gray strata that
ring the containers. She drains her wine cup, migraine thumping,
lights a Kent. The miasma of cigarette and pot smoke and sweat
and booze and incense and fried chicken has for now cloaked the
disconcerting international fragrances of the shipping containers, scents that she's acclimated herself to over the months but
which can be, to the unprepared olfactory nerve, challenging in
their exotic spectrum: traces still linger in each container, hinting
of their past international ports of call—Alaska salmon, crude oil
from Yemen, alkaloid residue from transistor shipments from
Peking, bananas from Brazil, pineapples from Oahu, Goodyear
rubber, chocolate, plastics, cured beef, fertilizers, Detroit engines,
drums of animal fats, Colombian coffee, bales of green onions,

Oregon timber, molasses . . . a mélange of essences more powerful than any pharmaceutical, a fortune's wheel of sensory assaults that alter those who pass through these chambers: states of despair, delirium, ecstasy, violence, eroticism, boredom, anxiety, metaphysical alienation, peace, and feelings she or even Monk can't describe . . . then there are the few containers welded shut, rooms they cannot bear to revisit or are too afraid to even step foot inside . . .

At the kitchen table at last, she lights another cigarette, tops off her plastic cup of wine. *Where the fuck is Monk, anyway? Out in the city somewhere, in his own world, escaping from all this, from a girlfriend and the baby.* Shit, there's Maurice—Fallouja Awahli now that he's a Muslim—approaching, shaking his shaved head disapprovingly: crisply pressed black suit and white starched shirt with black bow tie, gold lapel pin sparkling, engraved FOI, Fruit of Islam. "Dear Karmann—or should I call you Rosaline?"

"Who?" Karmann's looking for a way to escape, hoping one of the girls will saunter over and take her arm.

"Rosaline, who waits in vain for her Romeo even as he falls in love with Juliet. Why do you poison yourself with alcohol and tobacco?"

"My spirit is weak, Maur—Fallouja." Karmann sips wine, trying to exhale cigarette smoke away from his brown forehead.

"Your body is a temple, you should set an example for your black sisters. We must all set an example for our people." *A temple with an occupant,* she smiles wearily. His voice is soft, learned, soothing, always a grin on his lips to counterbalance the preacher born in him.

"I know, I know," Karmann sighs, "I'm living in sin too."

"Ah, yes. Monk should marry you. I hope one day God touches you and you are blessed with many babies, bringing glory and power to our people." Karmann bites her lower lip and smiles. "This is the only way our people will rise from the ashes."

"I didn't know we were in the ashes," desultorily flicking an ash, watching it float down toward the iron floor.

"Forgive me for speaking to you this way, but Karmann, you need a good, firm, godly man . . . a Muslim husband . . . you know I've known Monk since we were children and, well, you know, he's always going off in a thousand directions . . . Monk has no direction in life."

"He's lost, all right, lookin' for a sign." She drains her wine: whenever she starts clipping off those final consonants in her speech she knows she's getting drunk. He's right, Monk does have some crazy notions: buying a barge and floating the containers out into international waters where he could declare the sovereign rights of a separate country, issue passports, turn Boxville into an offshore tax-free bank and floating casino. Her head swims, the migraine a relentless throb of electric pain. "Excuse me, I have to go to the bathroom."

Behind her, Felonius angled, framed in a hatchway, talking on Karmann's wall phone. "Come on, baby, come meet me . . . shit." He drops the receiver and staggers away, the telephone swaying, bobbing against the metal wall like a pendulum. A tinny female voice drones from the receiver: *If you want to make a call, please hang up and dial again . . . if you want to make a call, please . . .*

She weaves down another tumble of crates and into a blue-painted Cronos container. A naked yellow bulb casts a faint gold light in the chamber. A cracked mirror on the wall reflects the navy-gray-painted toilet purloined from an old merchant ship. Nadine, a light-skinned girl in black hip-huggers, dabbles powder on her cheek before the mirror. "See you topside, honey." She smiles, blows a kiss, high heels echo and click away. A stick of incense by the old iron sink tapers smoke. The water reservoir behind the toilet is lidless, no flushing here, gravity plummeting all waste down into the Pacific below: instead the tank is filled with fresh-cut wildflowers and strips of newspaper Monk has carefully cut for toilet paper. Karmann picks up a scrap of newsprint:

Margaret Dumont dead, romantic foil in Marx Brothers movies. Featured in several of the comedy team's movies, Dumont played aristocratic dowagers fending off the romantic orchestrations of the brothers, usually Groucho, as they played a series of bungling suitors competing for her attentions. An open portal reveals the brick facade of the Crescent Warehouse between daisy-print curtains. An oval hatchway is latched closed near the gray navy ordnance of the toilet, two deck chairs stenciled USND on either side. Karmann unscrews the lug bolts and flips the rusted rings, heaving open the iron door. Below, lapping, glinting in darkness, the Pacific. She collapses in a chair, lighting another Kent cigarette, staring down into the lens of the ocean, at the empty chair: where is he? Below, the waters lap and surge. A deep metallic groan shudders through the steel room, the currents pulling, pushing, grinding the pylons somewhere deep below the container's welded mazes. She glowers at the empty chair, a queen waiting for the king's return. Some king. Why is he always leaving her? Going off on his strange tours with his weird notebook and graffiti drawings: sometimes she feels so mad, so empty. Maybe this time he won't come back . . . the baby, it's all finally too much. *Stop it now, stop doubting him.* He'd better move his black ass. The whole world's spinning like her head: all his so-called friends stealing his liquor, feasting and partying, even trying to steal his woman, offering her impromptu rings of promise. He'd better find his way home fast. Karmann drops the cigarette down into the glistening maw, a glowing red ember, then a soft hiss as it disappears into the sea. She'll wait and Monk'll be back, a good man: if any man can read the signs and find his way home again it'll be Monk. Yes, she'll wait, not patiently knitting, she doesn't have knitting needles, but she has a phonograph needle, and she will spin all their records, weaving song by song until his return.

2

Americo Monk stands on the corner and studies the traffic signal: recessed in their steel scalloped sockets, the bulbs follow their programmed progression, green, yellow, red, but something is wrong; the red light flickers with darkness, as if Edison, no longer able to regiment the ghetto's grids, has installed these sputtering *fourth* signs through the city's 'hoods. The signal turns to green. Now Monk can see a blackbird fluttering inside its nest webbed in the light's cowl.

He crosses San Pedro Street, walking east down 112th Street. His worn red Keds seem blood-orange in the dying sunlight. Run-down salmon-painted apartments and power poles flank one side of the street. Every door and window is open, surrendered to the sultry, stagnant heat. He passes a liquor store and a barbershop. Three men hunch on the curb, drinking beers from brown paper sacks. A little girl with no shoes pedals a tricycle past Monk, her reflection passing through his dark sunglasses like a sprite. A languid, suspended summer: Mother's Day—the fifth of each month, when welfare checks arrive—has come and gone, and now the money's drying up; soon it'll be Fathers' Day—parole days are on the first or last day of the month, and black men and long-gone fathers and husbands will return with empty pockets. He pauses, looking up at a billboard that shimmers through the smog behind the liquor store; a student of semiotics, he remembers the sign: a black man posed with a beautiful black woman as they toast a forty-ounce bottle of beer. OLD 88 MALT LIQUOR, in giant letters under their beaming faces, IT'LL KICK YOUR ASS . . . UMPTIONS . . . but some guerrilla urban artist's attacked the billboard, pasting two giant white triangles—masks with black eyeholes—over the faces of the black models, transforming them into cartoonish Ku Klux Klan.

Rampant vandalism. Monk shakes his head, grins. He stops before graffiti sprayed in yellow on the brick facade of a padlocked storefront. Three numbers hyphenated like a birth date inside the drippy double loops of a capital *B*: 6-20-13. Monk opens his tattered blue notebook, a thick sheaf of papers, notes, diagrams, drawings of the city's graffiti and street art: ink and pencil sketches of gang symbols, tagger signatures, homeboy art, margins filled with his crabbed, neat printing about locations, explanations, questions, affiliations, styles, leitmotifs, connections. He thumbs to an empty page and copies the graffito: numbers equal letter placement in the alphabet, 6 *F*, 20 *T*, 13 *M*, FTM, Fuck the Man, *B* for the Businessmen Gang, Watts area, 13 also marijuana, marking territory for drug selling. Monk copies the tagger's autograph: a lowercase *t* with an arrow pointing up, Lil' Tea from uptown.

Turning south, Monk walks on. Sun's setting, he better catch another RTD Freeway Flyer bus back to the harbor. Karmann's gonna be pissed off; the big rent party. He smiles: she's a good woman, she'll wait for him, like that Volkswagen convertible that shares her name, always free and open, not just her legs but her mind, heart, soul. Back home where the containers offer him some faint chance of *containment*, warrens and levels of iron shields that might stop the inundation of signs and input that he suspects will one day drown his sanity in infinite white noise and static; but Karmann, with maddeningly practical female radar, always laughed at him and said no, it wasn't containment that he sought in the iron wrens of the harbor but compartments: his life was an endless series of compartmentalizations, a vast accretion of disparate selves and moments, switching off with every closed iron hatchway and on again with every opened bulkhead. And now the baby coming . . . *Ready or not, boy, it's not gonna wait for you to get your shit together.* His T-shirt sticks to his sweaty copper skin. Summer in the city always seems endless, an unbroken chain of tinder-dry days and humid airless nights, the seasons, nature herself suspended in urban purgatory: his friends had a term for it, *ghetto time*, when minutes, hours, days, and nights fracture and blur and compress into a searing Now—as if the atmosphere itself teeters on the verge of sparking into flames—everyone senses this, a jittery, heat-exhausted edge in dripping faces and dark burning eyes, every soul waiting to be consumed.

On the corner of 113th Street, he stares down at the sidewalk: seven pennies in a row. Above the pennies a tiny Dixie cup filled with water. Below the copper line of coins, a chicken wishbone, a greasy black thread tied taut between the prongs of the bone. Gris-gris, a hoodoo sign, pointing east, watch yourself, Monk.

A car horn blares and he squints up through the dark filters of his glasses: a burgundy '63 Pontiac Bonneville rolls by slowly, windows down, four gangbangers in front and back seats. Two black men flanking passenger-side windows press their fists to the outside door panels. Monk's thumb crooks inward toward his curved index finger as the Buick chugs along the curb. The fists pressed against the passing car doors curl, answering Monk's sign with identical salutes: thumb and finger for G, the Gladiators, all brothers here, cool. The Riviera skulks behind a corner.

He explores this no-man's-land with, if not immunity, then a kind of fragile grace. These tenement streets, abandoned alleys, shuttered brick-fronts, desiccated apartments, frame houses bunkered with grates and iron bars in every window. The gangs—Slausons, East Side Loco Boyz, Eight Tray, and the rest—suffer him free passage, a fleeting transit through their interstices, battle lines and war zones all but invisible except for the sign-posts sprayed on walls, which you ignore and fail to decipher at your own peril. A motorcycle cop sputters on his Harley-Davidson, faceless behind reflecting eggshell helmet—now the cop imperceptibly nods in Monk's direction as he grinds gears east down 113th Street. Officer Reynolds. He knows almost all the cops, they too have sanctioned him safe routes, another gossamer passport through the city's shadows. His clutched, bulging notebook is a badge, papers that usher him past subtle checkpoints and border crossings: the urban graphologist and graffiti semiotician has lately proven of interest to all the city's fractious councils. The gangs and the police need Monk's arcana to track enemies, gather intelligence about new gangs, outlaw splinters, incursions, ever-shifting balances and loyalties and territories. So he moves, a double agent, inviolate—for now—through the city, recorder, code master, pawn: but who is using whom?

At Avalon and 113th Street, two men argue in front of a pawn-shop. "Motherfucker!" They walk down the sidewalk, shouting, hands gesticulating in the air like dark birds. Children laugh and splash around a broken hydrant, water cascading in the gutters, iridescent curtains raining down on soaked cotton shirts and torn pants. Where the pavement meets a low, crumbling wall skirting a weedy vacant lot, a graffito as if folded, half painted on the sidewalk, then extending up the wall: two black spray-painted hands, palms outstretched, thumbs joined in the center like some kind of craning head, splayed with a fringe of fingers like ragged wings, a night demon taking flight. Monk sketches the figure out in his notebook, scribbling the location and the artist's tag in the margins: *smOG . . . Las Sombras.* A legendary East L.A. gang from before the war, back in '41 or '42 . . . Are they coming back? Hard to tell; the Mexican gangs have an added veil of secrecy, their street Spanish. Monk's seen a pattern in his notebook, the black gangs seem to be creating their own Negro, underground slang and symbols, learning from their Mexican rivals. He'd seen smOG's (OG for "original gangster") work only once before. Maybe some kind of splinter group or homage here, tagged on the sidewalk.

Pneumatic brakes hiss, Monk turns: a fire truck idles before the broken hydrant's sparkling geyser. Firemen in soaked yellow ponchos cap off the valve, shooing kids sloshing across the huge street puddle away from falling panes of water. An angry little boy skims a trash-can lid across the puddle, bouncing it off a slick poncho.

Sunset smog glowers over rows of bleached tenement apartments like the spine of some prehistoric behemoth. Avalon and Imperial now, cars and trucks shimmering in the heat. A car horn bleats across the street. Piñatas and purple candy skulls festoon a tiny grocery store; a beauty parlor, Afros ensconced in hairdryers, undergoing secret transmutations; another liquor store; dingy bail-bonds office. Monk passes a shattered telephone booth reeking of urine. *Fuck Bitches* drips cursively on a plaster wall. Sometimes he wants to erase, blot out all these atavistic scrawls of division and hatred, but it's impossible: all he can do is catalog it, try to glimpse the glittering, infinite cosmos of these urban signposts, or be lost, swallowed into the blinding noise of unparsed glyphs. This city is always changing, shedding its skin of underground signs and languages in paroxysms of destruction and rebirth, seething in a secret war between the dispossessed, who write its street histories, and the cops and power structures, who destroy unsanctioned communication through anti-graffiti paint crews and incarceration and intimidation: he will be their historian.

South toward 115th Street. In an alleyway behind a burned-out car hulk, two winos sharing a forty-ounce bottle of that Old 88. One bum leers at Monk: "Brother, can you paradigm?" *What'd he say?* Now the wino's in the middle of what looks like a world-record swig when his companion yanks the bottle from his mouth, foaming beer down his greasy shirt: they tussle, the bottle smashes over someone's head, beer dripping down a chin as they fall backward into clattering trash cans. A black ghetto rat, big as a cat, skitters from the rolling trash cans, glass eyes glittering at Monk as it wedges its rippling fat fur through a hole in the brick wall and disappears like some kind of plague night's apparition: Jesus, is it his imagination or are those monsters getting bigger, gorging on who knows what kind of garbage here in soul town, trash cans full of ribs, grits, fried chicken, Old 88. Monk passes the alley, knowing that the city's signs are sometimes more insubstantial than his spray-painted taxonomy: a fist blossoming into a probing gang sign, a stranger's threats, a child's angry missile, a car horn, a smashed bottle—the city's usual progression of violence as day flees from the sway of night's darker forces. Now, in the final, smoggy prisms of the sun, women return to these blanched apart- ments and besieged homes, retreating behind locked doors and barred windows and security grates: thousands of the city's women returning from work, not men—the Negro men are gone, taken by the police, drugs, booze, the open road, games of chance, pimping, girlfriends, whores, pool halls, death—women returning to their families, to children who no longer ask about Daddy, to silences and empty spaces that deafen and blast their souls.

White concrete traffic barricades have been erected on 115th Street, channeling traffic, a detour toward Central Avenue. Already a Businessmen tag spills across a barricade, no virgin canvas of white immune from spray can and bandanna-masked face: even this graffiti has been answered, crossed out with a clashing, rebel-red swath of paint from the Slausons. Barriers the Depart- ment of Public Works carefully entrenches in key sectors and corridors of the city, coordinating with LAPD not to facilitate flows of traffic but to siphon, control the grids of color: blacks and browns must stay within their quadrants of containment . . . (not yellows, Asian gangs are underground) . . . in secret com- mand centers bunkered throughout the city, municipal controllers hunch over blinking traffic panels and monitors and cold foam cups of black coffee, watching for any breaches, any vehicles that may slip beyond their vectors. Monk makes his way toward the Red Line bus stop. Better get back home: Karmann's waiting. When it comes to women, there's always some man waiting to take your place—better hold on to Karmann, his grounded, swollen-bellied goddess. Across the street, a derelict glares at him, silently rambling, lips sputtering, rants to himself—or is he speaking in some noiseless tongue to Monk? Candles and waxy glass jars encircle the sidewalk corner beyond the demolished stumps of the bus stop— votives left for the dead. Virgin of Guadalupe candles, glass bowls of wax painted with the crucified Christ, dried flowers, faded cards, a Popsicle-stick crucifix. But here there are darker powers mixed with the signs of light and redemption: a dirty string with three knots, seven pennies piled in a stack, an arc of white brick dust gleaming in tonight's dusky shadows, portending a mixed warning to Monk, perhaps a path home more enigmatic and twofold than he'd like.

Monk turns right, trudging down Stanford Avenue. A brother, leaning against the sunbaked brick front of Ace Liquors, nods as Monk passes. Across the street, sunset glows and engulfs jagged rooftops and crooked antennas and looping telephone lines. The parked cars flanking him still radiate today's pulsing heat.

Will cops and gangs let him pass? His notebook is a kind of spy's black book for them, an intelligence coup for cops tracking the gangs' ever-shifting territories and feared alliances, and a grail to the gangs, locked in constant war and turf incursions; so they wait, because the historian must write the history before it can be seized. He's always been able to pass, neither black nor white, through these battle-scarred streets. In certain lights and times of day and angles of refraction he looks Caucasian, sometimes light Negro or copper. His hair is black, curled but not kinky, suspended in loops and ringlets: African, or, in other lights and to other people, disheveled or straightened; others see Mediterranean, white, Arabian—a walking Rorschach mirror that perhaps reflects more of the beholder than the subject; and the eyes forever hidden under those ebony teardrop sunglasses. His grimy red Keds step off the curb now, toward 116th Street. Monk clutches his sky-blue notebook to his sweaty chest like St. Paul with his Bible, his face, like the saint's, wavering, darkening as he trudges into the dusk faintly smoldering with today's last, fading light, deeper into profane pilgrimage.

3

The smog sunset casts the gray-and-white Buick into a strange, faded doppelganger of a police cruiser as the old sedan careens south down Avalon Boulevard. "You better slow down." Ronald twitches a chrome radio knob, the new Stones song, "(I Can't Get No) Satisfaction," throbs from tin speakers: . . . *Baby, better come back maybe next week / Can't you see I'm on a losing streak.*

"Fuck that, my brutha from another mutha." Marquette guns the Buick through a yellow light at Eighty-ninth Street. In the waning light the passing storefronts, weedy vacant lots, billboards, shuffling winos on corners, broken bus benches long abandoned by any municipal buses, everything is leached to sepia tones in the burnished sunset, the car itself darkening from white to gray to a blur of grimy steel veering over the blacktop: ghetto light changes with every second of the sun and even the moon's arc, as light travels through its mediums of smog, heat, iron, black skin, reflecting and refracting on the jagged cityscape in dynamics not yet fully explained by any known laws of physics.

Ronald turns up the radio volume. It's no use talking to Marquette when he's like this, edgy and sullen with vodka and this endless summer's heat wave. At Ronald's apartment, they drank drippy screwdrivers in front of the electric fan in the open window until the vodka was gone, and now they're late reuniting Mama with her Buick.

Marquette lights another cigarette, pointy Florsheim stomping the gas pedal, the Buick lurching through a yellow—no, too late—red light at Ninety-second Street. His gaunt black face glares into the rearview mirror with suspicion, bloodshot eyes hidden under the dark crescent of his folded chocolate brim hat. His saffron Arrow sports shirt is stained with sweat.

Coming south like a burning pinpoint in the sunset, red light and siren Doppler behind them, echoing down the shadowed artery of Avalon Boulevard. "Shit! Cops! I tol' you to slow down, Marquette," Ronald says, twisting back for a look beyond the backseat.

"It's cool," Marquette squinting in the rearview mirror: a motorcycle cop, siren pealing, red light bathing the Buick through its grimy back window. Marquette sucks on the cigarette, pulling over, gently brakes at the corner of 116th Street. "We good," turning off the engine, rolling down the window, avoiding Ronald's anguished face.

The police officer's long black boots push the kickstand and he leans the Harley-Davidson as he dismounts. The cop pulls off his black gloves and slaps them on the motorcycle's saddle. A nose, thin, colorless lips, and a jutting jaw are the only signs of any kind of human visage; the rest of the face is obscured by chin strap, mirror glasses, black-and-chrome helmet. A big man walking slowly up to the open window beneath a dissipating cloud of smoke. 116th Street and Avalon: a few tidy, poor houses on 116th, patched and worn since the boom back during the war when they were built, now have fresh paint but black iron bars brood over all doors and windows; another ubiquitous liquor store on the southwest corner, Joey's Jug; on the northeast corner, at the Muslim Oasis Shoe Stand, the rag buffing a customer's shoe stops as the shoeshine stands, both men watching the Buick and the cop. Heat waves shimmer from the hood in the fading light.

"License, please." The officer leans in closer, studying the two black men in the front seat. "You had this ol' Buick goin' pretty good."

"Think I was goin' only 'round forty, officer," Marquette says, pulling the license from his wallet. He grins but his voice is strained.

"Just sit tight." The cop walks back to his motorcycle, reading off the license number into his two-way radio. Two houses down on 116th, two women step down from their porches, watching the traffic stop from the sidewalk. The thin woman dabs at the curlers in her hair, a fat woman rubs her hands on a cotton apron.

"Don't argue with him, fuck." Ronald's wiping sweaty palms on his trousers.

The officer walks back to the car window. A third man over at the Oasis Shoe Stand watches as he sips from a brown paper bag.

"I smell alcohol on your breath, sir." Only Marquette's face reflects back from the officer's mirrored glasses. Ronald licks his lips. The silence is like an unseen presence hovering between them.

"Fuck," a hopeless whisper from Marquette. "Just a beer, sir," louder, trying to smile. He's careful to keep his hands on the steering wheel.

The officer nods. "How many?"

"Two, only two, sir. Look, officer, I'm fine. I live just 'round the corner. I had a fight with my woman, you know how it is. I ain't tryin' to diddlybop nobody."

"Mr. Bonds, will you step out of the car, please? We're gonna do a field sobriety test." To Ronald: "You just sit tight, okay?" The officer steps back from the door. Two young black men, loitering in front of Joey's Jug, cross Avalon for a closer look.

"Goddamn." Marquette shakes his head, rail-thin body stepping out of the Buick, flicking the cigarette butt into the gutter. He pushes the hat high on his sweaty brow, lips curled in silent anger: the sport shirt is sopped with dark stains of sweat under his armpits.

A black-and-white patrol car coasts south down Avalon and silently pulls over in front of the Buick. The two cops exit the cruiser, one conferring with the motorcycle officer while the other waits near the patrol car. "A deuce." The cop nods.

A man and woman, trailing two lanky teenage boys, watch from another front yard on 116th: the man is shirtless in the sweltering heat, a beer can and cigarette in his hands. The motorcycle officer passes his index finger slowly back and forth in front of Marquette's sullen face. "At this time, Mr. Bonds," the officer squeezing Marquette's left wrist, "I'm placing you under arrest for driving while intoxicated."

"What? I ain't intoxicated!" Marquette trying to free his wrist as the officer pulls handcuffs from his belt.

"Don't fight me!" The motorcycle officer spins Marquette around and pushes him against the Buick's front fender. Two cops are now pinning Marquette against the still warm metal, one handcuff crimped painfully on the thin left wrist as they try to bring the right arm around his straining back. A black boot crumples the brown porkpie hat beneath them.

Now a small crowd has overflowed from the street corners, congregating at the end of 116th, silent in the summer dusk, watching the arrest: an old man with a cane, the lanky teenage boy, a woman wearing an apron as she totes a baby against her sweaty bosom, two men from the Oasis Shoe Stand, children, two men with beer from Joey's Jug, three more women stepping out the doors of houses.

"I ain't goin' to jail!" Marquette shouts, struggling. Both cuffs are now on his wrists as the two cops drag him toward the patrol car. "Police brutality! Mutherfuckers!" His Florsheims seem to kick at phantoms in the glassy heat waves undulating from black asphalt.

"Leave him alone!" Ronald scrambling out of the car. The third cop pins Ronald against the Buick, the officer's baton a stabbing weight that compresses Ronald's chest against the car doors.

"Wha'd I do? Wha'd I do?" Marquette screaming as the two officers try to push him into the rear seat of the cruiser, but now he's kicking, squirming. "I din't do nothin'! Police brutality! White mutherfuckers!"

"What the boy do? Leave him be!" someone yells from the crowd.

A cop knees Marquette savagely and the prisoner screams: for a second his eyes flash with some other light, a fathomless brilliance, as if conjuring to unleash some otherworldly force into the vacuum of the retreating day . . . He collapses into the rear seat of the patrol car.

"They killin' him!" The crowd surges closer. "Tha's my baby! My baby!" A woman breaks through the crowd, a big woman with curlers in her oiled hair, gray sweatpants, cotton blouse sticking with sweat to her great heaving chest. The woman jumps on the back of the motorcycle officer, almost sprawling him into the street.

"No, Rena! No, Mama!" Ronald hurls free from the baton and runs to the woman, now on the ground, screaming as she's hand-cuffed.

"She didn't do nothin'! Police brutality!" a woman screams from the crowd. "Just like Selma!"

"Get out of here fast," a cop hisses to the motorcycle officer. Marquette, Ronald, Rena are all jammed in the backseat of the cruiser, pounding on windows. The Harley-Davidson coughs, revs up, peels away, down Avalon and into the darkening horizon. As the two cops scramble into the cruiser, the crowd surges around the patrol car, a fist pounds on the trunk.

"Just like Selma! Motherfuckers!" Now, as the police car squeals from the curb, a can of beer arcs from the crowd and into the twilight, amber spirals corkscrewing out like rocket fuel—a final tendril of sunset gleams from the tin can, then it bangs against the roof of the black-and-white as the patrol car flees into the night in its beacon of ruby light.

It is night.

The crowd spills forward. "They beat that woman for nothin'!" A woman's shrill voice: "She pregnant!" Bottles and a rock fly toward the cruiser but it's too far away now.

There will be no more light.

4

On the corner of Stanford and 116th, Monk hears a siren: sometimes the sirens seem like inanimate muses, calling, directing him
toward scenes of police action or tragedy where he finds some new
or strange graffiti for his notebook—but this wailing fades north
to silence. Studying the pavement, an iron fence, peeling houses
across the street, a bullet-riddled stop sign, its pole bent by some
old automotive assault so the sign tips to the west. Monk heads west
down 116th: signs are everywhere, it's just a matter of tuning oneself to receive.

Near Avalon he stops. A huge crowd throbs in the intersection,
people shouting. Bottles explode against brick like muffled mortar
rounds. At the corner he pushes through a knot of shirtless young
men, beer bottles clutched in hands. "What's goin' on, man?"

"Fuckin' cops killed some brothers and a pregnant gal." Cars
glide along Avalon, slowing down as they pass the gathering crowds.
Across the street, a heap of trash is on fire in a vacant lot, tapering
black smoke in the darkness like a funeral pyre.

A green Ford Falcon slows, a young white couple staring out
at the fire and the throngs. "Go home, whitey!" someone shouts
behind Monk. A rock bounces off the Ford's hood and the car
accelerates away.

Monk heads south, down Avalon, no signs literal or otherwise now, just away from the crowd, which seems to be growing with each passing moment, spilling up and down Avalon. He can feel the fear, a tension in these summer silences between distant sirens. Passing Joey's Jug, a handful of young men smash the windows of the liquor store, grabbing bottles and cases of whiskey and vodka. Across the avenue, at the Muslim Oasis Shoe Stand, a blind man leans propped on his white cane, his steel-wool beard and crazy, duct-taped black glasses seeming to nod over at Monk. Distant sirens echo, coming from the north. Behind him, a wall of flames licks up toward the night: the vacant lot is engulfed, a pulsating orange carpet of fire.

It is Wednesday, August 11, and this is ground zero.

Three cop cars wail past. Up ahead, sounds of shattering glass as two men run across the dark band of Avalon between street lamps. Avalon is not a good place to find an RTD Freeway Flyer. Monk heads west on 118th, then south on San Pedro Street. Sirens peal in and out of the humid blackness that presses like a shroud against Monk. At 119th, two brick-front stores, a furniture place and a pawnshop, are engulfed in fire, flames and black smoke billowing from shattered windows. Another mob converges over sidewalks and the street; a knot of men rock, then turn over a parked Ford Fairlane. Fear and excitement, a visceral electricity shocks through him as he walks faster, shaking his head: *Man, what the fuck is going on here?* Two patrol cars screech sideways, blocking the intersection: four officers scramble out, forming a line, leveling shotguns at the crowds running, breaking up in the darkness like night phantoms. Monk is skulking along the shadow line of an old tenement, hoping to slip past to 120th Street. As he passes a dingy doorway, a whisper: "Brother, come inside, take sanctuary."

Monk turns: two huge black men in ebony suits and bow ties, wearing purple fezzes. Their coat pockets are stuffed with pamphlets bannered *Muhammad Speaks*. Before he can answer, huge hands guide him gently but forcefully down steps and through the peeling door, Monk clutching his blue notebook with its sheaf of renegade and unspiraled paper to his chest like a shield.

Inside the apartment has been converted into a great lobby, wall lights shaded with blue cloth sconces, casting a cobalt sheen on rows of purple-painted doors and bronze-tinted tapestries unfurled on cracked walls. The two giants escort Monk through the lobby, past conference tables, men hunched over stacks of papers and open files, men on telephones or sitting at small tables, legs crossed, drinking from teacups: all black men, no women, everyone dressed in dark suits and bow ties, crew-cut hair, no banks of cigarette smoke, no beers or cocktails on tables. Monk notes the purple fez many wear, with its crescent and star symbols, and the gold letters pinned to lapels: FOI, the Fruit of Islam.

They lead him through two great paneled doors and into a large foyer. In the center is the biggest rug Monk's ever seen, woven in a web of interlocking Arabic glyphs and symbols. He resists the urge to copy the strange script into his notebook. Sitting at a massive oak desk in the heart of the dizzying rug, a shrunken old man gazes up at him with milky, rheumy eyes shadowed beneath his purple fez. "I am Elijah Muhammad," rising, extending his hand. "Welcome to the temple."

"Nation of Islam." Monk, shaking his hand. "Monk."

"You've heard of us? Allah be praised!" Elijah beams. "I am gratified whenever fine young black men have heard the word. Please join me for some hot tea. You must rest a short while, it is dangerous to venture outside now that the great siege has begun," steering him by an elbow toward a tea table near another closed door. A basket of fruit on the table, figs, dates, apples, oranges. No bananas: the profane, phallic fruit banned from all Islamic tables.

"Great siege?" Monk protectively places the notebook on his

knees under the table. Another FOI enters through the great doors, balancing a silver tea set, past those two bodyguards, who now flank each side of the door.

The FOI pours tea: all these matching suits, bow ties, crew cuts, they all look like undertakers. "Thank you, Brother Shabazz." Elijah nods curtly and the server stalks away silently. "You are aware of our teachings?"

"Oh, you know, just what I hear around the 'hood." Sipping tea, waiting. *I'm being interrogated by a man wearing a purple fez and a bow tie.*

"We, in the Nation of Islam, are always eager to recruit clean young men, such as yourself, Mr. Monk."

"Well, I ain't so clean, Mr. Muhammad," passing dirty fingers through his long locks.

"Your hair is only an affectation of the ghetto. It is easily cut. It is only a pathetic trend from Africa, the atavistic fantasy of the jungle nigger."

"Well, maybe I'm just too jungle for your organization, ah, I'm just tryin' to get home, sir." Monk steals a glimpse of the bodyguards still framing the doorway. *How the fuck do I get out of here?*

"And where is home, young man?" Pouring more tea in both cups.

"Ah, around Los Angeles Harbor." Monk's fingers secretly glide over the springy spine of the notebook under the table.

"It will be impossible to reach your destination tonight. Please accept the hospitality of Islam and stay the night. You may have your own comfortable room and a good dinner. In the morning, it will be safer to continue your journey. Tonight the first battle has begun of a long-prophesied war, the siege has begun. Tonight will be the Night of the Jinn, the night of the fire demons."

"You keep talkin' about this siege, man." Monk sips the hot tea; the old crank's drinking from the same pot, so it must be safe.

"Young man"—setting down his teacup, a disturbing light

dancing in his eyes—"you are witness to the end-times prophesied in the book of Muhammad . . . the final war between black
Islam and our oppressors, the degenerate white Christian race.
The epic confrontation of good and evil, a struggle that has raged
since the Crusades and further back into the millennia." Narrowing his wizened eyes suspiciously: "You are not an idolater or have
been brainwashed by their white Jesus, have you, brother?"

"Well, ah, I'm kind of on the fence, cosmically speaking."

"I was young once and full of mystical fantasies," smiling, "but
you will see the path. Watch and see how your brothers and
sisters are treated by the white oppressors. You will come to Islam
in time. Don't let them kill your spirit with their false gods. They
will try to teach you love and compassion, to turn the other cheek
so they can strike it with their police batons. Don't pray for and
love your enemies, destroy them ruthlessly before they destroy
you. That notebook: the brothers think you are a police spy, but I
think you are a writer. May I?"

Monk frowns, sizing up the old man, like a dark wizard in his
purple cap. He slides the blue notebook across the table. Elijah
thumbs through a few pages of graffiti symbols neatly copied in
pencil and ink, labels and arrows, margins scratched with his
cribbed, voluminous notes. "I study graffiti and gangs, I'm kind of
an amateur urbanologist."

Muhammad flicks through the notebook and loose papers, as
if searching for something. Monk, getting that sour feeling in the
pit of his stomach, reaches tentatively for the notebook. Muhammad frowns, closing it, slides it to Monk. "I know who you are
and what you do. These too are signs long prophesied by the
holy book. When cities begin to sprout this filth, it is the cancer
manifesting in the body. It is the first sign of the beginning of the
end. Rome too had these obscenities scrawled on every column
and portico before the end." Monk remembers a photograph in a
history book, an ancient graffito carved into a Roman basilica:
Illegitimi non carborundum—Don't let the bastards grind you down.

Elijah shakes his head. "These gangs, brother killing brother, black against brown, young man, all this too is part of their conspiracy. It is not an accident that whites have isolated us in urban zones, eliminated any economic or industrial bases from these zones, then flooded us and the Mexican *hordes* from the south with cheap guns and unlimited drugs. The Nation of Islam is the sword of the new Negro. The white man and Uncle Toms like Martin Luther King, Jr., have anesthetized the Negro. Their dreams of a Negro middle class and integration are just that, my son— dreams. Only the Nation's way will bring us salvation, will smash white imperialism." Monk drains his tea, nods, forces himself not to gaze toward the guards and the doorway from the temple. "Some will accuse the Nation of fomenting the coming rebellion. They will say the Nation cached arms and explosives, that we ordered gangs and secret undercover operatives to fan the flames of revolution. They will use their white propaganda machines to try to destroy us, mark my words. Perhaps," the old man sighs, sets the teacup on its plate, "you will set the record straight in your book."

Elijah Muhammad stands. "I have prepared a room for you," beckoning Monk to follow.

"Ah, I really should get goin', sir." *Get the fuck out of here, boy, get*— But Monk can't think, the old man keeps talking . . . it's as if Monk's mind has slowed, submerged in some kind of foggy static . . . everything is confused, jumbled . . . how can he be in this Islamic temple in the middle of the ghetto? What is really going on outside in his city? The spark of some kind of riot . . . or the gathering of night armies into a great race war?

"You are not a prisoner. But please stay, if only for a hot meal. I've already made arrangements. Leave after you gain your strength, or in the morning, I hope, when it will be perilous but safer. You are under, as the white man's TV commercial says, no obligation." Muhammad opens another door.

"Thanks, sir, but I—" Monk walks inside a large apartment,

soft lemon light dimmed by a thick curtain over a window. In the room's center is a dining table, a service of silver domed platters, porcelain plates, and cloth napkins neatly pyramided, set for two: sitting facing him is a black woman, her red lips and jade eyes made even more strikingly beautiful by the hijab covering her hair and neck. The abaya Muslim gown she wears covers her entire body, but even this medieval armor can't disguise the voluptuous curves under heavy black cloth. The door clicks behind them.

"Laylah Nefertiti," extending her hand. The faintest smile plays under her eyes.

"Americo Monk." The food smells good as he tries to clear his mind: *Think, boy, get the fuck out of here, back on the street before that shit out there gets worse.*

Her smile broadens. "A name at once ecclesiastical and adventurous. Please sit down, eat." She uncovers silver platters: orange roast duck and roast beef garnished with onions and carrots.

"Ah, I really need to get goin', ma'am," glancing at the door.

"Don't worry about Elijah." She laughs, forking a pink slab of beef onto his plate. "There is no relationship, we are . . . free agents."

Monk reluctantly sits down, his notebook next to his plate. "What, no clams or oysters on the half shell?"

She smiles. "So the old man gave you the usual speech," scooping vegetables onto his plate, "about the Nation."

"Yeah, I guess." He's starving. *A hot meal, I have to eat something, then I'm out of here.*

"Elijah is a fanatic. Be careful, when fanatics have power, they are dangerous." Nefertiti pours Monk a cup of hot tea.

"You dislike him." Monk sips tea: beyond the draped great window, muffled sirens wail in the night.

"The Nation only cloaks itself in religion, it is a political organization. Elijah only cares about amassing wealth and power and, of course, concubines and beautiful consorts." Her green eyes sparkle above the steam from her teacup.

"Well, you are beautiful. You don't have to lie about having no relationship." Monk smiles, slipping a carrot in his mouth. "You his wife? Is that why you hate him?"

Her eyes flash. "I apologize. You are not a fool. I am not his wife, only a mistress. One of many. He has twenty-one children out of wedlock. He's planted what he likes to call his divine seed in half the women in this ghetto. He sermonizes against *zina*, Islam for adultery." She forces a bitter laugh. "Women are chattel for breeding. He treats you like some princess out of the *Arabian Nights*, but if you get knocked up you're back on some bus bench on Crenshaw Boulevard. I am lucky. I cannot become pregnant, so he gave me the Islam name Sh'laylah, Laylah, Lilith, Hebrew for 'night.'" A rueful smile. "The succubus that lay with Adam and begat Cain, the first monster unleashed in the world. He is the satyr god, whose holy mission is to multiply the fruits of the Nation, to create some crazy future dream of a world ruled by black men."

Nefertiti stands, pulling him up, whispers in his ear. "You are in danger, come, where we can talk." She leads him to a pile of giant gold-embroidered pillows where they sit near the draped window. "He won't stop until you've joined the Nation, he sees you as a possible caliph, a kind of successor, perhaps." She nods over to the notebook on the table. "You are a young scholar, as he was. Beware if you betray him. Six months ago, Brother Malcolm discovered his dirty little sex life and was assassinated." Her lips move close to his, her lilac scent envelops them, jade eyes drooping sensuously. Beyond the window, a faint cry of sirens. "The only way you can be safe is to become a Fruit of Islam."

She claps her hands and another door opens from an adjoining suite: two other black women in translucent silver sarongs prance into the room, wiggling down into the golden pillows between Monk and Nefertiti. Hands with copper bracelets caress his thighs, lips brush against his as a tongue from somewhere nibbles on his left earlobe.

"Ah, ladies, I should be going." Monk presses back as gauzy breasts brush against him. "I have a woman waiting for me at home." A siren, muffled beyond the draped window, screams forlornly as it dies away: *Sirens, too many sirens, can't think.*

"How *jejune*." Nefertiti's green eyes blaze as she stands and claps her hands twice. The two girls rush to their feet, then are gone. "Pity, I must be losing my gifts." Laylah Nefertiti stalks to the doorway. The door closes behind her exquisite abaya-curved secrets.

The adjoining door opens again: a black arm spills from a silver silk sleeve, bronze bracelets jingling, her hand motioning him. "Quick! Follow me! A fire escape."

He follows the woman through a dark, musty corridor, terminating in a blacked-out window. "Hurry!" she whispers as he bangs the rusted latch free and pries the ancient window open. "Be careful, the Nation wants your notebook. They are dangerous. They are stockpiling weapons, he's planning some kind of race revolution." Monk's making a heroic effort to focus on her frantic eyes instead of the dark nipples heaving under diaphanous folds. "You've written a phone number, somewhere in your notebook. You must call the number, keep trying until someone answers. He will help you."

"Who?"

"They're coming!"

Monk jams the notebook under his belt and he's over the fire escape's rusted railing, out into the night. The sirens are louder now, as if converging upon him. Hanging from the fire escape he sees, below the dark strip of 120th Street, a few street lamps flickering toward Avalon: somewhere to the east is an orange radiance, fire beyond the tenement blocks ahead. A metallic thumping, and he gazes up. Elijah Muhammad stands on the grating, purple fez gleaming in the night like some wizard's cap as he raises some terrible weapon to smash Monk's hands gripping the warm rails. Monk lets go, drops to the next railing six feet below, grabs hold, legs locking around the rusted ladder as it creaks and echoes, pulling away from the brick walls with a terminal groan of distressed bolts.

But it's not a weapon raised above Elijah's fez, it's a guitar Monk sees as the old calypso troubadour slings it around and starts strumming. "You'll be back, my son, into the Nation's waiting glory."

A final, terrible iron groan as the rusted ladder fails and Monk plummets toward just another ghetto death here by misadventure: not free-falling, the ladder telescopes down, gliding Monk past bricks and windows until the rungs jar and lock to a stop, extending eight feet above the sidewalk where he sprawls. Up and he's running, cuts into an alley off San Pedro, calypso guitar and the old imam's sweet falsetto fading into the night. Blocks ahead is Main Street. He walks toward the distant lights and sirens, his fingers brushing the notebook still safe beneath his belt.

5

East on 121st Street to Main Street. Sirens wail from the north. On the corner, a crowd of young men drinking beers, huddled around a transistor radio crackling music from the curb. Monk heads south on Main, past a cubbyhole shoe-repair shop, front window smashed, display shoes gone, only a single ivory wingtip on the sidewalk. Cop cars speed past, sirens and lights flashing. Across the street, a crowd in front of Mama's Boutique, a dingy thrift shop: someone hurls a trash can through the plate-glass window. Up ahead, the yellow-and-green neon sign of the Tote 'Em Mart, still open. Monk ducks inside, past the plastic totem pole jutting crookedly near the glass doors: plastic Indian faces leer down at him, grinning redskin masks that betray no memories of prairie genocide.

"We are closing early," the dark Indian clerk lilts in his Babu, north India accent from behind the counter: Ganges Slurpadavedjahpad gazes anxiously out into the night beyond the still pristine front plate-glass windows. Monk pours a small inky coffee from the machine. The store is empty except for two little boys at the soft drink machine. The children grab jumbo plastic cups and fill them, passing them under every plastic nipple along the machine, frothing jets of cola, root beer, lemon dew, cherry,

Dr. Pepper, riffling up and down the spigots like virtuosos flaying a piano keyboard. "Hey!" Ganges waving his hands, shooing the kids away from the dripping machine.

"Come on, Mr. Ganges," one boy pleads, "make us one of your Indian drinks." Ganges's drinks are popular in the neighborhood, a little invention he stumbled on one day a few months ago when he was cleaning the soda dispenser: drinking a jumbo lemon-lime chock-full of crushed ice, he elbowed it down the hopper of the vanilla ice cream machine. Cleaning the tank, glops of green slime were collected in a bucket. In a moment of madness or inspiration he dipped a cup into the sludge and tasted. He started making the concoctions for the kids, who nicknamed it "Slurpee" in his honor.

"No time," waving the boys out the door, "drinks are free today from Mr. Ganges, see you tomorrow." Ganges locks the door, peering out into darkness. To Monk: "Please hurry, sir, we are closed."

At the counter with hot coffee, flipping through his book for a small scribbled note he dimly recalls in a lower margin: there, a double-crucifix graffito from Rosecrans Avenue, the letters *SK* for the Sand Kings, a neo-Nazi gang, and the number 7339969. He remembers the Kings are desert rats, mostly around the Mojave area. The double crucifix is a telephone pole.

The plate-glass front windows implode in a shower of crystals. "Discount night, motherfuckers!" A voice in the crowd pushing in from outside.

"The back way!" Ganges shouts. Monk runs after the clerk. They head through a door stenciled THE SOUTHLAND CORPO-RATION, "THE SOUTH SHALL RISE AGAIN."

Ganges bolts the door. They're inside a darkened stockroom, dim light filtering through a grimy skylight above. Ganges presses a finger to his lips, signaling silence, grabs Monk's shirtsleeve, pulling him deeper past boxes, stacks of foam cups, syrup jugs, cartons of cigarettes and candy and Twinkies. They slide down a rear wall behind stacks of metal shelves.

"The South shall rise again?" Monk whispers.

"I know," Ganges shakes his head, "very bad company." He stares nervously at the bolted door in the shadows. "I am the first Indian to buy a franchise, the white stockholders are very unhappy," whispering. Monk smiles and nods. "When I bought my store they required me to go to this board meeting in Texas. Have you ever been to Texas?"

"No." Beyond the door, muted sounds of shelves clattering to the floor, running steps.

"It reminded me of what we Hindus call *Naraka*, or hell." Monk laughs, then covers his mouth, too much noise. "A circle of old white men, they forced me to pray with them . . . I was very frightened. They informed me that they are changing all the store names to Seven Eleven . . . with the seven a number but eleven a word, an alphanumeric code because they believe the world will end on the seventh day of the eleventh month." They listen and watch the bolted door, but there is only silence. "So I said, 'Okay, November seventh, but before I purchase my store, can you tell me what year?' But they would not say." Monk grins and nods. "Very strange and alarming men," Ganges whispers. "I think they are gone now." They walk to the door and Ganges slowly slides back the bolt and cracks open the door, a sliver of light spilling over his black eyes as he peers outside. "Oh my Ganesha, my store," he moans as they step out. The looters are gone, having left piles of groceries scattered on the floor and display racks crumpled and stomped; sludges of green Slurpee slime and green boot prints everywhere.

"I'm sorry about your store, man." Monk shakes his head.

"Better go now." Ganges ushers Monk through the smashed glass front door, padlocking it behind him. "Terrible," he hears Ganges mumbling behind him, "the Southland Corporation will be very unhappy . . ."

Monk follows a dark alley and he's back on South Main. Mobs of young men spill over sidewalks. Above the rooftops of the shops, businesses, tenements, tapers of smoke curl up from distant blocks. Every rooftop in the ghetto—by secret covenant among white developers, media telecopter units, and the LAPD— is stenciled with huge black address numbers to track the denizens below . . .

Traffic is light, cars slowly rolling down Main. Monk trudges past Sweet Tooth's Donuts, glass doors shattered, the dim interior jumbled and ransacked. As he heads south, roaming groups of young men tote looted bags, boxes, chairs, six-packs, handfuls of merchandise indistinct in the gloom between sparse working street lamps: glancing up, he sees almost every other light's been shot out. What are they doing to his city? He gazes around in disbelief: these streets he loves, these spray-painted codas and rainbow-spangled graffiti walls, the underground voices to hear and heed if one only listened—are they going to burn it all down?

He passes Mercury Check Cashing. The store is in flames, smoke ripples into the night, one or two men still lobbing bricks and sticks through burning windows. No banks here in the ghetto, only these corporate chains that bleed every black paycheck 10 percent before a brother can even buy a beer on payday. Across the street, Mad Mel's Radio & TV disgorges men and women, running, stumbling with loot through the smashed windows as alarms blare, lost in tonight's sirens. On each block Monk hopes the destruction and the mobs will disappear, that this madness is localized, a few burning scars raked through his city, but each new corner brings another burning vista. A little boy cradling a huge radio, walking across the parking lot when this black man in black gloves and an army jacket snatches the radio from the boy and pushes him sprawling to the glass-sparkled pavement.

Monk stops at a stucco wall, takes out his notebook, and sketches on a blank page: the base of the wall's been spray-painted *Farmers* in blue and black; the letter *M* is inverted, for Watts . . . the graffiti is low on the wall, a warning that the gang is new and rising . . . but Monk has his doubts: sometimes gangs paint phony tags as decoys or to draw out traitors . . . he's heard rumors that even the cops are doing it to infiltrate the city. He knows that sometimes signs are like the new physics, that the rules break down; the semiotician struggles in the twilight of uncertainty: message, sender, receiver, meaning can shift, change in time and space.

A lowered purple '61 Impala SS idles slowly to a stop, tinted window rolling down: a huge Mexican behind the chrome-chain steering wheel, bald, black glasses, evil grin above bouncing double chins. "*Que onda puto?*" he laughs.

Monk's terrified, his mind frozen with animal fear . . . he has to *throw* fast, and he better not make a fatal error. He's pretty sure these *vatos* are with Las Sombras, the Shadows gang. He presses thumb to index finger of the opposite hand, throwing up the S sign for Sombras.

"*Buen trabajo, hombre,*" grinning, a gold tooth glinting in the night. "Where you goin', *ese?*" Another banger, a black scarf tied to his head, smiles around a toothpick, bloodshot eyes squinting out at Monk.

"Trying to get a bus to the harbor, man." Monk hopes his edgy voice doesn't betray his fear.

"Ain't no buses runnin' through this shit storm. You never make it tonight, bro. Hop in, we're rollin' some that way." The Impala's rear door opens, a third Sombra, wearing a tank top and cradling a bottle of tequila, beckons him in. Monk steels himself and climbs inside: safe passage once he's thrown the sign, unless they cross any other gangs tonight. The driver's huge body blobs across most of the front seat, wedged against door and steering wheel, black glasses and double chins nodding in the rearview mirror.

The Impala turns, glides east on 127th. Monk stares out the window: on the corner, a wall of mostly young men lobbing rocks and beer bottles at two police cruisers wedged in a V formation in the intersection. The Sombra swigs tequila, rolls down his window, shoots a street lamp out with his .22. "*Pendejo*," the huge driver laughs, turning down Avalon. Police cars scream past. A beer bottle bounces off the trunk. "*Chingaso*," Sombra laughs, passing the tequila to Monk. Monk fakes a gulp and passes the bottle. The Impala thumps over a house lamp abandoned in the street. Turning down a dark, quiet street, looks like Towne Avenue. The lowriders, lights out, creep into a driveway: an old whitewashed Craftsman house, barred doors and windows, four Sombras standing guard in the porch shadows with rifles and pistols, glowering beneath bandanna headbands.

"Please accept the hospitality of Las Sombras before you leave," the giant's gold tooth gleaming as they pass through the iron-grated front door, bars that seem to augur some future incarceration. Monk frowns: another delay, but he has no choice, he tells himself, talking away his fear. His frown crinkles to a faint grin: he's safer with these cholos right now than out there in the streets.

Inside, a dozen Sombras sprawl on ruined couches or stand around in a haze of smoke. The windows are covered with sheets and blankets, tequila and beer bottles and overflowing ashtrays everywhere: there is no air, only a fetid gloaming of booze, sweat, cigarettes. They sit around some kind of long steel ammo box that doubles as a coffee table, littered with bottles and cigarette butts. Young Mexican girls in clinging, sweaty tank tops bring food and beer from the kitchen. "El Gordo Pedo." The giant swigs Jose Cuervo, munching a taco from a plate the girls set on the steel box.

"Monk." Wedged against his back, the cardboard cover of his notebook digs under his shirt, like a blade under his belt. Guitar chords softly strum in a corner: a trio hidden under the great black-and-gold mushrooms of their sombreros, one of the ballad-eers sitting on his accordion.

"This is Slinky," jabbing a fat finger at the Sombra from the Impala's backseat. "Show him, *wey*. You, Quatro!" Quatro, a skinny Sombra in a knit cap, stands, frowns, puts a cigarette in his mouth with a shaky hand that Monk sees is missing a pinkie finger.

Slinky pulls a Slinky from his baggy pants and whips the toy's steel coils through the cigarette smoke. The Slinky flashes an inch before Quatro's flinching face, snapping the cigarette in half as the coils spring back into Slinky's hand like some kind of me-tallic, darting snake. "He spent months sharpenin' those coils to fuckin' razors, man. Quatro's name used to be Pancho," El Gordo shrugs, "but Slinky's gettin' better."

"Pretty soon you can call him Tres." Slinky laughs, drinking tequila.

"Call me Uno," Quatro giving Slinky the finger.

El Gordo grins. "Now, *El Jefe* will pass the sacred *yerba*." He lights a yellow joint the size of a stogie, sucks in, passes it to Monk. El Gordo exhales, filling the room with several cubic yards of dense, sweet smoke. Monk takes a polite token toke, passing it down the circle of Sombras.

Monk's impressed: the drug is incredibly sweet and, well, powerful—the cracks on the whitewashed Craftsman's walls seem to be crawling . . . and El Gordo, is he somehow *expanding*, a giant Buddha with gold tooth and black glasses swelling toward the ceiling?

"This is Coyote." El Gordo points to an empty chair. "He's a ghost. You don't believe me? We see him sometimes, *simon*?" to Slinky, who nods solemnly. "Coyote was a Sombra, man. Couple years ago some *maricón* shot him right between the eyes. *Esos tipos buen tiros.*" Laughter all around. "Those fuckers were good shots.

We were goin' about eighty too. Sometimes he sits there, sometimes we just see the fuckin' bullet hole floatin' above the chair,
like some kind of red eye or something."

"More like a red *culo*," a Sombra says: everyone laughs.

Monk must look skeptical. "You see a lot of strange shit, you
live in the barrio long enough. Ain't exactly your *West Side* fuckin'
Story." El Gordo sucks in the reefer. "Sometimes Coyote rides
with us. Sometimes we leave a cerveza on the chair and it's empty
in the morning." El Gordo's eyes are hidden quotients behind his
sunglasses. "When we roll, he always sits in the front seat, man.
Riding shotgun, that's where he got shot. When we talk, I see
everything differently, it's like," whispering now, "I have three
eyes, this other eye in my forehead where I can see the night and
trees and all around me, like I'm seeing through Coyote's bullet
hole . . ."

El Jefe claps his hands. *"Mi corridistas!"* The trio appears out
of the smoky air, sombreros, Mexican serapes glittering, guitars
strumming, the accordion breathing a snappy bass line. "My personal balladeers, to sing of the glory of Las Sombras gang." The
guitars twang and the accordion wheezes into tune as the three
sing a cappella:

> They shot Coyote between the eyes,
> But a Sombra never really dies,
> Now *El Jefe* has third-eye vision,
> The spirit guides his every decision—

They toast El Coyote as the *corridistas* bow and strum away,
fading toward the corner with a final accordion sigh. "This is some
powerful shit here, man." Monk's grinning. A girl offers him a plate
of flan.

"Yeah, it's this weird albino weed." El Gordo spoons a dribbling wedge of flan. "Only grows in certain places under the sewers. And only we know where," chuckling. "Maybe it's all that

barrio shit and piss and booze and drugs and shit, but it's the weirdest, white, shiny plants growin' in the darkness, almost *glowin'* . . . and man, does it fuck you up."

"The original Las Sombras," Monk takes a small bite of flan, "they go back to the forties, don't they? The Pachucos riots—"

"We are *los originales, ese.* My old man, Slinky's *padre,* Coyote's *tío,*" El Gordo sweeps his flabby arm around the room, "all of us are *la familia de Las Sombras.* I got my old man's zoot suit and fedora hangin' in the closet. Man, those *vatos* had some sharp threads." Everyone laughs. "Sombras were here before the black and white gangs. We go back to the thirties, man. *Sureños* straight outta Mexico . . . It was natural, see? We spoke Spanish, had to protect ourselves. We invented the throws," twisting his fingers into Sombra and Gladiator signs. "We painted the first *placasos,* spray cans weren't even invented, man, back in the day we used fuckin' shoe polish. My old man rumbled in the forties, used to tell me things weren't too bad till the gringos stole Chavez Ravine from us."

"Fuckin' Dodgers." Quatro shakes a pinkie-shorn fist in the air.

El Gordo's black glasses dip in agreement. "Squeezed all the niggers and beaners into the barrios, probably on purpose, hoped we'd wipe each other out. Since then nothin' much has changed, just sellin' a little green dope to put *pollo* on the table, protectin' our turf like everyone else. Sombras don't fuck with you unless you fuck with us. We're family, not a gang."

Slinky uncoils his razor Slinky, bouncing it in a silvery arc from palm to palm: "We're a social club." More laughter, Monk grins.

"Back in the thirties." Monk's eyes sparkle with light whenever he navigates the mysteries of signs and wonders, words within worlds, worlds within words—back in those storied days, when the first Mexican gangs' graffiti used heavy, black Old English lettering and stencils to copy the font of the daily headlines: it was their own underground news, to counter the official, white narrative of the city's newspapers, each morning edition that ranted against the blacks and the Mexicans, all the *hoodlums* that had turned their ghettos and barrios into *squalid districts of shanty-town shame . . . and vandalized every wall with their gangster and drug-dealing underworlds . . .* "That's when El Tirili supposedly founded Las Sombras."

Silence. El Gordo's fat arm frozen in mid-swig of a Cuervo shot glass, Slinky's razor coils retracting on his palm with a final rattle, Quatro's mouth open with a suspended tortilla chip. El Gordo: "What you know 'bout El Tirili, homey?"

"You know, just the legends, what people say." Monk striving for a casual tone here. "I like to study graffiti, the *placasos* and tags around town. Just kind of a hobby. They say El Tirili was the greatest *pintor*. That he started the Shadows back in the thirties. That he disappeared after the sailor riots in the forties, rumor is he went underground, but some folks say he's just a folk legend, never existed."

"He's real, man." El Gordo lifts his black shades, his bloodshot eyes transfixing Monk for a moment, his teal teardrop tattoo like an icy stigma freezing Monk, then the shades drop down. "My old man met him once." Slinky and Quatro nod.

"They say some of his *placasos* still exist somewhere in the city." Monk cautious here. "I'd like to see one. Some people say what he did was amazing, crazy, even—"

"Impossible?" El Gordo nods. "*Simon, ese.* We've seen one or two. Some are hidden. Some we've painted over with watercolor to protect his *obra maestros*. The lettering, his *estilo*, it's what the fuck, Slinky, *sobrenatural*?"

"*Sí, El Jefe.*" Slinky nods. "Supernatural."

"*Vatos* say all kinds of shit about El Tirili." El Gordo rubs his chins in thought. "How his lettering, his pictures have hidden signs of, fuck, *antiguo*?"

"Ancient," Slinky cascading his razor coils around his neck like a metallic python.

"Ancient Azteca powers . . . even the colors, colors like you've never seen in your fuckin' life."

Monk wants to show El Gordo the notebook, two or three tags and bombs he's sketched, where the colors, the puffy lettering seem to shimmer with a depth and geometric gravity of lost jungle pyramids and temples, and dusky artisan hands long turned to dust.

"Yeah, they say some strange shit about El Tirili." Slinky swigs Cuervo. "About *placasos* that are portals, about taggers disappearing into fuckin' thin air—"

"Hey, talkin' about disappearin' in thin air," El Gordo seems a little eager to change the topic, "remember Chicken? Back around '60, when I was just startin' out, one of our, what do you call it, *chinga de madre*, our instigations—"

"Initiation," Slinky scratching his groin, a faint rattle of muffled metal coils.

"Yeah, our initiation was you had to play matador, see. We'd go out in the Chevy, lights off, hammer the pedal, almost sideswipe cars. If you was fresh pussy you had to stick your head out the window and pull back just in time, only Chicken, his timing was a little off." They laugh. Slinky passes the joint to Quatro. "The fuckin' car cut Chicken clean in half. That's how we got our badass reputation, man. The cops said it was, what the fuck?"

"Retaliation," this time from Monk.

"*No te rajas!*" They all stand, chink beer cans and tequila bottles. "You don't chicken out!"

"We seen some shit, *vatos*," El Gordo wiping a tear of laughter from below the black glasses: no, not a tear, it's the faded blue tattooed teardrop.

"*El Carro Fantasma*," Quatro whispers, crossing himself.

"*Simon ese*," El Gordo nodding, sips tequila. A girl leaves another tray and he grabs a giant fist of pork rinds. "One night we was rollin' dark down Crenshaw and this Cadillac passes us, lights out too, then this *pendejo* blinks his lights at us, and it's on, *cabrón.* You know you never light up on a *vato* unless you ready to throw down. So we both skid around and make a pass, I got my twenty-two out the window and Slinky's aimin' his sawed-off, and Coyote, he says somethin' ain't right with this fucker and the Cad goes past us and we blaze on it, and nothin' happens, it's like the fuckin' bullets bounce off and shit . . . and the driver, man, he's wearin' a black hood and it's dark but I couldn't see his face, it's like he had no face . . . So this fucker roars past us, goin' maybe one twenty, hauling ass. Then this cop car flies by us but it's chasin' *him.* So we take off and follow 'cause I never saw a ride like this fuckin' car, man. It must've been a '56 or '57, black, those big tail-fin lights. We got closer and you could see every time this fucker hit the brakes this chrome skull face would light up in the rear window, glowing red eyes and teeth, it was fuckin' tight, man." El Gordo spews out a mountainous cloud of blue smoke, passing the joint to Monk. "And hangin' from the rearview mirror, a huge pair of fuzzy pink dice. So the cops are closin' in behind him and . . . You tell it, Slinky, he won't believe me."

"The pigs are on his ass," taking the joint, now the size of a cigar butt, from Monk, "the Cad belches this black cloud of smoke and the engine screams. The car, it just kind of glided up and it shot through the sky . . . we saw it bank left above Crenshaw and Normandie, weird green flames spittin' from silver tailpipes, then it was gone, that chrome skull head glowin' and grinnin', then nothing."

El Gordo props a huge boot up on the ammo box. "So where you tryin' to go?"

"Get back to my woman." A girl in a sleeveless blue sweatshirt sets a plate of rolled corn tortillas on the ammo box.

"Homemade." El Gordo nods toward the plate. "*Papadzules,* Sombra specialty."

Monk tentatively gnaws an end of the tortilla. Instantly his mouth burns with choking heat. He gulps a beer.

"Hey, Maria!" El Gordo shouts toward the hallway that leads to the kitchen. "He don't like your *zule*."

Monk hears silverware crash from the kitchen, then a woman's shouts: "Fucking *gilipollas criticó mi manjar . . . la verga*—" Maria stands in the hallway with a butcher knife, guacamole and salsa stains on her apron. She steps closer to Monk as Slinky moves beside her, the razors of his metal coils glinting in his palms: Monk, eyes still watering, pushes back against the cushions, his notebook digging into his spine. Maria raises the knife . . . and slips it into her apron's sash. El Gordo roars with laughter as Maria grabs a rolled tortilla, smiles, munches, saunters off toward the kitchen.

"Back to your woman? *Donde?*" The gold tooth glints as it bites down on a lethal *papadzule*.

"San Pedro."

"*No mames*, that's gonna be hard. We're burnin' down this fuckin' city, then there's the Rollin' 60s, the Eight Trays, Gladiators, the Slausons, all the rest of those motherfuckers." El Gordo pours Cuervo. "You gonna need *la mano de Dios*, or *la mano de Diablo*."

Monk staggers to the door, slips through the iron grating. A sphere of ruby light glows all around him . . . inside floats a bandanna-shrouded face . . . El Coyote, the third eye . . . Monk shields his eyes from the terrible, burning orb and runs down the steps.

"*Vaya con Dios!*" Echoes behind as Monk steps toward the corner, coughs, weaves down the sidewalk. As he turns back down 129th, a distant *corrido* fades into the night. Monk shakes his head: *Get your shit together, boy, getting high . . . find a phone booth that's not firebombed or ripped up.* Karmann's depending on him, that rent party's probably some kind of siege by now, his girl surrounded by all his so-called friends. Maybe he's just as bad: how could he leave her like that, pregnant, surrounded by wolves?

If he could just hear her voice, maybe talk to Maurice, he was the most responsible one, maybe he could keep those alley cats in line, though Maurice too always has that look when he's with Karmann—Monk walks faster, toward the diffuse ivory light that must be Avalon Boulevard.

6

South on Avalon. The night is now pierced with a constant Doppler effect of rising and falling sirens. Monk passes mobs spilling back and forth along the avenue, lobbing bricks and bottles and cans at the trickle of dazed traffic that weaves past patrol cars. In the distance, police cars have barricaded the next intersection, a line of officers in black standing ready with shotguns. The night sky above Monk seems to splinter as the air thuds and roils. He looks up: the first *ghetto bird* of the night hovers past, helicopter blades scudding through the darkness, its searchlight fanning across the boulevard like an incandescent tunnel. "The city is under emergency curfew," a loudspeaker blares like God from the sky, "stay in your homes or you will be subject to arrest."

Bottles explode, somewhere ahead a shotgun booms. Monk passes smashed-out windows gaping from dark brick-fronts. Across the street, smoke tapers behind a junkyard. He cuts into a huge vacant lot between darkened store facades, past the trampled chain-link fence, moving east toward distant smoke rising somewhere along Central Avenue.

Monk trudges through weeds and trash-strewn dirt. Past heaps of shattered wood, abandoned mattresses and rusting refrigerators and ovens, old tires welled with stagnant water. Beyond an avalanche of bricks from a broken wall, the earth deepens into weedy darkness: this lot seems to be immense, a swath of weeds, dead bushes, piles of garbage that wind through the city for blocks. Monk freezes: ahead, glowing in the flickering aureole of a sputtering electric lamp, standing in the clumps of weeds and trash, Christ crucified.

A black man in denim overalls, shirtless, arms extended like a cross. Monk can see a strange light coming from a miner's hard-hat lamp glowing on his head. Monk moves closer, skirting around a huge puddle of muddy water that gleams up from the weeds and piles of trash. A mosquito whines past his ear. The apparition moves and the cross is broken: checking his wristwatch, picking up a clipboard next to a silver metal suitcase near his muddy boots. The lamp beam transfixes Monk. "Evening," in a deep voice as the man scrawls something on the clipboard.

"Just passing through," Monk says warily, smiling, just another encounter here with one of the countless madmen who haunt the ghetto night.

"Don't be afraid, I work for the city, dig?" Tapping the metal box with his boot toe. The case is stenciled LAMA: LOS ANGELES MOSQUITO ABATEMENT.

"Twenty-two strikes in ten minutes." The man extends his forearms like a needle addict for Monk to inspect: dozens of tiny red bites up and down his big black arms like some terrible rash. "That's a Class Two infestation, pretty bad." He's buttoning up his work shirt. "They breed in these puddles, old tires, anywhere they can find standing water." He extends his big hand. "Mosley Terrance." A handshake, Monk waves another mosquito from his ear. "Friends call me M.T."

"Don't those bites, ah, bug you?"

"All the time," chuckling. "I've banked a lot of bug juice through the years, I'm immune to the little bastards. Fact, I've got so much insect bacteria in me that they usually get sick and die. LAMA entomologists have discovered squeets are specially at-

tracted to dark skin pigment, it's always us brothers, ain't it?"
Laughing. "Dark skin and body odor . . . so a squeet's idea of the
ultimate bug buffet would be your Negro bum."

"You get paid to kill mosquitoes, cool."

"That's right, but we like to say 'control.'" M.T. squats down
and opens a silver case. He snaps on a rubber glove and extracts
a purple pellet from a glass vial. "Die, you spawn from hell," grinning as he lobs the pellet into the center of the huge inky puddle.
"That'll get all biblical on their bug asses."

"Lot of puddles in the ghetto."

"Yeah, job security. More puddles, drains, sewers, clogged
tanks, abandoned swimming pools, flooded alleys, and leaking
pipes than you can shake a pump sprayer at." He stuffs the glove
and clipboard into the case, closes it, and hefts up the handle.
"Where you goin'?"

"South, toward the harbor."

"Got another call goin' that way, give you a ride. You can be
Mosquito Jesus." He measures the alarm on Monk's face, then
laughs. "Just fuckin' wiff ya," and slaps him on the back.

They trudge in silence for a few minutes as Monk tries to
think. What the hell is happening to him? What was that madness with Elijah Muhammad? Then a risky encounter with the
Sombras gang . . . but it paid off with a ride a little farther south,
and now another ride coming his way, this bear of a man braving
pestilence from the night skies while the city burns. Karmann
always said he's lucky, maybe so, but sometimes he thinks there's
more than luck, he can't explain it, more like a feeling, something
on the periphery, just beyond his grasp: a kind of grace or light
that's kept him mostly on track; he smiles at the strange wonder-
ment of following this ghetto spirit's hard-hat lamp through the
darkness. "This lot is huge," Monk says as they travel east.

"Yeah, we got maps over at the LAMA offices, but some of
these lots aren't on any city maps. When they are, you go there
and they're different, smaller or bigger, always changing shapes, a

wall breaks here and there, someone builds in this corner or that, damn lots is always changing like some kind of creature." M.T. chuckles as they move past a gigantic mound of demolished-building debris. "You see some shit in the 'hood," shaking his head, the miner's lamp scanning across the wasteland of weeds, puddles, broken battlements. "Back in '61 I was out doin' my rounds with a partner, found a vacant lot over off of Willowbrook. There was this big puddle, bigger'n the one back there. He lost his balance, fell in, mutherfucker disappeared. I grabbed a pole from the van, jabbed it into that black shit, hoping he'd somehow grab on, I guess. I couldn't even reach bottom with that ten-foot pole, must've been some kind of weird sinkhole or some shit like that. Later that summer the puddle dried up and there was nothin' there, just cracks in the dry mud, never did find his body."

The lot jags southeast now, past a weed-choked pyramid of old tires, rims soaked with fetid water, and circling mosquito squadrons. A rancid mattress and a heap of rotting clothes and rags. Monk notes the graffiti on a crumbling whitewashed wall: a black, drippy number 8 with a red 3 painted over the 8's right half, sign of the Eight Tray gang. Finally, the street lamps and fugitive headlights of Central Avenue. They scrabble through a trampled chain-link fence and they're back on the sidewalk.

Traffic is lighter, as if cars are abandoning the city. Down the block, police cruiser lights flash as sirens fade. Men lope across the streets like scattered foot soldiers and into shadows; alarms bleat somewhere in the night. Monk and M.T. round a corner: out in the middle of the street, in darkness between burned-out street lamps, the dim outline of a manhole cover pried up, two glowing, feral red eyes blazing at them from the depths, then the demon vanishes, the sewer cover slamming down with a clang of rusted iron. "Did you see that?" Monk frozen.

"Like I said," M.T. heading for a long white utility van parked in the gutter, "see a lot of strange shit in the ghetto." The van's side windows are painted over with LAMA and the city's seal.

They drive south down Central. "Sewer rat." M.T., lighting a cigarette, taps one loose in the pack for Monk.

"That fucker was huge." Monk waves away the cigarette pack.

"They get fat down there," M.T. exhaling smoke. "Seen 'em big as dogs. Willy—he works the South Side—tol' me one time he saw one like a goddamn bear." Outside the windows, looters stream in and out of a ransacked furniture store, toting armchairs, coffee tables, lamps, rugs. "Man, they're tearin' the city apart."

"You've seen them? The rats, I mean."

"Huh? Oh shit, yeah. See, LAMA ain't just after squeets and bugs. We maintain most of the city's infrastructure. Our charter is to eradicate all vermin. Bugs, rats, weeds, bats, pigeons, you name it. Workin' the sewers is the worst, man. Sometimes you see these huge shadows and mutherfuckin' red eyes glarin' at you, some of these shadows on the curved walls lookin' *too big*, them darting eyes way too high off the ground, man . . . you'd fire a few warning rounds and those things would disappear. While back, my flashlight caught one of them tails as it flicked away, must've been six feet long . . . You seen how that bastard lifted that manhole cover with its head? You ever try to lift a goddamn manhole cover?"

Smoke billows from store doorways as Monk stares out the window. "Someone told me there's this white dope growing in the sewers."

"Hey, that's right. *Cannabis albina sinistras*, only grows in ghetto sewers. Down in the West Side, it don't grow in any white folks' sewers, not enough soul food down there I guess. Falls under LAMA's mandate, we're supposed to wipe that shit out too, under the supervision of the DEA," M.T. laughs, "when we're not sneakin' it home and smokin' it. Up on the streets they call it Narco Blanco, Albino Dyno, Rat Smack, White Weed, Sewer Shit, Underganjaground, and Moby Dope. Gangs sellin' and killin' each other over it, mutherfuckers tryin' to grow it but it only grows in the sewers, man. It's a sight, baby. You see these big milky plants growin', clingin' to the sides of those tunnels, roots dippin' in the stream of shit between your boots. Must be some kind of mutant strain of dope. The stems, leaves, buds, it's all this shiny white. Shit gets you seriously fucked-up—or so I'm told," chuckling.

M.T. slams on the brakes as a knot of skinny men in sweaty tank tops bolts across the boulevard. A bottle smashes over the van's hood. "Fuck this." He spins the steering wheel, the van lurches around a corner, down a darker side street. "I know those fucking rats are eating that white weed, 'cause you can see something extra crazed in their beady eyes. That albino hooch makes 'em nuts, you can see mountains of food and garbage they chew through, cans of beer and bottles of booze, some serious-ass munchies . . . you can hear 'em squealin' and humpin' each other against the walls, all they do is party, baby."

This street is dark, subdued under August's balmy night. No lights, only the faint glow from barred windows of little houses. M.T. pulls the van to the curb, parks, shuts off the engine. "I gotta stop for a quick dinner break. Come on back." He opens a cargo door behind the seats and they climb into the rear of the utility van.

The interior of the van seems strangely elongated, receding into booths of rainbow-colored plastic beaded curtains that still sway from the ride. "I dig your beads, man."

"I'll give you the tour." M.T. parts a beaded curtain and Monk follows: a small love cushion and stereo; through another shimmering veil of beads, a still-sloshing water bed bathed in the jade glow of a lava lamp. "For the chicks, baby," slapping Monk on the back. They pass through narrow, zigzagging corridors of tinkling beads: *How big is this fuckin' van?* Monk shakes his head. A beaded cubicle with toilet and mirror; a crescent of beads enveloping a tiny couch in front of what Monk guesses to be the rear window, which M.T. reveals by pulling up white shades. "My love palace on wheels, baby. Every night I just back into any million-dollar view I'm in the mood to eyeball: the beach, perhaps the green cliffs of Palos Verdes, or the city lights over the gods themselves, Mount Olympus."

The maze of plastic beads tinkles apart and they've somehow made it back—to the front. They sit on chairs M.T. pulls from wall panels before a tiny stove, mini refrigerator, and storage lockers bolted to the van's side panels. He pops a ceiling vent, opens the cupboard, removes boxes and packets of tinfoil and frying pans, lights up the stove.

"Hungry?" He pulls spices and bottles from a rack.

"Actually, I just had duck à l'orange, unwisely topped off with some questionable Mexican food," Monk says, grinning.

M.T. cocks an eyebrow. "Too bad. I'm preparing peanut soy steaks with nut glaze, mashed peanut butter squash, and peanut faux rice with spicy barbecued nuts. Yeah, ever since they discovered that Moby Dope growin' in the sewers, strange *events* start gettin' reported with these damn rodents." M.T. ladles steaming food dark as coffee onto his plate; the van fills with the cloying stench of roasted peanuts. "Reports of giant rats appearing furtively at street level, raids into kitchens and food storage, everything chewed and torn apart . . . old ladies and children disappearing in the night, you know, shit like that and the cops hush it up, but every once in a while down at LAMA we hear reports of home invasions, doors gnawed through, windows smashed, only homes and apartments of women alone, you dig, the women sayin' they was *intimately assaulted*, descriptions of red eyes, clumps of coarse hairs in the victims' fists."

M.T. opens the fridge, offers a dark wedge of pie to Monk. "Try this, peanut meringue with honeyed nut husks."

"Quite a peanut diet you're on there." Monk tentatively nibbles the oily pie.

"That's all I eat is peanuts." M.T. polishes off the pie. "Listen, brother, the peanut is a secret soul food—"

"I know, George Washington Carver."

"Yeah, well, did ya know every American Negro owes his life to Carver? Old George was born right at the end of the Civil War, and lucky for you and me, he was obsessed with the nut. Share-croppers was starvin' when he showed 'em how to grow peanuts and make peanut butter. Then the whites tried to steal it from us back in 1895, when that mutherfucker Dr. Kellogg stole Car-ver's secret recipe. See, Dr. Kellogg was a head-shrink, and he discovered that when he fed peanut paste to the lunatics inside his Battle Creek Sanitarium, they became strangely docile . . . then he started that damn giant cereal company and turned the mighty peanut into a goddamn breakfast spread for white kids."

Outside, the muffled sounds of sirens and gunshots sound closer. Monk: "Ah, maybe we should get goin'."

"Okay, let's roll." M.T. clatters pans into the sink, bottles and tinfoil into the fridge, boxes into the cupboard. "Listen, son, don't sell the mystic peanut short. People live to be a hundred and twenty on peanut diets, but the health companies and doctors have it all hushed up." Monk nods: *Don't sell the mystic short* . . . He won't, he'll try to go with it, with this luck or whatever force it is that carries him south. "Somethin' else, peanuts is an aphrodisiac, or what I like to call an *Afro . . . disiac*," chuckling. "You can churn the butter all night, brother." M.T. latches the cargo door behind them. Back in their seats, M.T. guns the van down the darkened street.

They drive south down Parmelee Avenue, paralleling Central. Sirens pulsate up and down Central, to the east. Monk opens his notebook, studying the page he last perused while fleeing through the secret panic rooms of the Southland Corporation.

M.T. glances at the strange graffiti symbols and scrawled notes on the frayed pages. "You ain't a tagger, are you? If so, then I'm aidin' and abettin' the enemy." Chuckles. "'Course, half my damn crews moonlight as taggers, sprayin' everything so in the morning they can clock in and paint over last night's shockin' vandalism. Job security."

"No, it's a habit of mine. The college word is *urbanologist*."

"Kind of an *infrastructuralist* yourself, heh?" M.T. says to Monk. "What you lookin' at there?" Passing 134th Street now: a car crumpled into a wall, a mob pulling the driver out through the smashed window; a parking lot lit by smoke and flames from distant exit doors, shadowy looters pushing shopping carts heaped with boxes and merchandise.

"It's a number I found sprayed on a wall." Monk is dazed, transfixed by the smoke and flames that blur past. "Someone said I should call it." But he's got to call Karmann first; she must be on her second or third pack of Kents, worried about him. His dubious friends there, feasting and boozing. Maybe the party's breaking up, everyone eager to get home. Are they watching the riot on the news? His old TVs barely work. Are they scared? Are their houses cinders? Are their families safe? Maybe all they have is a few radios, three or four brothers always with transistors pressed into their Afros. What if they can't leave? No one knows how far the riot's spread; the whole city could be burning, all the way south to the harbor, maybe Long Beach, the entire coast in flames . . .

On Piru Street, two cop cars block the intersection: M.T. slows but the cops wave the county van through.

"Maybe those cops'll hold 'em back. Looks quieter. Crazy night to be workin' a shift, but here we go, last stop." M.T. pulls the van in front of another vacant lot off Central. "You can cut through here to Hillford Avenue. I gotta go back north up to LAMA."

The lot is black dunes and scrub brush and weeds in the night. Monk sees the dunes are heaps of slag and asphalt and bulldozed dirt left from some past demolition. They trudge through weeds, pyramids of old tires, rotting lumber piles, mounds of trash. M.T.'s silver case gleams under tonight's hidden moon. Blocks of graffiti concrete jut from the earth like spray-painted ruins.

"More mosquitoes to bomb?" Monk carefully skirts a large puddle whose black depths reflect a fathomless night sky. The air reeks of fire and smoke.

"Smoke's a bad sign. Smoke raises the ambient temperature, makes things nice and tropical for squeets. After fires, sometimes we see squeets that are, ah, unusually large and aggressive . . . but this report here ain't squeets, it's worse," M.T.'s hard-hat lamp shines past abandoned rusted rolls of corrugated steel. "Bees."

"Don't like bees." Monk kicks a bottle, staring across this ruined, hopeless scape of all that's abandoned and forlorn in this city: dark weeds strangle over white summer blooms . . . below, black beetles and black widows and black earwigs lurk beneath this rubble, scrabbling in their own miniature inner cities . . . above, black crows and blackbirds wheel through ghetto night skies . . . it's what he's always suspected, the ghetto projects on many levels, beyond the safe three dimensions of any city planner's maps . . .

"Me neither. This way." M.T.'s light illuminates twisted strands of iron and cable stabbing up from the ground like alien stalks. "Look at this shit." M.T. flicks on a flashlight, scattering the beam on the ground up ahead: green, purple, pearly, crimson bushes and plants dapple up half hidden by weeds and trash. "St. John's wort, Rubicon, nightshade. Them's voodoo plants and herbs, seein' them more and more these days, crazy-ass voodoo doctors and witches and shamans and shit always startin' or stoppin' ghetto curses."

"Ghetto has its own flora and fauna."

"Spoken like a true urbanologist," M.T. says. "White man looks around and sez shit, shor is a lot of black folks around here, so he moves his business to the West Side or retreats toward the Valley. Pretty soon the city is checkered with boarded-up buildings. Next,

white folks get the wrecking ball and haul away them useless buildings. Now we got vacant lots, more and more every year."

"Spoken like a true *infrastructuralist*." Monk grins. "But the
urbanologist might say that these are more than just vacant lots.
Only about forty years ago, back in the twenties or so, this city
was like most other cities, still filled with trees and wild places
and gardens and open lands. Swaths of wild oak, firs, cedar, pine.
Then the white folks come and there's this big land grab. In just a
few years, most of the trees and fields are gone as the clapboard
houses spread. But there's something else going on here. Black
folks secretly gathered in these wild refuges. The gardens, the wall
of woods, the tangled arbors were natural dens where they could
talk, sing, love, dream, read forbidden books and newspapers,
slipping away from a master's bonds only for an hour or two. So
white folks bulldozed all these sanctuaries away, only goddamn
weedy lots left. Now these lots take on a life of their own. Each
year they morph into more and more of a new kind of jungle, an
urban jungle, a ghetto jungle, man. The ghetto jungle's got its own
beasts too, mosquitoes, bees, flies, dung beetles, snakes, rats, black
widows, crows, pigeons, sparrows, finally bums and gangs. And
it's not that the white man is making more of these city velds, it's
that these wild places are slowly growing, *evolving*, until they
swallow the city and all that's left one day is ruins."

"Jesus," M.T. chuckling, "you're the *infrastructuralist*. But you're
right, I seen strange insects, weeds, *night things* that exist nowhere
in the world but here in the ghetto. You gotta meet the boys down
in LAMA. There it is." His flashlight transfixes a heavy, bulbous
gray sack hanging down from a rusted pipe bent from a crumbling corner facade, the sack tapering off to tendrils of glop plas-
tered around the pipe. They step closer: a few bees float around
the hive's obscene spout. M.T. shines the twin beams of his hard-
hat lamp and flashlight on the hive, etching it in a brilliant sphere
of light.

"Fuck, they're huge," Monk's whispering now: perhaps it is the darkness, the angle, but these insects look as big as locusts.

"Don't make any moves or noise now, shit, I didn't think they'd get this far so fast." M.T. slowly kneels and opens his silver case.

"What are they?" Taking a step back.

"They're African bees, we call 'em killer bees, some of the boys call 'em brother bees." M.T. laughs, slowly extracting a bronze cartridge pistol from the case.

"As in bees from Africa?"

"Back in '57, this biologist in Brazil was crossbreeding African and European bees to make a bee that was tougher and could survive the jungles. The African bees escaped, of course, and bred with every other damn bee in South America, creatin' this killer bee hybrid. About a month ago, LAMA brought in some of these hybrid hives for a secret experiment. Bees pollinate plants, and we want more plants instead of weeds, which crack our sidewalks and freeways and in general fuck up the infrastructure. More bees, more plants, just control the queens so they don't breed with our American bees, a simple plan except—who could see this coming—the queens escaped."

M.T. snaps open the barrel of the pistol. "Their escape is the subject of some interesting although unfortunately classified memos." He slides a copper lozenge into the chamber, locks it. "Memos rumored to outline their aggressiveness and uncanny, you might say unnatural, intelligence in a kind of hive thinking to *learn* how to unlock their apiary cages . . ."

"You're gonna shoot them?"

"Incinerate 'em. A very powerful charge of plastic explosive." He trains his headlamp on the quivering hive. M.T. hands Monk the flashlight. "Keep her steady on those mutherfuckers and don't make any hostile moves." He aims the pistol at the gray hive humming in its halo of wavering light.

The hive is vaporized in a cobalt ball of flames: perhaps a little too much C-4 here, as the entire wall explodes, shards of brick and metal pipe whizzing through the night. "Fuck and duck!" M.T. dives to the ground as Monk drops behind a block of rubble. "You okay?" M.T.'s voice somewhere in the rising dust and bits of weeds floating down. Monk raises an eye above the concrete block: gooey bits of hive and bee thoraxes mottle his face and hair. Beyond the smoking ruins, a giant *shadow* rises from the blown-out wall. "Oh my god." M.T. stumbles back, kicking up on his feet, the hard hat toppling to the ground, its light beam etching his face in horror. "The queen . . . run!"

Scrambling past a rusted-out car, Monk cuts across the lot, past teetering sentinels of old tires. Along a mangled fence, tripping through a torn curtain of chain link, he's on Hillford Avenue. On the corner, standing in its feeble nimbus of pearl light like an inanimate savior: a phone booth.

Monk slams shut the booth's door, afraid to look back. Catching his breath, he hears nothing, he's safe for now. He jams a nickel in the slot and dials home; the rotary wheel clicks and spins counterclockwise in agonizing slow motion with each number. The receiver buzzes with the terminal metallic pulse of a busy signal. *Shit.* He slams down the receiver. Rent party: some deadbeat always on the phone, running up his bill, he'll never get through. Is she all right? He pulls out the notebook, sets it on the wedge of metal shelf. Thumbs through the pages to the number graffito. The nickel tinkles down the slot and his index finger slowly circles around the rotary dial, spinning out the number like a wheel of chance: 714 . . . 733 . . . 9969. Monk's eyes scan the graffiti etched everywhere on the booth's glass like spidery translucent script. A tin ringing in his ear as somewhere out in the remote desert far from the city another phone rings: a desolate moonscape of sand and yucca trees and bottlebrush. A dirt road scars into the sand, far from all vanished highways. *Let it ring a long time.* Crooked birch telephone poles loop black wires above the sand, paralleling the road, then finally descend to the phone booth, dark beneath its smashed-out light, only starlight shining on its metal and pulverized glass panes: forgotten, forlorn, the last booth on the grid; it is the terminus of communication on the very edge of nothing. *Let it ring a long time,* she said. This outpost is all that remains of—nobody really knows—a remote World War II secret base, or a forgotten Prohibition prison, or an old uranium mine that bodes slow death for any trespassers, or an Old West ghost town not found in any history books, or a shanty-town of desert misfits called Bone Beach or Flat World or Bad Locus or Omegaville. The rings pulse out into the night like the lonely call of some metal cicada: a shadow hobbles toward the glimmering steel stand. International Telephone (IT) should have dismantled the booth by now, but somehow *it* escaped the auditor's files, and now it is a secret nexus, where any human voice anywhere in the world might connect with the strange nomads who haunt this desert crossroads: mystics, travelers, drifters, gangs, madmen, the lost, pilgrims, and all disenfranchised sojourners of wastelands. The shadow passes into the booth's feeble, reflected starlight: an ancient man hunched, enveloped in a long, filthy blanket, dark as the night skies above. The smashed glass and steel is tattooed with multicolored layers of graffiti and signs and tags, like some Rosetta stone awaiting an urbanologist's deciphering book. The black telephone—a vintage, early '50s sculpted rotary machine—rings into the warm desert silence. The old hermit crooks a bleached white cane in the booth's corner. His gnarled fingers brush lovingly down the metal face of the phone; he knows this booth, all of these way stations along the grid, like a father knows his errant children. He slowly lifts the receiver from its rusted cradle—

Monk: "Hello? Hello!" A silence except the faint electric hum of some alien static. "Who's there? Hello?"

"You are my eyes." A deep, grizzled whisper as if the voice is transmitted not across miles but the gulf of infinite space.

"Who is this? What do you want?"

"Remember the shoe shine? We will speak again—"

"Wait!" The dial tone whines like an angry metal insect. Monk bangs down the receiver. Stuffing the notebook in his pants, he pushes open the door and walks into the warmth of the sirens and the night. *Shoe shine?* He shakes his head.

7

At the corner, a huge mob suddenly undulates down the street, overflowing onto sidewalks, pushing east. *That shoe-shine stand. What was it called?* Monk follows, keeping his distance; they're looping back toward Central Avenue: police cars glower by, bathing mobs on the sidewalks in blood light. Voices shout and chant: "No more Selma! Burn the fuckers down! Three for one!" Storefront windows are smashed in, looters crisscrossing the street with armfuls of bottles and bags and shopping carts heaped with swag. *That Muslim Oasis shoe-shine stand I passed on Avalon.* Monk remembers now the strange old man who seemed to glower at him, across Avalon at the shoe-shine stand, his woolly beard and duct-taped glasses, a blind man hunched over his white cane. *She knew I had the number, Muhammad's girl, what's her—Nefertiti . . . Maybe that number's Nation of Islam, some kind of trap . . . They want the notebook, fighting for power like the rest of them . . . and that shoe-shine stand, that's called Muslim too.*

A strange bicycle tries to avoid the crowd but a bottle explodes across the rider's face and the bike clatters to the ground. The cyclist, a Chinese man, holds his head in a daze and staggers away from the crowd. It's a delivery bike, a big gold-painted tricycle mounted with a large white box proclaiming GOLDEN PAGODA

CLEANERS. Monk rights the bike, wobbles on the seat, then ped-als down Central. Bolted to the handlebars is a friction lamp in the shape of a golden oriental shrine, gold tassels whipping in the wind, this amber light beam bouncing ahead, casting a strange copper halo as he threads into the night.

Perhaps it is only the tricycle's bent handlebars but it seems to push *left*. Monk grips the handlebars, pedaling, fighting to keep the trike southbound, but it sways and pulls left . . . maybe a wheel is bent. Bumping off the curb, Monk almost knocks over two yellow candles that drip and pool into the pavement, the candles fixed between two crossed matchsticks and three pennies: these signs of devotion, magic talismans, seem to be more common at the city's crossroads now as the fires and the terrors conflate across the night, descending block by block. He's stopped, glaring down at the candles and matchsticks and pennies, these spells cast on the streets, on the city, against unseen enemies . . . or maybe signposts to protect and guide. He's on the opposite side of Central now, facing north. Monk slowly pedals, the tricycle gliding easy and straight, its inanimate lurching vanished. "You know some-thing I don't?" Monk stares down into the amber light of the little shrine-lamp glowing on the handlebars. "All right, fuck it, let's go, Golden Pagoda."

Monk weaves the gilded tricycle in and out of looters, knots of drinkers, crowds hurling bricks and bottles. Each block takes him farther from the harbor, from Karmann: *What the fuck am I doing?* Four police cruisers block the street, doors open, a line of cops with batons and riot masks marching toward the mob. Past the police blockade, the great bleached dome and ivory plas-ter arches of the White Front Department Store: the building is on fire, flames licking up the arches like some ancient Roman siege, looters scattering across the parking lot as a fire truck tries to brake into position. Monk grins, pedaling past: a karmic debt now being repaid for opening a store in the ghetto called White Front.

Streets blur past in darkness and flames. *Turn around, what the fuck are you doing?* Monk clatters by geysers of foamy white water blasting into the darkness from monkey-wrenched open hydrants. Is he fleeing from her, from the baby? The water rises, seeping over curbs and gurgling into flooded drains. The bicycle tires splash through the pavement, past throngs of black children, shirtless, some naked, squealing, playing in the thundering fonts. These street kids, chasing through the torrents, flitting across the golden beams of Monk's pagoda light, look like black sprites materialized from some watery lair.

He steers the bike north, up Hill Street, in and out of shards of glass that twinkle iridescent rainbows from the cascading water—no pressure when the fire trucks finally arrive, firemen retreating under barrages of bottles and bricks, waiting for police escorts that will never arrive, their hoses limp and dripping impotently. *Let these fuckers burn their own shit down*, nothing to stop the flames as they search out tonight's victims.

The tricycle lurches right, down Gin Ling Way, as if pulled by some secret feng shui under the great arch of red-tiled pagoda roofs, Chinatown's West Gate; carved into its pillars, strange gods and dragons seem to watch him pass. Monk looks back: smoke and flames billow from the city's hazy silhouette, sirens and helicopters fan through the darkness. He shakes his head. *Looks like Godzilla got tired of Tokyo and decided to give the ghetto a good ass kickin'* . . .

He pedals past ramen shops, apothecaries, souvenir booths, market stalls piled with fruit and fish, the Lucky Bean Cake Factory. Red lanterns, strung across the narrow street, sway and glow. The tricycle veers into the curb in front of twin gilt-lacquered Buddhas and a blinking incandescent sign: GOLDEN PAGODA CLEANERS. Above the shop, a ramshackle restaurant extends for half a block over the storefronts, its dark windows and chestnut camphor wood peaked with a red tile roof and arches like a shrine: a great pale willow tree towers through the center of the mansard roof, up into the night, its boughs gnarling out over the rooftop in a huge, shaggy canopy of bearded moss. A blue neon sign crackles beneath the gossamer willows: LOTUS PALACE RESTAURANT.

Monk glides the tricycle into an iron rack in front of the cleaners. "Hope you didn't steer me wrong." Its amber pagoda headlamp dims, flickering as if winking at him, then sputters out as it rolls to a stop. An old Chinese man with thick glasses in a white uniform gestures wildly from the doorway. "Where you go? You *filed!*"

"Filed?"

"Filed! No job!"

"You got to hire me first. Just returning your bike."

The old man squints up at Monk. "You not Lee! What you do with Lee!"

"I don't know no Lee. Just found your bike," turning to leave.

An old woman standing behind the counter squeals out in rapid Chinese. "Wait!" The old man touches Monk's elbow. "You give back bike. We give you something to thank," sweeping his hands toward the laundry.

"That's okay, I have to go."

"No! *Vely* bad luck. Please!"

Inside the shop: racks of clothes suspended from the ceiling, a gold Buddha in the corner, smiling above a sign chained around his thick neck: NO CHECKS! Steam billows from hot presses in the back. The old woman crouches like a shriveled chestnut behind the counter, huge scissors in her hand, needle sticking between withered lips. "Eat dinn*ah*, drink bee*ha*, no charge," gesturing toward a staircase in the corner, sign above on the wall: LOTUS PALACE RESTAURANT. The old man shouts Chinese up the staircase. A waiter appears, wearing a gold brocade coat and bow tie, waving Monk to advance. Monk shrugs: hot tea sounds good, he's exhausted. He ascends creaking wood steps.

The old man turns and walks back into the steamy shop to work in hermetic silence next to his wife, only the soft swoosh of steam until the old man pushes a button under the counter and

chains clink from suspended racks above: the clothes slowly re-
volve, ratchet down tracks, descending out of steamy banks like
disembodied ghosts. There are pants, suits, shirts, gowns, uniforms: they pass along the grinding chains, rolling back into the
steam, but sometimes the machine is stopped and the old man
grabs the hanger from its hook and places the clothes on the
counter before the old woman; this teal dress belongs to that snob
Mrs. Chang (who always insults them behind their backs), and
the old woman opens a jar under the counter, fingers a dab of invisible powder across the back of the dress—mandrake extract,
to ensure Mrs. Chang is afflicted with horrible diarrhea. A white
shirt, Mr. Sing—who insulted their daughter—is treated with a
pinch of pig's liver under the starched armpits, which will cause
him to constantly sweat. Her lips curl as he lays the cop's black
uniform on the counter. The department's litany of crimes against
Chinatown is legendary: graft for every opium den and whorehouse in town; beatings, rape, extortion; murder and terror to
clear shanties for Union Station back in '39, the great terminal
that brought Pullmans full of blacks from back east and the
South, though they never saw the magnificent station, all coloreds
were forced to detrain at Central Avenue—no blacks in the
Union unless you were pushing a broom or shining a shoe. Negroes to rob Chinese of work in the new war plants; brutal en-
forcement of the Exclusion Act, which stripped away all human
rights; back a century when this cop's Irish forebears were cruel
Pinkertons overseeing the Coolie slave labor, building iron train
rails in the days of the pueblos. Now, cop by cop, the Chinese
laundries across the city exact ancient revenges born from the
mystic chi arts of the motherland: a snuff of *Forsythia suspensa* on
this starched collar brings terrible neck aches . . . a little *Datura
metel* inside Sergeant Armstrong Trench's uniform shirt and his
breasts will burn and grow . . . a spritz of *Tintorius notorious* on
this rookie's shirttails precipitates horrible stomachaches . . . a
dusting of tiger penis on the zipper of Officer Napoleon Wilson—

from Precinct 13—has the unfortunate effect of arousing uncontrollable tumescence accompanied by homoerotic urges . . .

Monk slouches in a shadowy booth. In the center of the restaurant, a great willow tree rises through a hole cut in the floor, its trunk disappearing through another hole in the ceiling: branches twist out against the ceiling's exposed beams, straining across the room, lime tendrils of willows hanging down like mossy curtains. Just some green tea to fortify him, then he'll be on his way. The walls are designed with interlocking golden lotus petals; a fountain tinkles in the corner as he sips hot tea. He gazes at the great willow, which seems to be growing into the camphor walls. The waiter sets a plate with a small, round green cake. "Ah, that is the pride of Chinatown, the Anna May Wong Tree, donated by Paramount Studios in the thirties. Isn't it magnificent? Moon cake, Mandarin delicacy, on house," bowing. "The tree is at one with the architecture. Amazing, isn't it? This restaurant was designed by the great Frank Lloyd Wright. Oriental organic." The waiter disappears beyond the mossy willow tapestries. Monk eats a spoonful: mint, ginseng, faint almonds. A Chinese girl appears in a long gold brocaded robe, smiling, setting a fortune cookie before him. Her eyes linger, then she glances away, disappearing beyond the suspended fringes of willow. Monk sips tea, feels warm. A groaning sound, muffled somewhere above, like *distressed* wood. The golden-petal lotuses on the wall seem to shimmer and vibrate.

He peels the cellophane from the cookie, unfurling the fortune's tiny paper: *You are in danger.*

Standing, he sways, pulling the white cloth from the table, green tea spilling across linen, plates clattering to the floor as he crumples to the red carpet.

•

"Wake up!" Faces slowly sharpen into focus. Two Chinese men frowning down at him: an old man wearing round glasses and a lemon-shade suit, the other middle-aged in slacks and T-shirt, thin mustache, chain-smoking. "Who sent you?" blowing smoke in his eyes.

"What, ah," trying to move his wrists: they've tied him to a chair. He gazes around, head filled with cement—a long dark room lit by two dim orange paper-shaded bulbs. A gagging, sweet stench cloys the stale air, the room filled with iron clouds of smoke. The walls are lined with rickety wooden bunk beds, emaciated old Chinese men and women slumped in rotting blankets on torn, stinking mattresses, clutching long white clay pipes, vacuum eyes staring into banks of smoke. "No one sent me, man," shaking his head: *What is this, some kind of Asian nightmare? So much for that don't-sell-the-mystic-short bullshit.*

"You spy for Yang, huh!" More smoke in his groggy face.

"You like cookie, perfect, huh?" The other interrogator holds a fortune cookie in front of Monk's nodding head. "Maybe too perfect . . . Yang send you!" crumbling the cookie in his face. The old man turns to his companion and hisses out a barrage of Chinese. The other inhales his cigarette and fires a guttural torrent of Chinese back. "What? I can't *undahstand* you! Cantonese is *foh* dogs!"

"Your Mandarin sounds like monkey's fart!"

"Enough! What is your name?"

"Americo Monk. Would you please not blow smoke in my face?"

"*Amelico* Monk! Bullshit! We see! We make you talk!"

"What?"

"Lotus-eaters!" the other barks, exhaling smoke in Monk's face. "Shen Shen!" A diabolical grin that reveals, well, yes, *yellow* teeth, then they're gone, a bolt thrown behind the closed door.

Then a fat Chinese man in a disheveled plum robe stands before Monk: Fu Manchu mustache, clutching a clay pipe, red pupils shrunk like fiery pinheads, looks like that Keye Luke after some booze- and pill-fueled Lionel Atwill party . . . "I'm Shen

Shen. Don't worry, it's cool," untying the rope from his wrists. "You don't have to smoke, unless?" offering the smoldering pipe.

"No thanks." Monk rubs his wrists, stands on wobbly legs: drugged eyes gleam with disinterest from their shadowed cubbyholes. "What the fuck's he saying, lotus-eaters?"

"The lotus, the flower of dreams . . . of myths . . ." His Fu Manchu crinkles into a grin. "You're a wanderer, blown off course by ill winds, as it were."

"More like uptown by a fucked-up tricycle. What the fuck is goin' on, man?" Angry, glaring at the door, waiting for those two jive-ass Chinamen to come back in so he can throw a punch.

"Don't worry, he's a little nuts. That's Yin, the one in the yellow suit? He owns the restaurant below."

"Below?" Monk rubs his numb wrists as he calms down.

"Yeah, this is the third floor, ye olde opium den. Pull up your chair, Yin'll spring you in an hour or two when he comes to his senses. He's a devotee of the seed too," tapping the clay pipe. "Makes him a *tad* paranoid. This is a dangerous year for Yin. The Chinese calendar declares this is a yin year, not a yang year, therefore it is a year when Yin may be able to prosper or advance his objectives. The heavenly sign this year is wood, very lucky for Yin, considering his superstitious devotion to the sacred tree that grows through the center of this restaurant. But the zodiac's earthly sign is the snake, treachery, a foreboding omen for Mr. Yin."

Monk pulls the chair closer to the bunk, rubbing his temples: no time to think, only confusion; where is his grace or luck? There is only a dull flicker that he should do something, but then this thought too fades into a bewildered inertia. "What's this spy shit?"

"Old Yin says he invented the fortune cookie." Shen laughs, inhaling smoke. "At the turn of the century, Yin arrived in San Francisco with the usual wave of Yellow Peril. He set up a bakery in Chinatown and was struggling like everyone else. One day, to surprise his girlfriend, he got the idea to write her a tiny love note and he folded it in a sugar cookie and baked it. The fortune cookie was born, or so Yin says. The cookie catches on and he's selling 'em like crazy in his little bakery, he and his girl staying up all night, writing good-luck slogans that soon turn to simple little fortunes. Yin calls them Lucky Cookies. The bakery expands, Yin gets a little money. He hires a couple of people to fold cookies and write fortunes. Things are great, Yin and girlfriend are engaged. One day, this cook named Yang strolls into Yin's shop and eats a fortune cookie. Soon Yang opens a restaurant down the block called the Fortune Cookie. He serves the little cookies free for dessert and business booms. Of course Yin is pissed off. They become enemies, competing to make faster, cheaper, tastier cookies, each one jealously guarding any breakthroughs that come."

"So he thinks I'm a spy for Yang?" Monk shakes his head.

"They're still going at it." Shen laughs, lighting his pipe. "In those early years, around '04 or '05, they start experimenting with machines. Yin installs this great steam cookie machine in a secret room behind the bakery, pledging his staff of Fortunists and dough folders to secrecy. Yang has his own secret apparatus of pneumatic pumps that suck the cookie dough down slots that fold them. Later, Yang's spies smuggle diagrams that reveal Yin can superheat cookies and fold them with steam-driven blades in seconds. The two men are locked in a battle to produce the fastest cookies. Fortunists are hired for amazing handwriting speeds . . . wood-and-ink stamps are introduced, then printing presses. Buddhist monks are hired with secret copying techniques from China . . . adepts are found that can write ambidextrously. Then, in '06, Yin's machine is mysteriously blown up . . . dough covers the streets and horrifies passersby, a cloud of confetti fortunes floats down over Chinatown. Yin's bakery burns to the ground—but everything is wood back then, and Chinatown burns to the fucking ground, as does half of the city."

"You're talking about the great quake?"

"Quake! That's all white-man crap." Shen, exhaling smoke, cackles like a disturbing Buddha. "Once Chinatown was burning, they had the excuse they were waiting for and smashed every ghetto in the city . . . Chinks, Japs, Mexicans, blacks, everything was burned out and knocked down. The cops, all Micks back then, right? The cops, the best they could come up with was burn down old drunk Mother O'Leary's barn and blame it on a fucking cow . . . That riot out there now, they're trying to clean out the city again."

Monk stares at Shen Shen's face cloaked in sweet smoke. "How come you know so much about it?"

Shen's shrunken eyes twinkle. "Because I am the most wretched and lost of men, I am a *writer*. I was once employed by Yin. I was his greatest Fortunist, until I too, like all who become ruled by the damned cookie, was cursed by madness. You see, Yin and Yang not only jealously guarded their cookie machines. They also developed a stable of writers whose identities and talents became as coveted as the great cookie engines. Fortunists would duel in the streets, murder, poison each other over stolen styles and insulting aphorisms and purloined epigrams. Much of history's reports of Chinatown tong wars were in fact the secret mayhem between Yin and Yang." Shen sucks thoughtfully on his pipe. "For a year or two haiku became the rage, Yin and Yang both employing great poets from Japan and the motherland. Finally, Yin had the master Ibuki, and Yang secured the rising haiku genius Bo Gong. An epic battle of haiku kept Chinatown mesmerized for months. Then, one rainy night, on Gin Ling Way in the center of town, the two versifiers faced each other in a kind of sonnet showdown . . . Crowds of fortune-cookie enthusiasts lined the clapboard sidewalks, gowns and slippers sunk in torrents of mud. Zabatsu, the young rebel, volleyed the first haiku:

Spring, I strive to see
Your view but can't get my head
That far up my ass.

"The crowd is silent in awe. It is a great haiku, complete with the *kigo*, the season word. Now all eyes turn to master Ibuki, whose voice thunders out in the rain:

Verse blinds like winter
No answer but question: were—

"Silence, the crowd waits. Has the master stumbled? Zabatsu sneers, sensing ignominious defeat for the old poet. Then:

Your parents siblings?

"Zabatsu grows pale. In his arrogance, he'd forgotten the crucial *kireji*, the pause for righteous contemplation in the haiku's second line. His humiliation is complete, he's lost the contest. His knife gleams under the strung paper lanterns as he slices his throat, red geyser spurting into the muddy rain."

Monk's head is beginning to spin: far too much of this cloying smoke—a sound, muffled scratching, seems to be coming from somewhere beyond the peeling walls.

"I am blessed—rather, cursed—with a gift of clairvoyance that this mystic flower," tapping his clay pipe, stubbing a white substance into the bowl with his big dirty thumb, "seems to precipitate. I began writing fortunes for Yin that often came true for his customers: *You will acquire a sum of money . . . You will fall in love next week . . . Your pain will stop soon.* Yin's business skyrocketed. As always, Yang was spying, hiring his own psychics from China, and another secret war was fought by the two archenemies. A battle of psychic Fortunists, each smuggling *misfortune* cookies into the other's shops: *You will go blind . . . Your brother will die . . . Your sister will be raped.*" Shen lights the bowl, closes his eyes, inhales deeply. "Yang brought in a mysterious hired gun from Peking who wrote curses that came true and Yin almost died. Only through the agency of May Tip, Yin's first wife, the girlfriend who inspired the invention of the cookie itself—you've met her, she's the old woman downstairs in the laundry—was Yin's life saved. We answered by developing a secret message that upon reading the victim dies instantly . . . but Yang, nearsighted, had an assistant read it; he collapsed and the assassination attempt failed. Cryptic fortunes passed from Yin to Yang and Yang to Yin, driving both men to the edge of sanity: *Be at the south window at four o'clock . . . Beware of May ninth . . . Chang is the one you suspect . . . Is it in the green tea?*"

Shen Shen exhales a plume of cobalt smoke, contemplating Monk's gaze. "You don't believe me? Mask!" A shadowed lump stirs on a bunk bed, then this effigy draped in blanket shuffles toward them: an old Caucasian man, emaciated face, blind milk-cloud eyes shivering above the stinking blanket's hem, a skeletal hand gripping near his throat. "The cursed oriental cookie has a mysterious history that is seldom glimpsed by the sane. Even stranger things have happened than my little history. This is Targum Maskull. He was a rich socialite back in the thirties, owned several of those Long Beach oil wells." Shen Shen removes a small pouch from his robes and extracts a pinch of white paste. "Sing for your supper." Monk, dizzy, sits on the floorboards as the old man grunts down on the chair. Shen holds the clay pipe in the shaky, bony hand and sparks a match over the bowl. The old man inhales greedily, white orbs rolling back under blood-tinged eyelids.

"It was back in '37. I was young, rich, single, so happy," his voice rasps, exhaling smoke. "One evening I dined in this cursed house, in the Lotus Palace Restaurant. After dinner I opened the fortune cookie. It said *Love Gate red umbrella*. Love Gate is the east gate of Chinatown. It is carved with the symbols of maternal bliss and motherly love. In those days it was where lovers often met. I knew the area well because my grandfather, so I was told as a young lad, had several importing businesses there. I was a young turk on a lark, so from the restaurant I walked the blocks to the gate. A woman appeared dressed in black with a crimson paper parasol. I introduced myself, showed her the fortune. She was the most beautiful woman I'd ever seen," a tear rolling from his blind eye, "a Chinese goddess, long raven hair, skin like snow, full red lips, cyan eyes that twinkled with veiled promises. Qiao was her name. We laughed at the coincidence and she agreed to meet me for dinner the next night." Maskull lights the pipe with a palsied claw. "We became lovers. Her lust was insatiable. Soon our lovemaking became more and more adventurous. We coupled in a feverish dream in sedans, in alleyways, in parks, under bridges, behind the market booths on Old Arcadia Street, every-where, every night, she was like a beautiful demon that sucked all the energy, all clear thought from me, until I could think of nothing but the heat of her pried-open legs. One night, we met for drinks not far from the East Gate and she was terrified and began to cry. She told me her landlord was foreclosing on her. He had mysterious, dangerous men and she begged me not to inter-fere. I must do something, I roared. Reluctantly she said if I were to cosign a loan paper she could escape the disaster. I signed the papers and melted one last time into the intoxication of her em-brace." The old man exhales sweet smoke that envelops Monk in a reeling cloud. "A few nights later we met at our usual assigna-tion beneath the willow trees on the benches by the East Gate. Two men accosted her, shouting, clutching papers in their fists. Of course, I knew who they were. Qiao begged me to leave. I was a white man, an outsider, and should not dare to interfere. A fight ensued and I was knocked unconscious. I awoke on a bamboo mat in a barren bleached room, racked with fever, deathly sick. In the room's center was a red plate with a single fortune cookie. My trembling hands cracked open the baked crescent. I unfolded a black-and-white photograph. It showed a cute little Chinese girl, perhaps six or seven, smiling, posing between two young teenage boys—it was Qiao and the two men who had accosted her. On the reverse of the photograph, a cryptic message neatly scripted in a feminine hand: *Ninghongs 1922, K7-954.22.* Of course, all my money was gone, those papers I'd signed, my house emptied and sold, even the oil wells were transferred to some mysterious entity in China. I found out *qiao* means skillful; oh, she was brilliant. I almost died from the sickness. Doctors found needle marks on my arm and ran tests. Those bastards had injected me with pure opium, and I was hopelessly addicted. Withdrawing from the drug would kill me. I began to haunt opium dens, the pipe was my only refuge from the nightmare my life had become. I staggered through the city in the night, that faded photograph clutched in my hand, searching for her, for an answer, for death. Sometimes I would see a glimpse of cherry parasol turning a corner, or raven hair through a window, but she had vanished like the succubus she was. Finally I showed the photograph to a young man on the sidewalk and he pointed to a building down on Flower Street: the Chinese Library. Staggering among the rows of books, I realized the mysterious figures were subject numbers. K7 is Chinese History. I found the other numbers on the worn spine of an old book and slumped at a table. *Chinese-American Genealogy and History, 1890–1925.* My finger feverishly traced up and down the columns of pages. Qiao Ninghong had been born in 1915, her two brothers in 1909 and 1910. Her father, Tan Ninghong, married her mother, Jia Liou, in 1907. The father's history revealed nothing. But the mother, Liou, had been born in Chinatown in 1890. I can still quote you those terrible words: *Liou, Jia, remitted to Chinese-American Orphanage 1890, mother, unknown . . . Many of the women who immigrated to Los Angeles from the Liou clan regions were sold into white slavery. In the notorious pleasure houses of the East or Love Gate sections of China Town, women were forced into opium addiction by their brutal white masters, the most notorious of whom were Captain Jack Sullivan and Big John Maskull . . ."*

Shen Shen tamps the blind old man's pipe with another pinch of dreams. Maskull's milky eyes seem to bore into Monk's as the old man wheezes, shuffling back toward the shadows of his bunk, mumbling: "So the son shall know the sins of the father."

"Well, a few old men, a handful of addicts, soon we'll all be dead, and the secret histories of the Fortunists will be lost forever." Shen ruefully stokes his pipe bowl. "The cookie is doomed anyway. Asian groups complain it fosters images of superstitious peasants . . . grammarians bemoan choppy Charlie Chan syntax . . . Christians protest heathen sweets with secret prophecies."

Footsteps creak outside the door. "They've come back." Monk staggers to his feet, hands curling into fists, almost drowning in the banks of cobalt smoke.

Shen Shen pulls a strand of red firecrackers from beneath his robes, his pinwheel eyes glinting insanely. "A diversion, then we escape."

"We not prisoners here, you stoned asshole," an old man sighs between rotted teeth clenching a pipe, deep in the shadows of his bunk. "Get fuck out so I sleep." He's at the door, which, through shifting clouds of smoke, reveals that the rusty bolt is on the *inside*.

Yin and his goon burst through the open door. Behind Monk, firecrackers explode in the air in blinding white puffs of smoke and flying bits of red confetti and Shen Shen's giggling voice: "Your success will be explosive . . ."

Monk stumbles over Yin and falls backward through smoke clouds and out the door.

He careens down the hallway, *Don't look back*. Footsteps chasing him, Yin shouts: "Stop him!" The floor trembles, a low rumble as some great subterranean branch sways below.

A gold-jacketed waiter, screaming, passes Monk in the opposite direction: "Demons!" Monk can see the great willow trunk now, rising through its aperture here on the third floor, the massive tree disappearing through its hole carved into the mansard rooflines.

He runs across the arbored foyer, past tendrils of moss webbing from the overhead boughs. Down the staircase, a curving branch above, as if Anna May Wong points the way toward a grease-stained side door.

He's in the alley behind the laundry. Ahead, wedged in the prism between steam wafting from wall ventilators and rows of garbage cans, is Gin Ling Way, strung with glittering red lanterns. Monk bolts toward Broadway.

The gilded Love Gate recedes behind him like the portal of some drug delirium that tempts the pilgrim's journey home. Monk heads south. The concrete under his shoes is only a patina: beneath are layers of asphalt and tar and sand, stratas of clay and stone where the first alleyway of old Chinatown is buried, the street that long ago was called Calle de Los Negros, the Street of the Dark-Hued Ones. The way that will lead him back into the city, burning now as the descendants of the city's dark ones rise against summer's molten anvil.

8

Classified: Inter-Department Only
Volume 6: Emergency Department Directives
923: When to Take Police Action
923.20: Use of Force
During declared emergency actions by the governor, officers are permitted to use any force necessary, in any situa-
tion, and shall be indemnified against future review or
inquiry.

Sergeant Armstrong Trench steers the cruiser east on Ninety-
second Street, toward Hooper Avenue, smoking a cigarette,
eyes scouting tonight's streets. Riding shotgun is Officer Vicodanz:
overlapping teal sevens are tattooed on his right biceps, as they
are beneath Trench's sleeve, for the 77th Street Division.

Shadowed storefronts roll past, shattered windows, smoke roiling from a deserted alley. Sirens peal in the distance, scattered
black men run across Ninety-second Street. The patrol car bumps
past Zamora Avenue.

On the radio, interrupted by squawks from their two-way, the
Four Tops croon "I Can't Help Myself (Sugar Pie Honey Bunch)."
The cruiser screeches to a stop in front of the burning facade of

Central Furniture: five or six men and women lug a couch and chairs from its front doors through billowing smoke. The officers jump out, pumping their shotguns above the suspects. The couch and chairs tumble to the sidewalk as the looters run across the street. The cops open the trunk, take out a couple of cold Pabst Blue Ribbons from the cooler, and lean against the fender, sipping.

"Natives a tad restless tonight." Vicodanz gulps beer.

"Better to err on the side of caution," Trench extracting a sawed-off shotgun from the trunk, checking the pump action.

"Remember the first time you took that thing to the police range, demolished your target *and* three others, I believe?" Vicodanz's grinning face glows in the red lamps of the cruiser's beacons.

They crush the beer cans in their gloved fists and toss the cans into the gutter.

Patrolling south on Compton now. Only a few civilian cars pass in the almost deserted, smoke-palled streets. Later, back at the 77th, passing the Crown Royal bottle in the locker room, much merriment and laughter trading tonight's adventures with the other guys, another night out in the Duck Pond. The ghetto is the Duck Pond, just chock-full of those rioting, crazy Negroes like thousands of black Daffy Ducks back home on the TV: where you can hunt all night long, every wound or kill an internal department investigation that always leads to a few restful vacation suspension days, or coveted desk duty where Trench and others can talk to girlfriends and mistresses on the phone, read the paper, play the horses, sleep, drink fortified coffee from thermoses, before closing out cases with the inevitable imminent threat or justifiable defense rulings.

Parked on the corner of 103rd and Compton, chomping doughnuts and drinking coffee. Across the street, a fire truck trains torrents of water up into a brick facade engulfed in flames. Music fades in and out of the crackling two-way radio.

"Betcha the hookers are still working that spot on Santa Barbara Avenue." Trench sips coffee.

Vicodanz chewing, glaze on his lips. "We could check it out. That new one, Angel, she's pretty hot."

"Gotta stay in our zone. You know Parker and his Sergeant Roddenberry Principle . . . space your patrols, patrol your space."

"Roddenberry, space patrol," Vicodanz shakes his head. "Sounds more like outer space."

"Did ya hear the niggers wanna rename Santa Barbara Avenue?"

"To what?"

"Martin Luther King, Jr., Boulevard."

"Mr. I Have a Dream? Shit, I got a dream, stay in your own neighborhood, burn it down if you want."

They head south down Compton. An APB blares from the two-way and Trench guns the cruiser west on Imperial Highway: rioters run and scrabble up and down the sidewalks and across the street, under the shadows of shot-out street lamps. They speed past patrol cars lined and pinned against curbs, officers in riot gear advancing through the darkness. Bricks and bottles thump and smash glass invisibly from secret trajectories somewhere along the brick facades and storefronts that belch smoke and coil flames into the cloudless summer night. On the corner, flames licking from windows, the Scylla, a stucco flophouse hotel, lobby windows shattered, knots of men running, lobbing bricks. A TV, rocked out a third-story window, explodes behind the cruiser. Trench whips the wheel, the car caroms down an alley behind the hotel. A bottle bounces off the hood. Ahead, in the cone of headlights, a skinny black teen running.

Monk watches as the upper-story windows of the Scylla Hotel overspill with flames and smoke. A rock plummets past his head, skimming his hair. Up on the rooftop, kids lob down sticks, rocks, bottles, chunks of plaster. A jet of water blasts over the parapet and Monk sees six teens running across the rooftop, drenched in water, their aerial assault vanquished. Across the street, a fire truck's water guns spray the roof and the smoke-filled windows. A mob outside the lobby hurls bottles and bricks at the scattering firemen. A Molotov cocktail sputters into the darkness and explodes against the windshield of the fire truck. Monk runs as the water guns blast the mob and two squad cars screech in front of the fire truck.

A cruiser brakes into the curb, cutting him off: Monk sees Sergeant Trench and shakes his head as the rear door pops open. "Get in." Trench grins. Monk slips reluctantly into the backseat and the car glides forward. "Keeping your nose clean, Monk?"

"Sure." Monk shrugs. Vicodanz grins back at Monk.

"Wearing your Felony Flyers, huh, kid?"

"What, these sneakers?"

"Sneaking away from some fire-bombing or looting maybe?"

Do I look like I have a fucking TV under my shirt? Play it cool: "Didn't know the riot was formal attire."

"Formal attire," Vicodanz snorts, "that's rich."

"How's your little journal coming along?" Trench cruising down Imperial: some kind of explosion and fireball erupting behind them. Monk's guts ache with the pressure of the notebook wedged beneath his belt: he's afraid, that word *journal* triggering the visceral fear that these cops knew and probably hoped would shake him, and now he's mad, angry that these motherfuckers can reduce him, splinter his intellect and his pride with just a word, like a master's sadistic pleasure in the slow taunting of his black boy.

"Nothing new. The Gladiators maybe moving down toward 115th, that's about it." Monk, patient, measured, careful not to betray fear or anger; he knows they'll be done only when Trench is finished with him.

"What about Las Sombras?" Trench slowing down as Vicodanz aims the sawed-off shotgun out the window and blasts a round above a knot of men milling on the corner: Monk flinches as the explosive concussion echoes in the car. The men scream and scatter into the night. Trench guns the cruiser ahead.

"They're about the same, still hanging around 120th and Main."

"Maybe Chief Parker'd be interested in seeing your little notes. Doing a little reconnaissance for the Gladiators or Sombras? Maybe carrying a few notes in there for your Islam friends with the fezzes?" Monk's stomach under the notebook twists into a gurgling knot.

The squad car brakes at Wadsworth Avenue, at the fringe of the Red Zone. Trench twists around, unlocks, slides the steel panel open. "Hand it over, Mr. Monk."

"Look, Officer Trench, you know me," Monk trying to control the fear in his voice, "it's just graffiti, art stuff, a hobby."

"Are you resisting an officer, boy—I mean, son?" Trench grins, rubbing his chin. "This is the Red Zone. Chief says Negroes violating curfew will be shown no mercy."

"Or we can do a fifty-seven on your ass," Vicodanz beams. "That's like Heinz fifty-seven ketchup, see? We take gangsters like you, drop 'em off in the wrong gang territory, march you out of the car right in front of 'em, tie one of them wrong-colored bandannas we got in the trunk around your head. Then you're like the ketchup, real slow to get out of the neighborhood, red too with blood—"

Heart pounding, Monk lifts his shirt and pulls the blue notebook from his pants, hands it through the grille panel. He clenches his fists, digging into the hot vinyl seat. Trench thumbs through the notebook, shakes his head, frowns. "Signs, spray-painted cartoons, numbers, notes, what is this shit?"

"Like I said, it's just graffiti. You know me, Officer Trench, I'm no gangster or spy. I'm just trying to get to San Pedro."

"What's this mean?" Trench suspicious, jabbing his finger at a page sketched with a graffito of *MFR* scrolled in pink sausage-shaped letters.

"It means 'motherfucker,' pink letters for pigs, for cops."

"Negro jargon, Parker said, remember?" Vicodanz to Trench.

"So, you Negro kids, when you're out there yelling," Trench tensing, struggling to utter the new, blasphemous word, "mother . . .

fucker to police officers, are the Negroes suggesting we have . . .
sexual intercourse . . . with *our* mothers?"

"No, it's just an expression, like . . . 'asshole,'" Monk trying not
to grin.

Vicodanz: "Parker says it's because in the slavery days the
master took the slave's mother into the bedroom."

Trench glares, shaking his head toward Vicodanz.

"Look, how about giving me a few days," Monk says, "then you
could let Parker see the notebook. See, I'm writing down the gang
signs I see in the 'hoods and, maybe in a day or two, Parker could
find some . . . pattern, something useful about the riot. I bet he'd
sure appreciate your good police work."

Trench and Vicodanz exchange a dubious glance. Trench tosses
the notebook through the grille. "Stay loose." Trench lights a cigarette. "We'll be in touch. We all have our little notebooks," tapping his Field Reports book on the dashboard. Sergeant Trench
scratches his chest, his nipples lately throbbing with a terrible
itching and burning . . . Monk nods and opens the door. The car
throttles away into the night, a beer can arcing out the window,
the radio fading with Petula Clark singing "Downtown."

9

Monk's determined to stay off the main avenues as he wends his way south, avoid Officer Trench and the fuzz, try to work the periphery around the worst of the flames and mayhem. He clutches the notebook tightly in his fist: he almost lost it to the cops. The little journal, Trench had sneered. *Fuck them.* Only gang signs and cryptic turf lines to the police. The book's his secret history: there's a gravity in it, he knows. The cops, the Nation of Islam, the gangs, the graffitists: for them the notebook is a kind of mirror to unlock the pieces that illumine their worlds, vices, and shifting balances of power; but the book is also the voice of the voiceless, an arsenal of this city's outlaw, spray-painted walls and manifestos that shine like flags of warning; the words and art of the dispossessed are weapons of change, and to ignore or crush these voices can only bring fire and destruction.

Police cars and desperate civilian vehicles glow down Wadsworth Avenue as roving marauders raid storefronts, then disappear into the dark side streets. He's reached 118th Street; he should find a way off Wadsworth, zigzag down these little avenues with their shot-out street lamps. He turns down 119th Street. His Keds feel like iron weights, it's everything he can muster just to take each step. The avenue is dark, only a distant street lamp a few blocks ahead.

Monk disappears into the shadows of a dark alleyway. Next to a dumpster, there's a feeble lightbulb glowing above a padlocked back door. He sinks down against the wall, stretches out his long legs, crosses his aching feet; tired, besieged, so many miles to go. He opens the blue notebook, turns the pages under the flickering amber light. The pages he almost lost, the secret ledgers and stories of the people and the city itself. Monk wipes his dirty hands. On a blank page he slowly, carefully writes in cursive: *Karmann*. He fills the entire page with her name but it is not just a name, now it's a talisman, a spell of love. If he were an artist instead of a street scholar, he'd spray, tag, throw down her name all over the city, on every wall and gritty surface and sign: Karmann stores, Yield Karmann, Karmann Zone, Karmann Avenue, No Trespassing Karmann . . . that's what they're doing, back home, some of their alleged friends, trespassing against his girl and his trust. Turning the page, he writes in his crabbed, dense print:

Dear Karmann:

You are sick with worry over me, but I am doing everything in my power to return to you. You're a dancer, you know how to play off them, feed their greedy emotions, never holding them too close or keeping them too far. Each time I walk these streets, the city becomes more alive to me . . . a living thing, in flux, too big for any single mind to grasp. Spray-painted manifestos and secret images and signs appear, disappear, transform, reappear like fantastic visions in an iron and concrete jungle. Do their meanings change, or do I change as I try to see them and understand? I am somehow linked to all of this, to the city, the signs, the voiceless rage and despair and hope, my obsessive recording, though I don't know why. Whatever riddles and truths

I might unlock, it's all mist, nothing compared to the unfolding mysteries of your love for me and the miracle you carry deep within yourself. If I could, I would build a magnificent cathedral or palace of devotion to you. I would command every artist and graffitist to create all the colors and radiance of our love . . . then I would strike it down and tell them to begin again, because it must be a pale shadow of your light. Know that I am not afraid. There is nothing that can stop me from returning to you, and since we are one, there is no force that can stop you from being with me.

He's wasting time writing. He rises, jabs the pen inside the wire spirals, closes the notebook. Monk walks down the dark alley that curves toward 120th Street. Maybe he should head west to Avalon Boulevard. Monk stops. Wait: Mr. Collins's old movie theater, it's just a few blocks from here. Monk heads south down Belhaven Street. At 124th and Central Avenue, marquee lights glow above the faded salmon and teal colors of the art deco walls and scalloped box office of the Argus Theater. Monk grins. He used to work in the old movie house for a couple of summers back in high school. Is it open? Now the movie titles glimmer down in their backlit bold black plastic:

The Sound of Music
Alphaville

That old marquee, some of his best work, those two summers when childhood's fascination with words, codes, anagrams, puzzles grew into a dawning awareness of the secret scripts of the city's signs and graffiti. Working at the Argus, he'd swept floors, ripped tickets, scooped popcorn, but he also changed the marquee each week, spearing plastic letters from their box, gliding each letter in its marquee runners, each letter magnetized at the end of his long pole, he was a semantic fisherman, a harpooner of language. It was a summer of semiotic discovery, old Mr. Collins always good-natured about Monk's weekly marquee adventures in *signology*, which began one week with a dubious motion picture titled *Last Days of Vesuvius*. Monk lettered his own tagline on the marquee: DON'T TELL YOUR FRIENDS IF IT BLOWS! A summer of matinee madness followed, cat and mouse between Monk's cinema codes and old Collins remembering to check the marquee, making Monk correct his youthful folly with his giant magnetic stylus. A baseball movie called *The Stitched Ball* became HE ITCHED BALL . . . unfortunate spacing advertised a Hemingway bio MY PENIS READY . . . and a Vatican spy potboiler teased THE POPE' SHAT . . . a purloined S from the word SLAYS and a new sword-and-sandal epic was born: HERCULES LAYS SAMSON; and Monk's favorite, a soaper called *So Does My Love*—until Monk left an *E* and *S* in the box: SODOMY LOVE . . .

Monk stands under the buzzing marquee, shaking his head: Mr. Collins has converted it into one of these new twin cinemas. More memories flooding back: the old drunks used to slouch outside the doors here, begging for nickels, exchanging Night Train–fueled film theory: "Them tornadoes in *The Wizard of Oz*, see, they's time tunnels them Munchkin motherfuckers use to trespass into the human world . . . that Citizen Kane, he ain't dead, see? He's disguised as Jedediah Leland, wants to see what his friends really think 'bout him . . . you know that *Mutiny on the Bounty*? Captain Bligh, see, he's the good guy, it's that mother Fletcher Christian, he falls in love with some island girl, it's Bligh's monogamy against the crew's *Bounty* of sexual adventures . . ."

"That you, Mr. Collins?" Peering into the graffiti-scarred ticket-booth glass. An old black man with snowy hair squints up from a comic book. "Remember me?"

"Sure," chuckling. "My penis ready. How ya doin', Monk?"

"Okay. You know they're burning down the city?"

"Yeah." Collins closes the comic book, revealing a .38 pistol on the counter. "Safer in here than out there, boy."

"When did you change it to a twin cinema?"

"Last year, landlord keeps raisin' the rent. Why don't ya come in? That *Sound of Music* is real good. No charge. Got plenty of seats to rest a spell, better if you was walkin' out there in the daylight."

Monk shrugs. "Thanks, Mr. Collins." He walks into the darkened foyer. Monk's dead tired, a few hours dozing off in a plush seat in the darkness sounds good, and there's something else, a weird feeling that perhaps he should stop fighting the city, that if he opens up a little, bends instead of opposing forces beyond any morning light's logic, the night will finally release him, that his return is still possible.

Red and lime neon lines flow around the dim snack bar with its yellow glass cases of popcorn and candies; sconces splash lavender light cones on the walls. Last time he was here, years ago when there was only one screen, the movie was *The Crawling Foot* . . . disembodied foot inching along, toes flexing, dragging impossibly slow along floorboards as the heroine screams trapped in the corner, Monk and the audience guffawing . . . *Don't open that*—too late, the cop opens the door as a cowboy boot kicks him in the face . . . the foot grinds, crushing down on the hero's throat as he chokes and struggles to wrench away the monstrous horror . . . Monk pushes through a door below a glowing sign: THEATER 1.

He eases into a chair in the darkness. Two or three heads silhouetted, hunkered in the front rows; smells of popcorn and sweat. On the screen, a preview for the new James Bond movie coming this Christmas, assassins in ebony scuba suits hunting Bond with spearguns through Caribbean waters. Monk grins as the super white man dispatches the bottom-dwelling, *black-suited* frogmen.

Then Monk is gliding over snowcapped mountains, alpine valleys, verdant, sun-dappled meadows as the camera swoops down on that Julie Andrews twirling, raising her frocked sleeves to blue skies:

The hills are alive with the sound of music.
With songs they have sung for a thousand years—

"Thought I'd find you here." Mr. Collins eases into the chair next to Monk, wedging his cane into the armrest. "'Course, I had a fifty-fifty chance." Chuckling.

"No more customers, Mr. Collins?"

"Nope. Locked the doors. Sandi, that's the snack-bar girl, she'll watch the fort. You want a popcorn or Coke, she'll give it to you, my treat. This is a good movie. They don't make 'em like this no more." Nodding his iron-gray head. "Seen it seven times," he says, laughing. "That Julie Andrews ain't too shabby. What you doin' out in this craziness?"

"I was just going to hang out this morning, do some work in my notebook, go to the library, maybe get a burger, take the bus home, then all this shit seemed to almost explode in my face, Mr. Collins."

The old man nods. "Still doin' your art, keepin' a notebook, that's good. I remember when you worked here, every break you had your face stuck in some notebook or paperback. You keep readin' and writin', you meant for somethin' better, little monkey." Mr. Collins chuckles. "Remember when I'd call you little monkey?"

"Sure, Mr. Collins." All at once Monk feels peaceful, grateful for the sanctuary of the movie house, the old man's company: Mr. Collins even smells good, scents of popcorn butter and some kind of crisp laundered smell from his neat tan and powder-blue cotton suit, like lilac.

"Out there, burnin' down their own neighborhood, what kind of sense does that make, boy?" Mr. Collins shakes his head.

"Everything's goin' to hell if you ask me, but no one's asking me. This was a good town, even when you was a kid, remember?"

"Yes, sir."

"Last few years, I don't know, it gets worse and worse. This new generation . . ." The old man shakes his head. On the screen, Captain von Trapp gazes up an ivory spiral staircase where Maria—Julie Andrews—smiles down at him.

"How's your mama?"

"She's fine, doing great."

"She still livin' on Hickory Street?"

"No, she moved to Arcadia, her sister lives there."

"Way out there, huh? You see her regularly? I know you do, 'cause you're a good kid."

"I see her all the time. Talk to her on the telephone too. I'll tell her I ran into you, she'll get a kick out of that."

"Please do. You tell her Mr. Collins sends his respects to Missus Lettie Monk, I sure do." The old man nods. "Yes sir, Missus Lettie was a good woman, you damn lucky she's your mama. All these damn fools out there burnin' down the town. You ain't burnin' nothin'. You know why? 'Cause your mama brought you up right. Now, I know your father was never around, just like half the fools out there causing trouble, no papa to teach 'em right from wrong. Your father, he was a good man, but you know those musicians, always on the road, they shouldn't get married if you ask me, 'course no one's asking me." Mr. Collins grins. "Missus Lettie, she was strong, raised you almost alone. Back then, when you was a baby, this town was still a good place. Big as hell, but Watts was a small town in a big city. Back in the fifties, I guess, when you was growin' up, people watched out for each other, including your mama. Kids could run around, play ball in the streets, get a ice-cream cone at the little store, not hafta worry about no gangsters or drug addict fools . . . You remember it like that, son?"

"I sure do. You're right, Mr. Collins, times now are different, very strange." On the screen, Rolf and Liesl are talking in a garden vestibule ringed with rosebushes.

"Strange is right. Yeah, you kids could play in the streets. All the streets were dirt, no sidewalks or nothin'. We used to call it Mud Town when it rained, remember?" Monk nods his head. "Yes sir, back then everyone—Missus Lettie included—had chicken coops and Sunday barbecues after church, folks gave each other a hand. Your mama, she'd get a few eggs from the coop, give 'em to someone down the street who was hungry, that's just the way it was. And those barbecues, man they was good." The old man licks his lips, nods. "You remember the William's Smokehouse over on 109th, near Central? You was too young. Well, Mr. William, he'd always give some ribs or somethin' to the families, bring a big box to the barbecues." Collins pauses. "Like I said, you was too young, but Mrs. William, she'd visit all the Negro babies in the neighborhood, including you. She used to tell all the mothers to pinch their baby's nose every day so they wouldn't grow up to be a big-nosed Negro." He laughs, shakes his head. "One day, Missus Lettie caught her pinchin' your nose and threw her out. Yes, those were good days. Folks looked after each other. I don't know what the hell is goin' on with people today. We used to get together, build a porch or a garage for folks, everyone pitched in. Didn't need no buildin' permits and a thousand dollars like today. Everybody pitched in, maybe 'cause it was after the war and people didn't just look after themselfs. You remember your neighbors at your mama's house offa Hickory Street? The Claytons, and that Italian family, the Rossinis?"

Monk nods. "I do. I used to play all the time with their son, Adam, we were about the same age." Lost memories flood his mind: the little rubber pool in the Claytons' backyard, playing softball in the field across the street in the rain—creatures covered in mud and blue jeans, Mrs. Rossini bringing over bowls of spaghetti.

Looming in the darkness, a puppet—a blond shepherd boy in lederhosen—dances as Julie Andrews jiggles its strings and sings.

"We built a porch for the Claytons. That's the way folks were." Mr. Collins pauses, looks at Monk, who seems lost in the movie. "Every Saturday you could stroll down the neighborhood. Folks, your mama too had old bathtubs in the yards filled with boiling water, washin' their clothes and kids' clothes and sometimes someone else's clothes if they was workin' or needed help. The women, they'd put the clothes on the line to dry."

"Mom would put the clothes on the line, then us kids would hop in the tubs for our baths."

"Tha's right." The old man rubs his chin, stares up at the movie screen. "I like this part here."

"Got to get some water." Monk feels dizzy. "Be right back, Mr. Collins."

Monk *reels* out into the lobby. He slurps from the water fountain, asks for a box of Raisinets. The snack-bar girl's face is bathed in lemon light, like a projection.

He pushes open a black door, heads down the aisle. The flickering projector beams seem like dust-swirling tractor rays that pull him deeper into the darkness. Mr. Collins is gone. Monk sinks in a velvet chair.

On the screen, like a black-and-white dream: trench-coat gumshoe and French tough guy Lemmy Caution bursts through a door into a seedy hotel room, neon signs blinking beyond the window. "Alpha-Sixty, drink up, you can't stop it." Drunk, a man in shadows offers Lemmy the bottle. Lemmy pushes him away.

Where the fuck is that Julie Andrews? Monk rubs his eyes.

"It's just a computer, Dickson. You were sent here to do a job."

Dickson laughs, swigs from the bottle. "That's what Dick Tracy and Flash Gordon said. They failed, so will you. You'll never make it back to the Outland."

When he closes his eyes the dizziness subsides a little. As if stirred by Mr. Collins's words, he sees those rusted, chipped porcelain bathtubs and his old neighborhood: Mrs. Whitaker, down the street, who hated kids and filled her bathtub with geraniums;

Mom's victory garden in the backyard, tomatoes and green beans and spinach and lettuce when food was scarce during the war; he remembered Mom working her garden, still a victory garden that filled her baskets and grocery bags with fresh fruits, vegetables, home-cooked honey bread he can still smell that she'd lug over to the Carmichaels, who'd lost his job, or to the Lewis family when their dad was drunk, or whoever had a hungry stomach to fill.

An engine revs, startling Monk from his reverie: on the screen, Lemmy Caution zooms down a Parisian freeway in his black Galaxie, beautiful Natacha von Braun next to him, her long hair cascading in the convertible's rush of street lamps like strands of twinkling stars.

Mr. Collins slips into the chair next to Monk. "Had enough of white people singin', huh?" He chuckles, sets his cane against the armrest.

"Guess I got lost." Monk grins.

On the screen, Lemmy slaps Natacha. "Tell the truth, von Trapp!" he shouts.

Monk rubs his throbbing temples. *Did he say von Braun or von Trapp?*

". . . you was just knee-high." Dazed, Monk looks away from the screen: Collins's been talking to him, but he hasn't heard a word. "Brings back memories of your mother too. Missus Lettie was a fine-looking woman. Now, your daddy, he was lucky to get her, yes sir. When he left you and your mama, well, excuse me for sayin', but that was a dirty shame. We all knew your papa was not a homebound kind of man. He was a good man in his own fashion, he had to find where he belonged, which was on the road or in the clubs, playing his bass. You put a man like that in a house with a young wife and a baby, well, he's like a fish out of water and can't breathe."

The city is flickering black-and-white on the screen; only angles of light and darkness, soot skies. Lemmy and Natacha pass under shadows of gray concrete. *Lemmy Caution, report for interrogation,* speakers echo. The walls glow with incandescent white tubes, neon graffiti, but it's graffiti of the future—numbers, equations, mathematical theorems . . .

"You lucky your mama was a strong woman, yes sir. Then Missus Lettie had to go to work, ain't that right, Monk?"

"Golden State Mutual Insurance, over on Forty-second Street, Mr. Collins." Mom went to night school, learned to be a stenographer. She'd come home tired, but looking fresh and beautiful and cook him a real dinner.

Monk watches as Lemmy and Natacha walk down the black-and-white lines of a hotel corridor, past prostitutes in spandex tops and miniskirts, their skin tattooed in numbers and equations like living graffiti. Lemmy bursts through a door, gun in one hand, Kodak Instamatic in the other, the room blinking in the incandescence of the flashcube. On the nightstand, the Gideon Bible's been replaced with a white book, a single black title: *Dictionary.* "The notebook's missing a word." Lemmy thumbs through blank pages. "*Tenderness.*"

Did he say notebook? Monk rubs his eyes.

"I don't know that word," Natacha says softly. "Alpha-Parker erases, prints new editions."

"Alpha-Parker?" Monk whispers. "When did it—"

"What's that, son?" Collins glances over at Monk.

"Huh? I'm sorry, what were you saying, Mr. Collins?"

"We were talkin' about how your mother had that job over at Golden State. But I'm sorry, I keep interruptin' your movie." The old man turns toward the screen: Lemmy and Natacha in the Galaxie, caroming through Parisian night streets, a city of installations and inhuman factories and concrete sloughs.

The rain-slick city in the background behind the Galaxie seems to flicker with Technicolor cobalt and green vistas of Alpine splendor . . .

Monk blinks. *What the fuck?* He closes his burning eyes. *Maybe some kind of side effect from El Gordo's drugs.*

"Your mother's a saint, she sure is," Mr. Collins says to himself as he watches the movie. "Workin' full-time and raising you."

Monk remembers Mother would talk to him, she had to be mother and father to him. She would talk sometimes about her job over at Golden State, how the Negro girls in the stenography pool made less money than the whites, but you had to take it, not get angry, remember your pride, things would change, things *were* changing, she'd tell him, if only he could imagine how bad things were when she was growing up in Texas.

On the screen, Lemmy and Natacha rush through the door. Lemmy snaps pictures with his Instamatic: "Reporter Ivan Johnson for *Figaro-Pravda* . . ." Bursts of flashcube incandescence as . . . Maria and Captain von Trapp materialize like ghosts in the flashes, as a boatswain's whistle shrills:

"Oh please, Captain, love them all!" Maria pleads.

"Yes," Lemmy says, "only lovemaking can override the cold circuits of Alpha-Sixty's logic."

Monk slouches, dizzy. *It's the drugs . . . no sleep . . . I'm dozing, dreaming maybe . . . Think of something else.* His mother opened the world to him because he was her world after his father left. She'd laugh and say she'd known just as many lousy Negro men as white men; most of them wanted to control you or change you; the world expected Negro women to be dominant because some Negro fathers were no damn good. She'd tolerated little foolery or stupidity; she was her own woman because, she'd ask him at the dinner table and ask anyone else who cared to listen, what's the sense of equal rights if women don't have them? You brothers hollering about keeping the nigger down—you better take a look at the woman on your arm.

The Galaxie barrels through plate glass and into the great computer banks of Alpha-Sixty. The machine's smashed to rubble, blinking lights fading. "*It is*," Alpha-Sixty drones, dying in a shower of sparks, "*too late . . .*"

"That voice," Monk mutters, "it's the chief . . ."

"Who?" Collins asks.

"Parker," Monk whispers.

"You okay?" Collins says. "You don't look too good."

Monk nods and stares into the flickering screen.

The old man rests his hand on the cane's handle and rubs his knuckles. "You remember when your mama came after you with that big ol' wooden spoon?" Mr. Collins laughs, slaps his thin kneecap.

"Yeah." Monk grins. He'd just started working for Mr. Collins, must have been thirteen or fourteen. He'd told Mr. Collins there was no school that day, so he cleaned up the theater, then hung around for four hours, watching the double bill: *The Ten Commandments* and *Around the World in 80 Days*. Mother tracked him down, marched into the theater, down the aisle, squeezing past patrons' knees in the packed center row, pulled him up by the ear in front of all those people as Moses, on the screen, was parting the Red Sea, and, propelling him up the aisle, took out her wooden spoon from her belted chiffon dress—lavender and rose colors he still remembers—and the spoon seemed to the little boy the size of a croquet mallet as she proceeded to thrash his behind until the spoon snapped in half and spun into the rows, lost on the dark, sticky floor amid popcorn boxes and soda cups.

Natacha's eyes, filling the screen like a giant black-and-white enchantress, seem to engulf Monk as she whispers to him: *"Je vous aime."*

"I love you too." Monk's eyes are closed. "I'm coming home, baby."

"You all mixed-up, like that Manchurian candidate," Collins chuckles. "Showed that movie a couple years ago. He was all brainwashed. Didn't know fantasy from reality, dreams from wakefulness, books from memories. I remember this scene, it was Frank Sinatra . . . his desk all stacked with books, a scholar like yourself . . . one of them books was called *Ulysses* . . . like you, too much livin' in the mind. Come on, boy." The old man tilts up on his cane. "You dead on your feet. You need sleep and I need to get home."

Out in the shadows of the lobby. "That damn Sinatra," Collins says. Monk blinks, grateful the celluloid kaleidoscope is fading from his brain. "When Kennedy, God rest his soul, was shot, that damn Sinatra and the Mob banned all the prints and the movie disappeared." The snack bar's closed, doors locked, marquee outside unlit like a slab in the darkness. "Mob didn't want no links to no presidential assassinations, public might put two and two together . . . Come on, you can sleep in the projection room." Monk follows Mr. Collins as the old man threads carefully up a narrow flight of stairs, rocking himself up step by step with the cane.

Mr. Collins unlocks a door signed EMPLOYEES ONLY. A small room, a great projector taking up most of the floor. It's a 1960 Century, big as a dynamo—notorious for its Berlin mirrors, which have a propensity to burn film—its great 35 mm reels clicking as the celluloid strip threads through sprockets, spools, looping into white light and gleaming lenses. A flickering cone of light churning with dust motes beams through the rectangular aperture in the wall. A stack of silver reel canisters gleams near the projector. There's a mattress and a blanket and pillow in the corner.

The old man snaps a switch on the projector and the light beam disappears, the big 35 mm reels slowly clacking to a stop. "It'll cool down in a bit. You can leave the door open. Get some rest, son." Mr. Collins points his cane toward the mattress. "This is where I catch a nap now and then, mostly during Westerns, I hate Westerns. You know where the bathroom is. Help yourself to a Coke or popcorn if you get hungry."

"Thanks, Mr. Collins, I'm wiped out."

"Sleep till noon if you want, no matinees tomorrow. Just let yourself out, door'll lock behind you. You be sure to say hello to Missus Lettie, now."

"Yes, sir." They shake hands. "Thank you, Mr. Collins."

"That's all right, did me a world of good seeing you again. You be careful out there, it ain't like the old days, Lord knows."

Monk hears the old man's cane tapping down the stairs as he collapses on the mattress. Somewhere beyond there is the click of the front door downstairs as Mr. Collins hobbles outside. Before sleep his mind seems to unravel in jarring fragments of dreams: iron hatchways and green and rusted rooms; a phonograph, the table invisible under wine and beer bottles and the plastic bowl half filled with rent money like a wilted salad; Lemmy, Felonius, Maurice, Maria, von Trapp, Marcus dancing with Dalynne; a Kodak Instamatic flashbulb flares as Felonius snaps a picture of Karmann; Maurice's fingers glide over Karmann's thigh in flash-cube bursts; Karmann, submerged in citrine waters . . . her open hands slowly waving to him, beckoning, around and around, treading water, weaving endless circles within circles.

10

Classified: Inter-Department Only
Volume 6: Emergency Department Directives
929: Emergency Communications
929.10: Deadly Force Directives
Use of deadly force directives may be communicated by
Chief of Police orally without written protocols during declared emergency situations.

There is only the quiet, the great Century projector under the
light, stacks of 35 mm film canisters, the fan droning warm waves
of air across Monk's startled face. He rubs his face, yawns, heads
through the open door and down the narrow staircase. The lobby's
deserted. In the restroom he urinates, splashes water over his face
and head. He steps behind the snack bar, fills a small box of popcorn, heads toward the locked front doors.

Northwest, a dim haze burnishes the sky above the rooftops;
a block east, scattered street lamps and headlights ebb down
Central Avenue: *Shit*, dawn . . . dusk? Munching popcorn, he
walks to the corner. The street looks quiet, a few cars and pedestrians in the gloaming smog, no cop cars. He walks south along
Central, eating popcorn: better cut over to a quieter street in case

he runs into any hot spots, what Sergeant Trench would call civil unrest. Walking west on 127th Street, the empty popcorn box slips from his fingers into the parched gutter: it's getting *darker.* He's slept all day on that mattress. Karmann must be worried sick and now he'll have to navigate tonight's streets.

Monk's thinking of old man Collins, how he'd said the city had changed so much since he was a kid. Will Monk still be *here* when he's an old man? All the graffiti and the signs—will people write on walls in the future? Maybe it'll be like the science fiction paperbacks he sometimes reads: his city alive, its grids interfaced with him and everyone else; computers conversing with people, buildings programmed for every human need and mood . . . cameras scanning the streets below; inside every building, lenses monitoring each passing face, tracking people of color . . . clothes, hair, body language . . . retinas are scanned, cross-checked against political and criminal databases . . . recorders tuned to any speaking in Spanish or Ebonics . . . iron doors and shutters automatically close, sealing off escape.

Midway down the block, Monk stops. Someone's tagged a *bomb*, a gigantic graffito across the stucco side of Payday Liquor. Monk walks along the wall, printing the letters into the margins of his notebook. Giant Gothic black and silver numbers sprayed towering up the wall: *12197820*, and an arrow pointing south. A simple code, each number but one corresponding to a letter: *LS, G, 8T*, Las Sombras, Gladiators, Eight Trays. An ominous sign, the city's three biggest gangs united? Impossible . . . and united against what or whom? The cops? This is intelligence Trench and all the pigs over at the 77th would be very interested in. Why don't the fuckers leave him and his notebook alone? He wants to just pass through the city, unmolested by all factions and agencies, studying the signs, quietly compiling his urbanologist lore. And the arrow? South, either toward safe harbor and the woman he still hopes waits for him with a grace wearing as thin as the vinyl records she spins down, the needle and the groove her own clock counting the time until he returns, or to some other fate. At the end of the spray-painted wall, near the chained and padlocked glass doors of Payday Liquor, Monk squats down, inspecting the graffito's tagline. As he suspected, scribbling in the notebook, closing its tattered cover: he'd know that style anywhere, those black numbers ghost-lighted in silver, no drips, that Number Seven Regal Silver spray paint, the bold, assured strokes . . . smOG's struck again. Monk steps back from the wall: it's like the store and the wall have disappeared, all you can see at first is the graffiti, like smOG's blown up the store. "It's a bomb, a graffiti bomb." Monk labels the page he's copied in his notebook, *BOMB*, underlining it twice. "Most powerful weapons don't kill us, they change us."

Monk rattles the chains on the door, peers through the glass: three white clerks huddled behind the counter, two of them pointing shotguns at the front door. Monk shrugs, walks on as sirens, cop cars hurtle past.

Once he gets to Belhaven, he'll be southbound, in the general direction of smOG's acrylic arrow and perhaps some kind of state of grace, back to the harbor, to home. An old man passes him, in a hurry, trying to get off these streets. Near the corner, four black men hanging around, talking, pointing up the street. Monk ambles past a billboard shrouded in barbed wire—a beautiful black model, straightened hair, rubbing a cotton swab against her high cheekbones: BE THE WOMAN OF HIS DREAMS . . . WITH OUR CREAMS . . . SNOW WHITE LIGHTENERS. The sign's mast is graffitied with the usual tags, nothing notebook-worthy here, a Grape Street Gladiator crossing out an Eight Tray territorial incursion.

A woman, her face hidden under a red cap and white veil, rushes around the corner at Belhaven Street and slams into Monk. The shopping bag clutched against her chest falls to the sidewalk, record albums cascading from the ripped bag. "Sorry!" a husky voice blurts out. She squats down, slipping the albums into the bag, carefully sliding some of the vinyl records back into their jackets.

"Here you go, lady." Monk bends down, gathers up a few albums for her: Roach, Mingus, Getz, Coleman. "You got some great jazz here." His father played with half of these musicians. He's looking at the last album, a black-and-white photo of John Coltrane in profile, stamped *A Love Supreme/John Coltrane*.

"Thank you." That deep yet feminine voice again, jarring from such a wisp of woman as she reflexively bows: she's wearing a ruby old-fashioned tam-o'-shanter beret, a gossamer white-net veil blurring her face. She takes the record from him; a small tattoo on her right hand, between thumb and forefinger: a single rose, black stem with red petals yet to blossom open.

"Miss Toguri."

Behind the veil, her eyes widen in alarm as she stares up at Monk, then red lips, mottled in shadows behind the veil, slowly smile in recognition. Her hand sweeps back the veil: a Japanese woman, middle-aged, pale, one of those Asian faces that betray no wrinkles, the only signs of aging a kind of weight and gravity in the cheeks and worried mouth. "Mr. Monk. Are you okay?"

"More or less. Just trying to get home."

"Be careful, please, Monk."

"Yeah, you too. It's turning into a hell of a riot."

"From riots come revolutions." She smiles cryptically. "You are still writing in your notebook?"

"Yes."

"My story too?"

"Some notes, yes. Is that okay?"

"Yes. Please write it all down. All the stories. Not just your signs, but the people who scrawled your signs. Soon, after these fires, the city and its signs will change . . . many of us will be gone."

"You too? I hope not, Miss Toguri."

Again that smile that seemed to conceal torrents of unspoken words. "Soon I might perhaps complete one more . . . final chapter of my story for your notebook . . . Goodbye, Mr. Monk."

Clutching the torn bag to her chest, she propels herself east toward Central Avenue, beret and veil angled down to the sidewalk and her hurried steps, as if pushing into a gale or some force instead of the distant sirens and black-smoke night sky.

Monk lingers, staring at her retreating figure. Back in February, wandering around Los Angeles Street and Eighth, he'd found this strange graffito, numbers arranged inside the outline of a red rose with a black stem:

931
5

He couldn't figure it out. A few days later he showed up at the Watts Towers. Behind the iron pinnacles, under canopy tents with folding chairs and wood tables, people would gather for a class or a panel or an exhibit or speech or anything else these poets, professors, activists, gangs, Nation of Islam, citizens, and hundreds more, wanted to organize. There Monk found Big Morton Lighthouse—a black scholar and amateur historian, a kind of fixture and gadfly around Watts, whose shaved round head and stout seven-foot frame suggested an avatar of his surname. Lighthouse laughed, tapping his finger on the graffito in the notebook. "You said around Eighth Street, huh? That's near Little Tokyo. Let's see, that thirty-five number runs up and down, that's north to south, that's latitude thirty-five north. Longitude's east to west, so you reverse that top number, gives you 139 east. That's the coordinates for Tokyo. That's Iva. She lives not too far from there."

"Iva?"

Lighthouse grinned. "You might know her better by her stage name, Tokyo Rose."

"*The* Tokyo Rose?" he'd asked in astonishment. "From the war?"

"Oh yeah. In fact, she comes around here sometimes . . . active in the community . . . you might even say a rebel-rouser."

A week later, after a few discreet inquiries in Little Tokyo, he'd found her little apartment and knocked on the door. She was gracious, made him tea, said she could talk to him, help him with his notebook project, his history of the city, he explained.

Monk showed her the sketch of the rose graffito. "The Tokyo Rose," she sighed. "I've seen a few around town."

"If you look closely," he traced the outline of the drawing with his pen, "the stem and the two sides of the rose are shadowed, forming the letter Y. Is that a Japanese gang?"

"Y for 'yakuza'? Could be . . . there is a connection to the rose."

"A connection?"

"I will tell you . . . in a few minutes." She poured tea.

"Maybe it's a Chinese gang . . . Y for the Yow Yees, their turf is nearby. Or maybe it's the 880s . . . Y for yellow, their color, of course."

"That's a lot of Ys."

"Whoever it is, why do they invoke your name and your past?" Monk asked.

"I'm sorry, I don't know. But I'll tell you about the yakuza and the rose. I want to tell you everything. You're a scholar, you can put it all in your notebook and later figure out what is important."

"You were born here in the city, Miss Toguri?"

"Yes. Just a few miles from here. I went to Compton High School. 'Course, it was more white back then, but I never fit in anyway. I was raised a Japanese American, second-generation, a Nisei. I am a Methodist!" She laughed and sipped tea. "My uncle Ito, the old atheist, used to scold me when I was a little girl coming home from church on Sunday. 'You are Japanese, you are *kami no michi*, Shinto . . . you take the gaijins' god and forget about Japanese gods . . . it is foolish to turn your back on the kami . . . your path will not be easy.' No shit, Uncle Ito. The old buzzard was right. Sometimes I think it was all Uncle Ito's fault. Maybe he was an agent of fate or the tool that *kami no michi* possesses to punish treacherous spirits."

"You know Mr. Lighthouse?" Toguri nodded to Monk. "He said you had the incredible bad luck to be visiting Japan when Pearl Harbor was attacked."

"Yes. Uncle Ito, back in Tokyo for his last years, was dying. I was twenty-five and sent to Tokyo to represent my family for Uncle's last days and funeral. December seventh was the day my life ended. I became a . . . spirit in limbo. A life that was a death in life, a series of . . . confinements both mental and physical that would never end. Stranded in Tokyo when war was declared, I was branded an enemy alien by both countries. And so my ordeals began. POW camps in Yokohama and Mito. I can still feel the rough cotton prisoner's uniform that seemed to grow magically each week as my emaciated body wasted away. Dirty water to drink, just enough insect-infested rice and bean soup to keep the human skeletons alive. I began to hate my own people. Can you understand this? I was an American, I wanted to return to America, to join the war effort and prove my loyalty. I finally got a letter from home. My mother had a market on Flower Street, just a few blocks from here. She lost it all, they herded everyone onto buses at Santa Anita Racetrack and took her away to Manzanar, out in the wasteland. Overnight, Little Tokyo was empty . . . during the war the Negroes moved in . . . did you know it was called Bronzeville for a while?"

"Shit." Monk laughed.

"*Relocation camps*, they called them. My hatred spread to all Americans and then . . . I began to hate myself . . . I was this . . . hyphenated half-spirit of all I despised. The kami were truly punishing me. At the Mito camp, I met my only friends, but the kami spirits would make sure these friends would be agents too, like Uncle Ito, in my . . . unraveling." Her eyes never blinked, as if she were slipping into a trance; Monk had the feeling she was looking through him, somewhere beyond. "Major Cousens-san and Captain Ince-san were Allied prisoners of war, Cousens an Aussie and Ince a bookish Filipino. Ince-san was starving, the camp guards saving their most creative cruelties and beatings for Asian POWs. I would save a crust of bread or a handful of dirty rice for Ince-san when I managed to eat. One day Cousens-san approached me. The Japanese Ministry of Propaganda had offered him and the captain jobs on the state-controlled radio. I spoke English too, he could take me also. A chance to survive, ride out the war. Of course I said yes, and the kami smiled with sardonic laughter. They worked for NHK Radio in Tokyo. Major Cousens-san became producer of the show. He and Ince-san wrote my scripts. Fifteen-minute spots between American swing songs to keep the GIs tuned in. I didn't want to lie to the servicemen, didn't want to get them hurt or killed. Major Cousens-san agreed, and he and the captain played cat and mouse with their radio censors, whose limited English provided the means for my friends to write scripts that kept my anti-American banter limited to girly flirtations, scoldings, and . . . threats that were so over-the-top, I could only smile and imagine every GI stuck in a foxhole laughing and reading between the lines. All I needed was a handle, a name, so the major baptized me Orphan Ann, *your favorite enemy*. Later they would give me another name, the curse that would obliterate my identity. Shakespeare was wrong, a rose by any other name would smell—period."

"Your name wasn't Tokyo Rose?" Monk asked.

"No, only the Americans called me that. Countless GIs huddled around their radios in huts, jungles, camps, fields, villages, cities, and towns scattered halfway across the world, looking forward to a cigarette and Orphan Ann's sultry voice during *The Zero Hour*. I tried to help the soldiers when I and my writers could, even slipping in warnings when Major Cousens-san learned some rumors about an impending attack . . . a pun, a lowering of my voice to a whisper, an American slang phrase—once

I remember I blew a whistle impersonating an American drill sergeant, the whistle blasts in Morse code. After a year or two, our
secret efforts backfired . . . because we'd warned the Americans
of some attacks, I began to . . . spook the GIs. Some said I could
tell the future, that Orphan Ann knew the next victory or defeat,
which ship would sink, which fighter plane would crash . . . what
was worse, some soldiers thought I was whispering, flirting with
them personally, speaking *only* to them . . . that I knew, like
God, who would live and who would die . . . When Japan finally
surrendered, I thought my long exile might end. A military tribunal, with the testimony of Major Cousens and Captain Ince, and
the evidence of some of the scripts and broadcast recordings,
found me innocent of any war crimes. It was noted in the record
that I tried to aid American servicemen whenever possible, that I
was coerced into the propaganda effort along with many other
POWs. But the kami spirits are patient . . . I am only a paper
candle-lantern . . . the kami blow the lantern across the dark
waters of my life until the candle extinguishes itself. My visa and
papers were delayed. The U.S. government was at odds with the
tribunal's ruling in Japan. By this time I was in love with an
American serviceman in Tokyo. A baby girl was born, Fumiko. The
baby was very sick. I tried to—" Toguri broke off, her lips trembling as she sipped the last of her tea. "This is difficult but I want
to say all this now, quickly, get it over." Suddenly she squeezed
Monk's hand across the table. "Promise me you will write it in your
notebook."

"I promise," Monk said, and finally she released his hand.

"I tried to feed Fumiko but there was no milk in my breasts.
When I held her, she was light as a balloon. All the hospitals were
bombed-out, food and milk were hard to find, and the baby was
sick. She needed doctors and hospital care in the U.S. My visa
and papers were held up. A month later, in November, Fumiko
died. My lover disappeared. I fell on hard times in the rubble of the
city. My radio friends went back to their old lives and countries.

The Japanese and the Americans didn't want me. The tribunal and the U.S. government didn't want me. I lived hand to mouth, odd jobs in Tokyo as the months passed. My daily visits to the consulate brought no relief from my limbo. Because of my English, I worked in bars sometimes with the GIs, but I was no longer young or pretty. I never prostituted myself. I held myself in grace even among the most drunken and dishonorable American soldiers. The bars were run by yakuza, but they were not unkind. They gave me some money, clothes, food, sake. Obatsu, my gangster boss, a big Buddha with two fingers missing, chopped off due to the usual yakuza misunderstandings, was a kind of father to me. One rainy night, because I asked, Obatsu took me to a dingy pachinko arcade, where, in a back room, an old man ran a tattoo parlor for Obatsu and his underworld friends. The old artist—forced by Obatsu, because it was a shocking societal lapse to tattoo a woman—inked a beautiful rose on my hand." Toguri raised her pale hand from the teacup and stared in silence for a moment at the small, black-stemmed solitary red rose between her thumb and forefinger. "A rose by any other name . . . a rose for Fumiko, the sansei, the third generation that will never be, the red petals that will never blossom."

"The Tokyo Rose graffito I saw." Monk placed his teacup in its saucer. "It has a personal meaning—the loss of your daughter— but it's also a Japanese gang, maybe offshoots of yakuza during the war."

"I suspect so, but as I told you, I don't know. It could also be a Chinese gang, as the yakuza made many inroads into China, when the Japanese overthrew Manchuria during the war."

"Miss Toguri, if I were to guess what you mean to these gangs . . ." Monk slowly twisted his teacup in its saucer, gathering his thoughts. "Graffiti is communication . . . but it's also war for hearts and minds, for more power . . . it's communication that's weaponized . . . you were used as a propaganda weapon . . . but you turned it back and used it against your real enemies, who were finally defeated. You were the weakest victim they could find . . . a woman, a prisoner, an orphan in a strange land, destitute . . . an abandoned mother who lost her only child. And yet you found a way to help destroy one of the greatest evils in history."

"I don't know." Her gaze seemed to search into Monk's eyes.

"How did you get home?"

"Finally the visa materialized and I returned to Los Angeles. My parents were dead, no family, the Flower Street market and Little Tokyo shops long gone in the . . . shuttering and land-grabbing orgy of theft and violence after Manzanar. I worked down in the Garment District, anonymous behind banks of sewing machines under fluorescent lights and giant fans, forgotten, but not by the cruel spirits of Shinto. In '49 the government finally came and arrested me for high treason."

"Mr. Lighthouse showed me a history book with your arrest mug shot in it," Monk said. "You're actually smiling, like . . . that Mona Lisa."

"Why not? We live in an upside-down world where the innocent are guilty and the guilty innocent." She paused and looked into his eyes. "A world where those that see may be blind, and those that are blind may see." That Mona Lisa smile again. "My court-appointed public defender was as well-meaning as he was powerless. It was 1950, they were burning not witches but comic books and immoral novels. The American Legion and the Legion of Decency were making America safe from flesh peddlers, Commies, and freethinkers. The Rosenbergs were arrested for atomic spying. My public defender said the radio star Walter Winchell was broadcasting raving tirades demanding my arrest and imprisonment. Winchell had the ear of Senator McCarthy and his House Un-American Activities Committee . . . my defender called it the House *of* Un-American Activities." Toguri smiled and gazed for a moment into the mysterious patterns of the tea leaves in the bottom of her empty cup. "I was caught in this madness, a cold war world all the more evil for trafficking its violence and injustice underground. I served six years. Now I have finally found my way back to my city. It draws me . . . like the war, maybe it suits my dark destiny."

•

Monk lingers, watching as she marches with her shopping bag toward the immolated heart of the city. Now another kind of war rages in the streets, and she's returned. Her figure, a wisp of red and white, disappears around the corner. He turns and walks down the sidewalk. To this spiritless world, to her tormentors, she would always be Rose.

11

"Sugar, I know you're worried. He'll be fine, honey."

Karmann nods and takes a deep drag from her cigarette. She and Dalynne are sitting at the kitchen table, smoking, drinking wine from paper cups. Through the open hatchway, music and voices rise and fall from the adjoining container. "I know," she answers softly, unconvincingly.

"Monk knows that damn city better than anyone. Better than the police. He'll make it back." Dalynne pats Karmann's hand.

"Maybe I should go out there, try to find him."

"Are you crazy, girl? In your condition? They're burnin' the city down!"

Karmann frowns and taps her Kent into the ashtray heaped with lipsticked butts and ashes. Flames, smoke, blackness: she can't think about it anymore, it's worse than death, this limbo, as if hell had somehow impinged on them and the city, engulfing them all.

"Look, I didn't mean it like that." Dalynne sips her wine. "It's dangerous, but Monk'll be all right, you'll see, honey. He knows how to stay out of trouble. He's smart, clever, can read all the signs, right?"

Karmann nods.

"Just stay put. Wait a little longer. You can't go out there, it's too crazy." Dalynne lights another cigarette, decides to change the subject. "I love your hair, it's so glorious. I hate this damn Ultra Sheen." She flicks a thick shoulder-length strand.

Karmann smiles; she can see Dalynne's roots, tinged with sienna from the lye straightening parlor.

Outside, a bottle smashes and loud laughter echoes off the iron walls.

Dalynne gazes at her friend for a moment, the empty, dark eyes, Karmann's face lined with exhaustion and worry. "Besides, you gotta make sure these fools don't burn down your house . . . or sink it or whatever."

"Yeah." Karmann grins for the first time tonight. "I just feel so . . . so damn helpless."

"Now, we might be a lot of things, but helpless ain't one of 'em. Listen to those fools out there, they just boys, not a man around. You lucky you have Monk, you got his back." She sips her wine and nods. "He's like, I don't know, something different, something fine. You're protectin' him, though you don't think so." A little drunk, she points her cigarette at Karmann. "And I know he's watchin' over you and the baby, in his way, gettin' closer to home."

"Hey, girls." It's Cooky weaving through the hatchway like a black scarecrow with an Afro. "Hey, wine, wine's fine." He's swaying above the table, his junkie face gaunt, chalk-gray, holding up an empty plastic cup.

"You gonna make yourself sick, Cooky," Karmann pouring red wine into his cup.

"I'm real good, real good." Cooky cheers, gulps wine, and staggers away through the portal.

"A ship of fools." Karmann exhales smoke.

"Like I said, girl, not a man out there, 'cept Maurice."

"He ain't no good either." Karmann sips wine. "With his Islam mumbo jumbo, all he wants is slave women."

"Yeah. Them Muslim men get to have harems, don't they?"

"He's tryin' to recruit me as one of his concubines."

"Conk you what?" They laugh and sip wine. "Is that on their damn leaflets they passin' out in the ghetto?" Dalynne exhales her smoke. "I'm surprised every nigger in town ain't linin' up at the temple."

The girls laugh loudly and squeeze hands across the tabletop; it feels liberating to laugh, an animal joy that short-circuits too much thought, too much worry and fear.

"Honey, you blessed you found Monk, don't you worry about him. Now, Marcus, he'd sign up for that harem in a minute. No damn good. You lucky, girl. Only two things Marcus likes." She refills her wine cup. "The sound of his own voice when he's speechifyin' about all us still slaves, you'd think Lincoln got shot yesterday . . . with his long gray beard like a black Moses."

Karmann inhales her Kent. "I've seen that beard up close. There was, let me see," she's buzzed, counting off on her polished fingernails, "crumbs . . . cheese dip . . . drops of chicken gravy—"

They're laughing, slapping the tabletop. The wine bottle is almost empty.

"And the other thing that man loves to do is look 'n' try to touch every woman he can find." Dalynne frowns and empties the bottle into her cup.

"Let's go see what these fools are up to," Karmann says, smudging the Kent into the overflowing ashtray.

•

In a Triton container, knots of people dance around a plastic radio blaring pop songs, or stand around drinking beer and wine. A girl in a beret and a frowning man with a black T-shirt and sweatpants nod to Karmann as she walks past; she doesn't know who they are. Two couples are making out on the car seat in the corner; others crowd around the window torched through the iron walls, gazing at something below. Slim-Bone and three men are sitting on crates, playing poker, smoking, a bottle of Monk's whiskey in the center of face-up cards on the floor.

Karmann and Dalynne climb metal steps and clamber into a Matson container room: blue and yellow lightbulbs on strings cast the room in strange velvet shadows. Two couples slouch on pillows on the floor, drinking wine and talking. A few young men are hovering around a table, picking at cold fried chicken and potato chips. Karmann has to step over puddles of wine and shards of broken beer bottles. Near the opposite hatchway, a glint of golden light in the indigo shadows catches her eye: it's Felonius, grinning, his gold tooth sparkling. He's on the wall phone again, slouched down on the floor, the phone cradled in his sweaty neck as he sips from a bottle of Monk's brandy. Lamar's sitting next to him, nodding his black sunglasses, mumbling to himself.

"Motherfucker's always on my phone." Karmann threads her way over to Felonius. She glares down at him. "Felonius, you gotta get off the phone."

"In a minute, baby." He sips from the bottle and taps the receiver. "You should meet this girl—no, not you, baby," he mutters into the phone. "Says her name's Jazmin, like Jazz, you know?"

"Jazz," Lamar grinning, stoned, mumbling incoherently.

Karmann grits her teeth, her heart racing; the line has to stay open, what if Monk tries to call? She grabs the receiver from under Felonius's chin and slams it back into the wall cradle.

"Fuckin' bitch, why y'all gotta get nasty like that?" Felonius's bloodshot eyes glare up at the women.

"If you don't like it, why don't you leave?" Karmann says.

"You girls should be sweet to a brother," Felonius says. "Use honey, not vinegar . . . I could give you somethin' sweet—"

"Sweet and short," Dalynne says.

Lamar grins up at Karmann. "Shame," mumbling something she can't understand, "sweet piece of ass . . . Monk done knocked you up. Nigger ain't comin' back."

"Fuck you! Get out!" Karmann shouts. Now, for the first time, Karmann feels this surge in her belly, the faint but unmistakable kicks of the baby inside her. "Oh my god," she whispers, rubbing her stomach.

"What is it? Come on, honey," Dalynne steering her away. "You don't need this shit." Turning as they walk away: "Fuck both you motherfuckin' losers."

Another hatchway leads into the double-wide Sea-Land container. A half-dozen revelers are gathered around the Zenith TV towering above them on the crab trap, its baling wires for antennas snaking up the riveted walls. On the screen, black-and-white images materialize, then fade away, coalescing between white storms of static, a newscaster's voice fading in and out. Karmann and Dalynne watch the screen: a dark avenue, the blinking lights of police cars behind a white reporter speaking into a microphone. The reporter, the news camera seem to tower over them like some hellish sky god. "This is Mr. Gonzalo Gomez with MAPA—the Mexican American Political Association. Now, you're saying, Mr. Gomez, that Mexican Americans are angry at the Negroes?"

Gomez's face is covered with a bandanna, only his eyes visible as he stares into the camera. "That's right . . . Negroes are getting the jobs . . . making gains . . . we're tired of it."

"Jobs?" Someone next to Karmann. "What's that motherfucker talkin' about?"

"We don't get on the white man's news," Gomez says. "Mexican Americans are more passive than Negroes . . . we would never riot in East L.A."

"Shit, why that beaner wearin' a mask?" another voice nearby.

"He prob'ly not even Mexican."

"You know what I think? I think he's white . . . maybe works for Channel Five news."

"Yeah, or a cop . . . anything to keep us at each other's throats, black against brown."

"Fuck 'em, burn it all fuckin' down."

The voices around her fade, her ears are ringing, waves of nausea grip her as the room seems to sway, then Dalynne's holding her by the waist. "Let's get out of here. He's okay, he's okay," Dalynne steering her toward iron steps, Karmann's palm pressed against her belly.

"You okay?"

"Yeah. Thanks." Karmann looks around, feels better now; they're in the Hanjin cargo room, with its lime-painted walls. Here, someone's blaring one of Monk's bop records on the hi-fi turntable atop its rusted-crab-traps countertop. "Dalynne, when Felonius was on the phone. I felt for the first time the baby! The baby kicking inside me."

"Oh, honey, that's wonderful! And you're just what, fifteen weeks?" Karmann nods. "Fifteen and already kickin' up a storm! That means a boy for sure."

"It was when I screamed at Felonius . . . like the boy was trying to kick him."

"Kick him out!" Dalynne laughs. "That's right! Let's celebrate! We need more wine." She guides her past milling couples and drunken men, all strangers. *Who are they all? How did so many people come?* They find a table strewn with empty beer and wine bottles. "Shit, they gone and drank every fuckin' thing."

A black girl appears, wearing a pink halter top and jeans: her jet-black Afro seems to mushroom out from a pink headband. A hand, thumb and four fingers wearing silver and gold rings, extends a smoldering joint to Karmann.

"No thanks."

Dalynne takes the joint and sucks in a voluminous hit, passing it back to the girl, who wanders off. "You got any more wine hidden away, honey?" she gasps, exhaling cloying, pungent smoke toward the peeling iron ceiling.

"Dalynne! I been lookin' for you!" Marcus appears out of the green lightbulbs and haze, like some nightmare of a ghetto troll. Another stranger stands beside him, a middle-aged black man with short hair and round wire-rim glasses, smoking a menthol cigarette. "I been lookin' all over for you, where you been?"

"Just hangin' out with Karmann."

"This is Etaoin Shrdlu. Just met him at the party. He's a real gone motherfucker. Works at the DWP. This is my girlfriend, Dalynne." He's waving a beer bottle in his hand.

Dalynne, having rolled her eyes at the word *girlfriend*, smiles and extends her hand. "Nice to meet you."

"This is Karmann, our beautiful hostess." Marcus grins hungrily at Karmann, letting his eyes slowly gaze down and take in Karmann's breasts under her blouse, her tight jeans.

"Pleased to meet you." They shake hands; she wants to get away from Marcus, from everyone, these strangers, this rent party that the riot's turned into a siege: how can she demand anyone leave when the city's on fire? What to do? Go to the bedroom and sleep. Get drunker. Guard the telephone and hope he'll call. Keep patrolling their home, try to keep these men from descending into god knows what depths of mayhem and depravity.

"Nice to meet you too," Shrdlu says in a nasal voice, sucking in his menthol cigarette.

"Show 'em, show 'em," Marcus says, slightly slurring his words, sipping his beer.

"Are you sure? They are disturbing."

"Yes. They should see!" Karmann notices a new glob, looks like guacamole, clinging in Marcus's woolly beard.

Shrdlu pulls a stack of cards from his pants pocket. "I collect certain antique postcards." Eyes gleaming under his glasses, he moves between the girls, slowly shuffling the cards so they can see. Karmann, in this cloud of menthol cigarette haze, gazes down at each postcard.

"Oh my god!" Dalynne whispers.

Karmann looks down, her lips grimacing in horror at the black-and-white or faded sepia photographs and tintype engravings and daguerreotypes, each image engraved or etched with a postcard greeting or legend: a black man in a suit and bow tie hanging from a tree: *Greetings from Biloxi, Miss, 1912* . . . a little boy gazing up at an oak tree, a naked black man suspended from its branch: *Hangman's Tree, Helena, Montana* . . . a cinder corpse on a dirt road, carbonized hands still tied with singed coils of rope: *Burning of the Negro G. Jones, Marietta, Georgia, 1930* . . . a naked black woman hung from an iron bridge: *The End of Negro Mary Thorn, Clanton, Alabama, 1926* . . . a black man, shirtless, hanging on a gallows in a town square; a crowd of men, women, and children wave to the camera: *Scenic Greenville, Texas, 1933* . . .

"Why do you— I don't want to see," Karmann turning away.

"That's just it. No one wants to see!" Marcus waves his beer bottle. "It's like I been tellin' you. We're still slaves to them. That's how they see us! Nineteen thirty-three, that's yesterday! Nothin's changed. Instead of rope, they use M16s and police shotguns! That's why we got to burn it all away, burn it all down."

"Marcus, you and your damn crazy theories." Dalynne shakes her head.

"Crazy?" Marcus's bloodshot eyes widen. "You know what I think, Mr. Shrdlu? I think some brothers should go out there, take pictures of beatin' some white ass, then we can mail our own, watcha call it, commemoration postcards . . . Greetings from Watts, Motherfuckers . . ."

Etaoin Shrdlu nods, sucking his menthol cigarette. "In the water department, where I work, my cracker coworkers secretly trade 'em with all the city departments, like fucking kids with baseball cards."

Dalynne frowns. "If you paid half the attention to me as you do goin' on and on about slavery—"

"Why you so selfish? Why don't you listen to what I—"

Karmann's gone, across the hazy green shadows, their voices fading away. She wants to smoke, take an aspirin for her pounding head, lie in the darkness of her bedroom, wait in the cool darkness, wait for him.

No one seems to see Karmann as she passes through each iron chamber like a ghost: perhaps she's invisible because she doesn't want to see them . . . she feels as if she's in a trance, floating back through each chamber and container, each stairway that descends or ascends, each torched window gouged through the iron walls, windows that reveal nothing, only the darkness beyond.

Like a sleepwalker, the only thing Karmann sees is that tiny gold light penetrating her nightmare, like a portent of danger that dimly breaks through to register on the dreaming brain: it's Felonius's gold tooth again. She walks under the cones of blue and yellow bulbs in the Matson container, light shrouded in cigarette and pot smoke. Felonius is on the phone again, slouched on the floor, brandy bottle empty between his legs.

She heads upstairs on the steel rebar ladder Monk has welded between containers, and steps through another hatchway. The WestCon container reeks of sweat and beer. Men and women, some shirtless and topless, sway and dance drunkenly under amber strobe lights; they've set up two big radios in the corner that blare rock and funk music: the sounds echo from the metal walls, creating delays and jarring distortions. Pressing through the dancers toward the open hatchway, now she can see they've stolen five or six of those yellow blinking lights, pried them from the wooden sawhorse signs the traffic department uses, and strung the lights across the room with wire. A thin girl grabs Karmann as she passes, spinning her around, the girl's exposed breasts jiggling and flouncing: Karmann sees a flash of black nipples like inky silver dollars, then the dancer's eyes, empty, void of even a hint of reflection or life, then she breaks away. Near the hatch door, two shirtless young men smoke cigarettes and watch her sullenly; one man turns away, but not before she can glimpse the pistol jammed in his waistband . . . Karmann slips through the portal.

Karmann's on the rusted roof of an Evergreen container. The evening is thick with August's heat, no breeze, just this warm oppression that seems to squeeze her body, her brain itself. A sliver of moon wavers above like a mirage. Down below, the Pacific seems a dark mirror that only reflects the heat back into her bones. Karmann walks toward the steel boat ramp on the southern edge. Distant shouts, laughter rises through the thick night air, and Karmann pauses, turns. Behind her, toward the docks, a couple of containers down Boxville: some of the revelers have tied a rope from a beam they've jammed through a rusty big crane hook on the container's roof, and now they're taking turns swinging on the rope, leaping naked into the inky Pacific below. In her mind a flash of light—light dead from the past, ghostly reflected in faded antique shutters and prisms and powder flashes—sears the night as the naked black boy swinging on the rope seems to be hanging from his twisted neck . . .

Karmann turns away and strides across the boat ramp. She has to step over the thick iron ribs that divide the roof of this Atlas Maritime container. Beyond the harbor, north into summer's night, ominous ribbons and towers of smoke glower in the dark sky. *My baby's out there . . . stop thinking stop thinking.*

Trudging up the wooden plank, finally almost running across the Matson observation deck, past the white plastic chairs and table, to the far railing, the edge of the world.

She descends the welded steps that angle down the side of the container. Each time her hand grips the crooked, thin pipe handrail, she remembers him bending it, welding it piece by piece, perhaps his rusted, galvanized fingerprints are still here, meeting each touch of her hand like a ghost, like one of his damn signs.

Safe, alone in the candlelight now. Their bed waits in the corner, a mattress under piles of blankets, beyond Monk's shelves and crates jammed with their paperbacks and junk: a bed too empty, too forlorn to look at now. Karmann pours merlot into a plastic cup, finds aspirin in the nightstand drawer, swallows two pills, empties the cup and refills it.

Her fingers riffle through the records that fill an orange crate on the rug, pulling out one of Monk's jazz albums. She sets the vinyl on the turntable, a finger gently guiding the needle to the groove: side two of *Undercurrent*. Karmann needs another Kent, but her fingers brush her belly, and she settles for the wine. "Thirty-three and one-third revolutions per minute." How many orbits, songs spun in the air like spells, until he returns? By the time she gets through side one and Bill Evans's piano goes into her favorite song, "Dream Gypsy," the Kent pack and the bottle are almost empty. She stares down at the cover, the blue-tinted, underwater photograph she loves titled "Weeki Wachee Spring, Florida": the profile of a woman in a long white gown, barefoot, floating on her back languidly just beneath the water's surface, her head half submerged, her face invisible, still clinging above in the air and the light, blending into a soft, mysterious radiance beyond . . . her black hair and palms suspended under her in repose, peace . . . but it's not death to Karmann, it's as if the woman is almost free, rising from dark, murky depths.

12

Monk stands before a billboard on the corner facing a boarded-up storefront. The street lamp here is broken, only starlight dampened through smog and smoke. Up on the catwalk of the towering sign, shadows move: a man dressed in black works over the billboard. Monk stops, watching the tagger, dwarfed under the huge advertisement of giant packs of gum hurled in the air as a crowd of white hands wait to catch them. The man in black scurries along the catwalk, unfurling, pasting big cutouts against the billboard. Now, flying through the air with those packets of diet gum, there are several images of red bricks and flaming Molotov cocktails.

The tagger spray-paints his name in the bottom corner of the sign with a lightning stroke of silver, jumps down from the iron ladder hanging from the billboard's side, stops, nods at Monk, only his eyes visible, visored between a black bandanna and black beret. "Nice work," Monk smiling. "I think I saw your work down on Central, around Seventy-ninth." Monk slips his notebook from his jeans, fans through several pages. "Yeah."

The shadow pads over to Monk and gazes into the notebook. Monk's sketched a full-page picture of two black parents beaming, doting over their baby boy, who's standing inside his playpen, clutching the bars with his tiny dark fists as if in a rehearsal for some future, preordained incarceration. Monk's indicated where the playpen manufacturer's name has been blocked over with PICKANINNY PLAYPENS and, below the smiling toddler, another paste-over: NOW WITH NEW ULTRA-LEAD PAINTED BARS!

"Thanks." A green VW convertible whines over to the curb, headlights out. A cute girl smoking a cigarette is behind the wheel, brushing long brunette strands from her face. He throws a canvas equipment bag into the backseat. Monk can't tell, by the strip of eyes and brow and forehead above the bandanna, if the shadow is a black man or just smudged with grease and dirt.

"Are you going south? Anywhere south, I got a long way to go, man."

"How can I say no to a fan?" To the girl: "He's cool." Monk jumps in the back and the VW lurches out of the darkness and down 132nd Street. "This is Sofia."

"Monk." Sofia salutes him with a wave of cigarette smoke. "Got a few of your works here, Jaxsy GK," Monk tapping the notebook. "You should open up a gallery."

"Friends call me Jax. A gallery, yeah, the pigs would dig that." He pulls the bandanna down around his neck: a black man in his thirties, handsome, with a neatly trimmed mustache.

"Man, it's weird." Monk shakes his head. "I don't know why . . . I pictured you as a white man."

"Why?" Jax's rubbing paint from his hands with a rag.

"I don't know. A white Madison Avenue type . . . fired from his job, seeking revenge on all those billboards."

Jax laughs. They pass a pawnshop, knots of shadowed men smashing windows. Sirens drift somewhere down the blocks of smoke as looters scurry in the dark interstices of shattered street lamps. "Hope you don't mind a few stops."

"Sure. What's the GK stand for?"

"Giant Killer, for the billboards." Jax takes a hit from Sofia's cigarette. Jax is well-known in underground art circles, but Monk's never heard before the explanation for the artist's initials. Jax bumped up his notoriety a few years ago in New York, when he famously—despite cameras and security—tagged the foundation of the Statue of Liberty with a red, white, and blue stencil: TORCHES NOT TORTURE.

"The city is our canvas." Sofia smiles, kills the headlights, pulls to the curb.

"Wanna come?" Jax's impish grin lights up his face. "I could use a lookout."

"I have to get home."

"It won't take long," Sofia says, turning toward the backseat. "Then we'll go south." Now Monk can see her face: olive, translucent skin, full lips, brown eyes so dark they look like obsidian mirrors.

Monk nods. "How can I say no to Jaxsy?"

The two men jump out, Jax grabs the canvas bag. The VW disappears around the block in a puff of exhaust and cigarette smoke. They trudge across the street and hop a crippled chain-link fence. Before them looms a huge Foster and Kleiser billboard, the massive advertisement glowing under its canopy of flickering fluorescent lights: an attractive white couple sitting in a bar, toasting with frosty glasses of Pabst Blue Ribbon beer as they watch the TV over the bar. The man's hand rests lightly on the girl's waist as they watch a horse race on the television screen. Great glowing lime letters read INVITATION FROM YOUR TAVERN KEEPER . . . COME AND WATCH THE RACES . . . PABST BLUE RIBBON. Jax unzips the canvas bag, telescopes out a collapsible aluminum half-ladder with hooks. He pulls the bandanna over his face, hooks the ladder up around the bottom rungs of the signpost's iron ladder, straps the bag around his neck, and hoists himself up onto the catwalk. Monk sketches in his notebook as Jax goes to work with incredible speed. A few quick slashes of spray paint and now a black man sits in the bar with his white companion, his dark hand unspeakably caressing her waist. A sticker's pasted expertly on the board, background browns and grays already perfectly matched, then a silver-painted scrawl in the bottom corner, tagged *Jaxsy GK*, and he's done, already clambering down and unhooking the ladder. Monk doesn't have time to finish his sketch as he laughs and they run back through the fence. They jump into the waiting VW and Sofia peels away into the darkened street, headlights out. Monk watches the billboard pass behind them: INVITATION FROM YOUR TAVERN KEEPER . . . COME AND WATCH THE RIOTS.

"Sorry, man," Jax sharing Sofia's cigarette, "we have to backtrack a little, Sofi's turn now, but we'll get a little more south." The VW rattles along light traffic west down 135th Street.

"Maybe we can get some news." Sofia twists the AM radio knob.

"You're listening to KABC and this is Joe Pyne. We're back with Negro militant Ernie Smith."

"Have you heard this crazy white man?" Monk grins and Jax nods.

"Mr. Smith," Pyne's voice is shrill, "are you going to tell me that your fellow Negroes burning down stores and looting merchandise is *my* fault?"

"You damn right, it's your fault, and every other white man in power that's keeping the Negro down!"

"You are just like the Muslims and the other Negro militant nationalists. What about the good Negro leaders like Martin Luther King? Why don't you tell your people to integrate peacefully?"

"King and Dick Gregory and all the rest of them are nothin' but Uncle Toms. *Integration* is a white word to keep the Negro down. It took the Civil War to end slavery, the white man don't understand peace—"

"You, sir, are just a Negro hoodlum," Joe Pyne's voice blares in the radio static. "Your organization and the Muslims and the white hipsters out there, you're all Commie liberals who advocate the violent overthrow of the United States!"

"You should go on his show, Jax!" Sofia shouts.

"You whites are afraid of the black man unless he's weak," Smith's voice rattles from the radio. "The black man does everything better, even the wrong things! He's stronger, makes more babies, gets drunker, fights harder, lives faster, and screws better!"

Everyone laughs, Sofia's eyes wide with feigned shock and amusement in the rearview mirror.

"How dare you!" Pyne shouts, then an announcer's voice crackles over the radio: "KABC will return after station identification."

Jax snaps off the radio. "Everyone's going crazy," smiling, "maybe this is the last summer before everything gets all biblical and burns."

"All these stations with new talk shows, angry white men," Monk says. "What the fuck do they have to be angry at? People driving in their cars, isolated, through all these streets and freeways, listening to these fools . . . no wonder everyone's pissed off and insane, afraid of everyone else."

"They clog all our senses with their propaganda." Sofia waves her hand while she talks. "Eyes, ears . . . they'd inject their lies or wire our brains if they could figure out how, but we'll take it back, one street at a time."

The warm summer night buffets Monk in the backseat. A helicopter scuds over them, choppering east toward Compton. They pass a gas station, police with shotguns guarding pumps. "We're almost there," Jax says. "Won't take long. Sofi's more of a hit-and-run artist, guerrilla art."

"Jax is into iconography, using corporate ads' own weapons against them." Monk watches Sofia's eyes in the rearview mirror.

"Ike said beware of the military-industrial complex." Jax smiles. "But it's the advertising-media complex that holds all the power. They project their own reality, then they can shape public thought to their own ends."

"Jax wants 'em to think, but I'm more into artistic rape and pillage. I think the greatest canvas would be if they burn this entire city to the ground." Sofia exhales smoke.

"You're an anarchist, Sofia?" Monk yells as cop cars, sirens pealing, careen past.

"Call me Sofi." She brakes the VW to the curb. Half a block ahead, a big General Outdoor billboard shines above the street: a smiling white couple sitting on the grass with a picnic blanket and basket. Near them, a little girl squeals as she arcs into the air on the park's swings, her little brother waving at Mom and Dad from the top of a metal slide. COME HOME TO GARDENA GOLD MEDALLION HOMES. In the lower corner of the sign, smaller print: *Models do not reflect ethnic preferences.*

"We're a team, like Frida Kahlo, Diego Rivera." Jax slides behind the wheel.

"Like Abbott and Costello." Sofia grabs the canvas bag.

Jax thumps the VW into gear, and they lurch down 135th. Monk turns around: Sofia's walking in the shadows toward the receding billboard. "She never answered my question."

"Sure she did. She wants to burn down the city, but only for aesthetic reasons. Therefore she is an artist, not an anarchist." They're heading back, around the block. On the corner, three young men smash windows.

"Done already?"

"Sofi's fast, hit-and-run," pulling over as Sofia jumps in the passenger seat and they throttle down the street. Monk stares at the billboard and laughs: all she's done is slap a paper over two words in the bottom corner of the sign: *Models always reflect ethnic preferences.*

North now, up Vermont Avenue. Not the way Monk wants to go, but Jax said they'd eventually swing back south. Monk realizes he hasn't thought about Karmann since he stumbled on Jax and Sofia, but his surprise and pangs of guilt have already faded; this rush of outlaw exhilaration seizes him, he can't believe he's found this Bonnie and Clyde graffiti duo, kindred masters of the city's secret scripts and shadow signs . . . in this cramped, hot backseat, even with all the mad rush of the burning blocks rushing past, there's no place he'd rather be but with them, here and now. Cop cars flash, cordoning off a retail store, smoke and flames churning from its windows and rooftop. The sidewalks overflow with crowds watching the police and the fires. Fire trucks honk past them. "Beautiful," Sofia says, lighting a cigarette.

Past 126th Street, Jax pulls over near a darkened alley. "Ten minutes, I'm going to do them both." Jax climbs out, stubs his cigarette under his shoe. "Our last hit for tonight," to Monk, "then we'll get you south." He grabs the canvas bag and pulls the bandanna over his grin.

"Watch your ass." Sofia revs the VW down the street.

Jax lopes down the alley, then jumps a wall. He's in a dark triangle of a city lot, behind a glowing, towering MOB billboard: Mobius Outdoor Billboards. The huge sign is a great V, two billboards connected by a single steel catwalk above the iron posts. Jax hooks the half-ladder to the bottom step of the sign's suspended rungs and scrambles up. Looming before him, a colossal panorama in color beneath the cowling of fluorescent lights: it's Pat Boone, posing in slacks like a casual giant, a tennis racket in the crook of his elbow. Behind him, a Falcon station wagon, roof rack loaded with fishing gear, skis, luggage. GOING PLACES THIS SUMMER? TAKE IT EASY, TAKE DICKIES CASUAL SLACKS.

Back on Vermont, Jax scrambles into the VW, bandanna stylishly curled back into his shirt. Monk nods like a critic at an exhibition as they gaze up into the illumined vista of the billboard that now assaults the senses of tonight's stragglers: the tennis racket's vanished, Mr. Boone now cradles a shotgun . . . crouching on her knees, her cheek resting seductively on the thigh of those pressed slacks as she gazes up at him, blouse very unbuttoned, is an expertly painted black woman. "Check it out." Jax holds the steering wheel as they grind gears down Vermont. Sofia and Monk turn in the summer warmth rushing above the convertible. The second MOB billboard glows down behind them into the street lamps of Vermont: DEL MONTE ROUND-UP! It's *Bonanza's* Lorne Greene and Michael Landon in a grocery store, commandeering a shopping cart heaped with cans of spaghetti sauce, ketchup, corn, tomatoes, applesauce, pears, pineapple, the two cowpokes pointing six-guns as they roll down the aisle: but now, in Jax's still wet spray-can strokes, two black men stand before the shopping cart, hands in the air . . . behind the *Bonanza* boys another black man runs, a TV in his arms.

"Still using that number-seven nozzle?" Sofia turns east on 120th Street. Down the avenue, knots of men chase two teenagers across the avenue. Jax nods his head. "Nice work, baby." Ahead, police cars barricade Hoover Street: cops toting shotguns slowly wave a single lane of cars through the intersection, shining flashlights into windows.

"Stay cool, baby," Jax says to Sofia. "They're lettin' everyone through. Cops want us Negroes and cholas to go home."

"I got this." Sofia idles behind a Corvair, slowly passing the roadblock. Down Hoover, smoke and fire trucks, an apartment spewing flames and ash into the night. "They're gonna burn down this whole city." Sofia's eyes nod approvingly in the rearview mirror. "The city's the ultimate canvas, the flame God's brush."

"Yeah, the city's the canvas," Monk watching the flames, "and people are painting it, changing it, trying to take it back, maybe," tapping his notebook. The VW turns right on Avalon Boulevard, finally southbound.

"All this graffiti everywhere?" Jax lights a cigarette. "Yeah, it's beautiful, man . . . fuckin' subversive and all that shit, like my little adventures in advertising . . . urban art, takin' the city back one street at a time, one mind at a time, that's where it's at."

"You guys are dreamers," Sofia laughs. "The only way is to

burn it all down, then keep moving, keep burning, till nothing's left." Flashlight beams splay into the convertible, across their faces and dark clothes, the canvas bag hidden under the backseat.

Jax turns back to Monk. "Don't mind her. She wears the combat boots in the family." The flashlights wave them past and Sofia accelerates down the street. "You know what I'm sayin'. We're cultural jammers. Throwin' monkey wrenches into their propaganda machines. Gotta keep jammin' their frequencies until everyone sees through their lies. The boards we hit—you know what most of 'em are selling?"

"Booze and cigarettes."

"Yup, then hair and makeup products." Jax exhales smoke. "Booze to keep us natives sedated, cigarettes to kill us faster, then all that makeup shit—black girls want to look like white girls, white girls want big lips and wanna be black girls."

"Advertising is white money, white culture domination." Passing headlights strobe Monk's face. "But the taggers, the muralists, that's color money, black and brown, color culture fighting back. There's hope, man, 'cause on the reverse of all your billboards there's anti-billboards—signs tagged up or covered with graffiti. Maybe the underground advertisers will one day catch up to the big boys."

"Hope it's not too late." Sofia accelerates, the VW whining past patrol cars and sirens on El Segundo Boulevard.

"Hey, check out Cooper's Donuts!" Monk gazing west out the window, toward Main Street: the giant glazed concrete donut seems to hover above the haze and smoke, like some stoner's hallucination.

"There's a sign that demands a guerrilla art attack," Jax laughs. "I could get all Freudian on that shit!"

"No wonder this place is crawlin' with the fuzz," Sofia says, "it's holy Mecca for every cop in town!"

A few blocks before 135th Street, police barricades, fire trucks funnel the street down to one lane, then rows of storefronts smashed, engulfed in flames. As the VW approaches, cops in riot gear fan down from the lines of barricaded police cars, advancing on a huge mob throwing bottles and bricks and waving sticks and bats and pipes. "Just like Selma!" Chants fill the night between rising and falling sirens.

"Let's get the hell out of here." Sofia wrenches the wheel and the VW squeals into a U-turn, back up Avalon.

"Hang a left on 132nd," Jax shouts into the wind. Sofia nods, downshifting. Monk hangs on to the door handle. This street is quieter, there are only closed storefronts, a few passing headlights. "What we have to do now is zig when the cops are zagging."

At San Pedro Street, the southbound lanes are blockaded; cop cars ring City Bank, shotguns ready. Northeast, smoke and fire cloud the night sky. Fire trucks rumble past. Sofia turns right, guns the VW up San Pedro. Police cars and barricades funnel traffic north, past El Segundo Boulevard, then 127th and 126th Streets. Every intersection's barricaded, the cops squeezing traffic north.

"Sorry, man." Jax turns toward the backseat. "We're not getting you very far south, but that's a real shit storm down there. Plus I don't think the fuzz would be too amused at my little bag of tricks."

"That's okay." Monk nods. "I don't want to be anywhere near these cops, either. Maybe Main Street is more mellow. I'll work it out."

"Shit!" Sofia slams the steering wheel. "They've closed Imperial here too!" The VW whines north, past Imperial Highway and blockades of flashing police cars.

"This is fucked, sorry, man." Jax shakes his head.

"It's cool," Monk says.

The VW revs past 112th Street: no cruisers, only darkness. "This is good, make sure the pigs are gone." Sofia drives past another dark street, then pulls to the curb at 110th Street: the sidewalks are empty, a few lights on beyond the iron-barred windows of the silent houses and porches guarding dying lawns.

"Good luck, man." Jax and Monk shake hands.

Monk climbs out of the idling car. "Thanks, man, you too." Pausing at the window, he doesn't want to go: for a mad second he wants to say something, blurt out that he'll ride with them awhile, even *north* . . .

Sofia smiles up at him, exhales smoke over his head like a ragged halo. "I have a feeling we'll meet again, Monk."

"She's funny like that." Jax leans over, grins, steals Sofia's cigarette. "It's a Mexican thing."

"Watch yourself out there." Sofia grinds the stick shift into first gear. "The city doesn't care who it burns." The VW lurches away, Monk watching the little dark bug as it whines into the night, toward the street lamps and headlights flickering beneath distant pyres of flame and ash. *The city doesn't care who it burns.* He feels the metallic spirals of his notebook digging into his ribs. In the notebook, in his wanderings, with every sign and note he sketched, he'd always gotten this feeling that the city was alive, that every tagged wall or mural or paint-bombed alley or the altered code of sprayed lettering on signs and billboards was the city's way of communicating: how else could all this brick, stucco, and steel draw the painter, the artist, the street scholar? There had to be an invisible force, an attraction that flowed both ways, inanimate to animate. Monk trudges down the darkened street. At the mystic interstice where the mind and the beating heart held the brush or the spray can and the paint touched the inanimate skin of the city, who could really say where one began and the other ended?

13

Classified: Inter-Department Only
Volume 2: Field Operations
225: Community Profile
225.40: The Inner-City Negro

Today's American Negro is the descendant of slaves. Generations of slaves were tortured and beaten mercilessly. As a result, only the strongest males and females survived to reproduce. Today, most Negroes are natural athletes and possess strength and endurance superior to Caucasians. The field officer therefore must use extreme caution when engaged with Negro suspects, and be prepared to use weapons of force.

Ten blocks from the Imperial command post. A mob, hundreds, overflow and surge up Main Street: mostly men, T-shirts sopped in sweat or shirtless, black bodies deeper shadows in the night, lobbing bricks, bottles, anything down the street toward squad cars blocking 108th Street, a line of officers in riot gear slowly marching toward the crowd, flashing red lights reflecting in their face shields. Along Main, shop windows smash, furniture, pawned appliances, shoes, clothes, and merchandise boxes fill looters' arms,

funnels of black smoke churn from splintered doorways and im-
ploded windows. *Just like Selma! No shame!* and other chants rise
between shrill sirens.

Telecopters thrum overhead in the darkness, circling like
great ghetto birds, pointing video cameras down at the mobs:
above the telecopters, police choppers hover, raking the streets
and flames below with swaths of searchlight beams. Tonight the
telecopters don't just report the news, they create it: the news
choppers track the rioters with telephoto lenses, radioing to the
police, locations, movements, everything from loiterers to traffic
patterns down in the streets. On those streets, scrambling near
the protective phalanx of advancing riot police, TV newscasters
report from live-feed mikes, the long whip antennas of their news
station wagons swaying in the smoke, or shoot the rioters and burning buildings and running looters with handheld Bolex 16 mm
cameras: most of the white folks, huddled behind locked doors
back in their redoubts in the Valley, watching their black-and-white
TV sets, will only see telecopter aerial shots, godlike views of the
faceless savages below, down in their dark tenements, where they
will soon be stopped, contained. Street-level views are for the riot's black devils only, haunting their gutters and alleyways, oblivious
to the stars and firmament above: no white men on these streets,
where cold statistics accuse two out of every three black men of
having violent or criminal tendencies . . . Only the police force
dare venture down here in these burning streets, a force that Biff
and Jane and little Biff Jr. and pigtailed Doreen back in the Valley, in the glow of the Philco, pray is a deadly force, a magical
wall that will crush this obscene onslaught. But tonight there are
a few brave souls here at street level, camera crews, miked newscasters, reporters dodging bottles and bricks with their cameras,
and, reporting breathlessly into her mike, TV newscaster Brey
King.

"The devastation out here is unbelievable," she shouts into the
mike before the rolling camera: peroxide blond, late twenties, gray

lusterless eyes, red lipsticked mouth, gray V-neck sweater, tight but knee-length brown leather skirt. "The gap between police and rioters is closing . . . a clash seems inevitable . . . we'll stay as long as we can to give you this live report of . . . of a city under siege!" The camera pans in for a close-up of Brey's face, white skin tightened with thousands of dollars of plastic surgery and lifts and tucks, every year the scalpel slices another wrinkle, another crow's-foot, another chin line in a merciless race against male anchors who have twenty years' more professional longevity than any talking head cheesecake like King can hope for.

Monk's walking behind a few black young men scattering past the news crew, away from the advancing police line. "Young man! Young man!" King shouts, cutting Monk off from the sidewalk as she thrusts the mike to his surprised face. "Why are the Negroes rioting?"

"Ah, social inequalities, I guess," softly. "The inherent racism of a police force that's trapped in a Jim Crow past." Monk, realizing that being interviewed about the cops on TV is probably light-years from cool, slinks away. He scowls back at the white woman: *What's the use talking to white people?* He knows he shouldn't think like that, boxing her into some kind of simple racial equation, but she and her kind, aren't they doing the same thing to him? Most of the time the only communication between whites and blacks seems to be self-conscious, patronizing chatter about race . . . spoken words are signs too, and these feeble attempts at communication from the White Power Structure—the WhiPS graffiti copied in his notebook—are really miscommunication, static that walls in ignorance instead of tearing it down. Monk frowns: perhaps there is a limit to empathy, a gulf that can never truly be bridged between others.

Brey turns the mike toward a black youth in a sweaty green tank top. "Why are the Negroes rioting?"

"Rioting? Lady, we ain't rioting. This is an insurrection. This is the Civil War part two!"

"You are telling our viewers this is a protest against prejudice? A civil rights movement—what about the looting, the burning, the hooliganism?"

"Hula what? We're tired of gettin' beat up by the pigs and not havin' nothin'! Chicago, now L.A. White people better learn or it's gonna burn!" He trots away into the darkness.

She grimaces into the camera. "You heard that young Negro of the streets. To him, the police are . . . it sickens me to even repeat his vulgar street slang, the police are . . . inhuman pigs. This is Brey King live from Main Street in Watts!"

"We're out," cameraman Peterson yells.

"Okay!" King's spooling the mike cord around her elbow and palm. "We'll cut that first boy—the smart one—just use Mr. Hula what," grinning, "perfect." Riot police march past them—half a block up, the mob presses forward, chanting, pelting debris down the street: bricks and shattering bottles explode ahead of King and her news crew—a soundman and two shooters lugging a Bolex 16 mm and a video camera on a tripod. They scramble ahead, rushing along the brick-fronts and store facades. Jiggling camera shots of looters smashing windows, grabbing merchandise, angry men chanting or lobbing bottles and bricks. They're close to the front line of the mob, past the ranks of cops that slowly march forward like a tide of metal shields and batons and black boots crunching over glass shards.

Into the mob now, soundman holding the remote feed as King shouts into her microphone, "It is a war zone down here, folks . . . there in the middle of the street, a bottle bomb has just exploded against that store. These bottle bombs, I'm told, are called Molotov cocktails. The rioters fill a glass bottle with some kind of flammable liquid, ignite a rag or paper fuse, and throw this handmade bomb. Perhaps its Russian name points to a connection between these Negroes and the Communist influences often cited by police. Here a young Negro carries what appears to be a case of beer, and another young man has boxes of something, perhaps merchandise . . . there behind us, you see the LAPD slowly advancing in full riot gear . . . Chief Parker has warned us that tear gas may be deployed . . . but we will stay and give you these live reports as long as humanly possible . . . it looks like one block south of Main Street, a fireball has erupted over what appears to be a gas station . . . Why do they do this? They seem to be burning down their own communities, why? Young man, will you tell the cameras why, what are you doing here tonight?"

A thin black teenager, shirtless, big gleaming Afro, a boxed radio in his arms. "What you done foh us?" pointing into the camera. "No jobs, no money, no hope. Watts is on fire tonight, tomorrow maybe Beverly Hills. Fuck you, honkies!"

King turns to the video camera, ashen-faced. "There you . . . you have it . . . raw and uncensored, direct from the streets. Tomorrow Beverly Hills, or your town. That seems to be the fear, the response we've been hearing lately. Everyone is afraid, perhaps even the police and the city's leaders. Parker's warning, that the police are the thin blue line, all that separates us from violence and chaos, seems to be heavy in everyone's minds. Police are on edge amid reports of lone Negro provocateurs drawing officers in chase down alleys, only to be ambushed by waiting mobs. And there are reports tonight that gun shops, pawnshops, army surplus stores—any store where one can purchase a gun or rifle— are under heavy guard by police and armed store owners. Citizens are arming themselves, buying every gun available for miles. There is widespread fear—perhaps only rumor, perhaps not—that Negroes and gangs and militants are targeting these gun shops under cover of the riot, leaving burned-out stores to cover their real haul of stolen weapons." A black man hustles across the street in front of King. "Sir, sir! Why are you out here tonight?" She holds the mike up to a middle-aged black man who's drinking a 40-ounce golden bottle of Brew 102.

He looks her up and down with bloodshot, rheumy eyes. "Mmm, you a fine-lookin' white girl," mumbling as he pats her on the ass.

"How dare you!" The camera jostles. "Van Zanger, cut!" She shouts to the other cameraman. "Cut!"

The crew scrambles across the street, dodging flying bricks and bottles. At 110th Street they duck around the corner, a shadowy buffer zone between the closing police and the mob: a shoe store and coffee shop; across the street, boarded-up abandoned brick-fronts. Two black men run under the burned-out street lamps. "Hey! Young men! Come here, please!" King waves her mike. The two men walk over, smoking cigarettes. "Get ready to roll on my mark," she hisses to the crew. "Here's twenty bucks," pushing a wadded bill into one man's sweaty palm, whispering, pointing behind her. The two men shrug, nod their heads. "Roll!" The cameras flash on: the men heave bricks, smashing through the restaurant and shoe store windows. They grab some Florsheims and, puzzling over the broken plate glass of the restaurant, grab a coconut layer cake on its silver pedestal.

"You next, white people!" A black face leers over the white cake and into the camera. "Fuck the man! Black power, baby!" Shaky Bolex footage follows them as they disappear down Main Street. On every black-and-white TV across the cities and valleys, the contrast of the melting white cake below the black face is as stark as lightning flashing in the void: camera lights, cathode-ray-tube dots, even the black ink printed on tomorrow's newspaper headlines and photos can only reproduce every black face in the darkest, glowering tones, black masks that the day's technology cannot refine to show any human nuances of anger, pain, sadness, fear.

"The brutality . . . the raw, animal desperation," King's panting into the camera, "is almost palpable here on the streets . . . is this America or some dark, distant land of upheaval . . . Perhaps some of the liberal pundits are correct, is this another Vietnam?

Have the Negroes and the white war protesters united in besieg-
ing Los Angeles in another guerrilla war of fire and attrition? Reporting live, this is Brey King . . . and we're out."

The line of officers crushes against rioters. Billy clubs rain
down on black faces and arms; pipes and sticks smash against
helmets and shields; bottles and bricks push officers back. Clouds
of tear gas explode into the mob, spilling knots of men out into
the side streets and ducking into ravaged buildings and storefronts; Molotov cocktails burst in fiery blooms behind the ranks of
cops, and the police huddle, groups pulling back or surging forward
into the chanting and sirens and screams.

"I'll give the suits ratings," King hisses, waving her crew north.
She's working behind the police lines now, approaching 107th
Street. Behind them, riot police and mobs clash in the churning
glower of tear gas and firebombs, oscillating in the ruby lights of
distant patrol cars and chopper searchlights from above. "Screw
Cronkite, right here." They've stopped on a sidewalk under a
flickering, still working street lamp: in the distance, a burned-out
shoe stand and, down the block, a dark fireball of the engulfed
gas station. "Peterson! You know what to do! Hurry up!" They set
up the video camera and remote feed, King glancing around nervously, no one nearby. The crew tears up Peterson's coat and
shirt. He lies sprawled on the sidewalk. Brey extracts a bottle of
ketchup from her strap bag and squirts it over Peterson's hair
and face and chest. "Roll!" She crouches down near Peterson.
"We've found this poor man . . . an ambulance is on its way . . . a
human face to the senseless violence that rules the night . . . Sir,
can you speak? Can you tell our viewers what happened?"

"They jumped me," Peterson chokes out, grimacing in pain.
"Four or five Negroes . . . God help me."

"Channel Eleven News. We're not going to report just from
the safety of the telecopters . . . we're here live on the battlefront,
in a city gone mad," shaking her blond curls. "Will you be next?
This is Brey King, live in Watts."

Small crowds have worked around the riot line, smashing windows and lobbing Molotov cocktails at the barricaded police cruisers: more sirens are closing in from the west. The intrepid anchor and crew make it just north of 107th. Bottles fly, rioters crisscross around them under patches of smoke and shot-out street lamps. "King! Let's get the hell out of here!" A disheveled, ketchup-smeared Peterson screams, trotting toward the news station wagon, lugging the heavy camera. King, her high heels clattering, runs behind. The soundman throws his equipment in the backseat, jumps behind the wheel as Brey King and Peterson pile inside.

Van Zanger's trudging up 107th Street toward his station wagon, the heavy Bolex on his neck strap. The mob and police line seem to have melded into the next block east. A police car passes him, sirens wailing. Up on the corner, a knot of black men trot into an alley: behind the alley, a pillar of thick black smoke bubbles into the night sky. On Main Street, he walks toward the station wagon, its whip antenna a metallic line that points toward the smoky shroud muffling the skyline. Where are those guys? He sets the camera on the hood, unlocks the door with its Channel Eleven crescent blue logo. He straightens his narrow emerald tie, tucks in a white shirttail under his thin alligator belt.

"What you comin' in here wiff your cameras and shit?" Two black men approach: a tall thin man with a baseball cap, shirtless; the other paunchy in a sweat-soaked T-shirt and sweatpants.

"The newscast is over. I'm leaving." Van Zanger lifts the camera, opens the station wagon door.

"Why don't you stay in your own neighborhood? We don't need you taking pictures for the cops, whitey."

"Whitey? Who do you think you are talking to, young man? I'm a journalist."

The tall man with the cap steps in close and puts his hands on the camera. "We'll be takin' that, motherfucker."

Van Zanger grabs the Bolex. "Now you listen to me, you hooligan. Do you have any idea who you're—"

A fist rams into his stomach. Hands twist him spinning, strangling by the narrow tie. Pinned against the station wagon, a punch slams his jaw, then his ribs: he crumples to the ground, panting. Lying on his back on the hot asphalt, the world is upside down: the smoky night sky seems like a glowering floor, the whip antenna a sinister metronome that ticks away a new kind of time—the world and time are fractured, changed; Van Zanger lies wheezing on his back, the two black men with the camera alien shapes moving from his field of vision: he's in shock, not about the bruised rib, fractured jaw, stabbing inhalations of breath, it's that he's somehow entered a dark universe, a strange, inverted world where a Negro would dare think, would dare insult, would dare strike a white man.

14

Arcs of white electricity bolt from the gaping maw of the giant dragon, its gold scales shimmering, crimson eyes locked in baleful, reptilian malevolence at the towering apartment building as its tile roof explodes in a shower of crumbling concrete, dust, flying tiles and beams. A great dinosaur foot smashes down on the street below, crumpling cars and light poles as a prehistoric growl thunders, its bass wail shattering windows far below. The dinosaur plows like the bow of a great ship slowly through high-tension wires and buckling towers. The saurian's dwarfed, tweezer-like claws throttle the undulating, serpentine neck of the dragon as electric rays shoot from the dragon's mouth, exploding down several blocks, demolishing two office buildings and fleeing cars . . . but two more dragon heads rise from the smoke on weaving golden necks, spitting electric bolts into the dinosaur's smoking neck and chest as the beast roars in pain, falling backward like some prehistoric avalanche, the iron girders, electric lights, silver storage tanks of the Mitsubishi Refinery exploding and crushing under the titan's rolling body. Above, gliding out of dark clouds and rising pillars of black smoke like a flying nightmare, a gargantuan moth beats its silvery powdered gossamer wings down toward the bleating Medusa heads of the dragon. The insect's multifaceted eyes reflect the destruction below like hellish mirror balls as its bloated thorax swoops above rooftops and billboards and bent telephone poles: suddenly the giant moth falls and plummets into cars and splintering houses of wood, raining blue tiles and dust—

"Cut! Cut!" Honda bellows into a megaphone, leaping from his chair: a middle-aged, short Japanese man with a jet-black crew cut.

Above the smoking rubble of Tokyo, grips and technicians and puppeteers scramble along scaffolds and catwalks, reeling in spools of wire from hoists bolted to tackle beams that fan out over the set.

Honda's screaming into the megaphone in machine-gun Japanese as the special-effects crew blasts the set with geysers of white smoke from fire extinguishers. "You incompetent idiots! We're behind schedule! I'll have your balls for this!" Strands of harness wires gleam in the clouds and smoke-like silvery webs.

Cables winch and the puppyish, green puffy head of Godzilla rises into the scaffolding like some kind of fantastic decapitated apotheosis. Now the lifeless, droopy golden necks of the three-headed dragon lift on wires into the rafters and clouds and klieg lights, dragon heads whose chimerical, slanted eyes and royal, blazing gold suggest an evil origination that Japanese moviegoers will not fail to identify as the diabolical, genocidal Chinese: Godzilla's mortal enemy, King Ghidorah. Godzilla stoops, picks up a bottle of Suntory whiskey that's hidden behind an apartment.

"Now we have to do another take," Godzilla says. The monster looks as if an angry, tough-looking Japanese man's head has been transplanted onto its green, scaly neck. Godzilla, mustache, mottled skin, a sweat-soaked rising-sun bandanna on his shaved head, gulps down a mouthful of whiskey. "Good. Maybe King Shithead can stay on his marks this time."

"Fuck you, Nakajima!" a young, angular Japanese man shouts,

dripping sweat inside the chubby dragon's rubber suit. "You hog all the camera angles! I am the star!" King Ghidorah swings at Godzilla, but the great green lizard ducks.

"Are you insane!" Honda screams into the megaphone. "Get off the set! Prepare the next shot! I have to bring this piece of shit in in three months!" Technicians and grips pull the giants from the smoky set, Godzilla twisting Ghidorah in a headlock as they trip over camera lights and cables and fans. A knot of men finally separate the monsters. "We'll shoot if it takes all fucking night!" Honda lights a cigarette, twists it into his silver cigarette holder. A script girl pushes a glass of whiskey and ice into the director's hand. Modelers and technicians and pyrotechs work on the set feverishly. "Okay, we must wait!" Honda throws the megaphone on the director's chair.

•

Honda broods in the warehouse's makeshift office. A single halo of light from a desk lamp illuminates the smoky room. The director sits behind a desk, sipping another whiskey and ice, sucking on his silver cigarette holder between clipped shouts into the black telephone. On the desktop, piles of script pages, shooting schedules, contracts, drawings, storyboards, ashtrays heaped with cigarette butts. Outside the window, in the warm, summer night of this strange and magical city, sirens and hazy lights drift in from the darkness. "No! I want Gamera! I think he's going to be a big star! Mothra is not box office! And Mothra's tiny, singing pixies! Are you people insane! Even little kids won't buy this shit . . . no! Mothra's in every goddamn movie, huh! Mothra's a whore! How can I work with this shit, huh!" Honda exhales a cloud of smoke, chugs down Suntory whiskey. "Talk to Daiei Studio! How much does Gamera want? A hundred thousand yen! Is he crazy? Top billing too, huh? Over King Ghidorah? You think he can break into the big three, huh! He's no star! Are you all drunk on sake? Who? Baragon? I don't want fucking Baragon! Who the fuck—

Hello! Hello!" He slams down the receiver. Smoking, he sips whiskey, gazing out into the dark void beyond the window. Somewhere
out there, the city of his boyhood dreams, Hollywood, the valleys
and hills where the legendary American directors he idolized,
Ford, Huston, Curtiz, and others shot their classic movies. *And
what am I doing? Shooting another goddamn Godzilla picture. Fucking actors whine about typecasting, I'm a typecast director. I'll die in my
boots, carted off some goddamn set between rubber monster suits.
Meanwhile, they kiss Kurosawa's ass. He gets to shoot whatever the fuck
he wants, samurai Shakespeare movies that don't make any money,
while they shit on my* kaiju *movies that pay all the bills . . . they give me
ninety days to shoot this crap, push me ahead of schedule and that
prima donna Kurosawa gets two years. I should retire, just do Suntory commercials. Try to get some independent financing for my
scripts, like Welles.* If only he could shoot his own project, a World
War II movie involving kamikaze pilots and flying saucers, but
Toho's not allowed to shoot any war movies or they'll lose government financing. The closest he's gotten to his dreams is half a reel
of Godzilla fighting Gigan with giant samurai swords in *Godzilla
Yakuza Assassin* before studio execs pulled the plug and ordered
Honda to take a four-week vacation. They want him to read treat-
ments with titles like *Godzilla vs. the Space Hippies* and *Godzilla
Goes to Prison* . . . Godzilla is his blessing and curse, he hates and
loves the fat rubber bastard, tears the suits apart in drunken rages,
pummels the beast with a cane for blowing a shot; but he could
be protective too, shooting past schedules and budgets to get the
right scene or light on the beast, weeping and raging when spine-
less American distributors superimposed flames from Godzilla's
maw because they didn't want to be reminded, thank you, of past
atomic holocausts by his radioactive spray in the original prints.
Now he just wants to get these shots in the can and go back home.
It's enough to make any man drink: sitting around for hours while
the *tokusatsu* crew rebuild their models and sets and wires and
explosives, all for a shot that lasts maybe a minute. Honda steps

to the window, leans over the sill into the warm summer night. There, out past that sloping dark rooftop and nest of TV antennas, is that smoke? This place is another world to him, filthy streets and slums, Negroes everywhere: he'd heard Negroes liked giant monster movies . . . he should feel indebted; perhaps they identified with Godzilla, who's feared because he is misunderstood, persecuted by white technology, whose very name itself means "gorilla whale," a great, wild blackness on the screen. He longs for the safe feng shui—*fusui* of Japan, the comfortable geometries of rice fields, white paper houses, swept streets, cherry blossoms.

Downstairs, the crew finish the set for the next shot, winching wires through pulleys suspended from the scaffolds, dabbing paint on model buildings and houses and temples, covering explosive wires with paint and paper, framing miniature streets and cars in camera angles. Godzilla and King Ghidorah stand in full costume near the set as cameramen measure their green and gold rubber suits with light meters. Godzilla, through an immense plastic straw snaked down his rubbery throat, slurps from a pitcher of whiskey and ice. "Hey, Matsuda," a voice deep inside rubber darkness, "is it true your father is a Chink?"

"Fuck you, Nakajima!" Ghidorah head-butts the King of the Monsters with a terrific assault from all three dragon snouts and Godzilla pitches backward, a light tower shattering beneath his armored scales, whiskey and ice arcing over the flopping monster in amber splashes. Godzilla scrambles up, throttling a golden, shimmering neck as Ghidorah kicks his nemesis's foamy crotch.

The crew in sweaty tank tops and shorts shout and cluster around the rolling, twisting monsters. "Twenty bucks on Matsuda-san!" Everyone's peeling wads of yen bills from their pockets.

"You're on!" A cameraman pulling bills from his wallet. "Twenty on Nakajima-san!" The crew slap down bills in a pile atop Honda's Suntory rolling wet bar.

The two behemoths square off, warily circling each other. Nakajima clenches his green claws into fists.

"Eeee-yaaahhh!" Ghidorah karate chops Nakajima across the neck as Godzilla sinks a right punch into the rubbery gut of the dragon. The Titans of Terror roll across the studio floor, past still-smoking buildings, crushed automobiles, tangled power lines . . .

The beasts topple down a concrete stairwell, piling up in front of double steel doors. Godzilla pulls Ghidorah to his stubby feet but the diabolical Matsuda-san seizes a fire extinguisher and hurls it at Godzilla: the red cylinder caroms like a giant missile off the dazed leviathan's snout as the green lizard smashes backward through the double doors and out onto the dark sidewalk.

Godzilla pounds on the door. "Let me in! I am Haruo Nakajima! Japan's greatest stuntman! I'll have your jobs for this!" Green claws pounding on cold steel. "Fuck all of you for betting against me!" Godzilla shrugs: it'll be a couple more hours till they're ready to shoot, plenty of time to nick down a couple of drinks. The monster stomps down the alley.

Lumbering east on 120th Street. Stench of sweat and whiskey inside the rubber suit. Nakajima, through slits cut in the throat of the monster, can only see sidewalks, buildings, signs directly ahead, framed in rubbery rectangles. Godzilla stomps past a bullet-riddled sign, WELCOME TO WILLOWBROOK, but there are no rivers here, no gurgling brooks, only sirens, Negroes with sweat-stained shirts on sidewalks and drinking beer in shadowed doorways. Two teenagers pass, exchanging raised fists of black-power salutes with the monster.

Monk stops on the corner, almost drops his notebook: down the street, lurching toward the melted hulk of a torched car, is that . . . *Godzilla?* He laughs out loud as he realizes that he's almost *not* surprised at the hallucination, just one more aberration in this endless night of fire, signs, and wonders. How should he read this sign? The beloved monster that haunted so many of his childhood matinees stalks southward, in Monk's direction, toward some bums beyond the twisted car hulk: he shrugs, steps off the curb, and slowly trails the great lizard.

Godzilla moves south, toward the county park, Monk following a block behind. Nakajima's stuntman instincts, perhaps fueled by alcohol and a fierce personal code of method acting—despite that it's 112 degrees inside the suit and he's close to passing out—propel the veteran *kaiju* into the brackish olive waters of the park's lake. Godzilla's great claw rises dripping out of the depths and smashes down on a hapless radio-controlled white boat someone's abandoned in the dark waters. Godzilla slowly ambles from the lapping waves, lumbering onto the shore, towering as he looms past a wino huddled under a wad of newspapers on a park bench, the bum's paper-bagged Colt 45 malt liquor can slips from his fist as he sprawls in terror on the dirt.

The monster reels east on 121st Street, perhaps attracted by distant twinkling light, a single, throbbing orb that looms up into summer darkness and smoke, atop the Watts Towers. "This is where we part, old friend," Monk grins, watching as Godzilla disappears down 121st Street, the finned green tail sweeping a clattering beer can to the curb. Monk crosses the avenue and trudges south, still smiling: maybe he should let go, just drift, see where all these strange currents carry him; in the moment now he feels happy, a little reckless . . . he'll keep going south, but Karmann will wait . . . this is the time, he realizes, with his city in flames, that the semiotician should record the signs and wonders in his notebook, before the fire burns away these shadow-words and the city is scourged, voiceless.

Godzilla gazes in behemoth wonder, shaking his foamy muzzle at the singed, dead lawns in front yards: how could the armies of Japanese gardeners, his own countrymen, allow such a disgrace?

From blocks around, from certain angles refracted through smoke and night and smog, from basement apartment windows, from downhill grades and streets, people watch in horror as the monster seems to tower above the cityscape rooftops and smoke and electric wires, transfixed by beams of white light as it glares toward the distant red blinking glow of the latticed eponymous towers. Yes, it's every Negro's nightmare, they've rehearsed it every Saturday night in darkened musty ghetto theaters, smells of sweat, buttered popcorn, Afro Sheen, booze in paper sacks, the house is packed as this week's bad horror movie plays out in garish, scratchy color on the old, patched screen, everyone laughing after the obligatory shout-outs that are the real show: *Don't open that door! Run, nigger, run! You better hope that's some kind of flashlight gun, motherfucker! Dracula's got more pussy than Tom Jones! I got a dark house, ain't no bitch takin' off her clothes in my house! You scared of Transylvania fog, try walkin' in Compton smog!* Now searchlight beams lock on Godzilla's growling face, blinding him. The city must make a stand here against the marauding invader, keep it away from the blinking ironwork tower that seems to be a kind of beacon to the monster. "Freeze! Police!" Megaphone voices beyond the blinding lights. Godzilla lurches backward, rolls in titanic slow motion down a concrete embankment, smashes through a chain-link fence, and plummets through the darkness. A cataclysmic splash as the monster plows into the muddy waters of Compton Creek. A lifeless green mass floats down the river—is the monster really dead this time, after so many battles with Rodan, King Ghidorah, Mothra, King Kong . . . or is this only another boozy blackout? Godzilla bobs down the concrete channel, past its graffiti spray-painted on 45-degree walls tilted up like a profane gallery to the heavens, southbound, toward the converging, paved tributaries that empty into the Los Angeles River.

15

Classified: Inter-Department Only
Volume 6: Emergency Department Directives
150: Baton Holds During Civil Unrest
150.10: Sanctioned Baton Holds
1. The American Strangle: baton under the chin, grip with both fists.
2. The Japanese Strangle: twist the right arm behind the back, push the baton against the side of the neck.
3. The Negro Strangle: place suspect into full headlock. Insert baton between forearm and carotid artery. Push baton handle forward to incapacitate or break suspect's jaw.

Monk is on 122nd Street, trudging west toward Main. It seems the farther south Monk gets, he somehow ends up going north, as if the city's magnetized, drawing him back like black iron filings. Now he can see Main Street's intersection is blocked with flashing patrol car lights. He heads down an alley. On 124th passing the graffiti-scrawled broken wall of a vacant lot: he hears a woman's shrill scream to the east, or sirens, it's impossible to tell. He feels hopeless, weary down to his bones; too many sidewalks, streets, everyone—the city itself—running on pain and fear, the harbor and Karmann a universe away. Here he sprints across Main Street, between barricaded blocks, passing a pawnshop and thrift store, smashed and gutted, straggling looters lugging cases of beer, booze bottles, cartons of milk, bundles of clothes, lamps, framed paintings, kitchen chairs. Some of these looters' names will later be found in commission reports, newspaper articles, morgue inventories, police blotters, victims like so many others of mayhem and violence and *misadventure* in the nights of fire—but some of these transgressors' fates are darker, victims of forces not understood, unfathomable chains of cause and effect: the stolen whiskey bottle that provokes a fight that takes the looter's life; the carton of cigarettes that conceals the waiting Lucky Strike that will engulf that Beauty Queen mattress and incinerate its sleeper; the black thrift-store clothes that reflect no headlights as the car grinds over the jaywalker; the stolen car that sails over the guardrail of the Harbor Freeway; the doll little Shawna dangles from the window as she slips and plunges into the night; purloined guns and knives sold in the streets for cash or drugs that weeks, months, years later return in deadly force in the hands of accosting strangers; bras and panties cursing looters with infidelity and sexual diseases, hair pomades that precipitate death by mistaken identity, scarves and shirts blue or red in the wrong 'hood that bring showers of bullets from passing cars in the dead of night, fans that short-circuit and incinerate window-barred rooms, vinyl LPs playing loud music that masks evil's turning doorknob and footfall, GE White Light bulbs that fail as descending Florsheims miss and slip down darkened staircases, wristwatches that propel victims to late or early fates as they tick out final moments too slow or fast in ghetto time.

In the distance, the lights of Broadway glow. On either side of Monk abandoned or looted storefronts pass in shadows. A car roars past jammed with young black men, radio blaring, then it's gone. Silence, glass crunching under Monk's sneakers, a siren pealing somewhere. A block up on South Spring Street, tucked under the stucco canopy of a padlocked shop, Monk hears a metallic, plaintive ringing, like something urgent, alive inside a phone booth. He runs toward the booth, its lights smashed out, like a dark coffin set in the concrete sidewalk. The ringing is deafening, filling his mind as he slams through the broken doors and lifts the receiver.

"Hello! Hello!"

"Take Athens Way." That old man's grizzled voice again.

"Who is this? Please—"

"Some call me Tyrone. Friends call me Tyre, around and around, like the rubber on a ol' tire . . . maybe I'm just tired, old and tired."

"Who is this? Where are you? Please, what'd you mean I was your eyes?" A dial tone bleats from the receiver. Monk stares down at the black plastic phone in his shaking hand. He toggles the silver switch in the telephone's cradle. Silence, the dial tone is gone. "Fuck!" Monk slams the receiver again and again into the cradle, then stabs his index finger into the zero on the rotary disk and dials. "Operator! Operator!" Silence. He pats his pockets, no nickels or dimes. Calm now. "Okay." Monk gently sets the receiver back in its cradle and steps out of the booth.

In the smoky distance, fires and the flashing red lights of Broadway's scattered working signals glow in the night like brimstone beacons. On the corner, knots of men and teenagers gulp beer and pass a bottle, smoking cigarettes, hunched on the warm curb and the steps of shuttered buildings. Someone throws a nickel in an upturned hat on the sidewalk, and a couple of winos, sharing a bottle in a greasy brown bag as Monk passes, dance and croak out a raspy duet:

If if was a fifth,
We'd be drunk,
If hip was a whiff,
We'd be crunked—

If cool was a fool,
We'd be jive shuckers,
If bullshit was a big hit,
We'd be singin' mother—

Monk walks north into a pitch-black alley that parallels Broadway. "Okay, Tyrone." He cuts through a vacant lot and crosses Broadway, heading west on 122nd Street. Athens Way: a dark street fringed with back alleys, fences and walls, iron-barred tiny houses, towering electric power lines that parallel, to the west, the rising concrete stream of lights and engines of the Harbor Freeway overhead. Monk turns south and pauses, sketches a few new outlaw murals and graffiti—puffy spray-painted letters and words—as he passes: he's seen most of these works before, but there's some fresh *throw-ups*: he's recorded this new word in his notebook, some of the taggers calling their work throw-ups because speed of execution is a point of pride, but they're hip to other associations of the word, like throwing bombs at the Man and vomiting their disgust and pain into the public. Huge looping words, cloudy glyphs, veiled threats—*UR Next . . . Look Behind U . . . RU4 Da End? . . . Krip Keprz*—and spray-executed, harsh lines in bright reds, pinks, limes, oranges, turquoise, symbols of angels, demons, fire escapes, mushroom clouds, blood drops, floating heads and hands, magnifying glasses, and spiral purple vortexes: the sonic mania of Ameba88—88 for Eighty-eighth Street, where the mysterious artist was rumored to have been born. Athens is one of the main galleries in the city. Every house, wall, gate, power pole is a canvas, even horizontal planes of sidewalks, driveways, asphalt road. Ameba88's works command the surfaces of the most inaccessible areas: only those who can seek him out are worthy of judging his work. His murals are not of the world but underground, where only graffitists and wandering scholars with notebooks view his anti-galleries of spray-painted icons and intricate scripts on iron hatch plates high atop power-line towers, along twenty-foot walls beyond coils of razor wire, roof-tops, the concrete pylons and overpasses and exit signs of the Harbor Freeway—no height or barbed-wire spools or spiked fences or padlocked bars or rushing cars or gravity itself can stop Ameba88's assault: some of his work seems sprayed from impossible angles or composed from vantages where no steps or scaffolds exist . . .

On this wall Ameba88's sprayed black and brown men who glide above the dark cityscape on wings of flames. The wall corners into an alleyway where Ameba88 has attempted to continue the mural, but there are only a few strokes of a red angel's wings and then the spray stops, dripping toward the pavement. Monk looks down: he sees the crosshatched imprint of sneaker bottoms stained in red paint, a couple more half-prints down the alley, as if something made Ameba88 stop and run.

Across the alley, at the base of a tall fence, he sees two black candles half burned in saucers, three broken twigs, and a Dixie cup full of something reddish. The corner house is an old Victorian three-story that towers above the row houses. The white picket fence and the house's bright lavender panels and indigo moldings are the only surfaces not tagged or sprayed.

"You can pass this way." Monk turns, hearing a woman's voice. An old black woman is stooped in the open doorway of the house's octagonal tower. Her long frosted hair blends with a white knit shawl draped around bony shoulders hunched over her cane.

"I'm just going to El Segundo Boulevard, ma'am."

"You want to go south . . . through the house is an alley that'll take you there." A soft, gentle accent, perhaps Southern. Monk nods, walks up the pathway. Her sable eyes are milky, almost blind. Her cheekbones are drawn, her face pale, shrunken like a gourd, only a bronze wisp of color seeps back into black skin under her eyes. "My name is Mab," closing the door behind him. "My friends call me Queen."

"Mab? I'm not Mercutio, am I?" tucking his notebook in his pants. They stand in the entryway.

"More of a dark Romeo, but with a kinder fate in store, let us hope." Above them, a spiral staircase ascends into the shadows of the octagonal tower.

"You're some kind of voodoo queen. That's why your house isn't all tagged up." Past the staircase, a large parlor, faded tapestries on the paneled walls.

"Please. The word is *voodooienne*. Voodoo is a force, neither good nor evil, but it can be a kind of shield. Please come in." A fireplace crackles in the center of the far wall, though it is stifling summer outside. A round maple table with a green cloth is in the parlor's center. White candles flicker from sconces on the walls. A great window fills the east wall, but it is blocked with heavy burnished copper drapes that wrinkle over polished floorboards.

"You knew I was goin' south."

"Did I? Perhaps. Then again, this street runs north and south. A fifty-fifty chance."

"What else do you know, Miss Hoodoo?" Monk stares into her milky eyes. "There is a voice on the telephone. A blind man. I think I saw him once right before the riot began. His name is Tyrone or Tyre or something. He told me to take Athens, towards you . . . Who is he?"

"I . . . I don't know," a slight edge in Mab's voice. "But before I can let you go—"

"Aw, come on, Queen, I'm just trying to get home. Let me go if you can't answer my questions. I'm not burning or tagging nothing. Please don't curse me or stick pins and shit in your dolls or whatever you hoodoos do."

"Don't be so theatrical. How do you think you've got this far safely, with all that is going on out there? Voodoo ain't witchcraft, it's just a path that might work for you, just a state of mind if you like, or it's just nonsense." Her milky eyes bear down closer to his. "It does not require your knowledge or your belief to work . . ."

"Look, lady, if you don't mind, could I just be on my—"

"Of course, I only wanted to say that before I can let you go, please eat a little and drink a little with me, because if your soul were to pass through my home without this hospitality, it could prove dangerous . . . to me! Don't look so damned scared." She digs a silver crucifix from her withered bosom. "I'm Catholic."

They sit at the mint-cloth-covered table. The old woman pours tea, a silver plate with a knife and single peeled banana between them. The candlelight flickers over Mab's shawl, like a strange veil that's seeped into her kindly, wizened face. "Last time I had tea, bananas were forbidden."

"Then you must have had high tea with a Muslim." Mab smiles. "Superstitious lot," cackling in the firelight.

"Aren't you going to read the tea leaves?" Monk sips the hot tea: he's starting to sweat, the fireplace crackles, it feels like it's a hundred degrees in the dim parlor.

"I am not a charlatan or a fortune-teller. No one can tell the future." Tea steam rises into her cloudy irises. "I can only tell your *pastent*."

"Huh?"

"Your present, which is part of your past, your pastent."

"Not much of a trick."

"I told you, I'm not a trickster. You're going south, going home. The closer you get, the farther behind you in reality are . . . a woman waits for you, a woman you love, but there is danger . . . not for you, but for her."

"How'd you do that? What danger?" Monk's mouth is a little open.

"You see? The past and present is tricky enough!" Cackling. "Screw the future! I'm old!" Laughing, clinking teacups.

"Why can't voodoo tell the future?"

"Because the future doesn't exist. The future is a series of possibilities, but finite. There are . . . ways . . . to determine possible futures . . . some people have thousands of potential paths . . . some have only three or four . . . most people have six to eight, depending on age and sex and other . . . things."

"Well, how many futures do I have?" He dabs sweat from his brow with a napkin.

"We could find out . . . but do you really want to know?"

"What else can voodoo do?"

"Voodoo can only make the mind stronger or weaker. It can influence human action. Make a woman fall in love, make a man forgive, bring hate or love, protect or expose oneself or others to good or evil, protect a house from burning down out there, stop a hoodlum from spray-painting . . . create channels . . . where one's journey may be safe or perilous."

Monk picks up a silver knife. "No," Mab gently taking the knife, "we mustn't slice the banana, we must always break the banana. When you cut the fruit with a knife, you bisect the core of the banana, the inner stem, which, if you look, is the exact shape of the crucifix."

"Can you tell me about my paths?" Monk chews banana, sips tea.

"Perhaps. But only if your mind is ready." Mab's eyes drown out the candlelight. "These powers, these shadow things, are extensions of the mind . . . a zombie is a state of being, not a reanimated corpse . . . a night *loa*, a spirit, is a state of mind . . . no, wait, a zombie *is* a reanimated corpse," cackling, "just kidding!" She nudges his shoulder, sips tea. "Go to the window."

Monk steps to the copper-draped window.

"What's out there?" Queen Mab chews banana.

"Athens Way," Monk unbuttoning his sweat-sopped shirt. "The freeway."

"No. Out that window is a full moon. Fireflies glow above the swamps that trickle into Bayou Saint John . . . willows hang and tremble like old beards from mossy branches. Yellow gas lamps flicker around the crescent of Congo Square . . . people watch from the balconies atop the old stained and ivy trellises of mansion walls . . . as, down in the square, a naked black woman chants and dances, swaying with a black rooster over her wild, sightless eyes as the old hoodoos chant and circle 'round her, scattering white feathers and glass beads and rice at her bare feet, drinking from bottles and spitting rum on her glistening black skin. If you don't believe me, pull back the drapes and look . . . but be prepared to see the world for the rest of your life as you have never imagined it before, if I am right."

Monk's hand raises and touches the heavy curtain: but his fingers tingle; he's afraid. He turns and walks back to the table, sits down. "Good," Mab cackles, opening her ancient eyes. "You're ready." She opens a drawer in the table and extracts a blue velvet sack, stained with mud. "This is the earth, its seas and land," a black gnarled finger tracing the velvet. "Inside are the runes."

"Ruins?" Monk mops his sweating face: a log crackles in the fire.

"No. Runes. Stones with runic symbols, the ancient language of the first religion, long before Christianity. The Codex Runicus parchments may be the oldest written language. Move your seat so that you face the fireplace."

"Why?" Monk scoots over, the heat radiates from the grate.

"You must face north, toward Odin and the gods of long-ago ice worlds." Mab is rubbing the polished stones inside the sack with her fingers. "Choose four runes, a stone for each cardinal direction of life."

"And the four points of the cross."

"The cross existed long before Jesus saw one." Queen Mab's eyes gleam in the candlelight. "Four is also the axis points of the earth."

"I don't believe in all this Stonehenge stuff."

"My child, voodoo is our religion. It is a path to our old ways and selves. It is all the magic and power of the old country brought

here to this new country by us, by black slaves. Voodoo is the old
and new, the pagan and Christian, the Norse and South, the evil
and the sane. You must listen to me. I am Queen Mab. There are
no voodoo kings, only queens. We are a matriarchy, like the old
country, before men created the despotic kings of Africa. Listen
and set aside your prejudices. I am the mother's voice from the
mother country, the womb from where all civilization began . . .
Eve gave birth to Adam!" Mab cackles, slaps the table.

"And Eve was black."

"Black is beautiful, baby. So listen when I say the runes are
not confined to the old ways. There is power in these old signs,
just as all signs hold power. A traffic sign can kill . . . a mathematical sign can bring riches or poverty . . . an atomic equation can
bring the destruction of a world . . . a sign scrawled on a wall can
bring power or death . . . you should know that!" Mab taps his
notebook now.

"How'd you know—" Monk stops. "You could have seen me
through the window."

"That is one explanation. But I can assure you the runic language is still very important to your world. The runes have a long
and living history in this country. A secret language waged in a
battle for the nation itself, from the beginning and still fought to
this day. The destiny of America must be either white or black,
and these forces have been locked in enmity since the time of the
Founding Fathers. You can see the war is still being fought out in
tonight's burning streets." In the candlelight, Mab's white orbs
seem in a trance beyond him . . . the sweat, the dry buffeting heat
from the fire, he feels dizzy but now he's shaking, as if freezing.
"The war over slavery was often fought with the secret codes of
the runes. The so-called framers schemed bitterly over the slavery
question, communicating in secret languages, including runic,
using many clandestine organizations, such as the Illuminati, the
Sons of the Confederacy, and the Skull and Bones society. Slaves
fought back and adopted the same codes, but some say with the

codes, with the ancient signs, came magic too . . . there are accounts of slaves casting runes in circles under lynched brothers and sisters to bring the dead back to life . . . to curse cruel masters . . . to escape by powers of flight or invisibility."

"Yeah, but the Civil War, all that shit was a long time ago—"

"The war. Runes carved into cannonballs that never miss their mark . . . trenches cut into the earth in the horizontal configurations of runic signs . . . Confederate and Union troop movements under the protection of midnight stone-casting in gaslit command tents . . . runes scratched into the silver hilt of Booth's pistol . . . Don't be a fool. The struggle went underground mostly, with certain seismic manifestations—you just came from those streets, a city in flames. The war has never stopped. Black against white, night against day, darkness against light. You think it stopped a century ago? I don't have time for your foolishness. I'm an old woman. But consider this," patting his hand, stroking his fingers and thumb. "My, such strong hands . . . if I were twenty years younger," laughing. "Where was I? Oh, yes. Consider Old Yankee's Bell. You know it as the Liberty Bell, but I've been around for a long time. The symbol, the foundation of our land. Rung July 8, 1776, to call Philadelphians to the town hall for the reading of the Declaration of Independence. The bell's inscription echoes the great document and a new, free world is created: *Proclaim Liberty throughout all the Land unto all the Inhabitants thereof—Leviticus twenty-five, verse ten.* But the bell's historic tolling cracks its forged metals, some say because of others using occult powers. The bell is sundered like the newly born nation itself. Old Yankee's Bell is beloved—but only by abolitionists. In 1915, the bell is freighted by train to San Francisco for the Panama-Pacific International Exposition. It's a world's fair advertising the city's rebirth from the great fire and earthquake . . . a disaster that may have not been natural at all . . . more of an . . . *ethnic cleansing*, the latest volley in the secret war."

Monk's shivering even as the heat from the flames radiates from his face and warms his clothes.

"In the middle of the night, somewhere across the lonely plains, the train never stops but the bell's freight car is secretly breached. When the train arrives in Philadelphia's depot, the bell has been split in two along the fissure of its crack. Only half the bell rests in its crate, the other half never found. Inside the bell's demi-fluted remnant a new biblical inscription is discovered, etched in the ancient strokes of runic figures. *Cursed be Canaan; a Slave of Slaves shall He be to His Brothers—Genesis nine, verse eighteen.*"

He sneezes, buttoning his shirt, bathed in sweat before the roaring fire: *How the fuck can I be cold?* "You are cold because you face north, and Odin and the spirits of ice are gathering . . . you are almost ready to cast the runes." Queen Mab grins. "Nineteen forty-two . . . Negro soldiers are allowed to fight only in segregated units, deployed only in the worst, suicidal front lines. I could go on and on, but it's all out there," sweeping her shawled arm toward the draped window, "waiting for you—you are ready now for casting. Pick four stones and put them in my hand."

Monk slips a trembling, sweaty hand into the velvet bag and extracts four smooth pebbles, placing them in Mab's old claw. Mab polishes the stones inside her palm, glazed eyes looking through Monk's sweat-dripping face. "East," she rasps, placing a stone to Monk's right: black, sticklike lines, a crude letter *R*. "*Raido*, the Journey. This may be your best direction for now." She places a second stone to his left. "West." Monk stares down at the inverted V, its right leg cut in half. "*Laguz*, a lake or body of water . . . this is a dangerous direction . . . avoid it." A third rune is placed under the two on the green table. "South."

"W," Monk rasps.

"Fuck, excuse my language."

"What is it?" His teeth chatter, perhaps he could move closer to the fire.

"*Merkstave*." Her cloudy eyes reflect candlelight. "The rune is upside down. It's an M. Not a good omen. *Mannaz*, means men. There are men waiting for you south . . ."

"Well, I've been trying to get home to my girl. She's throwing a big rent party at our place and I'm missing it." He's wrapped his arms around himself, shivering.

"*Merkstave* means 'reversed,' in other words, one or more of them appear to be your friends but they are enemies." Queen Mab rubs the final rune and places it on the table to complete the cross. "North." The rune is blank, only polished bone. "Sorry," her gnarled black fingers flipping the rune over: the other side is blank too.

"What the hell's that mean, old woman?" Monk's staring at the flames, perhaps he could crawl into the fireplace, sit on the nice warm grate.

"The blank rune, the *Wyrd* stone . . . There is static in your reading. You are wandering, perhaps in thrall to a demon or an angel . . . or both, battling for your soul."

"What should I do? Which way should I go?"

Mab's milky eyes crinkle and she frowns, her ancient fingers rubbing the polished blank ivory stone: now Monk can see worry, perhaps fear in her silence.

"What is it?"

"It is dangerous to interfere," her voice pleading, "you should go."

"Help me!" Monk slams his fist on the table.

"There are angels and demons battling for your soul. This man, Tyrone—" She shakes her head, pauses, closes her wizened eyes as if weighing something, then opens them. "Oh shit, I hope I don't make things worse for you, young man . . . Tyrone is real. You were given his phone number by . . . the forces that protect you . . . Tyrone is a physicist, an engineer, a genius, a madman, the only Negro physicist to work on that atom bomb, I heard . . . he is many things . . . he helped design and invent the telephone companies, their newfangled computers and communications, I don't understand any of it, I'm an old woman. I heard he made all the phones, every line connect and work in all of Los Angeles and way beyond . . . but see . . . he was losing his eyesight, a disease . . . he raced against time and finished his final work, just a few months ago. He and some other scientists built this satellite called Intelsat One. They launched it, like I said, a few months ago and it's circling over our heads as we sit here. It's a communication satellite, and somehow, it beams phone calls—not just the telephone, but radio and TV and God knows what all . . . beams them across space to anywhere in the world . . . maybe beyond the world, for all I know . . . Yes sir, a genius . . . now he's blind, in hiding. They built that satellite for a mysterious international company called Comsat . . . supposed to be for communication only, to help mankind. Well, Tyrone found out Comsat was a military front . . . that they were gonna use the world's telephone networks for spying, or worse. But old Tyrone's one step ahead of them. Before he lost his sight and the world went dark, he rigged the satellite and the phone systems so's he can hijack it all. Now he's building up a group of like-minded folks, to sabotage, break down their systems."

"Why does he want to help me?"

"I don't know, child. Some say working on that atomic bomb made him hate authority . . . the government, the police, maybe he'll close 'em all down with his satellite and computers and second sight," she cackles. "Maybe he sees you and that notebook as an ally. You must go now. Come, come, young man," shooing him with her cane toward the back door. "It's positively roasting in here, why didn't you say something? 'Which way, what should I do,' how do I know? I told you I wasn't a fortune-teller." Queen Mab opens the door: beyond, the summer night and distant sirens. The draft warms over him and his shivering subsides.

"Are you really blind, old Queen Hoodoo?"

"So many stupid questions! Was the ancient poet blind when he sang of the odyssey every man's life must trace? Many have eyes who are blind, and some who are blind have many eyes!" Monk feels a cane nudging between his sweaty buttocks as he's propelled down the steps and the door slams.

The alley empties into El Segundo, south just as the old hoodoo said. The summer night feels good against his soaked clothes. Monk cuts under the concrete pylons and shadows of the Harbor Freeway overhead; the freeway is eerily silent, as if few cars dare to venture north into the Stack: the cloverleaf multiverse where the Harbor, Hollywood, Santa Ana, and Pasadena freeways interchange . . . invisible cars pulsing above and below, along the looping arteries of the transitions layered like engineered mazes that rise into the smog. A strange essence radiates from its concrete gyres, perhaps because the four-level exchange—the world's first—was built in '53 on the site of the old downtown gallows . . . its levels corkscrew into the night, promising ascent—cops, reporters, pilots shaking their heads, whispering about some nights when its loops arc up into a *fifth* level, where cars fade into smoggy banks and disappear . . .

Monk passes a chain of cop cars that ring the Imperial Cadillac dealership. Police and salesmen guard the new Coup de Villes and Fleetwoods and coupes under the lot's lights, corporate is trying to get the National Guard out here, yes, it's only a matter of time before every Negro in town converges on the lot for a joyride in the ultimate soul car . . . double up those cops around the convertibles, the black-, chocolate-, gold-painted models with those fine chrome wheels.

Railroad tracks stitch along Athens Way. Monk follows the tracks to 130th Street. The small lawns in the front yards of the row houses are all burned brown, like sepia-tone photographs from the past somehow leaching into the present: summer heat, fire, smoke have all conspired to kill any natural buffers between the erupting streets and iron-barred, barricaded houses. Acrid smoke layers the air, drifting somewhere from the east. He passes shops where black proprietors stand guard with shotguns and pistols and hunting rifles. Some plate-glass windows are intact, hand-made stenciled signs leaning against the glass, signs painted with black palms and extended fingers: STOP! I'M A BLOOD BROTHER!

At 131st, Athens Way is flooded with rushing water, lapping at the sidewalks Monk treads. Every hydrant's breached, shooting torrents of white foamy water hundreds of feet into the summer night and smoke, as if the night itself is engulfed. Fire crews and cops fight to wrench off the valves. The police can't shoot, they can only cluster around fire trucks in their riot gear as firemen are forced to turn their hoses on mobs of men and women across the flooded street lobbing bricks and rocks into the trucks and squad cars and flashing red lights and spraying torrents of water. The water's rising now, Monk splashing his way down the block, weaving around geysers of water and shouting kids; men smash windows and hurl debris, cops and firemen run for cover. He turns east toward Spring Street but the water seems to be channeling down here, torrents swirling down the narrow street until he's slogging ankle-deep in water and gurgling trash. Monk's reached another corner, Charybdis Circle, when some kind of under-ground explosion rocks him against a brick wall. Towers of water blast into the air, rocketing manhole covers through the sky. *Shit, Tyrone warned me.* He sprawls into the flooding waters: Monk's fingers claw at the curb as torrents swirl him into the street. He's scratching the asphalt, spitting out water; his red Keds kick and splash as he's swept down the street. "Help! Fuck!" He grabs a mailbox's iron leg but his hands are wrenched away. Monk gags, spits water, twisting on his back as the cascade slams his head against the curb. Ahead, a great vortex of foamy water, trash, sticks, papers, mud, and now Monk's motionless body swirls down the black maw of the sewer hole.

16

Shadows, dim light filtered through blankets nailed over windows. Two women and a man lie curled on a filthy mattress, sunken eyes watching. Monk's clothes are wet, soaked and clammy. His head and his left hand pound in pain as he looks in bewilderment at his swollen, bruised wrist: the last thing he remembers is walking down the alley from that old hoodoo's house. Two black men sit in the corner, lighting a glass pipe. Monk staggers across the floor strewn with clothes, newspapers, food, trash. In the ceiling's corner, a great spiderweb radiates out: no, it is only cracks that splinter down toward the door like etched lightning. A black girl sits on the floor with a glass pipe in her lap, she grabs Monk's hand as he passes but he wrenches away and staggers through a doorway.

Monk lurches between men and women who lie in sleepy tangles, or watch him with glazed indifference as they slump against walls, pillows, other bodies. His stomach churns, the walls seem to glow and throb as if somehow breathing. A sharp, stabbing pain stings his thigh. He digs into his soggy pants pocket and pulls out shards of broken, dark glass. Monk watches, uncomprehending, as the shattered, twisted pieces of his sunglasses slip from his fingers onto the floor.

An emaciated, naked black girl dances alone in the silence:

she raises her bony hand, beckoning to Monk as he staggers toward the door. A blinding flash: black men and women line the walls, spectral faces silent masks watching without emotion— then they are gone. He's in a hallway, alone, acid gnawing the pit of his stomach. His mouth tastes ash as he turns the knob and slowly opens the door to another room.

An ornate four-poster bed sits in shadows under the hazy puce nimbus of a crystal lamp. A woman is draped under the sheets, her breasts dark and heavy in the soft light; behind her, a small black boy snores, his large Afro pressed into a pillow. She is entwined in the powerful, dark arms of a demon, its head impossibly bloated, a giant's head bobbing, its shadow like a great planet floating against the walls.

"Shit, look who woke up," feminine giggling, her hand scruffing up the sheet modestly around her dark nipples.

Monk rubs his burning eyes, pinwheels and strobe lights fade from his throbbing head as he stares up in horror. Slowly his eyes focus and his reeling brain processes the monstrous shadow looming before him: a giant black man, over seven feet tall, Monk judges, dressed in gold silken pajama bottoms. His naked chest and biceps are gargantuan. A black silk patch covers his right eye; the left eye, bloodshot, glares down balefully at Monk: perhaps because of the patch, the solitary eye appears too large in the grinning, brutal face; great black sideburns darken his jowls like reversed African continents. The immense demon head, Monk sees now, is just the shadow of the giant's great Afro, the biggest Monk's ever seen: a black, impenetrable sphere of kinky hair that extends in a woolly diameter of a meter and a half.

"Where the fuck am I?" Monk rubs his pounding head, his heart thumps as he looks around: they're in some kind of concrete storm drain, a cavernous cement-block chamber with water gurgling on the floor, drain channels radiating out into darkness, iron-rung ladders on walls leading to drains and pipes and locked steel hatches, river debris and branches and trash clogging grate covers and spillways, drops of cold water dribbling from concrete above like a slow drizzle. Near the immense bed are stacks of steel storage boxes, chairs, tables covered in heaps of comic books, couches. Five or six black gangsters are scattered along the chamber: three playing cards, two weighing packets of white powder on a scale under a generator light, another man cleaning a pistol and drinking beer, wearing jeans and tank tops or shirtless in the subterranean warm, foul air. It's no gang that Monk can place.

"Don't cha remember, cutie?" the woman purrs from the bed.

"Shu' up, LaDot," the giant's deep voice growls, echoing across the slipway. "You deep in the Wood."

"Shhh, honey," the woman whispers, "you'll wake up little Ricky."

Monk rubs his throbbing temples and gazes around, lost in what must be a hallucination. The Wood? The river swept him all the way west to Inglewood? That means he's off course again. Towering heaps of gang swag rise from the concrete floor and channels like fantastic mountains: piles of guns and rifles, cans of beer, bottles and cases of wine and liquor, purloined watches and jewelery, white-powder bricks and chunks of cocaine, rows of motorcycles, choppers, pyramids of stereos and radios and TVs and phonograph players, pressed kilos of marijuana stacked like ziggurats that domino toward the dripping ceilings and drains, threatening to topple. Down the far end of the spillway, beyond the generator lamps, a great, rusted steel circular hatchway is locked closed. Monk recognizes the wedge-shaped hinges above the hatch as the iron doors he's seen along the flood channels, *los gatos*, the ones taggers paint into giant cartoon faces, their riveted hinges pointy ears: through the city's concrete riverbeds and channels and aqueducts, he's seen Happy Felix, Stoned Felix, Tom with poor little Jerry dead in his fangs, that Cheshire Cat disappearing behind his iron grin, Sylvester smoking a blunt, Krazy Kat rolling his eyes, red devils, hinges for horns, glowering balefully up into the barrios from their underworld lairs.

"Yeah, you dropped in." The giant laughs. Turning his great Afro toward the bed: "Make meat, bitch."

LaDot scowls but sighs and clambers out of bed. Monk's stomach churns as he watches her prance in a diaphanous powder-blue slip toward a bank of hot plates and a refrigerator.

Through Monk's seared brain, between flashbacks of blinding white light, floating glass pipes, and incandescent pinwheels, the fog of improbable memory breaks: he was swept away down a flooding street, pried from a mailbox, sucked down a torrential drain . . . washed through pried iron grates, half drowned and semiconscious down concrete channels and into a great subterranean chamber. The notebook. Monk pats his damp pants, relieved to feel the soggy but intact notebook still tucked under his torn shirt.

"Who are you?" Monk feels fragmented, as if his brain is amped to electric overload while his body is in some kind of slow-motion limbo.

"No, da *quesdon* is, muferfuckah," the giant pulls a .38 from the back of his waistband, "where you?"

Monk knows the telegraphic slang is a query of where he's from, what gang. A fleeting image flashes through his aching mind, *R60* sprayed on a pylon as he was swept down the muddy currents of the spillway. Monk's right hand curls into an R sign, index finger and thumb forming the loop, two middle fingers splayed out for the letter's legs, left index finger and thumb forming a circle, the other fingers curving to complete the number 6: Rollin' 60s.

"Good answer, man," from one of the gangsters playing cards: both men laugh.

The giant's eye glares at the card table. To Monk: "Shit, I was just fuckin' wiff cha, ol' Highbeam don't cap future clients," laughing, tucking away the gun.

"Le's see dat sign agin." Highbeam grins as he sinks into a black leather double car seat propped against a pylon. Monk flashes the R60. "Better'n you fucks," to the other two men.

"Like I told you, boss," says a short, stocky black man, no shirt, Afro crushed under a backward baseball cap. "We should make the fuckin' sign easier."

"Yeah, dig this, boss," from another, a cigarette smoldering from his lip. "See? WM. Easy. We just call ourselves Watts Monsters."

"No, Cronk." The other gangster flashes a hand sign. "Dig this, OX."

"OX?" Highbeam's eye squints skeptically.

"Outside Experts." Grinning, revealing rotten teeth gleaming with bluish metal caps.

"Nigger, get da fuck outta here, Blue-Cap," from Cronk.

"How 'bout this shit, boss?" Thumbs and index fingers make loops as the other fingers extend straight up, describing "BD." "Blood Daddies."

"Look here, nigger." Cronk's hands give the double finger to Highbeam: "Inglewood Imps."

"Go count da bazooka 'fore I cap you black asses." Highbeam waves them away with a cigar-sized blunt: he lights up, takes a huge drag, closes his solitary eye. A sweet cloud of marijuana smoke engulfs Monk. Highbeam offers the joint but Monk waves it away politely. "Frone!"

"Here I am, monster." LaDot's shrugged into a silk kimono and she hands Highbeam a huge plate piled with smoking sausages and slabs of beef. Highbeam holds up a dripping shank toward Monk.

"No thanks, I feel kind of sick."

"Yeah." Highbeam grins, tearing into the meat. "You won' be hungry for a week after doin' a blast." The bloodshot eye glares at LaDot: "Chivas, bitch." LaDot frowns, prances over to the banks of hot plates.

"Blast?"

"Bazooka." LaDot pours two tumblers full of scotch, hands one glass to Highbeam. She sips, lifting the glass to Monk's pale lips, but he shrugs away. Monk's stomach flips, his head burns, Highbeam's words echo now: *a future client.*

"Bazooka?" Monk's voice is a hopeless croak, beads of sweat on his forehead and under his arms.

"Yeah, dig this operashun, baby," Highbeam sweeping his hands around the chamber, big fists clutching a dangling string of sausages. "This is jus' da beginning. See, dere's money in blow, dig, but dere's fuckin' crazy money if you cook de shit."

"Cook?" Monk feels dizzy.

"We cook it, honey." LaDot smiles. "You cook cocaine and it leaves this paste in the bottom of the pot. They call it *basuco*, from *basura*, trash. They used to throw it away . . . until they found out you could smoke it. They've been doin' it in Colombia since the twenties, kind of a secret. Who'd you steal that recipe from, honey?"

"Sombras." He frowns and glares at her. "You talk too much, bitch." He licks his greasy lips. "Blast, Mr. Clean, corn flake, whitey, trash . . . Bazooka blows your mind."

Highbeam drains the glass, throws it against a concrete pylon half buried in broken bottle shards. "Bottle, bitch."

"The rooms . . . hallucinations," Monk's mouth full of ash and acid.

"You'll feel better, honey." LaDot hands the bottle to Highbeam, traces a black fingernail down Monk's damp chest.

"My harbor houses, up and down the Harbor Freeway," Highbeam says proudly, his eye closing as he drags smoke in from the blunt and hands the joint to LaDot. "See, what we doin' is givin' every brother and sister—like you—a complimentary ball-pipe of bazooka. I gots these dumps rented everywhere in dah ghetto, where ya all can hang and have another taste, for a reasonable fee," exhaling smoke. "I'm just a . . . wha's that fancy word, bitch?"

"A facilitator."

"Yeah, I'm just a facil-tader, takin' you to the house where you meet dah real host." Wafts of smoke ring the great Afro like a dark, smoky planet. "You wuz in number seven, topside, just above channel twelve."

Monk's brain throbs. Jangled memories—or hallucinations—of those rooms: hopelessness, sloth, lust, fear, paranoia. How long had he been there? Had he committed the seven deadly sins? Sloth and lust he remembers from his lapsed Catholic childhood, watch out for those demons, mortal sins that prey on a life that has—so far—maintained a kind of fragile grace, always on the brink of that black abyss of damnation: had he let lust come between him and Karmann? She must wait for him, just a little longer— "The last room." Monk feels dizzy, jagged.

"What room, honey?" LaDot lobs a jade bottle into Highbeam's paws. She smiles, takes a hit from the blunt.

Monk closes his eyes, sinks his burning head into his hands, but he can't stop the vision returning in his pinwheeling brain: flashbacks of an immense shadow staining the wall, perhaps a fantastic Afro, or a throbbing, monstrous black brain.

"Cow!" Highbeam bellows. Cronk, swearing under his breath, rises from the stacks of tiny plastic pendants of white crystals next to the gleaming scale. His footsteps echo away into dripping darkness. Metallic clangs reverberate down the spillway, from the iron-hinged hatchway below the spewing drain. "Fuck." Highbeam jumps from the throne, walks toward the hatchway's dim outline past a cone of vibrating light.

"Would it be okay if you showed me the way out?" In the distant gloom, rusty metal groans as Highbeam pries open the hatch plate with supernatural strength.

"Don't worry, baby." LaDot presses close to him. "Highbeam always passes out, then I'll get you out of here. He's harmless—unless you fuck with him. You're safe, you're a future client. You'll be okay, unless he does too many blasts before he passes out. Then sometimes he gets a little, ah, weird."

"He's not weird yet?" Monk's afraid, but his fear is fragmented, blurry, like something dark, fluttering on the periphery of his awareness: it's that new drug they've doped him with. The towering Afro gleams back into the splayed, dripping light beams. A man walks at his side, under the shadow of the great kinky penumbra.

"Hey, Standard," LaDot nodding coldly, sipping Chivas.

"LaDot." Standard's white, sweat-stained T-shirt stretches taut over bulging muscles. Out on the street, everyone knows blacks with bodies like Standard's come only from the prison yards, where they spend six hours a day, year after year, pumping iron and morphing into rippled strongmen as they grow angrier and bitter at the white folks who put them behind bars until one fine day it's parole time and another pissed-off, jobless Herculean black man hits the mean streets.

"VSOP," Highbeam orders, taking his throne, swigging from the green bottle. LaDot frowns and prances off to the hot plates. "Wha's the word, Standard, my man?"

"The word is good," Standard smiles. "One thousand, two hundred eighty-four." He lobs a massive rubber-banded roll of hundred-dollar bills into Highbeam's palms.

The Afro nods majestically. "Blue-Cap! One grand, two eight four!"

"Aye! Aye! Captain!" Blue-Cap shouts back. Monk watches as Blue-Cap, over at the scales, counts tiny bags into a paper sack.

LaDot returns with two glasses of brandy. "The word, then the world!" Highbeam shouts, clinking glasses with Standard. The men drain their tumblers. LaDot freshens their glasses with more amber brandy: for the first time, Highbeam appears a little drunk.

Standard's just come by the old Zephyr from San Quentin, where, by a clandestine and lucrative deal with certain guards, he's secreted away every two weeks from his life sentence without parole to purchase the yard's growing pharmaceutical needs. Raised fatherless, he spent most of his teen years in youth camps and correctional institutes: everyone called him Standard after he ripped a Standard-brand urinal from a detention center bathroom wall and beat another inmate to death with the porcelain bludgeon. Transferred to San Quentin in '59, he became an adept of the prison commode. The toilet became his safe, where by an ingenious rig of strings and weights and floats, a drug stash dangled in darkened pipes. The ivory throne revealed still more wonders: one night, while puking a tad too much cough syrup, cocaine, Malt-O-Meal, and whiskey, Standard heard, like the prophets of old, a voice whispering up from the gurgling drain. Voices, incipient madness, until he heard the whisper again: "Standard? Is that you? It's Cook . . ." Randall "Crazy" Cook, in the next cell over. In the months that followed, Standard experimented and refined the commode's amazing acoustical powers: by controlling flush patterns, bowl water volumes, through trial and error etched on his walls that the guards mistook for scratched calendar days, he discovered that he could converse with every cell on every deck . . . Soon the prisoners were communicating through a vast, secret web of interconnected pipes and drains: it was like some fantastic future machine, thousands connected through a kind of *inter-net* of invisible lines and devices, powered by what Standard understood to be the mysterious, little-known properties of water and wave propagation and sound amplification through liquid and metal media. Even the most remote toilets, over in the segregated blocks of Death Row, could be reached by Standard's remarkable tapping codes on the toilet's flush handles: the historic breakthrough code was back in '60, when Standard tapped out, in response to the watery coda clicking back from Death Row: *Mr. Chessman, I presume?* Gradually the warden discovered the illicit network and took steps to ban "potty talk." But the authorities were helpless. Restrictions like solitary bucket rooms, secret laxatives to jam transmissions and garble communication, flushing sabotage were ineffective. Stoolies and decoders were enlisted to break changing codes and intercept messages, or bomb communiques with explosive diarrhea. The warden studied toilet flowcharts, water bills, pressure spikes, plumbing blueprints, brought in wave technicians and sonic engineers, but Standard was always one step ahead. Nothing would stop the toilet drug traffic and gang pipelines of communication: Standard, like all the disenfranchised above in the city—blacks, Mexicans, gangs, musicians, graffitists, cons, even these new hippies— would always find their own underground languages and signs of communication and identification. And now Highbeam's creating another argot, his bazooka drug addicts. If Parker and the cops, the white establishment could only half-glimpse the secret babel spreading up from these hidden strata: subterranean, underground, street level, and beyond. Monk shakes his head. For the cops to understand, break, and arrest someone like Standard and these new gangs—the 1965 men—they'd have to filter through so many walls of code: the Negro, the Convict, the Gang Member, the Addict . . . then maybe they'd have the real Standard, unless he's cocooned under yet another semiotic cloak: the Jailhouse Preacher, the Assassin, the Militant, masks within masks.

Cronk returns with a frail Mexican girl in a filthy, ragged white cotton dress and shirt. The dress balloons over her bloated, pregnant belly. Monk stares into the dead vacuum of her eyes in her deathly pale, sunken face. Cronk pushes her to the throne. Highbeam, his single eye leering down, leans forward and rips open the girl's blouse. He squeezes a sagging, milk-bloated breast and she whimpers. His big black thumb and fingers pinch her nipple over the tumbler glass and white milk squirts into the Jägermeister. Highbeam swirls the liquor with a finger until it's pearly brown. He twists the breast toward Standard and the girl moans in pain.

"No thanks, man."

"Don't know what you missin'," pushing her away into Cronk's arms. "Give her a blast, Cronk." Cronk nods, leads her away beyond the generator lamps. To Standard: "Here's to bidness!" They drain the tumblers. LaDot fills their glasses with brandy. "Le's do a blast too, baby! Blue-Cap, get dah horn!"

Blue-Cap appears with a duct-taped baggie. Standard rips it open and extracts a pinch of this white goop, like gummy tobacco. Blue-Cap holds a glass pipe drilled with a metal bowl tamped with a wad of steel wool. Standard mashes the drug into the bowl as Blue-Cap sparks a match. "Motherfucker," Standard rasps as he exhales. Next Highbeam takes a hit as he closes his eye. Clouds of acrid smoke hover under the great Afro like banks of fog.

"You got dah treaty?" Highbeam's bloodshot eye opens, squinting.

"Yeah," Standard exhales smoke.

"Don't I get a taste, baby?" LaDot, pouting, rubs Highbeam's thigh.

Highbeam turns, high and drunk, to Blue-Cap: "Bazooka, bitch." Blue-Cap lights the pipe as LaDot greedily sucks down the swirling chamber of smoke.

"This is the only way I could smuggle it out." Standard grins, stoned, pulls off the tight shirt from his rippled muscles. He turns, flexing his shoulder blades. Monk steps closer: on the convict's chiseled back, a tattoo against the black canvas of his skin, a map of—Monk stepping closer—Watts. Highbeam snaps his fingers and Blue-Cap hovers around Standard, clicking pictures of the tattoo with a Kodak Instamatic. Monk, craning around the flashbulbs and Highbeam, tries to get a glimpse of the map's inked streets and arteries as they shift and glint against dark muscles under the generator lamps. Is that a red-inked route that meanders through the city, snaking south? Naomi Avenue south to East Fifty-eighth . . . the flashbulb explodes and the map disappears in white light . . . Monk sees a blur of inky map lines . . . Hooper south . . . East Seventieth to Miramonte Boulevard, then south. Monk sees a zigzagging trail down Makee Avenue to Compton Avenue, toward the blue-inked border of Florence—

"Tha's only haf duh treaty, bitch!" Highbeam growls. Standard turns, Monk's lost the map.

"Now, be mellow, monster," Standard smiles. "All the brothers got our backs this far through Watts, we got Gladiators, Grapes, Businessmen, more . . . the northern territories, dig? But farther south, gettin' down toward Compton and shit, yuh gonna need the beaners: Shadows, Boyle Street Boys, 190th Locos, and all them cholos. They got the other half of the treaty. El Tirili—the Reefer Man, a big dick with the Shadows and the Locos in the joint, he's got the southern half tattooed on his back. Then y'all can . . . *patch* it together." Standard seems to be grinning, but Highbeam takes no offense. Monk's hazy mind reels: then El Tirili is real? The Reefer Man still out there somewhere, almost as old as the ancient, mystical graffiti he left in the city, like an elusive grail. Monk spies a wedge of tattooed routes between the great Afro and Blue-Cap: he can't see the street name, are those Southern Pacific tracks?

"Where's dis reefer, mufafucker?" Highbeam's eyeball squints down suspiciously at Standard. Monk moves around Blue-Cap, sees an inky scrawl of tattoo line bending to Elsie Street, then the red route drops south again to Parmelee Avenue, blocks closer to home and Karmann. Monk's repeating the street names in his bazooka-blasted mind, trying to remember them, like a spell, a passage home . . . but he can't take out the notebook, risk losing it to these gangsters.

"Don't worry, boss." Standard pulls his shirt on, the tattooed palimpsest disappears under sweaty tight cotton, Monk frowning as the map, his safe passage home, vanishes. Standard hefts his duct-taped bag, nodding his gleaming bald head toward the iron hatch door. "El Tirili'll find *you*." The great Afro nods and the two men slip into the shadows toward the rusted portal and the dark waterfall churning from the elevated drain; Blue-Cap disappears toward the tables and scales.

"Mama, I'm hungry!" A little black boy wanders out from the

shadowed corridor. He rubs his eyes, a finger digging into, scratching, his big round Afro. Tiny red and blue Supermans swoop and fly, printed on his cotton pajamas. The boy Monk had seen in LaDot's bed.

"Okay, Freeway honey." LaDot scoops him up into her arms.

"Pancakes, frone!" the little boy hollers. Monk can see, in the boy's face and voice, a disturbing mirror of Highbeam's darkness.

"Blue-Cap!" LaDot shouts. "Blue-Cap'll make you pancakes, Freeway baby." Blue-Cap appears, takes the child's hand. "Go make Ricky some pancakes."

"His name's Freeway?" Monk asks.

"Nickname," LaDot answers. "When he was a baby we took him all the time, up and down the Harbor Freeway a million times, Highbeam building up his harbor houses and clients. 'Freeway' was the first damn word he spoke."

Monk has to get out of here, no telling when this stoned one-eyed giant in his cave might snap: it's all he can do to control his fear, he knows it's that newfangled, industrial-strength dope, but he has to escape before the terror, palpable as these dripping walls and shadows, engulfs him. "How 'bout that way out, LaDot?" Monk whispers.

"Ssshh," LaDot cinching her robe. "Wait till he passes out."

Rusted iron groans and echoes down the slipway as Highbeam, growling with inhuman strength, opens the hatch and Standard disappears. Monk's stomach drops as the door closes with a terminal metallic grind. "Bitch, we doin' big bidness." Highbeam staggers to the throne. "The dream is comin', baby," slapping LaDot hard on the ass, "and it ain't no fucked-up peace dream." He pulls a crystal pipe from the wiry depths of the Afro, collapses on the carseat throne, lights the pipe. "We gettin' da money, gettin' the guns, gettin' the brothers and sisters ready. See, we ain't just fucked-up gangsters. Got secret plans with that Castro mufafucker . . . he's gonna help us take over Haiti . . . gonna be all Negro Americans, can't touch us, Rollin' 60s' own economy of guns, money, bazooka, ain't that right, frone."

"Yeah, ogre," LaDot nods.

"What?" the wild eye throbs in rage.

"I said yeah, oh great," LaDot smiles.

Highbeam swigs brandy, his eye drooping closed. "There was a riot before dis one, long ago, folks forgot. I see da visions when I blast on the horn . . . a hot country, covered in sand . . . a great riot, all the fuckin' slaves rose up and killed their white masters. It was a . . . a wha' you call it?"

"Utopia," LaDot whispers, like a mother soothing her son to sleep.

"Yeah . . . we gon' have that in Haiti, Fidel's missiles back us up. Whites be our slaves . . . gon' have our own black Mount Rushmore on da biggest fuckin' mountain . . . big rock faces of Thelonious Monk . . . Malcolm X . . . fuckin' Gabe Jones wif his trumpet . . . and ol' Highbeam—" The bottle slides from his fist and shatters on the ground: Highbeam snores, slumped forward like a fallen oak.

"Gabe Jones?" Monk whispers.

"His favorite Negro comic book hero," LaDot whispers. "Jones, this commando in Sergeant Fury's squad, a jazz badass that blows his horn when they charge into every battle." LaDot's hands stroke his chest. "Maybe I'll blow your horn."

"Look, you're fine and everything," Monk gently pulling away from her. "Help me get out of here, please," he whispers: that black, strung-out fear tingles through him.

"Wait a few minutes, make sure he's out." Her dilated, drugged eyes fix on his face. "Call me LaDot, baby."

"LaDot?" he asks, eager to change the subject: "Los Angeles Department of Transportation, huh?"

"How'd you know?" LaDot grins, impressed.

"Seen it stenciled here and there in my city travels."

"Yeah," laughing. "My mama used to say I was conceived under the Florence Avenue overpass of the Harbor Freeway. She remembered lyin' on her back, starin' up at the rumblin' concrete bridge stenciled LADOT. Now I got little Ricky Freeway, guess it runs in the family. Well, Highbeam's asleep, I'll show you out, but it's a pity," gently brushing his lips with her fingertips. "There's a tunnel that'll take you up to Compton Creek, then you just hop the fence. Come on."

They walk across the spillway, toward the iron hatch in the shadows. Cronk is gone, Blue-Cap's slouched stoned at the card table, boots up on the table and scales, listening to music from a transistor radio, gazing off in the other direction. Monk pulls the notebook from his pants, fans through damp pages, scribbles names that are already fading from his pounding head.

"What you got there? You a reporter, a snitch?" LaDot leaning into the notebook.

"No, the map." Naomi . . . Sixty-seventh . . . Miramonte— "Fuck," he hisses: it's gone, it's all gone. Behind them, Cap groans, shifts his boots on the table as Monk stuffs the notebook into his pants.

"Sure you won't change your mind, baby?" LaDot holds his hand. "I got a cozy little pad off tunnel number seven."

Monk shakes his dizzy head. "You should get out yourself. He's crazy." The cones of light from the generator lamps splay across dripping pylons and angles of concrete channels and storm drains behind them.

"Highbeam's okay. You know they say that when you lose an organ, your other organs kind of overcompensate," smiling bravely. "No, you're right. I know that Negro island shit is crazy, but I've seen a lot of true heavy shit go down. Bazooka, it's bigger than anything, a revolution."

"A curse." Near the iron hatchway now: a canal sluices past the hatch, a channel of rushing water and debris moving in the gloom between dripping concrete pylons.

"I don't love him anyway."

"I know. You love bazooka."

"The feeling it gives me . . . it's better than anything. It's not just bazooka, that's the secret. We mix it with white pot . . . this weird, strong pot that grows only here, in the sewers . . ." Her voice trails off, breaks into a sad silence. Monk remembers M.T., the mosquito man . . . She entwines arms with Monk and whispers, "Let's change the subject. White men come down here. Black glasses and suits. That's who the map is really for. They're opening operations and houses in every big ghetto city, here, Chicago, Philly, New York, others. Highbeam got crazy strung out and told me, but it's the truth. They're CIA. They're funneling money from bazooka to expand the war in Vietnam. The map is safe lines of export and import." Water drips and echoes around them in the concrete and shadows. "The gangs have a truce for safe passage of the new drug . . . if you can follow it, maybe you can get on home . . . through the riot." Her eyes are pinpoints, far away. "Through the riot," she repeats softly. "Highbeam says the riot up there, it's just a cover, a smoke screen for his shipments."

Monk closes his eyes: tries to remember, but his brain is on fire; the route south to Karmann, Compton Avenue? . . . get out of here, try to draw the map, but it's already fading with each lightning bolt flashing across his retinas. "But it's only half a map," hissing to himself.

"You're cute and smart," LaDot's eyes twinkle in the darkness. "Rollin' 60s need the Mexicans to protect the routes farther south. But the brothers don't want to cut them in on the action." LaDot points to iron rungs that ascend into a dripping drain beyond a corner pylon. "There's your ladder to Compton Creek. Could be a big shit storm brewin' up there, be careful."

"Farther south, down to the sea. That's where I'm heading. El Tirili—the Reefer Man. If Highbeam gets El Tirili and the cholos, then there won't be fifty gangs. There'll be one giant gang." Monk shakes his head: a vast, countless underground guerrilla army, in some kind of final Battle of Los Angeles against every cop and white man in the city . . .

An inhuman roar growls through the splashing torrent of water as a greenish blob topples over the iron grates of the elevated drain, splashing into the muddy water channel at their feet. A black wall of scum and mud-water erupts and drenches Monk and LaDot. Behind them, in the distant splayed lights of the generator lamps, perhaps with ears more attuned after a catastrophic loss of vision, a scream answers.

Monk staggers back as the giant reptile's fanged snout looms out of the darkness: fuck, it's . . . Godzilla.

Highbeam stomps across the arc-lamp beams, his great shadow projected on the spillway's walls. "Run!" Monk pushes LaDot away. "Kill the generators!" They split apart, running back along the shadow lines and dark interstices of pylons and dripping channels.

"Who goes there!" Highbeam roars, his baleful eyeball a pinpoint of sparkling light under the dark nimbus of the Afro.

"*Nandato? Baka!*" a muffled voice answers beneath Godzilla's torn and soaked jade scales as the feisty dinosaur thumps his foamy chest with taloned fists.

"Nobody, my ass!" Highbeam's voice shouts, echoing across the concrete tunnels.

Monk, skulking behind a whining generator, snaps switches and half the spillway disappears in darkness as the machine coughs and sputters to silence: only a single lamp bathes them in a broken swath of amber glow. Shots ring out as Blue-Cap runs toward Highbeam, then freezes just beyond the cone of light: Godzilla's fangs are buried in a clump of Afro as the great reptile's bloated tail thrashes and buckles the black titan to the spillway. "*Usero!*" A muffled shout deep within the beast's snout. A gun clatters on concrete as Blue-Cap screams and runs disappearing into the dark recesses of the pylon rows.

Highbeam's grabbed his gun but Godzilla smashes it against a pylon, a metallic clink and an invisible splash down the channel. The flabby scourge of Tokyo has the black gargantua pinned between foamy thighs in a move the stuntman pioneered in *Attack of the Mushroom People*. *"Banzai!"* Godzilla roars, talons flashing from the ripped foam of his big belly: Nakajima raises the chopsticks he keeps tucked in his waist for set-break lunches and plunges the sticks below the writhing Afro that engulfs him.

An inhuman shriek peals and echoes. Monk turns away but not before he sees a looming, terrible shadow projected in the solitary lamp beam, the towering Afro swaying, whimpering, hands clawing the air. Monk, pressed against a cold, dripping pylon, silently moves toward the iron hatchway, following the sounds of water cascading down into the channel. He hears the wounded monster's wails and screams echo across the spillway. Monk's hands grip the iron rungs and he turns for one final look back: Godzilla's plucked a bottle of booze from a pyramid of cases and the beast's green muzzle tilts toward the dank ceiling as it guzzles an amber rivulet of liquor down its throat, ivory fangs clogged with tufts of gleaming Afro.

17

"It's me, Nozzy!" A spray-paint can, big as a man, yellow rubbery feet with black untied sneakers: red nozzle tipped rakishly like a fez, steel-can demonic eyes squint down above this leering smile, cylinder chest bannered BARRIO BLACK. "Paint yer way to underground fame and power! Now you have a voice!" Nozzy jumps up and down, the metal pea inside pinging. "Life's a drag till you tag!" A yellow arm rises to his red hat, black-gloved fist punching down the nozzle, a stream of black wetness burning Monk's eyes.

A slap stings Monk's cheek and his bloodshot eyes slowly open and focus. He rubs his throbbing cheek. "Jax?" A familiar face shadowed between knit cap and bandanna smiles down on him. He looks around, dazed. A taillight glowing red from a VW idling in the mouth of this dark alley: the cyclops's eye. "Where am I?"

"An alley off 119th." Shaking his head. "Some bum, you kept screaming his name was Nozzy, was pissin' on you. Come on, let's get the fuck out of here." Jax wedges Monk under his arm, steers him through the alley, past green trash bags crawling with rats and bums sleeping behind cardboard flaps and corners.

"Bazooka . . . Godzilla," Monk's mumbling, he stumbles, clutching Jax.

"I don't know what you've been taking, but it must've been good shit. Get in." Jax opens the VW door. Sofia, behind the wheel, turns her pretty face and laughs. "A wino, huh? You look like refried shit. And you smell like piss." She throws him a towel, he wipes his face and shirt.

"He's in disguise," Jax says, "the wanderer assumes many forms to get home, eh, Monk?" Sofia slams the VW into gear and they peel down the alley.

Jax shrugs around, facing the backseat. "I thought you were headin' south." He lights a cigarette, hands it to Sofia.

"Cocaine . . . they're cooking it," Monk mumbles: his heart is resuming some kind of normal rhythm, the city's flames and smoke and passing headlights seem to clear his fractured mind. "One-nineteenth . . . north . . . how did I . . . back where I started . . . I have to go fucking south—"

"You've gone south, all right," Jax grins.

"South," Monk mutters. He pulls out his notebook. "The way home." He's scribbling down Standard's human map, trying to remember, but his mind's sparking in haywire flashes. "Naomi Street, Sixty-seventh east . . . was it Palm Street? Fuck . . ."

"He's sick, Jax. Let's take him to the loft." Sofia's cigarette smoke drifts into the backseat.

•

"Monk! Monk!" He opens his eyes: he's curled in a fetal position. Sofia's face is framed in the open window of the VW, Jax behind her. "We're at the market. It's still open. There's cops guarding the doors, so it should be okay. We're gonna get some spaghetti and coffee and stuff. You just rest, okay?" Monk nods as they disappear.

He slouches up in the backseat, looks around groggily: Giant Supermarket, a sign in blue lettering on the roof. Mostly black people hustle in and out the glass doors with their shopping carts. Two LAPD squad cars are parked on either side of the front entrance, four cops standing guard with rifles and white helmets. A brown man in dirty overalls slowly heaves and rolls a long chain of shopping carts, interconnected like a great metal snake, across the parking lot.

"Hey, scoot over." Sofia opens the rear door. Jax sets two shopping bags on the seat next to Monk. "You okay?" Monk nods, sinks back in the seat, closes his eyes as the VW whines out of the parking lot.

•

The loft is in the back of a three-story run-down stucco office building off Hooper Avenue and Eighty-seventh Street. Grimy windows frame the night, streetlights, flashing red lights, plumes of black roiling smoke, blooms of fires blistering across the city and headlights beading toward Compton Avenue and beyond.

Two hooded metal lamps suspended from wires bathe the loft in soft white. Monk pulls the notebook from his waistband, tosses it on the cushion of an old green couch, and collapses on the sofa. He watches Jax open a can of chili with his knife as Sofia stirs something in a pot on a hot plate. A table is cluttered with plastic cups, a wine bottle, food cans, the two grocery bags. Half the room is heaped with Jax's tool bags, canvases stacked against a wall, precarious bookshelves of pine and bricks jammed with spray cans, brushes, glues, rolled-up posters, bottles, buckets, a few ragged paperback books. Beyond is a door leading into a shadowy bathroom. In the corner, next to a wooden milk crate with a candle and an ashtray, is a mattress with two pillows and a worn charcoal quilted blanket.

"This'll make you feel better, Monk." Sofia's fanning pasta into the boiling water. "My specialty, Left-Wingy Linguine."

"Pinko pasta." Jax takes out a box of macaroni and cheese from the shopping bag.

"Spaghetti, chili, onions, paprika, oregano," Sofia says, plopping a huge white gob of stuff in the chili pan. "Mayo and mac and cheese."

"Put hair on your chest." Jax beams, lights a cigarette. "Look what I got to stock up the cupboard." He pulls a can out of the shopping bag and grins. "It's a brand-new invention," tapping the red label with his finger. "SpaghettiOs!"

"How did scientists get it in that shape?" Sofia laughs.

"What will white folks think up next?" Jax flips the can in his hand.

"You don't have a phone here, do you?" Monk asks.

"No." Sofia shakes spices into the sizzling pan. "Half the time no electricity either. We share this place with some artist friends, pay the bills now and then."

"We have music, though." Jax switches on a transistor radio on the table. Martha and the Vandellas' upbeat soul vibrates from the tinny speaker: *Summer's here and the time is right for dancin' in the street.* "Wine?"

"No thanks, man. Maybe some water?"

Jax fills a plastic cup with tap water, hands it to Monk: a rusted tint in the cup, but he drinks a few metallic gulps.

"I don't think they're dancing in the streets," Sofia stirring pasta. Jax opens a bottle of red wine, fills two plastic cups, hands one to her.

Monk forces down more water, rises on wobbly legs: his stomach churns as he walks toward Jax, avoiding the window, where the lights and glowing blossoms of fires seem to follow him in disturbing contrails. "Getting ready for the next gig?"

"Yeah." Jax, cigarette jiggling on his lower lip, selects a Globe Master Rajah Red spray-paint can from the shelf, rummages through a coffee can filled with nozzles.

Monk studies the shelves: spray-paint cans labeled Red Devil, Kit-Kote, Jet-Eze, Wizard, Magic-Wick, Spraint. Colors he's never heard of: Al's Aluminum, Bazooka Joe, Android Alloy, Deep Druid, Ecru, Babylon Blue, Fulvous, Cloud Delirium, Mao's Mauve.

"How ya feeling?"

"A little shaky." Monk drains his cup. Martha and the Vandellas are fading out: *Way down in L.A. every day they're dancin' in the street.* "Martha should see the streets now."

"Yeah, well, we'll give 'em something to think about tomorrow night." Jax tosses a few cans in his satchel, then places some nozzles of different sizes and colors on the shelf. "Let's see . . . an NY Fatcap and an SEKT adapter, the old trusty Drip Flow." He places the nozzles in a pouch and tosses it into his satchel.

"You know your stuff." Monk watches as Jax duct-tapes some spray cans together, end to end like double-nozzled batons.

"A craftsman's only as good as his tools." Jax opens an X-Acto blade and Monk watches as Jax sets brown construction paper on the floor. "Stencil time." He kneels on the floor, expertly drawing large letters in some kind of script style, sipping his wine.

"This one's for Ford." Jax nods down at the stencil. "I've got it all planned out," tapping his temples. Monk's feeling a little better, the strobing light in his eyes seems to be diminishing. He can see paint stains on Jax's temples and in his hair and on his hands and fingers, and the floorboards scarred with thousands of razor-blade gashes.

"Come and get it." Sofia places shopping bags on the floor, grabs a plate from the shelf.

Monk sits down, his chair creaking alarmingly as it shifts into a slant but holds. "Sofi's soul spaghetti, just what the doc ordered."

She slides a huge plate in front of Monk, refills his cup with tap water, and settles into her chair.

An electric guitar, a dissonant assault with a twelve-string F/G chord from the transistor radio, then John Lennon's voice: *It's been a hard day's night.* "He has no idea," Monk says. Monk heaps his fork with the lumpy pasta, braces himself, stomach knotting as he chews a mouthful, eyes closed.

"Well?" Sofia's smiling.

Monk opens his eyes. "Wow, this is the greatest thing I've ever tasted."

Jax laughs. "She gets that every time. It looks fearsome, but holy hell, it's good." He slurps down a mouthful, refills their wine cups.

"So how long have you been stuck in this insanity?" Sofia sips wine.

"Truthfully, I'm not sure." Monk swallows food. "I slept a day or two . . . I lost track of the time . . . then some gangsters drugged me." Monk shakes his head, forks pasta from his plate. "If I told you half of the crap I've been through—"

"I know, man," Jax nods. "These are some heavy times, brother, strange days indeed."

"It's dangerous out there." Sofia chews pasta. "We're the wrong color. If they wanted to, the cops could mess us up." She squeezes Jax's hand.

"We'll be okay, baby." Jax smiles, drinks wine. "Works both ways. We're the right shade for the streets."

"I think I'm darker than you." Sofia twirls her fork in linguine and chili. "I heard light-skinned blacks are getting beat up, mistaken for whites. Be careful."

Monk sips his water. "I know. I'm melanin challenged."

"Where's home?" Sofia watches Monk as he eats.

"San Pedro. The harbor, Pier Thirteen."

"*Mierda,* you've got a ways to go. The pier? You live on a boat or something?"

"Not exactly," Monk says.

"Jaxsy, couldn't we give him a ride?"

Jax looks at her and Monk. "Sure, why not? We'll sleep in, do the Ford sign tomorrow night and get the hell out of town."

"That would be incredible. I don't know how I could—"

"It's no big deal, Monk." Sofia grins, drinks wine. "We have to help each other. We're all artistes," winking at Monk. "That's why I love my rebel boy." She plants a wet, chili-stained kiss on Jax's cheek and he beams, sips wine.

"You have a girl waiting back home?" Sofia's eyes twinkle.

"Yeah." The heavy food in Monk's stomach makes him feel grounded, each bite seems to dull his headache and push the pins and needles of strobe lights from his eyes.

"What's her name?"

"Karmann."

"You must miss her so much. She must be worried sick about you." Monk nods. "Well, you have to get home. It's settled, huh, Jaxsy? We'll give you a lift tomorrow."

This is KFWB news at ten p.m. A voice squeaks from the transistor radio. *Lieutenant Governor Anderson has just announced that the National Guard will be deployed to Los Angeles to secure the city and contain the rioting, which the police chief has described as, quote, out of control. KFWB has reported stories or rumors of a massive gang buildup . . . even a gang truce in retaliation against the police. Chief Parker has scheduled a news conference tomorrow at nine a.m.—*

"The National Guard!" Jax's fork chinks on his plate. "Fuck, it's gonna be Vietnam all over again."

"We better get out of town. And you're going with us," Sofia says to Monk. "Besides, I want to meet Karmann." She purses her lips, nods; she's made up her mind.

"That would be great." Monk smiles, scrapes a final fork of Left-Wingy Linguine from his empty plate.

"The Guard." Jax shakes his head. "Parker, the pigs, Governor Brown, they're all like Johnson, all they know how to do is make war."

"Maybe it's better if it all burns." Sofia sips wine.

Monk nods. "I don't know. Malcolm X is dead but his spirit is sure out there."

"Want a sip of wine, Monk?" Sofia offers the bottle to him.

"Sure, I'm feeling better. You'll have to give me that recipe too."

"I'll give it to Karmann." She pours wine into Monk's plastic cup.

"Those stores they're looting?" Jax says to Monk. "I'll bet most of them are the stores that charged them high interest to buy everything, from beer to washing machines. Sky-high interest, much more than the Valley or the white parts of town." Jax chuckles. "I'll bet the fire department will find all the arson started in the store's finance department, folks burned up their files that showed how much they owed.

"Tell him about your square father," turning to Sofia.

"My father's a Realtor. He's Mexican, but pawns himself off as white to sell houses." Her lower lip creases into a frown. "He told me he knows some agents that are called blockbusters. They go into a white neighborhood, buy a house themselves. Then they sell or rent it to a black family, sell it way under market price if they have to. So the white neighbors panic, have to sell their houses, at reduced prices, to the blockbuster. My father's a capitalist first and a human being second. So last year, when Proposition Fourteen was passed, you know, it struck down the fucking Fair Housing Act, right? 'Course, as a Realtor, he voted for it."

"Him and the John Birch Society," Jax says. "He's also a member of the Committee of Twenty-five, this secret group of cracker businessmen trying to drive Negro stores out of business. Maybe that's why you're such a rebel, baby. Well, Monk and me can clean up."

"Good." Sofia sizzles out her cigarette in her empty wine cup. "I'm going to wash my hair." She switches on the bathroom light, shuts the door.

Jax washes dishes as Monk dries plates and cups with an old rag, stacking dishes on the shelf. "Man, thanks for everything. I'm wiped out."

"I bet. You can crash on the couch. It's hotter than hell up here, but I have a sheet for you. We'll sleep in tomorrow, so you can rest. Tomorrow I'll finish my stencils and equipment, we'll split when it gets dark." He walks to the stacks of canvases, pulls off a worn sheet that shrouds half the pile, tosses it on the jade sofa. Back at the table, Jax drains the wine bottle into his plastic cup.

They splay on the couch. Jax lights a cigarette. They can hear the water in the bathroom as Sofia washes her hair. "Mind if I take a peek?" Jax nods at the blue notebook on the cushion. "I'll show you some of my stuff later if you want."

"Sure, man." Monk hands Jax the notebook, leans back into the cushions, closes his eyes.

Jax carefully turns the pages of the notebook: the cover's torn and faded now, only one tiny hole still fastened near the top of the mashed spirals. "Shit, you've found some amazing graffiti around town." He turns pages, nods. A few pages fall out, and Jax picks them up off the floor.

Sipping wine, Jax turns pages, silently reads some of Monk's notes, nods with each new page and graffito. "I like how you record exact locations, colors, surface descriptions, overlays, cross-outs . . . shit, you're an art critic."

"Maybe, but it's an art that's not recognized as an art. It's communication. It's language and code, hearts and minds. I think it's the city talking. My theory is that America is a collection of cities, right? These cities are all planned and built by rich white men."

Jax laughs. "You're right. I never heard of a poor or female architect, I mean the firms, they're all huge white corporations, right?"

"Yeah. So these developers have designed living spaces where they themselves don't live. It's like they built a city on Mars for Martians, then went back to earth. So now the people are left to try to survive in this artificial environment they had no say in making. The artists, the rebels, they're always the first to be the canaries in the coal mines and sing the alarm when death is coming. So they interact with the city and create these records. Visual and written records, a voice to both the inanimate and the have-nots. Anyway, I think it matters."

"Man, you really get it. Shit, this is incredible. This cat's really good," tapping another loose page. "smOG. His technique is amazing. Those drips he sometimes paints . . . they're *intentional*."

Monk nods. "He's a new voice out there."

Jax leafs through some pages. "You write stories too?" He's staring down at a handwritten page, its title underlined: _Mosley Terrance and LAMA_. Turning a few more pages, more hasty paragraphs titled _Shen Shen in Chinatown_.

"No, just some notes. People I've met, some of the places. A woman I met said I should write everything down . . . but I haven't had much time."

Jax nods, turns pages, stops. "Who's this? No way . . . this can't be."

Monk gazes at the notebook, nods. "I've only found two in two years."

"You think that's him, that's genuine?" Jax exhales smoke.

"I don't know. They've been copied over, traced, preserved by other artists. But there's a hint . . . the Aztec temples and jungles look three-dimensional . . . the impossible colors and depths . . . a kind of geometry that shifts and the eye can't nail it down—"

"But El Tirili must be dead, if he ever existed. He was supposed to be painting, when, in the forties?"

"The thirties . . . maybe the twenties . . . and before, in Mexico or who knows?"

"Fuck, you have to take me and show me this." Jax turns pages, sips wine. "You've seen him too? *Bozo Texino?*" Monk grins, nods. "Jesus. Texino, the ghost of the boxcars." Jax studies the graffito on the page: a sideways figure eight—like the symbol for infinity—bisecting an oval face; this horizontal eight is the floppy brim of a cowboy hat, the upper half of the face becoming the hat . . . the lower face shows slit eyes and a frown that always flows into a protruding cigarette or cigar jutting from the face. Under the visage are some painstakingly etched numbers and letters. "We're living in the days of signs and wonders. I saw one of these on a railcar in Oakland."

Monk nods. "This one's scratched on a tanker car in a switching yard along North Broadway. The tanker's from Oklahoma, and the date—1932—is scratched in it too."

"Thirty-two? Shit." Jax taps the graffito.

"Yeah, Texino's monicas are all over the states." Monk's animated, passionate about his notebook and its underground signs.

"Monicas?"

"Monicas, slang for monikers. That's what the hobos and tramps who rode the rails called all this early graffiti. This one, you could tell by the etching lines that it had been redone, scratched in over and over, to preserve it down each generation."

"Shit, to keep the movement alive, each Texino a fuck-you to the establishment, to the railroad," Jax excited, grinning.

"Yeah, a big fuck-you to the Pinkerton goons the railroad hires to beat up any riders it catches. But there's more going on with graffiti like this, man. Some of these signs go back to the Civil War, back to soldiers and blacks riding the rails to escape the South . . . Texino's face morphs over the years . . . carved into old wooden trains, then painted with grease and chalk onto iron sidecars, sometimes a slave's face or a plantation master's face . . . and there's more, codes within the signs. Those letters and numbers . . .

they're messages about paths to the North, locations of safe havens for freed slaves . . . even the position of his cigarette changes, pointing like a compass toward safe tracks or routes to avoid."

"You're amazing, man!" Jax shakes his head as he slowly turns the notebook's pages. Monk watches, thinking about his dizzying gallery of graffiti and tags, of Bozo Texino, the two—if they're genuine—of El Tirili's space-warping visions . . . and now that gangster Standard's living, tattooed signs: if he can only piece it all together, see the greater design in his path south, his journey; and something else, half glimpsed, perhaps some reason why he's a witness to all this destruction.

Jax's mustache crinkles into laughter. "Hey, here's yours truly." On the page Monk's sketched a large vertical drawing of a billboard advertisement: GOLD MEDALLION HOMES NOW IN GARDENA! An attractive white housewife leans over Dad in his easy chair, handing him a martini as he reads the newspaper. A little boy plays with a toy train on a throw rug. But Jaxsy's signature is spray-painted near the bottom, and now it's an art installation: Mom's left eye seems to be bruised . . . and her cleavage has been enhanced, as has the angle of the little boy's joyful face, now seeming to stare not at his father but at his mother's breasts in some kind of Oedipal rapture . . . and Dad's newspaper masthead and headlines read THE OUTER PARTY . . . CONSUME, OBEY. "Is it still intact?"

"It was a month ago. I've got four or five others of yours, stuff you did on walls, even that one off Grape Street, that big, abandoned office window where you painted faces, but their eyes are the clear window parts so it looks like the eyes reflect the empty office space inside. It's all still there. The taggers and bombers, they respect you, man, no one's painting you over . . . never even seen your signature flipped."

"Wait a minute! Man, you're too much, what's a bomber? What do you mean, flipped?"

"Some of these huge graffiti, they cover up and erase the

whole building or wall, like a fucking bomb destroyed everything but the message. Flipped is when the graffitist signs another tagger's name upside down as a sign of disrespect."

"Shit, you're schooling me, Monk." Jax drains his plastic cup of wine.

"They'll study artists like you someday, Jax."

Sofia steps out of the bathroom, a white towel wrapped around her hair, a plastic bottle of shampoo in her hand. "You boys still talking shop? You come with me." She crooks a finger at Jax. "You've got paint all over your hair." Jax shrugs, closes the notebook, sets it on the cushion next to Monk. "You're next," to Monk. "We found you lying in garbage," she grins, "you can't go home to Karmann smelling like a wino."

Jax walks past the big window, rummages in a coffee can on his shelves next to the rows of spray-paint cans, tosses a wide rubber band atop Monk's notebook. "Here. It's falling apart." He follows Sofia into the kitchen area.

Sofia leans a chair against the sink. Jax sits down, cranes his neck over the sink as she turns the faucet on over his black hair. Ray Orbison's crooning through the tiny radio, *Pretty woman . . . mercy.*

Monk pages through the notebook, but his eyes are heavy. He stretches the rubber band over the notebook and sets it on the floor.

Someone taps Monk's shoulder. He opens his eyes. Jax is standing there, the milk crate in his hand, cigarette in his mouth, drippy hair. "Your turn. I'm taking my nightstand and retiring. See you in the morning."

"Try not to burn the mattress up." Sofia kisses him. "Come on, Monk."

Monk sits in the chair wedged against the sink. He feels cool water soaking through his matted hair, then her fingers as she rubs shampoo into his scalp. He closes his eyes: her hands feel so good. An electric tingling races down his spine, into his groin; it's been too long since he felt a feminine caress, soft, little hands . . . Karmann . . . *Say something, stay cool.*

He opens his eyes. "So how'd you guys meet?" On the radio, Skeeter Davis sings softly: *Why does the sun go on shining?*

"Me and Jaxsy? In New York, around '63. There was this artists' commune, Fluxus, it's still there." Her fingers massage lather into his hair, it's like his brain is submerged and she's rubbing the spongy lobes and canals.

"Fluxus?"

"Yeah, it's an underground art movement, started in Amsterdam, then spread to London, New York, lots of places. Their manifesto is to purge bourgeois art, anticommercial, it's right up Jax's alley. Anyway, I was born in Mexico City. My mom's an artist in Mexico City, my dad, well, I told you about him. They got divorced a few years after I was born. Living with my mother, I wanted to be some kind of artist too. I ended up going to this great art school in Buenos Aires. I got into the underground art scene. Apprenticed with León Ferrari, he's this amazing *provocador*, a master of protest art and what we called *happenings*. He showed me this sketch he's working on, this sculpture of Christ crucified on a Vietnam War bomber . . . a fucking genius. We were trying to rattle the government and the pope, anything subversive. Installing mattresses around the city, encouraging people to fuck . . . hanging slabs of meat dressed in brassieres and panties," she says, smiling. "León knew some artists in Fluxus, so I ended up in New York. Working, learning with the group, you know, all avant-garde artists, that's where I met Jax, over on Canal Street, they called the studio Fluxhall." She begins to rinse his hair in cool water, rubbing, stroking his head. "He was dating this crazy Japanese artist, her name's Ono. I called her Oh No," laughing. "But one thing led to another and we got together. He helped me get my visa, then we split for Frisco for a while. He and some of his guerrilla buddies did this installation that blew everyone's minds. They draped this huge mural canvas down over one side of the Golden Gate Bridge, a perspective painting so it looked like the bridge and the road arced *up* into the sky and clouds . . ."

"That's fucking crazy." Monk grins.

"That's where Jax really found himself. You know, it was Dada and Duchamp in the air, making art by pasting things and using signs and found art, then reinterpreting it, jamming its signal. They called them ready-mades, so Jax saw a billboard and it was love at first sight. You're all done."

Sofia rubs a damp towel into his hair. He stands. "You smell better. Get some rest." She lights a last cigarette. "Good night, Monk." Smiling, Sofia pulls his face down to her with her wet hands and kisses him on the cheek. She walks toward the mattress in the corner, where Jax softly snores in the shadows.

Monk sinks into the couch, pulls the cool sheet to his waist. He closes his eyes, grateful for the darkness, the quiet. Somehow he's found this refuge from the blood and fire outside, if only for a few hours. Each minute with his eyes closed is like surrendering to an eternal dream of peace and warmth. Now these two souls that chance or fate or whatever ruled these strange days had found him, healed and trusted him, shined a light for him when he'd lost his way. His arm slips to the floor, his fingertips resting on the notebook, then he's asleep.

18

It's just past sunset as the VW chugs south down Hooper. They head west on Ninety-first Street, crossing South Central. On the horizon is the Harbor Freeway; traffic is light tonight.

"I'm glad you're tagging along—pun intended." Sofia's eyes in the rearview mirror crinkle in amusement and everyone laughs. Monk's wearing a clean blue T-shirt Jax gave him. He's feeling better after sleeping away most of today's light in their loft. He can't remember meeting anyone like them; he feels this instant connection with them, a mysterious forging of their souls. Monk knows they're best friends, but he has no idea how, maybe it's chemical or cosmic: even these silences between them seem like a glowing, kindred bond.

"We'll get you to the harbor, man," Jax smoking his usual cigarette.

"Look at this shit." Sofia shakes her dark hair and points at a huge, glowing billboard: a beautiful, light-complected black woman in a business dress and pleated jacket stands by the office cooler, folder in hand, chatting with her white, handsome boss. JACKIE GOT THAT RAISE! in bold white letters. RAISE YOUR EXPECTATIONS WITH SNOW COAL WHITE MAKEUP TONES!

"I've seen them all over town," from Jax. "Must be a lot of sisters want lighter skin."

"You mean the brothers want *them* to have lighter skin," Monk smiles. In the rearview mirror, he can see Sofia's eyes crinkle with laughter. "Most of my so-called friends, they're always trying to pick up white girls."

"They can't say we'll make you look white so you can get a better man, or maybe even pass as white." Jax shrugs around, grins. "So they use code words like *fair, Caribbean, pearl.* There's another company, called Nerola . . . they're on my hit list, I'm working on some designs for these motherfuckers, a little truth in advertising."

"Fucking propaganda." Sofia downshifts, stops at a stop sign. "Everyone on the street knows lighter-skinned blacks get preference over darker blacks. Who are you going to hire, Mr. light skin, straightened hair, yes sir no sir? Or Mr. black as outer space, kinky Afro, yeah man, noah man, sheeeeet?" Everyone laughs.

"And those skin lighteners they use have this chemical ingredient called hydroquinone, to destroy dark, unwanted pigmenting cells. Trouble is, it's highly addictive. Wanna quit? If you stop using their stuff, your skin turns even *darker* than its original hue . . . no consumer is more loyal than the addict."

"That billboard company, it's the biggest in L.A." Sofia shifts gears, hands the cigarette to Jax. "No accident their name is fucking Medusa."

"The Gorgon?"

"Media Environmental Displays, USA." Jax exhales smoke. "You know what happens when you stare into the Medusa." Jax widens his eyes, splays his fingers on top of his cap, waves his fingers like grimy black snakes. "Medusa and these companies have technology. This is the twentieth century, man! They have computers now. Brushes, spray cans, stencils, so quaint and nineteenth century. In New York, we heard they were experimenting with giant video loops . . . soon they'll be projecting 'em on buildings."

"On the clouds, raindrops, the fucking sky itself," Sofia says.

The concrete web of the Manchester Avenue off-ramps and the Harbor Freeway pass over them like a vibrating, rumbling crucifix. Down Flower Street now, Sofia cuts the headlights and pulls up in front of an alley. "Gimme fifteen, baby." Jax grabs the canvas bag from the backseat. To Monk: "Wanna come?"

"Yeah." Monk climbs from the VW. They watch a single red taillight disappear down Grand as the VW's headlights blink back on.

They move silently through the deserted alley. A few blocks ahead, a glowing bank of billboards rises along Century Boulevard.

"Here are the satanic windmills," Jax chopping through the chain link with a bolt cutter from the canvas bag. "Call me Quixote," pulling away the shorn fence. "After you, Sancho."

Walking behind the shadows of the steel scaffolding, "A fool's quest, then, fighting Madison Avenue?"

"No, I see signs, pun intended. Change is slow, but I see it. The graffiti you document in your journal, the murals and designs, some of it's like underground art. I see stickers, stencils, tags, each one a little rebellion, everywhere, growing. On walls, bus benches, overpasses, every surface. And it's not just the spray-painting, it's those surfaces too, using the canvases to make statements about the system itself they want to overthrow."

Monk nods. "Like smOG bombed the Water and Power building over on Vermont, so it reads Watter and Powerless. Watter's slang for Watts folks."

"You gotta show me that one, man. Only the old and feeble-minded take Madison Avenue at face value. There's a change coming, these fuckers' days are numbered. This is it," and points up at the glowing, massive billboard towering above:

New for 1965!
The Ford Comet

The compact blue car streaks across the billboard, a fiery comet's tail burning in its wake. Huge letters banner under its wheels:

Forward!

The letters *F*, *o*, *r*, and *d* are highlighted in silver.

Jax slings the rope ladder up, its hooks ringing onto the bottom iron rungs of the access ladder. Bandanna over his face, he heaves the canvas satchel over his shoulder and scrambles up the rope ladder. Up on the catwalk, he digs into the canvas bag and works quickly, deftly spray-painting, drawing and holstering half a dozen spray-paint cans from a utility belt like an old gunslinger, spraying the duct-taped cans, then spinning them in the air to spray the attached can; finally he unfurls a large sticker.

Down below in the shadows of the pylons and girders, Monk shakes his head, then staggers down the weedy embankment, lost in the scaffolded rows of the billboards. He leans against the cool iron of a pylon and rubs his eyes. The billboard looms as he gazes up:

New for 1965!
Ford
For war!

A huge red, white, and blue poster's been glued to the Comet's doors:

Robert Strange McNamara
President of Ford
Secretary of Defense
First the Edsel . . .
Now Vietnam!

Monk wanders under the scaffolded signs.

"You okay, man?" Jax grabs his arm, leading him toward the alley.

"That shit they gave me. It keeps coming back like a bad memory."

The alley angles back into Grand Avenue. The idling VW hulks in the darkness. They climb in, slamming doors.

"You all right, Monk?" Sofia shrugs around. Monk nods. She grinds into gear and the bug lurches off.

Jax pulls the flask from the glove compartment. "Take a swig, do you good." Jax hands Monk the flask as the VW chugs toward the hazy lights of Century Boulevard.

The windows are engulfed in crimson light as a siren wails behind them. "Cops!" Sofia's eyes go wide with fear in the rear-view mirror.

"Where the fuck did they come from!" Jax peels off his bandanna and knit cap, stuffs them under the seat.

"I don't know! One of the alleys we passed, maybe. *Hijo de puta* . . . Jax, what should I do?"

"Pull over! Be cool!" Jax trying to jam the satchel under the seat. Sofia glides the VW to the curb. They're still on Grand, the street is dark, quiet, the intersection lights of Century still ahead.

A cop appears at the window, bends down, shines a flashlight into the car. "Well, if it isn't Mr. Monk."

"Good evening, Officer Trench." Monk's voice is tight with fear.

Trench smiles, studies Sofia and Jax for a moment. "Shut the vehicle off, miss." Sofia turns off the ignition. "You folks are approaching Century but there's a roadblock. You should have taken the detour back on Manchester."

"We're sorry, officer," Jax says, smiles. "I guess we missed it."

"We'll check you out, then you can be on your way." Smiling down at Sofia, enjoying the smell of her perfume. "License and registration, please." Sofia swallows, digs in her purse, hands him her license. Trench shines the flashlight on the glove compartment as Jax opens it, rummages around, hands him the registration. "I'll be right back. You folks sit tight." His boots click away in the hot, still night.

Inside the VW, their exaggerated shadows loom in the red radiance of the patrol car's lights. Sofia looks over to Jax. "Fuck, I thought he'd see your flask."

"It's in my pocket."

"Jax, I'm scared." Sofia's fists blanch white as she grips the steering wheel.

"We'll be okay, baby. The license and registration's clean. It's the riot, they'll send us back toward the detour." He shrugs around to Monk. "The fuzz knows you?"

"They want my notebook," Monk rasps, shaking his head. "That cop, he's a real motherfucker."

"Fuck that." Jax reaches under the seat.

"Jax! Don't do anything stupid!" Sofia's voice is pleading, strained in panic.

Inside the open doors of the cop cruiser, Officer Vicodanz sets the radio receiver back in its cradle. "They're clean," tossing his clipboard with Sofia's license and registration on the dashboard.

"Maybe. Let's do a vehicle search, then we can take Mr. Monk and his spy book to the professor."

"Parker's dyin' for that book, huh?"

"Just trying to make us look good, partner. You take Monk to the car, and I'll search those two."

"How 'bout I search that Mexican little spitfire?" Vicodanz licks his lips, opens his door.

"Whose collar is this asshole?" Trench grins, slides his baton into his holster as he walks toward the VW.

Officer Vicodanz opens the bug's rear door. "Okay, red shoes, let's go to the patrol car for a field search."

"He hasn't done anything, Officer." Jax's voice measured, controlled as Monk steps out of the car.

"Jax!" Sofia hisses.

"You should listen to your lady friend." Trench at Sofia's window. "She's smart . . . and nice-lookin'."

Sofia's squeezing the wheel; in the side mirror she can see Vicodanz and Monk are halfway to the patrol car.

"Now I'm going to conduct a field search of your persons, then your vehicle." Trench leans into Sofia. "We'll start with you, miss. Go ahead and step out of the vehicle, and you, sir, remain inside the car."

"Sofi, go!" Jax shouts as a wire-thin line of Babylon Blue spray paint shoots across the front seat, just missing Sofia's face, no time to react, no time to see the can of Magic Wick spray paint with its strange chrome nozzle in Jax's hand, as the spray has already jetted into Trench's eyes. Sofia wrenches the key and the VW revs up.

"Ahhh, sonofabitch." Trench staggers back, rubbing his blind eyes; he's pulled out his service revolver but the VW's already yards down Grand, Sofia grinding it into second gear. "Vicodanz!" Trench shouts, reeling around blind, the gun impotently waving in his right hand.

"Fuck!" Vicodanz runs toward Trench as Monk stands at the side of the patrol car, legs spread, hands on the ivory roof: through the rear passenger window, he can see his notebook where Vicodanz had tossed it on the backseat. Inside the open driver's door, the clipboard with their license and registration sits on the dashboard.

"The med kit!" Trench shouts.

Vicodanz turns and runs back toward the cruiser, fumbling, pulling at his nightstick in his utility belt. Monk slips his fingers under the rear door handle. The big cop is yards from him, raising his baton. *Fuck!* Monk grabs the clipboard from the dash and runs back into the alley, toward the median strip where the breached chain-link fence leads back to the billboards and the vacant lots, a network of dark alleys and interstices of escape behind the parallel lighted barrier of Century Boulevard.

"That nigger's gettin' away!" Vicodanz, breathless, sprinting toward the alley.

"Fuck him! Get the med kit!" Trench rubbing his eyes: he looks like some kind of raccoon demon. He can see blue light from one eye squinted open: Vicodanz looks like a ghostly indigo shadow.

Vicodanz runs back to the patrol car and opens the trunk. He sets the med kit on the trunk lid, hands Trench a squirt bottle of tear-gas eyewash. "I'll get backup." Vicodanz leans into the cruiser, pulls out the radio mike. "Car twenty-two, request backup, over." His thumb releases the mike switch. Static pops and hisses, then a slow, bass male voice purrs from the radio, the drawling words, to their dawning horror, thick with a *Negro* resonance: *Keep it cool out there in riot land, baby . . . This is Sir Soul with another groove to burn, John Lee Hooker and his "Blues Before Sunrise" . . . Burn, baby, burn . . .*

19

They sit and stand in the muted glow of blinking, snowy static. On the Zenith, the reporter, the flames and gutted buildings seem to tower above them, like a pulpit of violence. Black-and-white images and crackling sounds fade in and out. Charred storefronts. Two patrol cars block the intersection behind, their lights pulsing in the darkness. "Police are warning that the riot is spilling to other areas."

"Riot my ass!" Marcus shouts, raising his fists like a crazed black Moses with his long woolly beard. "This is a rebellion!"

Lamar mumbles, stoned, like a weird black praying mantis in his dark sunglasses.

Etaoin Shrdlu exhales menthol cigarette smoke: the TV images reflect in his wire-rim glasses like tiny apocalypses.

Dalynne shakes her head, sips wine. Karmann stands behind her, with a cup of merlot: she wants to get away from the Sea-Land container, take refuge on the observation deck or back in the bedroom, but she waits it out for a few more minutes, hoping for some kind of good news, anything.

"Southgate . . . Lynwood . . . north to the Harbor Gateway . . . the rioters seem intent on spreading their lawlessness and havoc," the reporter's voice breaking into static. Jumbled shots of ransacked liquor stores, looters running down sidewalks, loading car trunks with boxes and lamps and furniture.

"What the fuck is the Harbor Gateway?" Another stranger standing next to Karmann says, pointing his beer can.

"Look at all that shit," Lamar mumbles. "Free for the takin'."

"Authorities are bracing for the terrifying possibility that these rioters and gangsters want a race riot . . . it seems to stagger the mind . . . will we see the fall of Culver City? The fall of Torrance?"

"Viet-Watts!" A shirtless man, another reveler Karmann doesn't know, hurls an empty beer can at the TV; Karmann's stomach churns; she can't tell if it's the baby or if she's sick with hopelessness.

"I'm gon' get my share while the gettin's good." Lamar weaves toward a portal door.

"Here's the latest hot spots, ladies and gentlemen! The battle of Watts . . . Live from our Telecopter Five!" Images and sounds on the Zenith fade in and out between white storms of static: swaying helicopter aerial shots of buildings on fire, plumes of smoke, chains of police cars flashing through the darkness: beaming across every TV in America, this white, godlike vision from above of the savages scurrying in the darkness below . . . Now from the TV, this prerecorded music blares in the background, up-tempo drums, a horn section . . .

"Motherfuckers playin' car-chase music!" Marcus shouts.

"Sounds like that fuckin' *Fugitive* show," Shrdlu says.

"Honky propaganda bullshit!" Marcus reaches up and topples the TV: the plug, baling-wire antennas taped to the iron walls ripping out as the TV thuds and crackles into his arms and he runs out the hatchway, everyone staring in stunned disbelief.

"No, Marcus!" Dalynne shouts, chasing him. Karmann, Shrdlu, the shirtless stranger run to the portal.

They're running across the rusted green roof of the Hanjin container, like a mob chasing some looter with his purloined TV set. "Marcus, you crazy asshole!" Dalynne shouts.

At the edge of the container, Marcus raises the TV over his head and hurls it toward the dark Pacific below, the Zenith swings back: the shirtless man's grabbed the dangling cord, and he catches the TV, laughing. Marcus, off-balance, windmills his arms as he pitches forward over the side . . . but Shrdlu and Dalynne have his shirt bunched in their fists, and they rock him back away from the precipice.

"I don't know whether to laugh or cry," Karmann says as they follow the men back through the hatchway.

"Laughin's more fun." Dalynne squeezes her hand. "Let's have more wine." But back inside the Sea-Land, Marcus and Dalynne erupt into an argument, and Karmann slips away.

•

In the kitchen area, all the wine and booze bottles on the counters and serving tables are empty. Karmann scrounges through the cabinets and boxes. "They've drunk every drop of Monk's liquor. Maybe they'll go home." *What if they don't go home?* "Don't think like that," Karmann says aloud, shaking her head. *What if the party never ends? How many days and nights have passed? It's like Monk's always talking about, ghetto time, where time can speed up, slow down, or even freeze in a kind of strange suspension . . .*

She settles on going to the observation deck; fresh air will do her good, and from there she can always go downstairs to the bedroom and sleep, or spin another record on the turntable.

Karmann rushes through the WestCon room, its party still going, sweaty bodies in varying stages of undress swaying, dancing under the stolen blinking amber road lamps. Radio music echoes, bouncing off the iron walls. She glances away from a shadowy corner, where five or six bodies squirm and fuck under blankets and sleeping bags. *Monk, you better get home soon.*

Stepping onto the roof of the Evergreen container, the rush of warm August night only feels like a suffocating shroud. Karmann resolves not to gaze north, toward the burning city.

A loud, shrill whining rises behind her as she turns: Lil' Davey flies past her, revving a red Vespa scooter, almost knocking her down. Two revelers—more strangers—burst from the hatchway, waving a green nylon jacket in the air. Lil' Davey turns the scooter precariously around on the boat ramp that connects the south edge of the Evergreen to the Atlas container. Karmann watches in disbelief as Davey races past her, motor screaming, hand throttle all the way open, his long legs bent outward, knees above the handlebars like some black giant on a children's bicycle. One of the strangers flicks and waves the jacket before him like a deranged matador as the Vespa plows through the jacket, the man jumping sideways at the last second.

"Toro! Toro!" The other hollers, swigging a whiskey bottle as Lil' Davey screeches in a cloud of black exhaust, turns and blasts past Karmann, popping a wheelie that almost knocks her down as she jumps back.

"Fucking asshole!" Karmann shouts.

Lil' Davey twists the scooter around the boat ramp again, flashing Karmann the finger.

"Toro Toro, motherfucker!" Voices behind her laugh.

"Fuck this," Karmann hisses, stalking back inside the West-Con. "Why don't y'all leave! Just fucking go!" she shouts. The dancers ignore her, turning, gyrating under the yellow strobe lights: it's as if she's a phantom. In the corner near the orgy of blankets and writhing bodies, a man leans against the iron walls, his pants curled around ankles as a woman with a gold-sprayed Afro swallows his huge cock deep into her mouth. Karmann flees out the hatchway.

Karmann sweeps through the containers in a seething rage, shouting at everyone to go home, like a mad noblewoman railing against the drunken peasants at a castle feast. Some nod and humor her, or laugh at the woman they don't even know; most ignore her and go back to drinking, smoking, whatever pleasures her tantrum had disrupted. "Oh," Karmann pauses, leans against a wall, her breath taken away as the baby kicks in her belly.

In the Matson container, Dalynne finds her. Under the blue and yellow strings of lightbulbs, Dalynne's face looks garish, her tears seem to glow like molten silver.

"What is it?" Karmann holds her heaving shoulders.

"I'm leavin'. Marcus . . . I can't stand him . . . I caught him . . . making out with some bitch outside . . . I'm sorry, Karmann . . . I got to go."

"Back home? It's too dangerous, honey. Stay here with me."

"No. I can't stand it . . . I'm done with him. I'll call you tomorrow, promise." She kisses Karmann on the cheek and weaves through knots of people, toward the hatchway.

Cooky's on the wall phone, shaky hand cupped over the receiver, probably talking to his heroin connection. "Get off the phone, Cooky!" Karmann hisses, standing before him, her arms crossed. Cooky raises a finger to his pale lips, then turns his back to her, his big Afro blotting out the phone like an eclipse. Karmann spins his scarecrow body around and rips the receiver from his bony hand. "Get lost!" She bangs the phone back into its plastic cradle.

"Man, you a bitch," Cooky mutters and shuffles away.

She glares at him for a moment, then picks up the phone. A metallic white woman's nasal voice—Karmann can always tell the sound of white voices—drones in her ear like a chanting curse: "If you'd like to make a call, please hang up and dial again . . . if you'd like to make a call, please hang up—" Karmann smashes the receiver again and again into the cradle, until a black shard of plastic flies into the air. "Goddamn it," whispering, jabbing the plastic button-tab inside the cradle. She presses the phone against her ear: "If you'd like to make a call, please—" Her eyes fill with tears as she drops the phone and it clatters against the iron floor, swaying on its black coiled cord.

Through the open hatchway, music blares, someone's ratcheted up the volume too high, she can hear the record player echoing from the Hanjin container. They'll blow out the speakers . . . it's one of Monk's old Charles Mingus records. She knows this song but can't think of the title . . . her mind aches . . . she wants to drink the last merlot in her bedroom, sleep . . . it's too late, all of this madness, what does any of it matter if he doesn't come home? These people . . . these things . . . the only important thing is Monk . . . Monk and her and the boy: she knows it will be a son. Now a refrain echoes: *Weird nightmare . . . take away this dream you've born.* A loud scratching sound grates her ear, then the record skips: *take away this dream you've born . . . take away this dream you've born . . .*

Karmann turns and walks back through the room, away from the chanting words: it's another one of Monk's omens . . . *take away this dream you've born . . .* there is no way she can decipher if it is an evil or good sign. She needs her bed, darkness, solitude, any last dregs of wine and just one more Kent. A sleepwalker out of time . . . not out but beyond time: a faint smile as she remembers one night when she and Monk had fucked gloriously for hours in bed, listening to albums; then one song began to skip over and over again, and Monk said it was a sign . . . he had this theory: whenever a record skipped, time stopped . . . seconds, minutes, hours lost secretly until the needle lifted or bumped on or power failed, in rooms scattered across the world . . . until no one knew how many years had been lost . . .

She walks across the roof of the Evergreen container, relieved that Lil' Davey and his Vespa and drunken matadors have vanished somewhere for now. Ascending the boat ramp, Karmann sees Maurice and another man conversing near the edge; they look like strange apparitions in their Nation of Islam black shoes, suits, bow ties, their Fruit of Islam gold lapel pins glinting in the moonlight.

"Good evening again, Karmann." Maurice bows his shaved head slightly, his eyes lingering up and down her body.

"Good evening, Fallouja Awahli." From here they've been gazing north, toward the burning city, but she tries to focus only on the two men.

"Karmann, this is Raheem Taj."

"Hello." Her voice is strained.

"The pleasure is all mine." Taj smiles: a strikingly handsome man with piercing cobalt eyes and close-cropped, oiled hair. Karmann notes that his bow tie is crimson, and Maurice's—he's always Maurice to her—tie is black, no doubt another of the Nation's cryptic uniform ranks or insignia.

"I hope you don't mind, we've escaped up here for a little air. The loud music, the smoking and drinking, it's a bit overwhelming," Maurice says.

"Yeah. I wish they'd all leave. What is this? The second night? The third?" Her eyes seem dark, lusterless, as if she's staring through them.

The two men exchange worried, fleeting glances. "If you wish, perhaps we could help, tell them the party's over?"

"No no," she blurts out, as if he's crossed some invisible line. "Monk . . . Monk will be home very soon, I know it."

Maurice shoots Taj a furtive glance. "Of course, I'm sure of it. Maybe he will take refuge in one of our temples, he'd be safe there."

"Then you could give him one of your pamphlets." Why is she so hostile? She's a little tipsy, wants a Kent so she can blow the smoke in his self-righteous face, then he can lecture her about defiling the temple of her pregnant body . . . it's just that she can see through him, knows he'd like nothing better than if Monk should somehow be out of the equation and Maurice could add to his secret harem . . . he's worse than Felonius and Lamar and the others, their lust for her is naked, clumsy, hopeless, but his is a cold, calculating series of moves, like some fanatical chess master.

"He might learn much from our literature . . . you too. We are only seeking the promise of our destiny, the freedom from white oppression. Look out there," he points north into August's smoky horizon, "the city is burning. It's not the first city, and it won't be the last."

"I hope it is the last."

"The fruits of Islam," Taj says, "will be harvested from the ashes of these cities."

"Maybe you're just another gang," Karmann says, grinning, "a very well-dressed gang."

"But Karmann," Maurice touches her shoulder gently, "we are not burning and looting."

"You got guns, hideouts, recruiting for new blood in the streets."

"Don't you want our white oppressors out of our businesses and communities and lives?"

"I don't know. White devil, black devil, I don't want to think like that."

"The Nation is misunderstood." Taj smiles. "If you open your mind, you would see that most Negroes agree with us. We are only saying that the Negro masses have been blinded by ten percent of the people—the white power structure. They used to control us with chains and whips. Now they use the media and money. It is the Nation that can free us."

Below, a muffled, sputtering motor chugs louder in the torpid night air. They gaze down over the rusted edge, into the mirror waters of the Pacific. A black rubber dinghy bobs into the pylons of the pier: three scrawny black teens wave beer bottles and holler from the raft. "Ahoy, motherfuckers! Beer for the party!" One boy, shirtless, tries to stand with a case of beer and falls back into the dinghy, laughter.

"Black pirates, give up your women!" Another boy's slicing the air with an oar.

"Oh my god," Karmann whispers.

Under the Evergreen container, a figure leans out from a window blowtorched in a bottom cargo box. "Hoist it up!" A rope whips out from the window, dangling above the dinghy.

"Please . . . I can't take any more." Karmann talking to herself.

"Me first!" A voice below. A shirtless boy in swimming trunks has tied a loop at the end of the rope. He stands precariously on the outer tube of the raft, one bare foot swaying inside the rope's coil.

Maurice extracts a pistol from under his suit coat.

"No!" Karmann hisses in horror, grabbing his sleeve.

"Don't worry. I'm just going to scare them away." Maurice gently frees his arm, aims and fires: the shot is muted, a soft clap in the heavy air.

Karmann looks down: the dinghy's hissing, collapsing into the water. "Fuck!" The standing boy loses his balance, splashes into the water as the rope springs into the air.

"What the fuck," a boy says, sinking into the water around the deflating raft, grabbing an oar.

"Save the beer!" someone yells from the window.

Now all three boys are thrashing in the water, two hands desperately holding the beer case above the lapping waves, but it's too heavy and he lets go as it sinks. "Motherfucker." They swim, disappearing under the pylons toward the shore.

Karmann bursts out laughing, then Maurice and Taj laugh. "Don't worry, they won't be back." Maurice slips the gun into his jacket pocket.

"Oh my god." Karmann presses her palm against her belly, breathing fast, her heart thumping.

"Are you all right, Karmann?" Maurice squeezes her hands, rubs them gently in his strong hands.

An electric shock seems to pass through her and she catches her breath, gazing up into his eyes. "Yes . . . yes, thank you . . . I'm so tired . . . good night."

"Of course. Good night, Karmann." Maurice and Taj watch her as she slowly heads up the boat ramp.

•

Up on the Matson, she is finally alone. Walking across the corrugated roof, she stops as a moth flutters around her, then disappears into the darkness. She smiles: It's already been three years since they'd first made love. Monk had scraped up some cash and they rented a cheap motel room for the night, a horrible place off Florence Avenue. Later, still in bed, they watched as an iridescent brown and blue moth circled above their bed three times, then bobbed around the white candle they'd set on a rickety table.

"Blow it out so it doesn't die," Karmann had said. Monk walked over and blew out the candle. "It circled us three times. Is that a good sign, Mr. Semiotician?" she asked in the darkness.

"With you, there are only good signs."

When Monk woke up in the morning, he found her outside, sitting in a plastic chair in front of the room, smoking a cigarette. In the weedy flower bed beside the entranceway, planted in the dirt, was a tiny cross made from two twigs and a knotted strand of grass.

"You buried that moth, didn't you?"

Karmann nodded and they laughed.

"A cross?" Monk had asked. "Are you sure it was a Christian? What if it was Jewish or Muslim?"

She exhaled and laughed again. "It was special. That was our love moth."

"You said a prayer too, didn't you? I know you. 'Dear Lord . . . bless this little creature . . . searching in the darkness for the light—'"

"You asshole." She'd wrapped her arms around him. "You do

know me. We have an hour before checkout time." And she'd kissed him and pushed him back into the room.

Karmann now leans wearily against the iron rails and gazes out into the night sky. The city to the north is bathed in moonlight. Fingers of black smoke rise over the burning city like foamy pillars frozen in the gloom, jutting into the smoky haze. She doesn't want to think of him out there, but how can she not? She becomes aware that her hands have been rubbing the beads of welded metal along the handrail, the drops of hot metal that Monk had left when he'd welded it together, as if each bead were a kind of rosary, a link to his hands, to him: she knows Monk would agree, it's another sign waiting to be read. Now, for a moment, the towers of smoke look like they're not rising but descending . . . mysterious, dark shafts that beam down from the haze and into the city's horizon. Karmann squeezes the rails, her hand resting protectively over her belly: it is as if the darkness is churning into the city instead of rising away. No, smoke must rise. Everything, everyone must rise. Tomorrow there might be fear, but here and now, in this moment, she is no longer afraid.

20

Monk walks south on dark side streets and alleyways, his thoughts black, exitless as tonight's avenues seem to be: *Fuckers took my notebook. My notebook!* Only a few cars creep along the gauntlet of Watts, Athens, Inglewood, trying to make it west toward the safety of the coast, or east toward Lynwood and the walled terminus of the San Gabriel River. *All my work, everything gone . . . the keys to a thousand locks . . . fucking pigs.* The Harbor Freeway twinkles with possibilities of escape: north toward the mountains, or south toward the harbor where, Monk thinks, some lights must still shine and illuminate Karmann's beautiful face now etched in worry and fear. Escape, his life, even Karmann . . . all of it a hollow, bitter joke without his notebook.

Monk's made it to 101st, a block east of Avalon with its gauntlet of police checkpoints every block. He jabs his hands angrily into his front jeans pockets. Huge black letters have been sprayed across a brick storefront: U.S. TROOPS OUT . . . Did they mean Vietnam or the city? *Fuck*, if only he can remember Standard's map: he has to go south, but cut east, toward Compton and Miramonte . . . what was that other street, sounded like Pamela? Two police cars roar past, flashing lights and sirens. *Jax and Sofia . . . hope they made it out . . . cops looking for me too.* Now his fingertips can feel the folded papers in his front pocket, Sofia's license and registration.

Monk needs to stay clear of these main streets, maybe cut south on Wadsworth or Stanford Avenue. Scattered bands of men prowl the sidewalks or cluster on street corners. Monk passes an overturned car as a ghetto bird hovers above, its searchlight stabbing down across darkened blocks and fitful wall shadows. The stench of distant smoke burns his nostrils.

He feels naked, defeated without his notebook: Trench and his Nordic goon partner; it's the worst kind of violation, a raping of the soul and spirit instead of the flesh. And what about Jax and Sofia? Had they only meant to save their own skins? Monk frowns. Was it thanks to them or in spite of them that he'd barely escaped?

Across the street, two taggers spray signs and dripping bombs on the front of a stucco office building, black and red paint slashing across padlocked doors: it's just the Gladiators expanding their turf. Monk tries to shake off his bitterness and suspicions. *Jax and Sofia are good people . . . don't let the poison into your brain.* The taggers scatter now as a crowd of *white men* march down the sidewalk: about twenty men with billy clubs, all wearing green berets with patches emblazoned JBS—the John Birch Society . . . *Shit.* Monk shakes his head: each night these streets become more and more like some kind of occupied no-man's-zone.

On the corner of 106th Street and Stanford Avenue, a church is surrounded by cops and fire trucks: Our Lady of Perpetual something, the building charred and gutted, the roof smoking and caved in. Firemen roll up hoses and tote equipment back to idling trucks as cops with shotguns watch him pass.

Another block south, only a few stragglers on the sidewalks or sipping beer behind iron grilles of tenement apartments wedged between abandoned or closed commercial buildings. Ahead, the gleaming lemon-and-avocado neon sign of another Tote 'Em Store.

Thirsty, Monk walks across the parking lot, pushes through the door. Inside, a nervous thin white woman in a gray pantsuit stands in front of the cash register. Two black women stand at the soda machine, filling big wax-cup drinks. A middle-aged white woman with a shopping bag waits before the cashier, avoiding Monk's eyes. A large white man, dressed in his yellow-and-green uniform, works the register, watching Monk, his thumb slowly sliding up from the hidden panic button under the counter, the *boogie button*, every store's first defense against Negro customers. Behind him, silver letters on the wall, THE SOUTHLAND CORPORATION, reflect aisles and lights and racks that seem somehow futuristic: chrome displays, silvery cases, frosted rings of cold halogen light, bags and bottles and boxes of products he doesn't recognize. He walks past racks of candies to the fluted, chrome fountain-drink machine: SLURPEE TIME! A sign above the silver spouts. Monk grabs a small wax cup, fans it under the nozzles, root beer, Bubble Up, cola, Dr. Pepper: good thing that Ganges Slurpadavedjahpad isn't here to see him commit this unauthorized soda scherzo. Monk's red Keds cross the floor's black-and-white tiles. He slaps a quarter and a dime on the counter, walks out in silence with the sensation that eyes are following his back as the chrome doors close.

Monk trudges south down Stanford. He grins: he can almost hear the locks bolting closed on that Tote 'Em Store's doors, white clerks and customers breathing a sigh of grateful deliverance.

His Keds mark off another section of sidewalk, each crack bringing him closer to the promise of harbor and home; but he's still subject to laws and forces unfathomable as this endless night of inferno and destruction: to the west Gardena, to the east Rosewood, the rose that hides the thorns of Compton. Fading church bells gong in the distance, a requiem for the dying city.

A car passes him, a white girl's face, afraid, examining him from behind the rolled-up window. Monk walks toward the pale-lit intersection of 109th Street, then stops.

On the curb, under a stop sign: an opened pack of Fatima cigarettes. An ebony sprig of flower with snowy petals and two pennies neatly placed on top of the cellophane. Monk picks up the flower, sniffs the sweetish nectar, carefully places it back on the pack. The cigarettes extend from the box in rising lengths, like paper steps. The final cigarette extends almost fully from the pack, a nicotine finger pointing west . . . *Like Texino's cigarette tilted toward a safe route* . . . Monk can only hope it's good gris-gris.

Monk walks rapidly south on Stanford. He's finally going south, but this won't be a good place to be if the cops or the Guard show up. He crooks his thumb but the few cars that pass don't slow or stop. Five men dart across the dark street, carrying iron rods, bricks, beer bottles. He passes an alley blocked by two rusted dumpsters heaped with burning, smoking trash. A stucco wall's tagged in drippy, blood-red spray paint: VIET-WATTS.

He sucks down the last of his soda rainbow, sets the cup in the dry gutter. Just a few more hours now until they start running the buses again, or maybe he can hitch a ride and get to Karmann. Walk those Keds, those Felony Fliers through this bricked incinerator until your scorched soles and soul reach sea foam and the rusted fortress of home.

Monk crosses 111th Place. Two cars pass as he waves his thumb. Behind him, eastbound on 111th, a burgundy Corvair Monza convertible screeches to a stop.

Monk turns: two black girls smiling up at him. "Where ya goin'?" the girl in the passenger seat says, plump, conked hair, paisley blouse, black leather pants.

"Anywhere south."

"Well, we're goin' north, up Central to the clubs." The girl behind the wheel's thin, pretty, with a short Afro and glasses, wearing a deep blue Jeweltone belted dress. She pouts her lips. "But if you don't mind hanging out at the clubs for a couple of hours, I've gotta take Sidney home . . . this is Sidney." The other girl waves. "She lives way down off Artesia Boulevard. We could drop ya off down there."

Artesia, that's a long way toward home. "That'd be great." Monk slips into the backseat. The Monza turns left, whines north up Stanford. "What the hell." Monk's sitting on something as he digs a metal buckle on a vinyl strap out from under him. "What's this?"

"It's called a seat belt." Sidney turns and laughs. "You might want to wear it considering the way Jaylah drives."

The girl behind the wheel smiles in the rearview mirror as she smashes the gas pedal. Monk's head bounces off the vinyl seat back as the Corvair revs into second gear. After some experimentation, Monk manages to buckle the harness around his waist.

"I'm Monk. Glad to meet you all!" Monk shouts into the buffeting, warm wind. The radio blasts the Supremes' "Baby Love" and cigarette smoke wafts in Monk's face as Sidney lights up.

They turn right on 104th Street. Ashen smoke roils in the distance, a burning, acrid shroud for the night. "What a stink!" Jaylah waves her hand in front of her nose. Rioters have set every tire dump and junkyard in the city on fire, from Crenshaw to Compton, Ladera Heights to Florence. Towering black pyramids of burning rubber, like monstrous ebony candles spewing charcoal smoke and poison clouds over a city already in flames. Water only exacerbates the poisonous runoff, so the rubber fires have to burn until their fuel is gone.

The Corvair turns left on Central, accelerates north. They pass boarded-up windows, black men sitting in chairs in front of shop windows, shotguns across their laps. Handwritten signs in windows are like talismans to ward off evil: *Blood Brother.*

"You girls picked a hell of a night to go clubbing!"

"We black, honey." Sidney turns in the front seat. "We cool."

"I heard the club section is okay!" Jaylah shouts. "Folks want to stay inside, party until sunup, when it's safer. They said it's worse over around Florence and Graham!"

The clubs begin around Sixtieth Street. He remembers a few of them from when he was a kid, his long-gone, ace-of-bass father having played most of the clubs back in the forties and fifties. He's backtracking miles, but that ride later to Artesia will make up for a few lost hours. *What's the rush now that they've stolen my notebook? Fuck it, we'll see what happens.*

A Byrds song wafts from the radio: *We'll meet again, don't know where, don't know when.*

As they barrel past Ninety-first Street, two cop cars fly by in a glowing red blur of flashing lights and sirens. "Hoowee!" Jaylah yells. "Somethin' to tell the grandkids!"

"You flipped, girl!" Sidney laughs. The Byrds song fades and a baritone man's voice reverberates from the radio: *Yeah, we'll all meet again, baby—*

"It's him!" Jaylah squeals. "That crazy DJ. He's all over town. Listen!" She cranks up the chrome volume knob. *Sir Soul here with you, baby, all night long . . . stay cool in the fire . . . gonna burn a little 'Pride and Joy' now, by Mr. Marvin Gaye . . . and stay tuned, 'cause later on Sir Soul's gonna have a special guest, till then, let's burn, baby, burn . . .*

A block east, Monk gazes out at the flames and churning columns of smoke peppering the darkness above the passing rooftops and storefronts. Street by street, alley by alley, fire trucks, squad cars, support vehicles are holding their positions down the ruined streets, gutted buildings, smoky black mounds of debris, and charred frames rising into the haze like monstrous wrens. Down Eighty-eighth Street as the Corvair whines past, Monk glimpses tanker trucks blasting foamy cannonades of water into still burning recesses. But this counterstrike is only a tentative probe east as far as Central Avenue: beyond, the city has vanished to islands of lights, flames, sirens, searchlights fanning into smoke and darkness.

"Wow! Better'n TV!" Jaylah slaps the steering wheel.

"I heard the National Guard's coming!" Monk shouts back.

"Mmm!" Sidney exhales her cigarette. "Young men in uniform! They can guard me anytime!"

"Sidney!" Jaylah turns, laughs.

The Corvair brakes as they approach Firestone Boulevard. Police cars have barricaded Firestone to the east. A line of headlights ahead as the cars wait to pass through the intersection. Monk can see cops with flashlights waving and scanning over the cars. At the checkpoint, cars are bayoneted with crisscrossing flashlight beams: some cars are motioned to pass through the gauntlet of cops and cruisers, interior lights winking off as they accelerate up Central. Other cars are rerouted, flashlights and toted shotgun barrels direct vehicles left to the shoulder, a barricaded search point ringed with glowing flares. Monk's guts churn: what if that asshole Trench is here?

As the Corvair sputters closer, a homemade sign rests against the trunk of one of the patrol cars: TURN ON INSIDE LIGHTS OR GET SHOT. A cop scans his flashlight over the convertible; Sidney smiles and waves at the young white officer. The cop motions them through and Jaylah revs the Corvair down the block.

Waves of exhaustion press Monk against the hot, sticky vinyl seats: time has been suspended here in the ghetto, there is only an endless chain of sleep, consciousness, dream or hallucination.

They've finally reached Fifty-ninth and Monk can see some of the distant neon signs of the clubs a few blocks ahead. "Here we are! Sin Street!" Jaylah shouts.

The Corvair idles at a red light. Monk can see the old clubs are still open. Through an open red door of the Freak Lip, two women's voices blend and wail out into the night, some kind of blues ballad floating over tinkling piano and throbbing bass. Their voices are like angels, a soul aria that seems out of this world . . . He opens the door, he wants to go to them, see the faces that command this heartbreaking dulcet force. "Hey, where y'all goin'?" Jaylah turns but Monk can't hear her, only the euphonious echo of the women's voices. He falls back into the seat, somehow tangled up in restraining straps, these goddamn contraptions new cars have called seat belts. Sidney reaches behind and slams Monk's door as the light turns green, Monk squirming in twisted loops of belt, lashed to the Corvair as it peels through the intersection. "Honey, you don't want to go in *there*," Jaylah laughs. "Them girls are so hot you'll *never* leave."

The Finale Club looms ahead and the car lurches to the curb. "Shit." Monk looks around: they're on East Fifty-seventh. The club's doors are open, FOI guards ringing the sidewalk, a drum solo crashing through upstairs windows. "Meet you back at the car, Monk." Jaylah grins, purses her lips. "Say, around three-ish?"

"Watch out for them soul singers," Sidney laughs, waving good-bye. The girls disappear in a line of customers trickling in under flashing neon. Monk, hands in pockets, heads down the sidewalk, trying not to dwell on forces that blow him back, circling, spinning, trapped in a loom of shadows and lights that only project linear progress, as he steps into the blinking lavender nimbus of Club Alabam, and the glow and music of Sin Street beyond.

21

On Sin Street tonight, the clubs are the only places in the city where you can still get booze, no curfew here, money buys anything. Monk passes Club Alabam, a few hookers testing the club's Fruits of Islam bodyguards at the front door. On the corner, the DownBeat is jumping; a huge black man in a porkpie hat and gold vest stands toting a sawed-off shotgun at the upholstered doors.

Monk walks a block. Ivie's Chicken Shack is jammed with people; men drink beer on curbs. There's the old Dunbar Hotel, brownstone rising into the night, its olive canopy over the sidewalk, neon signs splashing rainbow lights.

Two doors down is the Congo Club. This is the joint—and some of the others down Sin Street—where his father played, Damon "Pocket" Monk. A thin, tall man with a big stand-up bass sticking out of the backseat of his DeSoto, always on the road to the next gig. Monk only knows him from a few sepia-tone photographs his mother kept in a dresser drawer. Mother once told him his father had his own name tattooed on his chest so that the image in every morning's mirror would reflect his creed of the open road: *nomad.* In his lost notebook somewhere, Monk long ago scribbled an aphorism from some ancient scribe: *The son can never know the father.*

The sign blinks in yellow neon sizzling above Monk: TALL
TAN TERRIFIC COPPER COLORED CHORUS GALS. Bamboo walls and
fake palm trees line its facade; coconuts and Christmas lights
loop over windows and the black padded doors. FOI bodyguards
are stationed in the shadows of the jungle canopy. On each side
of the upholstered doors, big wooden speakers blare jazz music.
There's a cymbal crash as the song ends, then that radio voice
he's come to recognize: *All right, Sir Soul back here with you,
baby. Now, as I promised, I got a special guest DJ tonight . . . Miss
Compton Eve.* Now a woman's voice, slow, sultry: *Good evening,
this is Compton Eve . . . to all my brothers and sisters out there . . .
tonight I want you to love . . . and burn . . . baby, burn . . .* Monk
feels electricity jolting down his spine: *Good evening.* He knows
that voice too . . . vinyl records spilling on the sidewalk . . . the record jacket with the black-and-white photograph of Coltrane . . .
Eve for Iva . . . Tokyo Rose. *Brothers and sisters, they have oppressed
you too long. Words change nothing, only action brings change. Let
the fires consume all the symbols of their slavery and lies . . . let your
children build from the ashes . . . burn, baby, burn . . .* A gong
booms sonorously as Coltrane blasts four piercing alto saxophone
sonic notes, then his band lays down the rhythm as the sax blis-
ters into a solo.

The black doors open, spilling Monk in blue light. Saxophone
and piano and drums and bass thump and wail from inside.
Monk cranes his head over a few Islam fezzes, trying to catch a
glimpse of the old paternal haunt, then slips into the deep blue
jazz interior.

Black men and women are drinking, laughing shoulder to
shoulder, dark forms in clouds of cigarette smoke, beyond teak
African masks frowning from walls and green jungle vines swaying
in the smoke. Monk finds an empty stool at the jungle bar, next to
a fat black man in sweat-drenched cream pants and open lime
silk shirt, black sunglasses reflecting Christmas lights. "Coca-Cola,
please." Monk's already sweating. At the corner of the bar, a pretty

black waitress in a grass skirt and khaki blouse smiles at him as she sets drinks on a tray.

"Ain't you," a fat black man's deep baritone voice, "Monk's kid?"

"Yeah. My dad used to play here, back in the fifties." He pulls out a crumpled dollar bill.

"Tha's reet, no sheet," the big black man laughs like a great bellows. "Chu 'Hurricane' Reed." He shakes Monk's hand. There's a silver number five reed strung on a chain around his thick sweaty neck. "Well, I'm glad I hungover my hangover on this here stool, 'cause look who I bumped into. White man's money is funny here, lock it in yo' pocket," Chu pushing the dollar back into Monk's palm.

"Americo Monk, pleased to meet you, Mr. Reed."

"Americo?" He grins, sips beer. "That's beautiful. Call me Uncle Chu, please. He slides a bill toward the bartender: red paper, the number one above the words *One Skrill* printed in blurred black ink, two illegible signatures under an oval-framed silhouette of a man crowned with a huge Afro. Chu catches Monk's quizzical look. "Nigger Tender, Soul Specie, Ghetto Gold, legal tender wherever the lender o' presenter is black, brown, o' renowned. Got denominations for a new black nation. Brother Bucks, Watts Wads bearin' the *glims* of the founding hims: Booker Ts, John Browns, Lincoln's on the ten bill, got Carver— we call him Peanuts—Thurgood, you can really swing if you got X and King . . . all part of the movement . . . out there ev'ry night," Chu hooks a thumb toward the front door, "fightin' for the right, that uprising before the sun rising, fire 'n' pain to get on the soul train to a future black domain, to inde*hip*endence." Chu sips his beer. "I hope it takes this time, cuz after the fires comes the liars."

"The riots?"

"I've peeped all this shit before. You wasn't even a gleam in yo' daddy's bloodshot eye. Before I hooked up with ol' Monk. Back in '43, I was livin' in Detroit durin' the war, a young man, 'bout yo' age now. All this killin' and burnin' out there? Same gory story in Detroit, only 'round twenty years ago or so, seems folks forgot or like to pretend they forget."

"What happened?"

"Déjà voodoo. There was this project the government built, Negro housing they named the Sojourner Truth projects." Chu laughs. "It was supposed to be for black people but whites thought the neighborhood should stay soul-free. So one hot summer day fistfights turned into street brawls turned into burning city blocks, just like out there. Rumors spread like fevers . . . white men throwin' black mothers and babies into the river . . . white mobs with guns drivin' in from the hills . . . black gangs stalkin' white women in the 'hoods . . . lootin' and burnin' for days until FDR called in federal troops. Sound familiar?"

"Shit, I never knew."

"I know." Chu grins. "Like I says, folks like to pretend to forget. But, dig, Americo? That ain't even the evil of it out there. The evil comes later, the liars after the fires. Back in '43, the cops, the white people, newspapers, the city leaders and their so-called investigations. They discovered the shockin' truth, the riots was instigated by uppity, unemployed Negroes . . . and black and them Mexican zoot-suit gangs . . . now, you dig ol' Chu, same thing gonna happen in yo' time. Fires, then liars."

"But that's bullshit." Monk glowers across the bar, thinking of his notebook.

Reed shakes his big head, grinning. "Time will tell. You sound just like yo' daddy. Look like him too. Yo' pa was cool drool, a fucker of a plucker. I conked with Monk back in nine an' fifty, real nifty. He was a gone bass ace, you prob'ly a chip off the ol' wick wherever he dipped."

"I don't remember him."

Chu's big face winces with pain. "Well, I'm on my break, so fade 'n' I'll have another brew 'n' tell you true." He's nodding to the bartender, who slides a cold mug of beer across the bar top.

"Yeah, I remember pickin' up Monk—yo' daddy—a few times at his house. You was a little boy, frowning behind that little beat-up Wurlitzer piano."

"I was eight. Dad made me take lessons."

"I know. It's a foundation, he'd say, you can build to any instrument from piano."

"More like an off-key hell than a foundation." Monk laughs. "I don't know how my mom put up with it. Dad hired this white woman to teach me, a German lady, Mrs. Von Walpurgis or something like that. Man, she hated teaching me those scales as much as I hated doing them."

Chu sips beer. "I remember one gig yo' daddy was mad as hell, said you wrote stories and drawings all over the sheet music." Monk smiles, nods his head. "You still writin'?"

"I was," he says bitterly, "in a manner of speaking, yes."

"Well, tha's good."

"Dad wanted me to be a musician. I think Mom was relieved it didn't take."

"Life on the road ain't for married men. Now, old Chu's single and likes to mingle. Yo' old man and me, see our generation, well, there wasn't a whole lot a options for us . . . but if you could play an instrument, that was a golden ticket out of the ghetto. Sure beats bein' a Pullman porter, or if you was real lucky, working at the post office."

Chu extracts a canary-colored joint from his shirt pocket and a chrome Zippo lighter. "When we played together, Monk talked about you many times. He was torn. He felt bad, knew he wasn't doin' the right thing as a father, but he was proud to be a good provider, making sure you and yo' mother had money. Some cats I know blow all their wad on libations and sensations." Hurricane lights up the joint. "Back when we was playin' together in the fifties, you had to look hip, *zoot*, all *reet*. Monk spent half his paycheck at the barber's and cleaners, but man, his drapes were shaped, put the dares to the squares." Chu exhales a cloud of cloying reefer smoke over Monk's head. "A few years back, one gig Monk showed up after sleepin' in his swing suit, then for a while after that, all these folks would show up at the clubs with these copycat threads all wrinkled and frazzled on purpose, 'cause they *Einsteined* Monk must be settin' a new style profile with his *dweezled* front, when all he'd done was cop some *doss* after passin' out in his drapes." Chu laughs.

Monk nods as a vivid memory flashes through his mind: his father picking him up from Grape Street Elementary School, mothers and annoyed-looking fathers in dirty work clothes and all the other kids staring up mouths agape at the handsome, railthin black man in his sharp black-and-white silk suit, polished indigo Florsheims, pomade, conked hair, the thin mustache that looked too perfect to be real.

"Those early days, '50 or '51, us and the band, we'd play anywhere. Monk always made sure we had money. Shit, we'd play the Elks Hall down Central, or the Masonic Temple on Fifty-fourth. White folks' *skiffles* on the other side of town, where the white ho-dads had a two-bits-a-head invite to hear some *race music*." Chu grins. "The ho-dads grooved to the found sound and dug us Negroes with Happy Feet that like to groove all dim long." Chu speaks in this pinched nasal, accent-free white man's voice: "See Arnold, how happy they are. Why yes, Bob, so poor and not a care in the world." Hurricane laughs, returns to his thick baritone. "Sheeeet, regular *Negrotarians* . . . the hos never copped that all we wanted was their cabbage to keep another month off the agate." The unctuous white man's voice: "Why, Bob, don't you find their jive language *just marvelous?*"

Monk almost spits Coke, he's laughing so hard.

"We even played for the Mexicans at their parties in Boyle Heights, Pico Rivera." Chu drinks beer. "Every damn time those Mexicans would start drinkin' tequila and there'd be a fight and we'd run to the car with my horn and his ax, then we'd have to run back, dodging flying beer bottles and brawlers, to help Tritone

Cootie lug his drum kit piece by damn piece to the car. Have a brew on ol' Uncle Chu?"

"Okay, Mr. Reed. Just one."

Chu signals the bartender and a frosty beer mug slides before Monk. "Yeah, yo' daddy and me, we played all the clubs on Sin Street. The Alabam down the street, Memo's, Honey Murphy's, the Plantation Club. Monk was—is one ace of bass, yes sir, wherever he is, Chicago, New York . . . you ever hear from him?" Monk shakes his head. "Not even a postcard?"

"Nope." Monk sips beer.

"Tha's a shame." Chu sucks a deep drag from the reefer. "Yeah, we played with the best, Bumps Myers, Joe Comfort, Pee Wee Crayton . . . that was the twilight of bop. There used to be four times the clubs then as now, all the way from Washington clear down to Manchester. The Congo's the last of the sweet spots. The combo deck is good, the *boogfloor* is *fungshun*, craps tables in the back are still rollin' the bones and the usual African Dominoes action, upstairs might still even be a bordello or two, so I'm told." Chu slips down his sunglasses and winks a bloodshot eye. "Yeah, used to be Charlie Parker, now it's goddamn Chief Parker, messin' with folks in front of the clubs, searchin' brothers for drugs, any excuse to close down the clubs. You know what really made the cops crazy?" Monk shakes his head. "All the ofay college girls flocking like fine white birds into the clubs . . . that drove those cracker cops nuts. All these luscious girls chasin' after us jazzmen like yo' dapper dad and yo's truly, the man with the big horn." Hurricane grins. "Syncopation and fornication. Now, yo' daddy wasn't a bad man, he was just a man, and like I said, a wife and the road life don't groove. Women were everywhere, black and white. Hell, they still are. Those days the band, all the Negro bands had these groups of young fade chicks followin' us around, we called 'em our *bopsicles*, these *groupie* girls. You dig, Chu's an old cherry picker from way back, but Monk was quiet." Chu shakes his jowly head. "Jazz hounds, picture snatchers, autograph scratchers. *Studyettes* from every college of knowledge. Diggin' Negro blues, tryin' to be cool, or researchin' in Negro Heaven, scratchin' terminal term papers like 'Dionysian Ethno-eroticism in Race Music.'" Monk laughs. "It's hard to say no to the rabbit habit. So we dug the tails of these nightingales."

"When's the last time you played together?" Monk sips beer.

"Last chime we grooved was the last bright of the last decade, before the sixties and hippies." (December 31, '59, an auspicious year: on 113th Street, under cover of darkness, Elgin Q. Boyd slips his suitcase onto the seat of his station wagon and drives out of Watts, the Last White Man to leave the city.) "It was the twilight of bop, it was the hep of chimes, it was the bummer of chimes."

"I'd like to hear about that, Mr. Reed." Monk grins, for once not dwelling on his notebook.

"Tha's Uncle Chu, please. It was right here, in the Congo Club. We tore up the joint. No one played bass like Monk, maybe Big Jay McNeely or Mingus. That was the last time I saw him, said he had a gig in Detroit, I think. A little reefer madness?" Chu offering the stub of joint to Monk.

"No thanks, I'm good." Monk smiles, sips beer.

"I feel bad, I've probably spent more time with yo' old man than you."

"That's okay. I'm grown. My mom's around, she's cool."

A young white girl approaches Chu, black hair in a ponytail, wearing plum culottes and a crop-top pink blouse. "Mr. Reed, could I have your autograph?" She nervously offers a pen and this blue album cover that reads *City Blues*.

"Sure, baby." Chu takes the pen and album. "What's yo' name?"

"Carla," in a small, nervous voice. Chu scribbles words on the cover. "Mr. Reed, my friends and I have a bet. Should bop be called colored or Negro music?"

"You call it whatever you want, sweetie," handing her the pen and album. "To me it's just jazz."

"Thanks!" Clutching the album to her chest, she disappears into the plastic hanging vines and the dark tables across the club.

"See what I mean? Cute but a real cube." Chu sips his beer. "I wish you coulda seen the good side of Monk. This one time, I think it was over at the Finale Club, this young cat, a real gone sax player, Local 767 pulled him off the stage, that's the musicians' union, 'cause he didn't have no damn union card. So Monk paid his membership fee right then and there so this young man could play and get paid. Another time, I forget what club . . . I got to quit smokin' this shit," Chu laughs, stubs out the reefer in an ashtray. "We all got thrown out of this club 'cause he refused to use the segregated Chamber of Commerce."

"Chamber of Commerce?"

"Tha's what we call the toilet . . . as many an illicit transaction takes place inside and around the porcelain chamber." Chu laughs. "Now where was I?" Chu slips his dark glasses on. "Yeah, ol' Monk was one of a kind. Soul solfeggio."

"Soul what?"

"Solfeggio . . . he played only by ear. Couldn't read music. Tell you a little secret. In his bass case, he had a notebook of sheet music. But the sheets, they were all drawn on with cartoons and designs, and all these notes and stories about life and people."

Monk stares in awestruck silence at Chu's jowly grin under the Christmas-light sparkles reflecting in his dark glasses.

"I'll tell ya somethin' else too, Americo. Yo' daddy was an outsider . . . that's what we call a cool cat who plays against the melody, outside the notes. He had a vision . . . a kind of way of seein' how everything in his pages, in his notes, connected in the future. 'Course, in his case he didn't see the patterns, he heard 'em." Chu grins, his sunglasses locked for a moment on Monk. "Well, I got to go on, nice seein' you, kid."

Chu Hurricane slumps from the barstool like a dark mountain. Monk watches as Chu picks up his sax from its stand on the stage; three band members wait behind their instruments. Chu slips a silver reed into his saxophone, the notorious number five reed, which only the mightiest wind wailers can master. Behind the drums there is a small stack of nutmeg cans, the drummer's addicted to the stuff, Chu grinning as he remembers some girl last night remarked, *Look at all that nutmeg! You boys sure must bake a lot of pies.*

Up on the stage, a spotlight shines a dusty cone of light down at a black man with a red bow tie, white vest, silver suit. "Hello, ladies and gentlemen. This is your master of ceremonies, Pigmeat Markham. I have good news. I've agreed to stop performing stand-up comedy, and so the riots have officially ended." Laughter, a drumroll and cymbal crash from the drummer on stage. "I just came back from performing in Vegas . . . to a riot! Sinatra and the Rat Pack were at the club. Sinatra saved my life. After the show, two big guys were beating the shit out of me. Sinatra saw what was happening and came up, and he said . . . that's good enough for now, boys." Scattered laughter. "I bumped into Sammy Davis, Jr. too. Man, his hair reminded me of my wife . . . both used to be kinky." More laughs, snare drum and cymbal crash. "Now, ladies and gentlemen, let's hear it for mister embouchure, the king of winds, hittin' another homer outta the park, Chu 'Hurricane' Reed and his band!"

Chu takes center stage, red and blue Christmas lights shimmering above him like stars suspended in a firmament of cigarette and reefer nebula. "What's the word?" Hurricane calls out to the crowd.

"Thunderbird!" the audience shouts and claps. The band thunders into the bop assault of "Good Sauce from the Gravy Bowl."

Chu stares down into the copper gleaming funnel of the horn, as if falling down into its golden vortex. He's got to get *outside*, away from the melody, perhaps time itself, as if to find a key to somehow stop the madness and violence and hate *outside*, beyond the sound.

Hurricane's fat black Buddha's face is pale as his fingers blur and poly-chords ring the night, the S of the horn's piping a brass-plated serpent screaming, ascending toward some millennial key. The black ballooned mouth breathes life into the reed, into the recondite brass chambers and flanges: eerie chords that glissando higher, ninths to shattering elevenths. Chu's face is a black sweating mask about to explode as he inverts the notes and breaks through, moving *outside*, a long arpeggio anviling each screaming note higher. He's skirting the edge, a Bop Gabriel wailing toward a crescendo that not even he can transcend: a splintering twelfth note sustained for an infinite moment at perihelion before the sound and the solo finally diminish with Reed's last mighty breath: he leans against the piano, bellows cheeks gasping in air as the audience applauds and cheers. Outside, in the streets filled with blood and fire, has the sound, the soul, the energy they've released made some kind of difference?

"Bathroom?" Monk inquires toward the faint wisp of the bartender.

"Upstairs to your right."

Monk climbs a rickety staircase garlanded with vines and ascending African masks; below, the crowd yells and applauds as bass and drums play solo riffs. Monk brushes away vines. *Can't a brother just get home?* The dim hallway is shadow-suspended with smoke drifting from downstairs. *Where's that bathroom, left, right, fuck.* He lurches through a door. Rusted iron cargo walls, welded rungs fading into cigarette smoke, Motown music blaring from a scratchy phonograph. Karmann backs under blinking painted electric bulbs casting pastel shadows. Marcus and Dalynne sit kissing, coiled in piles of blue and purple pillows. Slim-Bone, Felonius back Karmann toward the pillows: she cups her hand protectively around the swell of her belly, dark wine splashing from her plastic cup . . . Monk grabs Felonius, they topple over strands of lights, the phonograph screeches, bottles of wine clatter from a table, rainbow lights flicker to darkness—

Monk opens his eyes: citrine waves and foamy surf ebb and flow above him, a marine-themed ceiling. He's lying on a bed. Monk bolts, sitting up. A white cat springs from the lap of a girl sitting beside him on the bed: raven hair laced with deep green strands like seagrass, so long it cascades and disappears under aqua silk blankets and frilly cream sheets like sea foam. Hyacinth eyes, black lipstick, a delicate child's face, pale, made translucent by the dark counterbalance of black hair. "Who the hell are you?"

"I'm C.C." Smiling, a black lacquered fingernail tracing down his sweaty arm.

"Oh shit, is this, ah," watching the ivory cat stretch its nails into a teal carpet, "a cathouse?"

"I prefer the word *brothel*." She sits up, tiny rose nipples under diaphanous green and gold.

"Oh shit . . . did we, did we—"

"Not yet."

"How old are you?" Monk scoots to the edge of the bed.

"Age is such an arbitrary concept," then laughter, deep like a woman but trailing disturbingly into little-girl giggles. "Don't be so . . . *insular*."

Monk's gazing around, blue-green submerged light splaying from a lamp: a dresser and a table with tiny fountains, a water wheel and a water clock all softly dripping and tinkling; a wall is centered with a great saltwater aquarium, bubbles glistening up in waters suffused under indigo electric bulbs, golden seahorses suspended in glowing space.

"Relax. You came in and had some kind of fainting spell. Kept mumbling 'Karmann' and something about a notebook. Is she your girlfriend?" That ebony fingernail gliding over his collarbone.

"Man, that dope downstairs is something else. You've got an interesting collection of, ah, water apparatus." The room seems

almost misted with the cool negative ions of the water clock-
works, wheels, tinkling fountains, gurgling ladders.

"Well, in a brothel time is money. I've always been interested
in horology—no wisecracks, that's the study of time."

"C.C. What kind of name is that?" shrugging away her hand.

"Canadian Club. Would you like some?" She stands, sways
toward the dresser, beautiful buttocks shimmering under the
gown, but there's a hint of adolescent, jiggling baby fat.

"No thanks. Just had a couple of beers with Mr. Reed." Seahorses stare dolefully out at Monk in their heliotrope sea, tiny
fins flapping, like limpid, yellow changelings.

She laughs, pours a shot of whiskey into a dusty tumbler. "Yeah,
he's a live wire, Sir C—that's what we call him, C for 'Chu.'" She
sits next to him on the bed, too close, scents of brine and lilac
and honey wafting into his nose.

"Is he your—"

"Pimp?" More laughter, she drains the tumbler. "No. All us
girls up here are independent contractors."

"Well, I have to go. Sorry I barged in on you." Monk stands
but her little hand squeezes his.

"What's your rush? Stay a few minutes. You look a little wobbly to me. I won't bite you . . . unless you want me to." C.C. takes
a pearl seashell brush from the nightstand and slowly combs her
long thick strands.

Monk rubs sweaty palms on his pants legs. The seahorses curl
and float in their purple world, snout mouths pulsing, perhaps
silently warning him? "Maybe just a few minutes," he croaks, light-
headed, gazing around the watery den, tongue thick. "I'll take that
CC now, please."

She saunters to the bureau, chinks a good shot in the tumbler. Monk drinks it down, opens his eyes: she's standing before
him, budding nipples inches from his sweaty face, dark thatch
shadowed between her legs under shimmering chartreuse, brine,
lilac, honey. "You came here for a reason."

"I was looking for the bathroom. Besides, I have a girlfriend."

"You don't understand, Monk," sitting down next to him.

"How'd you know my name?"

"You were saying all sorts of things in your little nightmare. Monk, Felonius, a notebook lost in a . . . trench? And Slim-Bone— I'd like to meet *him*," giggling. "The Congo brothel is . . . different. There's a lot of rooms up here, and each room is different, with a different girl and john."

Trench. Monk frowns. "Are they all—the rooms, I mean—as unique as yours?" The whiskey warms him.

"Some even more startling," C.C. laughs. "This place exists on many levels . . . for the hedonists, for those on the physical plane, there are the usual rooms, girls, and kinks . . . there's interracial for the hip, there's segregated fun for the squares . . . even *segregated* love-ins. But when the johns' proclivities explore more, how should I say, more cerebral, philosophical levels, that's when us girls really start the meter ticking. The man in the room for the love-in can't face just a single girl, but needs multiple girls because he himself is fragmented . . . there's a gent in Talia's room, she's tied him up, wants to know if the universe has a purpose? When his time's up he'll come out spent, exhausted, on the verge of belief in an extrinsic or intrinsic finality or purpose in all matter . . . in Mona's room—you should see Mona's room—an old man's crying in her naked arms, having experienced with— through—her a *panpsychism* breakthrough, now he sees all matter as sentient."

"What kind of whorehouse is this?" Monk wants to go but her legs, her breasts, the brine and lilac, the child's face with the dark eyes of an old sea nymph . . .

"This is a *metaphysical* brothel, honey." She pours another shot in the glass, Monk hypnotized by every curl, wisp of childish nakedness under diaphanous turquoise spangles. "You put your money down and we strip—strip you of any illusions or hang-ups or shaky worldviews. We'll give you the best fuck of all time—a mind fuck." C.C. sips whiskey, presses the tumbler into his hands, squeezes his trembling fingers. "Daphne's in her room, dressing, undressing herself. Is she the same girl or is she different each time? Her john's an endurantist, thinks objects never change, but she'll take off the leather pants, a painful bruise where she's laced them too tight, and john'll leave tonight, a perdurantist, every curb he crosses, every mailbox, every wall now in a constant state of *riot* and change."

"Until he gets Mona the next time." Monk sips whiskey: the wheels drip and turn, water time splashing by in echoing streams and gurgling mysteries. "Mental whores."

"You're beginning to dig," C.C. raking black nails over his thigh. "We know what our johns need, not what they think they want. You should see Theda's room. All white, no bed, furniture, zero. They come in and leave later with the greatest sex experience of their lives, because it all took place only in the mind. Her johns lie there, fully dressed, and Theda puts them in a mental construct of ecstasy. She's an idealist, the world only exists in the mind."

"Who's the object, the whore or the john?" Monk grins. "Who is the whore, what is the john?"

C.C. smiles, nods, then her black lips frown and in the aquatic lamplight she looks ancient and wise. "I'm afraid we're the whores, incorporeal yet objects at the same time. We have no metaphysical identities of our own. Empty vessels, reflecting only the strengths or cracks in each john's philosophy. It's not all fun and games. Some of the johns, they come up here all liquored up, you know, start acting like *swines* . . . then we become a kind of mirror. Be careful, there is danger. There is a . . . a cosmic mechanism that sometimes must be invoked . . . Last night, in Lara's room, her john had his cosmological thrill. Is the universe finite or infinite? She says, 'Imagine the edge of a finite universe,' but he can't, no one can. He jumped out the window. One time, a group of drunk white sailors came upstairs, wanted black girls to dress up like slaves. Sir C and the boys downstairs slipped a Mickey in their booze, shanghaied them. They woke up in the pitching shadows of an oak-and-pine hull, ankles chained to tarred floorboards, above them, through the iron mesh of rusted deck grates, Negro mariners marshaled the sails of their barque toward the port of Sofala, and the African markets that awaited their cargo of white slaves." She guides his hands over her tiny breasts. He can feel her heartbeat, her black lips part in a sigh, lilac warmth bathing his face.

"I gotta go." Monk pulls his hands free, trying to ignore the bulging heat beneath his pants.

"No, you can't go, I won't let you," she hisses. "Just a little longer, please?" Her voice is low and sweet, pale angel's face glowing up into his tired eyes. Only her spidery hand rests gently on his knee, but Monk feels as if an impossible weight holds him down, as if the gurgling and wheeling water machines themselves exert the gravity of submerged fathoms pressing against him.

"This is just a misunderstanding, please let me go." On the dresser, the ivory cat sits, jade eyes mesmerized before the purplish aquarium, studying the seahorses congealed in their violet, watery prism. *What's she doing? Some kind of hypnosis—*

"Don't be gauche. You're in a metaphysical brothel. There are no accidents. What'll it be, big boy," C.C. slipping a pale leg over his lap, "determinism or free will? You think your journey has been one of free will but every step has already been determined."

"Please, I have to get home." *Tell her she's too late, the notebook is gone—*

"No! You can't leave!" Hissing, her cinder eyes reflecting dangerous depths. "Once you taste me, you'll forget about her." She squeezes the hardness beneath his jeans. Monk closes his eyes, a powerless dread swooning over him. C.C. pulls his hand to her black lips, kissing his fingers. "Bitch!" Slapping away his hand, she jumps from the azure satin bed. "Moly." Tears flood her mascaraed eyes.

"Who?" Monk opens his eyes, an invisible weight seeming to lift from paralyzed limbs.

"Not who, what!" C.C. screams, stamping a naked foot. "An herb, your fingers stink of it!"

The gris-gris. Monk wobbles to his feet: the tinkling water wheels have stopped, one or two final drops plinking in their dark pools.

"You're under her protection, you can split now." She sits on the bed, a little girl, wiping mascara from her eyes. Seahorse eyes follow him. He walks, each step a little lighter as if he's emerging from invisible depths, and he's out the door, down the staircase, and into the smoke and vine-tangled light and the reassuring throb of the Congo Club's saxophone and thumping drums.

The club's almost empty, the jazz piping from radio speakers. Reed and his band are gone, the bartender's wiping down the empty bar top, waitresses filling trays with empty glasses. Monk sprints out the padded doors, bathed in lemon neon blinking lights as he jogs down the street to the Finale Club. He sees a couple of parked cars but no burgundy Corvair convertible, no ride home.

22

Monk turns and heads south down Central again. He passes Club Alabam, its front doors padlocked now. Those girls and their damn Corvair—without hitching some kind of ride, it'll take hours to make up his lost time, but even Sin Street, this late at night, is emptying out, only one or two cars rumbling past, ignoring his waving thumb. Ivie's Chicken Shack is dark, closed. Another block and he's trudging past the lemon neon and bamboo walls of the Congo Club again, feeling hopeless, like a pawn in a secret maze.

"Hey! Monk's kid!" Monk turns around: the bartender stands in the doorway of the Congo Club. "Phone call." The bartender disappears past the two towering FOI bouncers. Frowning, Monk follows, nodding up to the guards as he pushes through the padded doors.

Only a few stragglers finish their drinks in the shadows under the strings of Christmas lights. Waiters are setting chairs atop tables as Monk heads toward the bar. The bartender slides a black phone across the bar and hands Monk the heavy receiver. Monk licks his lips. "Hello," his voice hoarse, exhausted.

"Gage station." An electric current tingles through Monk as that old gravel voice rasps in his ear.

"Tyrone, who are you?" Monk pleads. "Who is this?"

"Downstairs . . . the book . . ."

Monk stares at the receiver as a dial tone blares, then a metallic busy signal bleats like an insect drone. He sets the receiver into the black cradle and looks up: the bartender has her back to him, polishing glasses. Monk quickly picks up the telephone and stabs numbers on the rotary dial. *Come on, baby, pick up.* Another busy signal rings in his ear. *Usin' up my booze and my phone bill.* He smashes the receiver into the cradle. The bartender turns and glares at him. "Thanks." Monk pushes the phone across the bar and stalks toward the padded doors.

He heads east on Fifty-seventh, away from Sin Street. The street is dark, no traffic, only distant sirens. Monk's walking fast, his feet numb but painless in his unraveling Keds sneakers. *Keep going south. Phantom telephone calls . . . Tyrone the blind madman with his satellites and ringing phone booths . . . maybe some kind of trap . . . the cops and the FBI spying from every phone in town.* Headlights twinkle as a car speeds past and Monk presses reflexively against a brick wall until the taillights disappear around the corner. *Trench would love me showing up, turning myself in . . . fuck him . . . get back to Karmann, then when it's safe, after the riot . . . come back with witnesses . . . get my notebook . . . private property they stole.*

Monk turns south on Naomi, then freezes: *Naomi, the street on Standard's tattoo.* Slowly, a street sign looms closer. His Keds count off grids in space and time, each sign bringing him closer to Karmann, to home. *Fucking cops think they can roust you anytime they want, steal your shit.* He starts at the sound of a bottle smashing against a wall as two teenagers run down an alley.

Naomi dead-ends at Fifty-eighth. "Fuck!" He can't remember Standard's secret route. Monk walks a block east to Hooper and heads south again. Hooper is quiet, but a block ahead is Gage, a major street: traffic and cops, maybe National Guard soldiers. Monk moves quickly through the darkness; any pedestrians caught past the curfew will be questioned, arrested: Monk doesn't need to dwell on the interrogation procedures the police would subject him to once they linked him to Trench's assault and felony evasion. *Those bastards have my notebook, all my work . . . like they've pried open my head and their dirty fucking pig fingers are thumbing through my dreams.*

Monk sprints across the red signals of Gage: there is a glimpse of flashing police cars, a blockade down the street, then he's shrouded again into Hooper's shadows.

He turns east on Sixty-fourth Street: Gage is behind him and he slows down. This street is quiet, dark. The silence is broken by a siren in the distance, fading down Gage. Monk passes a house and a dog howls. He moves faster. Three black men stand around a parked car, drinking beer and nodding to him as he passes. *Where the fuck am I going? Parmelee's up ahead . . . that's it, the street from Standard's tattoo . . . goes south to what, Sixty-ninth or Seventieth? Downstairs, the old man said . . . my notebook's downstairs in some room.*

The dark tunnel of an alley swallows Monk. Behind a brick wall, a stereo blares. The alley angles into Parmelee Street. A police car rushes past as Monk freezes in the shadows, then it's gone. His heart pounds against his rib cage.

Monk stops, licks his lips. *Don't do this to Karmann. She needs you now.* "Fuck it." *Forgive me, baby.* He turns and heads *north* up Parmelee. *How can I find it? Are you fucking insane? How can I get it back from a fucking police station in the middle of a fucking riot?*

In the distance he can see the blinking red traffic lights of Gage Avenue. *Tyrone called it "the book." How does he know all this shit? Who is he?* Monk thinks of the old black man with the strange, duct-taped sunglasses he saw at the Oasis Shoe Stand, waving his cane, ranting to no one, to the darkening night. *It really is the book, maybe the key to all this fire and madness . . . much more than gang turfs and vandalized walls.*

Ahead, a car crawls past the blinking red lights of the intersection. Monk slips into another alley just before the strobing ruby glow of Gage Avenue. The alley parallels Gage, east behind a block of storefronts and shops. He's going to walk into the police station, take his notebook, and walk out. Monk shakes his head; he has no plan, no chance. *Think. A few more blocks to go.* He silently, quickly passes trash dumpsters, padlocked iron doors, fenced storage areas piled with auto parts or stacked oil drums. One Stop Auto Repair, yellow metal sign glowing past under a lightbulb. An electric transformer box hums as he hurries on. In the distance headlights splash over the mouth of the alley: Monk freezes behind a telephone pole and the car is gone. He walks on and stops again. A dumpster, heaped with overflowing trash and cardboard boxes, under a cone of light from a utility pole. Beyond, another sign in the shadows of the stucco walls above another metal door: Tipsy Tom's Liquors. Monk stands, transfixed in front of the dumpster, staring at the flattened cardboard boxes heaped on the trash and stacked and piled on the asphalt. He picks up a square of cardboard and examines it under the dim light: Old Crow Sour Mash Whiskey. Monk folds in all the flaps, sticks it under his arm, and walks faster toward the end of the alley.

Monk turns left from the alley and onto Compton Avenue: he can see the parking lot of the Gage Division police station ahead. He swallows, his mouth dry as dust, walking faster now, his heart thumping. *Trench . . . don't think about it.*

He crosses over into the parking lot. The station's sign glows under lamps embedded in its gray stone walls. Two guardsmen flank the glass doors, rifles angled, ready in their hands. *Stay cool,* Monk keeps repeating to himself, *stay cool . . . every brother in town trying to get away from the police and I'm trying to break into the police.* Monk threads between rows of parked cruisers: as he passes the last patrol car, he quickly sets the folded cardboard against its rear wheel, beyond the sight of the guardsmen.

"I'm here to file a report—it's an emergency." Monk's voice is cracked, strained.

"Put your arms up for a weapons check." A soldier slings his rifle as Monk raises his arms. The guardsman pats him down quickly. "Go ahead."

Monk walks down the hallway. Two cops gaze into his face as they walk toward the rear doors. Monk is careful to look them in the eyes as they pass; fighting the urge to turn around, he measures each step along the white hallway floor.

The hallway opens into a large main room illumined by ivory frosted lamps suspended from the ceiling like glowing pearls. Cops, motorcycle officers, men in rumpled white shirts and black ties move around the room or sit at desks. The polished floors are painted with red and blue lines, marking various pathways to the departments within the large station, Roddenberry's idea of mapping, controlling space within the precinct . . .

Monk makes a conscious effort to breathe slowly. Rows of wood file cabinets line a wall; two women clack feverishly above typewriters on their desks; opposite is a wall of offices with opaque glass and wood doors; metal portable fans whirl and hum atop file cabinets, swirling the strata of cigarette smoke that hangs in the stifling air.

"Can I help you?" A big sergeant with red hair squints down suspiciously from a huge standing desk near one of the pillars that section off the floor. Behind him, suspended from the center of the wall, is a great framed black-and-white photograph of Chief Parker, his black-wire glasses gazing down at his force below, his men who toe the thin blue line.

Monk steps up to the desk as another cop with black coffee walks across the room, glaring at Monk's red sneakers.

"I'm here to file a report."

"A report? There's a riot goin' on, in case you haven't noticed. Come back next week." His pale, jowly face scowls down. "What're you doin' out past curfew, anyways?"

"Trench," Monk stammers, "Trench . . . Officer Trench told me to file a report."

"Trench? He ain't here, out on sick leave."

Relief floods through Monk. *Sick leave.* Monk represses a grin, thinking about Jax's double-taped spray cans. "Trench wants it right away . . . about the Slauson Avenue gangs."

The desk sergeant frowns. "Okay." He slips a paper from behind the desk and snaps it into a clipboard with a chained pen. Monk takes the clipboard and sits in a row of heavy wooden chairs along the wall beyond the big desk. He begins to fill in the form. The sounds of typewriters and police scanners and voices meld into a soft babble all around him.

After a few minutes Monk returns to the desk sergeant. "Can I use the bathroom?"

The sergeant sighs and jabs his thumb behind him. "Downstairs."

As Monk sets the clipboard upside down on the chair, he pulls the pen from its chain and slips it into his pocket. He walks down another hallway, toward wide stone stairs that descend to the next floor. A white woman, clutching a sheaf of papers, walks past him, averting her eyes from Monk.

He passes a sign: 2ND FLOOR BOOKING ANNEX. His sneakers pad down the steps. *Downstairs, Tyrone said.*

Another large room sectioned off with pillars, desks, offices and interrogation rooms, and a hallway in the distance. A cop walks past, sizing up Monk skeptically. Monk heads toward the hallway. Two officers, caps in their hands, approach him. A tall white cop stands blocking him. "You lost, son?"

"I'm looking for the bathroom, sir."

"What ya doin' here?" The other cop, chewing gum, grins. "Run outta gasoline?"

"I'm filling out a report . . . Officer Trench asked me to."

"Trench?" The tall cops nods. "He's out. His partner, Vicodanz's here, want to see him?"

"I really have to go . . . go to the bathroom."

"Down the hall to the right." The two cops continue toward the stairs.

At the hallway, Monk turns right. He passes a door with a metal sign plate: LOCKERS. Opening the door, he slips inside.

Rows of tall steel lockers on each wall, the floor divided by wooden benches. Behind the lockers, two men are talking, inaudible, muted in the sounds of water spraying from showers somewhere beyond. Monk quickly works down the rows, jabbing, testing each locked handle. One opens and he grabs the hanging clothes inside; another door opens but the receptacle is empty; more locked doors, then a locker opens and he grabs two shirts and a pair of boots; finally another locker opens and he seizes a motorcycle helmet and jacket.

Out the door, clothes and helmet bunched in his arms, he runs down to the end of the hallway and pushes through bathroom doors. Monk rushes into a cubicle, kicks the toilet lid down, and piles the helmet and clothes atop the toilet. Latching the door closed, he hangs the shirts on the hook.

Monk's going through the clothes, trying on a shirt, when he hears the bathroom door open as three loud male voices boom and laugh and speak outside the cubicle. Footsteps. "They ain't burnin' down Van Nuys." Laughter. Monk looks down at the polished black boots he's stolen, spaced on the tiles and pointing out like, he hopes, what one might see under the occupied door of a bathroom cubicle. "White people don't burn down their neighborhoods." Tinkling sounds of urination, then tap water gurgling and more voices. "Burn down the store, then you don't have to work there. Niggers." Laughter as paper towels rip from dispensers, and finally the door closing and silence.

He steps from the cubicle and gazes into the mirrors over the dripping sinks: a black motorcycle officer stares back at him. The leather jacket is zipped up, snug against his old shirt, his Keds stuffed into its pockets. The gray uniform pants are too big, but passable, tucked into his big rider's boots and worn over his jeans. Now Monk snugs on the white and black-trim motorcycle helmet: too small, a vice of pain, but it's on and hides his wild hair.

Down the hallway and past the interrogation rooms and offices. Monk's boots click up the stairway. His leather jacket creaks as his storm trooper boots echo past the desk sergeant, who's yelling into a telephone. As he paces down the hall toward the exit doors, he feels like some kind of astronaut about to exit his hatchway and go out into the waiting darkness and void.

Monk nods to the guardsmen, then crosses the parking lot. He turns and walks along a row of cruisers, picking up the flattened cardboard leaned against a rear tire. Monk walks on, resisting the temptation to look back at the guardsmen. Pausing at the second to last patrol car, he opens the rear door and sets the cardboard inside, folding the flaps until the box is assembled. Now, if the Guard or anyone else is watching, they see a Negro motorcycle officer removing a box from the backseat of a cruiser.

The guardsmen watch as the Negro motorcycle officer approaches, lugging a case of Old Crow Sour Mash Whiskey. "You boys want a bottle?" Monk shifts the empty box onto one arm, pretending to struggle and balance its weight as he tentatively opens a flap, then stops. "Sorry. I know, you're on duty. Maybe later." A soldier opens the glass door and Monk walks into the station.

Monk marches past cops, his head tilted down, eyes shadowed under the helmet's visor, past offices and clacking typewriters. The desk sergeant ignores the motorcycle officer creaking by. Monk descends the steps.

He walks across the Booking Annex, toward the hallway beyond the last section, passing the rows of offices and interrogation rooms. Under his helmet, sounds are muted, muffled, as if he's a sleeper lost in some whitewashed, authoritarian nightmare.

At the hallway, Monk turns left. A white cop walks past, ignoring him. Ahead, double doors are stenciled BOOKING and HOLDING

CELLS. He's in another cavernous room of filing cabinets, desks, cops, plainclothesmen. Monk keeps walking, surreptitiously looking for signs: a semiotician, who can't ask for signs but must seek them, has to appear found when he's lost.

Passing another pillar, he marches along a row of holding cells and interrogation rooms, some doors open or windows with blinds pulled up. From the corner of his eye, he can see some of these rooms are empty; one room has two detectives talking at a desk; in another room, a black man is handcuffed to his chair as two white cops sit next to him. There's an empty room, then Monk passes a door ajar where, in the wedge of light inside, he can see a black man sitting alone on a wood bench near the wall, his back to Monk, one wrist handcuffed to the rail of the bench as the prisoner's other hand holds a smoldering cigarette.

Finally a sign, real and concrete as its metal screwed into the door, yet transcending reality with its secret meaning that only Monk can read: PROPERTY ROOM. *Yeah, my fucking property.*

Monk's face is sweating as he lugs the empty box up to a lieutenant behind a desk adjacent to the door. "More hooch for Parker and the boys." Monk grins, setting the box slowly, heavily on top of the desk's corner. Under the cop's badge, his name tag says SULINSKI.

The lieutenant glances at the box. "Old Crow? I wouldn't touch that swill." He shakes his head. Monk feels clammy sweat dripping down his face. "Parker's Micks, they'd drink fuckin' piss if it'd get 'em drunk." He opens the center drawer and slaps a ring with a single key on the desktop.

"Yeah," Monk scoops up the key, "even the brothers won't touch this shit." He lifts the box carefully back into his arms, unlocks the door, and steps inside the room.

His elbow nudges on the light switch. Inside are metal shelves stacked with evidence, some tagged, most not: a baseball bat, labeled boxes, a bundle of bloody clothes tied with string, boxes of files, an old suitcase, a TV, boxes of booze and products, tagged wristwatches and rings, pistols and rifles and knives. Monk sets the empty box on a shelf. He rummages around the shelves. *Where the fuck is it?* There. On a lower shelf, near the dusty window, next to a box of files. He picks up the blue notebook, squeezes it, gazes at its thick sheaf of papers; loose, torn, waterlogged, stinking of smoke, but all of it, all of his dreams, all of the secret voices of the people and the narrative of the city itself: everything that those in power would burn away from memory . . .

Unzipping the jacket, Monk clips the stolen pen into the spirals and wedges the notebook into the loose waistband of the uniform pants and zips the jacket up. He turns off the lights and locks the door behind him.

Monk sets the keys on the lieutenant's desk. Sulinski doesn't look up from his newspaper.

He wipes his sweating brow as he heads toward the rows of holding cells and rooms. If only he could remove the suffocating helmet and leather jacket. He hears a male voice mumbling, talking to himself. "Hey! I knows you!"

Monk's frozen in front of the open door of the interrogation room: inside, a black man, black sunglasses and greasy hair, one wrist handcuffed to the bench, smokes a cigarette, but now he faces the doorway and grins, nodding at Monk. *Fuck. It's Lamar.* Felonius's friend, a thief and addict. "I knows you, motherfucker," his voice slurring, "Monk." He shakes his head, mutters incomprehensibly. "Youz a cop now?"

Monk hesitates, trying to process his shock: he's been passing through the streets and the nights unseen, like a ghost, and now this man recognizes him, as if some veil has been pulled away. "You a pig now?" Lamar asks, then laughs and waves his cigarette: he still looks drunk or stoned.

"I have to go."

"Fuck that. You tell me wha' you doin' here, motherfucker. Get me outta here." He rattles his handcuffed wrist against the bench. "Why you dressed like that?" Now he's muttering incoherently, shaking his head. "You get me outta here," raising his voice, "or I'll tell 'em I seen you, tha's worth somethin', motherfucker!"

"Okay, okay." Monk steps inside and shuts the door. "They get you for looting?"

"Fuck them honky stores! I want out! I'm gonna tell 'em you here!" Raising his voice. "You here to bust me out!"

"Okay, yeah, don't yell," Monk's voice pleads, but not just for Lamar, for himself.

"Shoulda stayed at yo' ol' rent party, things was goin' real good," shaking his head back and forth. He mumbles, then grins. "Why you leave tha' girl all alone, nigga? What kind of man is you? That Karmann's fine . . . maybe I'll go back and show her somethin' real fine . . ."

The room seems to glow with a pink aura as his temples throb and his mind somehow seizes, stops in suspended time. His fist clenches the dangling chin strap and he whips off the helmet, a blur of arcing white as he smashes it across Lamar's face. Lamar's body rocks violently into the corner, then the prisoner's unshackled arm swings wildly up, hitting Monk in the mouth. Monk slams the helmet into Lamar's face, blood spurting from the prisoner's broken nose, then Monk hammers the helmet again and again over Lamar as the man's free hand tries to impotently swat away the attack. Monk steps back as Lamar slumps off the bench, unconscious, his wrist broken, suspended from the handcuffs' taut chain. *Fuck fuck Christ what have I done.* Monk gazes down at the white helmet: drops of blood are spattered on it. He wipes the blood off with his palms and snugs the helmet back over his long hair as he steps from the room and shuts the door.

•

He has no memory of leaving the station, or the parking lot, or running through the darkness. He's back in the same alley off Compton Avenue, hunched against a wall, gasping for breath. Spitting blood from his mouth, his tongue experimentally probes a loose front tooth. Monk rips off the helmet and it clatters to the ground. He unzips the jacket, tosses it down, and pulls the notebook from the gray uniform pants. Setting the notebook atop the jacket, Monk strips off the pants and the motorcycle boots. *Christ, what have I fucking done?* Monk stares at the helmet, glistening on the pavement like some kind of evil ivory egg. He'd beaten the hell out of Lamar—a worthless bastard, but another brother. He's no better than the cops . . . is the notebook that important? He put everyone in danger, himself, Karmann, anyone who stood in his way. He chose his goddamn book over her.

His clothes are drenched in sweat. After a few minutes he can breathe. He sits against the wall, pulls his Keds from the jacket pockets and laces them on. Monk picks up the notebook. *All of this madness for this.* He riffles through the pages. One of the last few blank pages—the upper corner's been neatly folded. Monk creases back the paper. In a shaky hand, someone's scrawled a note in black ink:

M: VINES ON A METER

Monk trudges east in the shadows of the alley. He's lost hours after backtracking northeast to the Gage Station, and now he's back just a few blocks farther south from the clubs on Central; but he can feel the notebook pressed against his ribs. He can still taste the blood in his mouth and his broken tooth aches. Since the station he'd made peace with himself: Lamar is no brother and deserved whatever happened to him, and the notebook . . . it's part of him, Karmann realizes that . . . probably knows him better than he knows himself.

Past Compton, he's reached a small, dark street: Makee Avenue. Monk heads south. The smashed street lamps above seem to cast their own darkness. If only he can remember Standard's map: is it Sixty-seventh to Compton . . . or East Seventieth to Miramonte? He coughs, gagging in smoky air. Monk studies graffiti-sprayed walls and paint-bombed boarded-up windows, absently touching the notebook wedged in his waistband. Now someone's added another graffito to his notebook: *M: vines on a meter.* What does it mean? Too many people knew about the notebook: Nation of Islam, the gangs, the cops, whoever Tyrone is . . . Who knows how many others? *M: maybe for Monk, a message to me.* Too many dots to connect . . . it's vertigo, any patterns that seem to coalesce only fade like shadows: sometimes he's sure the city is one giant graffito, a sprawling, urban *uber*-text that one day, with enough notebooks, he might unlock to reveal all its hidden codes. Sometimes the graffiti in his thoughts and notebook blur into the city's spray-painted icons, until his mind and the streets seem like one vast network of rainbow messages, the convolutions of his brain and the corridors of the city fused into one myriad, fantastic structure, like a palace of graffiti.

On the corner of Sixty-sixth, he sees chrome gleam in the shadows: a phone booth. Monk slides open the folding glass doors, grabs the black, warm plastic receiver. "Fuck." Its dangling, severed, tiny red and white wires gape from the sliced black cloth cord. Monk sets the receiver back into its scalloped cradle. A random act of sabotage, or was it gangs, looters, even the cops? Did Tyrone know one of his myriad voices had been silenced?

Armored ambulances from the police tactical unit scream by, shotgun-toting cops and green-gowned EMTs in the lights of their cabins—Medical Armed Response Vehicles—MARVs, Chief Parker's latest brainstorm, lights flashing, speeding toward the looming, fiery outskirts of Watts and points south. A black car, headlights out, whines past, then staccato pistol shots ring out as it screams across the street. Monk runs into an alley, presses against cool bricks, waiting in stifling silence, only his breath wheezing in the shadows.

He turns, Keds squishing something: a plate of cooked rice, brown sugar, black-eyed peas, two twigs crossed on the rim. "Shit," wiping his sneaker on the wall.

"Quit steppin' in my *congris!*" A rain of sparks showers down on him. Monk spins, bumps into metal: the alley terminates in a wall of tangled steel rising like a shrapnel dam. Are those shopping carts? "I've been expecting you."

Up there, behind the gnarled bars of a wedged cart, he sees a robot's iron square face, its dark, glowering visor reflecting coldly down on him. Monk's mumbling *Klaatu barada nikto* when the visor flips up: an old black woman's face in the grid shadows. Monk steps closer. Only her snowy frizzled hair and iron eyes are visible in her sunken, grayish skin.

"Now I'm tired of this shit." Monk glares up at the visage behind meshed steel rods and rusting cart handles. "Another hoodoo. If you've been expecting me, then what's my name?"

"Names aren't important, boy." She opens a jagged section of steel network, like a thatched doorway. Something falls near his sneakers, a white flower on a black stem. He picks it up, sniffs: the gris-gris he'd found on that curb. "That's right, Sherlock Homie. Come on *up.*" Rungs are welded into the jumble of carts and Monk ascends into the wire opening.

She stands before him, short, wizened, with pink culottes, tennis shoes, lavender bowling shirt replete with flying pins and zooming bowling balls and a name embroidered over a vest pocket: *Earl.* Now he can see one side of her face is scarred, as if her dark skin was somehow burned, shriveled with wrinkles. She sets the welding mask and torch atop a rusted tank cylinder. "Just doin' a little home touch-up." A warren of stacked cages, welded from carts; every wall, floor, ceiling, like some kind of mad X-rayed structure, reveals jumbles of furniture, bag-lady flotsam, hanging plants and pictures, webs and knots of welded rebar, plastic roofing, rusted water pipes welded through cart walls, dozens of candles glowing.

"Please, sit down." Monk's followed her into another cubicle, ducking his head. They sit on an old green sofa in the candlelight. A round table, welded from cart handles and scrap, is draped with a lace doily. "I'm not a hoodoo, young man. I am a voodoo-ienne, a female practitioner of the craft. Lungwort tea?"

"Thank you, ma'am." The lattice walls are strung with pouches, jars, tin cups suspended on strings; welded sculptures of iron, wire, scrap metal fill recesses lit with white candles.

"Mojo. Call me Jo." She twists a nozzle flange on a dripping pipe, water sprays into a pot. Ancient hands prime and ignite the butane stove.

"You set that charm, the flower, the cigarettes." Dried talons of chickens or birds are looped from strings on the dripping pipes.

"The Moly? Doesn't prove nothin'. I put little things all over this town. Can't be too safe." She spoons bluish grounds into steaming cups.

"But C.C., this whore—ah, girl over at the Congo Club, she said I was under protection." Monk takes the cup from her.

Jo frowns. "I know that place. A water sprite. You must be tryin' to get back to the water. Sounds like more than coincidence now, heh, young man?"

"Then how come you don't know my name?" Sipping tea: licorice, minty.

"I do know your name!" Her voice angry. "I keep repeating it. You are a young man. That's all I see, all that I need to know."

"Why am I here?" The tea warms his stomach.

"You tell me. You're the one bangin' on my door."

"Well, I'm tryin' to get home, and some folks are tryin' to stop me. But you're gonna help me."

"Sounds good." The old woman nods, opens the pipe spigot, soaks a sponge, gently dabs the pale gray wrinkles that line her brow and seem to melt and run down the scarred, bleached side of her face. "Have to keep it moist," returning to the sofa. Light warms her iron eyes. "I sure enjoyed your little Chinatown adventure."

Monk stares at her, his eyes wide in disbelief, almost panic. "Voodoo?"

"Not voodoo, just a sensitivity." Mojo dabs her cheek with the sponge. "Think of me as a liberated Negro woman, a pioneer. Voodoo gives the power to women, not men. It's what your white folks call a matriarchal culture. I was kidnapped, didn't have time to be a Christian. Guess it's just as well. The Bible says the serpent gave Eve the apple of carnal knowledge." She sips tea. "But in the book of voodoo, the serpent gave Eve a better gift, gave her first sight, vision . . . every gal has some trace of it, call it woman's intuition."

"Kidnapped?"

"When I was six years old we moved out here. By train, there were no cars back then, that's how old I am. A voodoo king took me one night while my folks slept, and I was raised in secret in their church, in their society."

"Church?"

"The voodoos have secret churches. See, from the outside, it's a Christian church, with your pastors and Bibles and such, but inside, they're reading secret verses, praying to older gods."

"Like a coven of witches." Monk sets the empty cup on the doily.

"Well, you got kings and queens instead of warlocks and witches. Babies and children with gifts or born with signs—what white folks sometimes call defects. I was born with a caul, a kind of extra veil of skin on my face . . . remnant of the womb . . . some black folks think it's a sign . . . such strange children may grow up with the sight, may see things nobody else can. So I was kidnapped, they left a changeling in my place for Mama, so they told me."

"A changeling? But you were six years old."

"A double for me, a girl under the voodoo spell." Jo nods. "Happens all the time. Mama was happy to be free of such a bewitched child. Lot of black folks disappear from Negro cities. Sometimes it's the voodoo. Babies become voodoo and voodooiennes, each with their own specialty. Men disappear if they wrong the church, and women are taken to be brides or concubines, like that white bitch Aimee Semple McPherson," chuckling. "'Course, virgins are prized and lots of mamas in the ghettos make sure their little girls lose their virginity damn fast to keep 'em safe. I was twelve when I ran away from that voodoo king and his church. There was an orphanage that took me in, and later charity doctors operated on me, removed my caul. Left me with scars, scars that got worse as I got older. But they couldn't remove my . . . insight. I became a seer."

"If you're a seer, when will I make it home . . . or will I?"

The old woman sighs, rises, takes his teacup, rinses it under the dripping pipe. She removes a clay jug from a wire hook, pours something in the pot, starts the stove again. "I'm not a fortune-teller, honey. More like an old travel agent." Pours white liquid in his cup. "Warm milk. Child, you look beat. You need some good motherin'."

Monk sips warm, sweet milk, smiles. "Thanks. It's good."

"Sure is. Nothin' like fresh breast milk."

Monk sprays milk across the green sofa. Jo shakes her head. "That's good gris-gris you're wastin'. Helps you see through the eyes of the innocent. You're gonna need it for the journey." Monk wipes his lips with a napkin, disturbing images in his head of dank storm drains, monstrous Afro shadows, and a cyclopean, bloodshot eyeball.

Pings and taps echo from the tangled network of rusty pipes. The old woman leans against lattice walls, cocking her frizzy head near a dripping flange.

"What—"

"Shhhh!" A final clang and the tapping stops. "A message." She sets the sponge on the shelf. "Go south, but avoid all them main streets. The fires, the madness out there, it's gonna get worse before it gets better."

"Who was that? How can you do that?"

"That? That ain't nothin'. Black folks been doin' that forever.

Never needed white *tricknology*, had jungle drums long before electricity." Jo laughs, removes a bone-hued, long-stemmed clay pipe from under the table. "They took away our drums and logs, but we found talking trees in this new land, or left notes written in pebbles and broken twigs and stamped cotton stems. Now we in the ghetto, not payin' any bills and they turn off the juice, but we got candles, we got long-distance and local calls bangin' on pipes, signalin' with teapot whistles, window blinds, alphabets of laundry strung out on clotheslines, finger trails in dusty windows, gris-gris, you name it."

"Graffiti." Monk grimaces but downs the last mouthful of tepid milk from his cup.

The old woman opens a leather pouch and pinches tobacco into the white pipe bowl. "Now you gettin' it. Word is you're gonna meet a white man, a very bad white man. Stay with him until he reveals the way home. Remember that your enemies may be any color, human or inanimate . . . Beware of sunglasses . . . You don't have sunglasses, do you?"

"Not anymore."

"Good. Those that wear shades may be shades, spirits caught between this world and the next. Beware you don't become a shade yourself. One more thing, might help."

Mojo takes his hand and Monk rises from the couch. She leads him past the rusty pipes to a candlelit alcove of welded scrap-metal walls, thick black carpets under their feet. They stand before a sculpture, a kind of rebar-welded dome of iron ribs, gleaming dark jagged pieces of glass and seashells and gems cemented among its iron lattices. "Go ahead," she nods, "touch it, run your hands over it for a moment."

Monk traces his fingers over the rough, cool iron, the smooth glass baubles, the faceted gems. Under the candlelight, the glass and gems twinkle with dark, soft radiances: blue, green, amber, blue, green, amber—

He's walking along the railroad tracks just north of 107th Street. The sun sets into a layer of smog behind him. Up ahead, a man in a hat slowly ambles near the tracks. Closer, Monk can see dusty blue overalls as the man gazes down, scouring the gravel berms of the tracks as he walks: he's lugging two bent iron rods on his strong shoulders.

"Mr. Rodia!" Monk's reached him as the old man looks up and squints in the sunset light.

"Who's that? Monk's boy! How you doing?" Rodia smiles: his leathery, unshaven face is shadowed under his perennial dusty gray porkpie hat; sideburns, wisps of hair chalk white.

"What ya doing here, Mr. Rodia?"

"Well, you see this rebar?" Rodia taps the iron bars balanced on his shoulder. "Sometimes I come out here, stick one end in the tracks and bend it just so it's how I like it."

"For your towers?"

"It's our towers, your towers. *Para nuestro pueblo.*"

"What's that mean?"

"Our town, our towers."

"How do you know how much to bend it?"

Rodia grins down at Monk. "After a while, you can kind of feel when it's right. What are you doing out here?"

"This!" Monk digs in his front pocket and extracts a shiny round piece of metal, holding it up to the old man's face.

Rodia takes the metal and examines it, flipping it over in his gnarled hands. "A buffalo nickel all squished by the train, huh? Listen, you be careful, don't get squished too." Rodia squints and examines the coin. "Good work. You can still see that Indian's face, but he looks like he's melting. You know what? Tonight I'm going to finish the towers. Just these two rebars to go."

"Aren't you going to build more towers?"

The old man smiles down at Monk, his eyes shining under the shadow of his sweat-stained hat brim. "I have time . . . but no space. Tell you what. How would you like me to put your coin in the tall tower? Your nickel will be the very last piece to finish *Nuestro Pueblo*."

"Yeah! That'd be great! Wait till I tell Mom."

"Heads or tails? Which side do you want to see when you visit the towers?" Rodia balances the coin under his crooked thumb.

"Heads!"

Rodia grins. "You catch it." He flips the coin into the air. Monk's fist snatches it and slaps it down on the back of his hand. "Bad luck, kid."

"Whadaya mean? I called it, Mr. Rodia! I think the buffalo side should be heads. I like it better than the Indian side."

The old man laughs. "Good! You think for yourself too." Monk's inspecting a swaying rod of rebar, running his dirty hands along the ribbed, rough iron.

Monk's fingers let go of the rebar. He blinks and looks around: the old woman's gray eyes stare up into his, a wrinkled, scarred smile. Sweet smoke puffs out from the long white pipe clenched in her grin. The glass shards and gems twinkle green, blue, amber in the sculpture's iron webs.

"You put a spell on me."

"Must every daydream and memory be magic?"

"I'd forgotten," Monk whispers. "I must've been eleven or twelve."

"Eleven years ago he finished the towers. Come sit down, have one more cup of tea."

Mojo brings the teapot and they settle on the green couch; Monk fills their cups. "My nickel, that was the last object he put in the towers?"

The old woman nods, sips tea. "That's quite a coincidence. If you believe in coincidences."

"I'm gonna find that nickel one of these days. Coincidences do happen."

The old queen shrugs. "You can see I'm a sculptress, I too

work with metal, scraps, things you find. Thirty or so years
ago . . . Sabato . . . Mr. Rodia and I were lovers." Her gray eyes
glow with light as she smiles. "Don't look so surprised. I was quite
beautiful in my day, the scars and wrinkles did not really mani-
fest themselves until I grew older. In '54 Sabato completed *Nuestro
Pueblo* and moved away, up north. Of course, by this time, we
were no longer . . . intimate. But our bond . . . second sight, hoodoo, the electricity lovers share, call it whatever you like, your
boring coincidence, but our bond never wavered. A coin cemented
into the tower, perhaps coincidence. After all, some object must
be last to complete a structure. You'll want more. Young people
these days want more. Just a few years ago, they tried to condemn
the towers. The white city councils said it was unsafe, but the
truth is, they could not abide such primitive monuments to . . . us
poor folks, the outsiders, the powerless. To test the towers to see
if they were safe, they attached steel cables to each tower and
pulled them with cranes. Ten thousand pounds of pressure. *Nuestro
Pueblo* didn't budge."

"He was a great engineer, a great artist." Monk sips tea.

"Yes, he was . . . however, I've heard that . . . that kind of pressure against Sabato's towers . . . towers welded by hand with
rusted scraps and set just a few inches in hand-mixed concrete . . .
well, many folks, most of 'em white, can't understand it . . . but
you see," patting Monk's knee, "I . . . and many of us hoodoo
kings and voodooiennes . . . blessed and cast spells of protection
for Sabato, for the towers, before them cranes could roll up. And
your graffiti. Some places are holy, they project an aura. Since
'21 . . . the towers have never been trespassed with one mark of
graffiti . . ."

Monk's thinking of that other hoodoo, Queen Mab, her Victorian house and picket fence miraculously untagged. Did they
know each other? "Okay, Miss Mojo," Monk smiling. "I'll try to
keep an open mind. What do I do? Go to the towers? Find the
coin? Talk to Mr. Rodia?"

270 A. G. LOMBARDO

"No, no, young man. Go to the towers? Better wait till this . . . insurrection's over. Parker's ordered the Guard to surround the towers," she laughs, "damn fools. He's afraid Negro snipers will use them, or fix antennas up there for criminal broadcasts . . . and talk to Mr. Rodia? If only you could. Sab—Mr. Rodia passed away last month."

"I'm sorry, Miss Mojo." Monk drains his teacup.

"Yes. Well, he and I . . . it was a long time ago. You just remember those that wear shades may be shades . . . and watch yourself 'round those evil white men you're gonna meet." Mojo closes her eyes and sets the smoldering pipe against her cup, sinking back into the jade cushions. "Now, young man, if you don't mind showin' yourself out, I'm very tired."

Monk sets the cup quietly on its saucer on the table. In the sputtering candlelight he ducks through cage-welded corridors and descends rungs into the pitch-dark alleyway.

23

Monk is walking east on Sixty-sixth Street, staying clear of the boulevards like the hoodoo queen said. Is the horizon lightening toward sunrise, or is it only this unending night's fires and the charnel ruins of the city?

Maybe that old witch is right: wires slant from utility poles, lines and plugs coil and web from telephone transformers; wires droop and loop from house to house, chimneys to yards, or splayed over fences and brick walls. Monk's not sure if the power companies have rigged firetraps for the ghetto or if folks are just stealing watts from the man.

Miramonte: *Standard's street*. Monk heads south down the quiet avenue. Tiny bungalow houses, doors and windows grilled with iron bars. Some people hunker on stoops or curbs, talking softly, sipping beers in the summer night heat, gazing at the smoke-smudged, flame-ribboned horizon. Monk's mind is working, the sign scrawled in his notebook luminous, tantalizing in his mind: *M: vines on a meter*.

These blocks have a crimson hue. Red-painted window trims, red flower pots, wine-shaded windows, brick walls and walkways like rusted blood, even the flowers: roses, cardinals, lantana, scarlet sage: this is Gladiator territory, and these houses, these people languid in summer's moment, exist only by fealty to their gang overlords. Monk stops and stares up at the black street sign. Miramonte. The letters flash in his mind: *Miramonte* . . . *M: on a* . . . it's part of the message . . . *M: vines on a meter* . . . Tyrone, whoever wrote it . . . they somehow *knew* he'd take this street . . . Standard's street . . . who else knew, Standard, the gangs, the cops?

He's reached Sixty-eighth Street, his mind working through the code, burnished letters spinning like some kind of combination that might tumble and reveal a guarded secret. Subtracting *Miramonte*, the remaining letters are *v* . . . *s* . . . *n* . . . *e* . . . *e*—

"Seven." Monk's reached the corner, staring at the street sign: Seventieth. A black boy rides past on a bicycle with a fluttering red bandanna tied to its handlebars. "Fuck. Miramonte seven . . . vines on a meter."

Monk walks diagonally across the street and steps up onto the sidewalk: before him is an abandoned house, its white stucco walls covered with graffiti tags, bombs, drippy numbers and diagrams between its broken windows. On the corner of the wall, half hidden, sprayed in neon colors of graffiti, are smashed, rusted old electric meters strangled beneath knots of dead vines spidering up the wall.

He treads across the summer-bleached lawn, past the meters and vines to the southeast side of the house, invisible from the street. He stares up at the large spangled graffito painted over the entire side of the windowless wall: cubes of neon gold, red, and orange pyramids and temples—strange ziggurats that fuse Egyptian and Mayan pyramids into futuristic lines that have depth, dimension, a vibrating life . . . Monk gently touches the graffito to see if it is real. Beneath the impossible temples is a golden scroll, like a papyrus, blank and shimmering, a strange black pen poised above it, ready to write. "El Tirili," Monk whispers. Impossible but here it is, an El Tirili masterpiece that no graffitist would dare paint over. He steps farther back, gazing up at the mural. Rodia's voice echoes in his mind: *I have time . . . but no space . . .* "I see it now . . . graffiti's like the towers . . . it exists in time." Monk's talking to himself. "Graffiti travels through time, shaping the people, the city in its wonders and warnings . . . but it can't transcend space, it's fixed in cement foundations or sprayed walls . . . the papyrus . . . books, the notebook . . . the word travels through space . . . mind to mind, across the planet . . . but the pages are blank unless someone sees them, words are not signs until they're read . . . until they change us here, this city, then the next and the next . . ."

•

At the corner of Florence, Monk crosses the street, his heels crunching broken glass. He passes a news van parked at the flooded curb, a reporter, cameramen, two men adjusting klieg lights on stands. Channel Five's Wink Rover stands before the camera, bathed in the chalky glow of the lights, microphone ready, nodding as a man shuffles through the cue cards.

"Ready?" The card man's inhaling a cigarette nervously.

"Give me a minute." Rover glares at the cue cards, then at the Channel Five news van parked on the corner, its long whip antennas and their portable lights like beacons to him, *Hey, Negroes, we're over here, come and beat the shit out of us whiteys.* Next to the van, his co-producer is talking to the new token Negro hired by management to "team-cover" the riots. Wink suspects the Negro newscaster is secretly slipping messages into the broadcasts, codes to clandestine black operatives: where the cops *aren't* . . . which stores are *not yet* looted . . . city blocks ripe for larceny where the power is *out.*

"Okay." Rover nods as a tiny red light blinks on above the lens and the cameraman signals him. "This is Wink Rover with Channel Five News with live coverage of the riots in Watts. We are on Florence Avenue where the police have responded to a series of confrontations with Negro rioters. Channel Five News just hours ago brought you Chief Parker's press conference announcing the deployment of the National Guard. As I speak to you now, the National Guard is en route from Camp Roberts, but they are," Wink pauses, grimacing professionally into the lens, "some two hundred miles away. Meanwhile, armed gangs of Negroes seem to loot and then set fires faster than the police and fire brigades can respond. The police and fire departments are undermanned and spread too thin across this burning metropolis. A few National Guard units, including the Mechanized Infantry Division from Long Beach, and the First and Third Battalions from the San Fernando Valley, may arrive sooner with," Rover nods gravely, "God's speed. Indeed, because tonight there are reports of truckloads of Negroes with rifles and guns terrorizing the city. Some of these hoodlums wear scarlet armbands to identify their criminal brothers-in-arms, and to spread terror in the night as they rove the ruins of their violent handiwork—"

Another cue card slides into position as Wink glares into the camera: "We have *unconfirmed* reports from our police sources that hundreds, perhaps *thousands* of guns and weapons have been seized from Negro rioters and gangsters at police checkpoints throughout the city, guns, we are told," pausing, shaking his head, "even guns taken from scores of little Negro . . . children."

Wink's been working double shifts since the riots began; sometimes he stays late at the station, going over the kinescope monitors with producers, watching the magnetic tape recordings of the nightly broadcasts, when strange thoughts race through his exhausted mind. Watching the news feeds, the buildings, flames, faces seem to repeat in endless loops . . . are they showing the same footage over and over again? Images edited and broadcast across the country to fuel the fear, hate, and terror?

He nods toward the lens and cue cards. "Chaos and paranoia seem to fan these flames. Civil rights activists charge police with firing into mobs, while Chief Parker—at least publicly—has stated officers' orders are to fire above rioters. The chief yesterday stated that he fears the Negro unrest may be coordinating with large groups of the city's Negro and Mexican gangs. There is mounting concern that rioters and gangsters are gathering and concealing vast caches of guns, weapons, and bombs for an all-out assault on police, or a gang war of unprecedented violence—"

The camera's red light dies as the operator yells, "Cut! Cue!"

The darkened avenue seems to funnel into the red and lemon flashing lights of cop cars and fire trucks beyond the newscasters. A Molotov cocktail bursts in a flower of flames at the center of the avenue, illuminating crowds of rioters fanning across the street. "Let's get the hell out of here!" Cue cards flutter to the curb as the cameraman, light techs, crew, and Wink Rover run toward the news van. They pile into the van and it skids away from the curb, stamping a black tire track over a cue card printed NEGRO MEX GANGS GUN CACHE.

•

Monk's safely across Florence as a news van, followed by a police car, roars past. Now, from the open windows of the tenements above, from loudspeakers and radios and megaphones somewhere in the night, a soulful, amplified baritone echoes between waves of police sirens: *Brothers and sisters, let's chill with Coltrane's "Summertime" before we burn . . . baby, burn . . .*

Police cruisers whip past. Monk stops; it takes his brain a few seconds to process what he sees: following the cop cars are two olive National Guard trucks, their flatbeds filled shoulder to shoulder with soldiers in full khaki uniforms and helmets, carbine rifles and M16 machine guns glinting from their shoulder straps. A few Guard snipers hold rifles with experimental army scopes that can detect light from *dark* targets. A third National Guard truck rumbles past, bigger, with a camouflaged steel cargo box jutting up behind its cab, twin, huge steel RDF loop antennas revolving on their motorized bases atop the roof, triangulating closer toward the renegade broadcasts.

The convoy squeals around the corner. Now Coltrane's sax fades as a husky woman's voice reverberates through the night streets, a sonorous purr down the avenues and across the ruined city . . . Tokyo Rose: *We are one . . . Nation of Islam leader Elijah Muhammad is of Negro-Japanese ancestry . . . hand in hand with the Japanese Black Dragon Society since the war, fighting with yours truly Compton Eve against the white devils . . . make them burn, baby, burn . . .*

Squad cars brake in front of the iron staircase and boarded windows of a darkened pawnshop. Guardsmen leap up stairs, smashing through doors with M16 rifle butts and combat boots, cops scrambling behind, pistols drawn. In the night, Coltrane's tenor sax peals like a squadron of mournful angels in D minor.

Inside the dark building, flashlights dart past racks of musical instruments, glass cases of watches, jewelry, guns. The soldiers smash and topple shelves, barrel past collapsing, teetering aisles stacked with boxes and suitcases and appliances. In the corner, flashlight beams transfix a makeshift studio carved out of boxes and stacked lockers. A desk heaped with radio equipment and microphones, wires and cables snaking down into the darkness. An empty chair. Under a microphone, a turntable slowly spins, the needle scratching around and around, orbiting the jade paper-label center of a vinyl record. The flashlight beam illuminates the revolving, fading print: *My Favorite Things . . . John Coltrane.* Beside the humming phonograph player: a paper cup, half filled with water, a solitary dead black fly slowly wheeling in its center; three pennies point in shiny, copper reflected light toward the stem of a single rose, its dried, red bud forever closed.

24

Monk's a few blocks north of the bright streetlights of Firestone, Coltrane's final, sad sax notes echoing in his mind, keeping to the shadow-splashed sidewalks of Miramonte Boulevard. Heading south, but is he following Standard's secret gauntlet? Should he zig east and down Maie Avenue, or zag west and down Compton again? When he passes Firestone, the little barred houses transform into prisms of blue: light and dark shades of blue paint, cobalt blooms of baptisia, delphinium, periwinkle in flower beds, teal and sky drapes and furniture and doors, even dark blue cars, no longer Gladiator territory, instead the royal hues of the Farmers borderlands. On the dark horizon he can see the feeble twinkling lights of the Watts Towers rising over 107th Street, a skeletal beacon in the haze. *I have time but no space.* So many nights have passed, yet the fires still rage, and he's only twenty or so blocks closer to the sea and the lover who waits for his return.

A black man in rumpled street clothes, rags on his feet, looms on the sidewalk before him, transfixing him with strange, ghettoized sunglasses cobbled from duct tape, wire hangers, mismatched black lenses, feathers, silver chains. "Beware, brother, I see with the eyes of the blind. I can see the glow of the bigots, of the damned . . . armies clashing in the night . . . it is the time of no time . . ." Monk pushes past him. "Why you gots to push me? And their dead bodies shall lie in the streets of the great city," the old street preacher's raspy voice behind him. "I'm tired."

A turquoise-and-white two-tone '61 Chevy Brookwood squeals before Monk, its windows blacked out. The car's passenger window rolls down: a white gangster, shaved head glistening with tonic, brown eyes rainbowed with some kind of purple pharaoh's mascara and jade grease pencil, grins at Monk. "I'm tired," the preacher's gravelly whisper fades around the corner, "I'm tired, so tire—" A shock jolts through Monk's spine: *Tyrone*. Before he can turn toward the old preacher, the gleaming silver barrel of a .22 pistol levels out from the car window.

"Where you goin'?" The gangster whispers, instead of the obligatory *Where you from?*

"South, the port." A back door swings open, the gangster waves the gun barrel toward the rear door. "No, please, that's okay."

Eyes gaze sadly up into Monk's face, then the gangster whispers: "Little fly, / Thy summer's play / My thoughtless hand / Has brushed away." Monk stares at the gleaming gun, swallows hard, slides into the backseat. The Chevrolet glides forward as Monk stares out the tinted window, looking back, but the preacher is gone.

Another white banger sits next to him, shaved head, tattoos on his thick neck. He leers as his hands interlock, flashing Monk an S sign.

"Slausons?" Monk wipes sweaty palms on his thighs. "I thought you cats were Businessmen."

"Nah," the tattoo-neck laughs, "we use'ta be but those pricks sued us, copyright shit, so we changed it to Slausons."

"Lamb, how many times have I told you," glittering eyes turning from the front seat. "Don't talk business."

"Sorry, Asmodeous."

"Here, Nobodaddy," Asmodeous hisses, pointing out the front window: Nobodaddy, behind the wheel, slows. Monk leans forward. Telephone lines overhead, dipping over the street: old pair of sneakers dangle from shoelaces looped over the wires, toes pointing east. "Left here." Nobodaddy turns down another street, east.

The car brakes to a red light. "Let's go." Asmodeous opens the door. Lamb pushes Monk out and the three men scramble inside the cab of an idling big diesel truck. Nobodaddy squeals the Chevy into a right turn, disappears as the truck driver—another white thug in an army jacket, black sunglasses, shaved head—grinds gears and rumbles through the intersection. "Let's do some business . . . Monk." Asmodeous smiles. He opens a hatchway in the rear of the cab, descends three steps into the cargo container, Monk following as Lamb steps behind, his big hand clamped on Monk's shoulder.

The long trailer glows from fluorescent tubes above: a black sofa and lavender leather chair, table and chairs, a cubicle or hallway with built-in steel walls and doors blocks the truck's rear axle. Oil paintings—dark Flemish masterpieces—hang from riveted walls. Another white gangster sits in an upholstered chair, cowboy hat over his eyes, shirtless, a silver pistol on the table surrounded by heaps of green dope baggies and piles of joints—fifty cents each on every corner of Slauson turf. Two young white women lounge on the sofa, smoking cigarettes; smoke tapers up to the milky glow and funnels through open hatch windows in the roof, patches of hazy night rolling past above. One woman, long dirty blond hair, champagne halter top and cherry hot pants, the other short black hair, leather miniskirt, cutoff T-shirt. "Drink?"

Monk shakes his head. "How do you know my name?"

"You've been sent. This is business of the secret kind. Terror the human form divine, and secrecy the human dress."

"Sent?" Monk asks.

"Gris-gris, niggers tapping on pipes, whistling teapot signals." Asmodeous sips whiskey. "Get hip."

"Mojo?"

"No spooks, just business. All them bags of hoodoo hanging on her chicken-wire walls." Asmodeous glances over to the gangster slouching behind the table heaped with dope bags. "Just one of my dealers. Maybe there's a reason for all your night wandering. Mr. Monk, you seem to be doing quite a bit of dwelling in the *underworld*. Some are born to sweet delight, some are born to endless night."

"Why am I here? So you can show off your Blake?"

Asmodeous's eyes sparkle darkly from the depths of blue and purple shadows. "You're no fool. My father gave me my name, and the worn book that lit the nights of his prison sojourns—the collected works of the dark master." Gravity slightly pulls their bodies to the left as the truck gears into a right turn. "Sit down." Monk sinks into leather. The girls snuggle into him, scents of perfume and cigarette smoke, their hands patting his thighs.

Asmodeous nods, sits on his throne, a stuffed amethyst leather chair. "Tirzah." The blond in cherry hot pants smiles at Monk as she rises. Tirzah mixes Asmodeous another drink, plucks a joint from the pile next to the cowboy's pistol. She lights the reefer, extends it to Monk, but he shakes his head. Tirzah inhales, leans over Asmodeous, kisses him as he sucks in her exhalation cooled by her darting tongue. He exhales, sips whiskey. Tirzah passes the joint to the other woman, Lyca. "The road of excess leads to the palace of wisdom."

Brakes hiss, metal walls groan, everything tipping starboard. Monk: "Where we going?"

"Nowhere," Asmodeous exhaling smoke, rasping. "We're here. The Slausons are what you might call a mobile operation. I roll through the city, day and night. A convoy of offices. This is one of my recreational rooms. Cars, buses, trucks, each a room of my palace on wheels. Got a foyer, bedrooms, safe houses, gun rooms, dope processing, you name it. Always rolling, no fixed addresses, no cops, no stakeouts and raids. God gave me the ghetto, perfect cover to build an unholy kingdom. And did the Countenance

Divine . . . Shine forth upon our clouded hills? And was Jerusalem *builded* here . . . Among these dark Satanic Mills?"

"Trouble, boss," a speaker in the riveted wall reverberates, Jake brakes rumble, everyone balances forward as the great container slows.

"Excuse me for a moment." Asmodeous drains his whiskey. Lyca and Tirzah curl around Monk and pass the smoldering roach to each other. Opening the fore hatchway, Asmodeous disappears into the glowing light of the diesel's cab.

The engine pings and idles, Asmodeous gazes through the big windshield and into the night bathed in the beams of the Mack's headlights. Telephone lines splay over the intersection before them, a pair of gray calfskin Florsheim Imperial shoes knotted, dangling from shoelaces. "Shadows," Asmodeous hisses. "Call ahead, you know what to do." The driver nods his head, grinds gears, and the truck lurches forward.

Monk is wedged so tightly between the girls on the couch that he's wondering if they are some kind of bodyguards too, when Asmodeous descends through the hatchway. "Las Sombras," to Lamb.

"A slight detour," Asmodeous says to Monk and sips his whiskey.

Air brakes hiss, bodies sway. "Fuckin' Shadows." Fly turns his cowboy hat toward Monk. "That's why we're fightin'." Fly's thumbs and forefingers twist into an S. "Stole our Slausons sign."

"That's not why." Asmodeous's voice is soft. "Back in '55, we were kids. We called him El Gordo Pedo even back then—a fat Mexican kid on a chopped chrome Schwinn, baseball cards clipped to spokes for rumble sound effects. Had this fucking *attack Chihuahua* in his basket. Wanted to start our own gangs as far back as I can remember. Gordo stole my gang sign, the black handkerchief hanging from the left back pocket—that was my flag."

"Boss," Lamb scratching his shaved head, "is that legend true, that the bad blood between the Gladiators and Rollin' 60s started when Highbeam stepped on Lil' Conk's black shoes?"

"That's just a rumor," Monk says without thinking, "the real reason is the Gladiators changed a couple of street signs, and they were dealing dope for blocks inside Rollin' 60s territory for a year until Highbeam caught on."

Asmodeous bows his head. "The word on the street must be true, your gangster knowledge is encyclopedic. The word is also that you keep a kind of . . . graffiti encyclopedia?"

Monk is silent: *Stupid, can't you keep your big mouth—*

"I too keep a book, Monk. But first a little pleasure before business. Fly." The cowboy hat nods, pale hands tattooed with teal crosses tap white powder from a glass vial onto a small mirror ringed by olive bags of dope. Lyca leans over Monk and kisses Tirzah, a long, sensuous kiss; Monk presses back into cushions away from their dizzy heat. "Tirzah." She pulls away from Lyca, smiles, rises, mixes another whiskey tumbler for her master. "Do you believe in miracles, Monk?"

"Well," careful now, "I'm skeptical, but lately I've seen some crazy shit."

Asmodeous nods. "In an insane world, miracles seem . . . commonplace. I too keep a notebook, a book of miracles." Monk's skin tingles, the notebook chafes his lower back as he presses deeper into cushions. Asmodeous stands, whiskey in his fist as Fly hands him the mirror chevroned with white powder. "I keep a journal of sanctioned miracles. Phenomena beyond any natural laws. Not the superstitious miracles of medieval times, but a record of city miracles, corroborated, witnessed, true as the dark angel's light. Tell him, my *souldier*, what you have witnessed with your own eyes."

"Cops opened fire on me," Fly grasps his silver S Slauson belt buckle, "every bullet bounced off this, like Superman."

"They're all recorded here." Asmodeous holds up a green notebook. "A new bible for a profane world. Categorized, annotated, documented, *quoad substantiam*—miracles of the dead brought back to life, *quoad subiectum*—the curing of the sick, miracles of every degree and class. Pending miracles, Eucharistic miracles of holy apparitions and forms. Wonders of *pareidolia*— natural stains and patterns taking the forms of the divine—or the unholy. Miracles *vulgus* and *rarus* . . . of the flesh and spirit, of the animate, inanimate. The mural over on Ninety-fifth in Watts where real salt tears drip from the Negro faces of unknown city martyrs." Asmodeous's nose vacuums another powdery line from the hand mirror.

Thumbing through the pages, he reads: "A sparrow flies into the clubhouse of the Willowbrook Eight Trays, breaks its neck against the window. An hour later, their O.G., Tiny Playboy, goes through his car windshield, dies . . . Imperials' gang house. Eleven homies drink for nine hours from a single beer that never empties . . . Spoony Athens, from the South Side Scissors, straddles atop Southern Pacific freight train Engine Nine and surfs the rails, over a hundred miles through curves and tunnels and bridges and track switches, speeds up to seventy miles an hour, from Soldiers Home to San Pedro."

Monk hopes he looks disinterested but he's thinking of the page in his notebook, the mysterious graffito he'd copied from Engine Nine last year: the image of a huge hat, a sideways looping figure eight for its brim, a face with a cigarette dangling from frowning lips, and the train rider's mythic name scrawled below— Bozo Texino . . . the ghost rider who's haunted the tracks and rail-riding bindle stiffs for more than eighty years.

Asmodeous licks his fingers, then leafs through journal pages. "Miracles from *vulgus* to *rarus*. Cops chase Eight-Ball, from the Crenshaw Stones. He stops at a corner where a candle jar burns, a votive to Guadalupe. The two cops run past him as if he's enveloped in some kind of invisible benediction."

Above the green journal, Asmodeous's face is spectral under the vibrating fluorescence. "Mero Vato, head of the L.A. Santaneros. His house is engulfed in flames, he's trapped by the iron bars on every window and door. The fire department finds him unconscious but alive on his front lawn. Mero Vato's chest is striped with burns where he'd pressed himself against the red-hot bars. He said he felt himself passing *through* the bars before he blacked out . . . dead gangbangers whose bodies don't corrupt until their killers are killed . . . little kids shot in drive-bys, laid out in tiny open caskets, miracles of rigor mortis, their baby fingers fixed and curled into gang signs that reveal their executioners."

Asmodeous sips whiskey. "You must be thirsty, Monk."

"Just a Coke, or water if you don't mind."

"Fly, fetch our friend a liquid Coke."

Monk swallows hard. "Could have called yourselves Hell's Angels, too bad those new bikers took it."

"Yeah," Asmodeous chuckling. "*They're* afraid of us." Tapping his notebook. "Imagine the power if one could predict or perhaps replicate just one of these profane miracles. I have recorded one or two *rarus* miracles of graffiti too." As he reads, he studies Monk's face. "Rollin' 60s crossed out Bastard Gs'—from the Jordan Downs Huns—graffiti. At the exact same moment, Bastard G drops dead from a heart attack . . . the Reyes Locos paint *RIP 3 G ST 61865*— Rest in Peace three Grape Street bangers on June 18, 1965. When that day comes, three Grape gangsters are dead from bullets by the Vagabondos. You are afraid, I must apologize. If you were thinking clearly, we could discuss the law of large numbers—coincidence to the uninformed—to dismiss most of these miracles. But some of these events defy any probability, one has to postulate fantastic explanations that become more extraordinary than the miracle itself."

Fly hands Monk a frosty bottle of Coca-Cola, then pads away.

Asmodeous reclines in his chair. "Word on the street is that you also keep a journal, a kind of graffiti Baedeker. You know how rumors fly through this fucking city. Wild stories about graffiti charms and curses that protect or take life, spray-painted interdictions that no power on earth can trespass beyond, graffiti portals where taggers disappear through their magic thresholds." He closes his painted eyes. "A scholar like yourself no doubt recalls the infamous *graffito blasfemo.* The ancient Roman graffito of Alexamenos worshipping the crucified Jesus, the Christ portrayed with the head of a donkey . . . this underground image is the earliest portrait of Jesus we have . . . blasphemous, but it was the city's story to counter the official gospels . . . so too we need our graffiti, don't you agree? To give voice to the damned. Naturally, I am very interested in looking over your notes. Perhaps both texts will reveal some . . . holy key."

Jake brakes hiss, gravity pulls against Monk. "Good to go, boss," the intercom crackles.

"After you, Mr. Monk, please don't be alarmed." Asmodeous sweeps his hand toward the cab hatchway. "To my office for a little business." Monk walks on jellied legs to the hatch, trying to control his fear and marshal his thoughts: *I went through hell to keep my book, get it back . . . and now these fuckers are gonna take it.* The iron door opens; the driver nods, his black glasses and shaved head gleaming. Monk climbs down the steps of the idling big rig, wedged between the driver and another Slauson, no escape, only one step down onto the asphalt road, then up the metal steps of an opened bus door idling parallel with the truck. Monk sees a flash of the gray exterior of the long bus, Asmodeous's hand gently guiding against his shoulder. Pneumatic glass doors fold closed as they ascend into white light.

The bus rumbles, jars ahead. The driver's compartment is shuttered behind steel doors. They walk on thick burgundy carpets deeper into the silvery interior: recessed lights curve above, casting shining pools they pass through. The walls are padded, only a faint murmur of gears and the diesel engine, the windows blocked by reflecting metallic shades. All the seats have been removed as they reach the glowing nimbus of the vehicle's smoke-shrouded rear section: a great black onyx table, a ring of black leather chairs, wet bar against a padded wall. Slouching in the chairs is a white gangster, boyish face and blond crew cut, pale in a black button shirt and pants; another white boy, shaved head, tinny music from a transistor radio held clamped over his right ear; a beautiful woman, long black hair, silver knit top and gold hot pants; that old crazy Chinese gangster Yin in his round eyeglasses and rumpled lemon suit, oblivious to Monk as the aged Fiendish Oriental chain-smokes and leers at another girl in the next seat, younger, red hair, carnation halter top, cinnamon pants, Monk can see the broken tips of her angel's wings tattoo above the pink hem of her top. "You are a rucky rady," Yin's palm sliding toward her breast as she swats away his hand. A giant black man smokes a fat cigar, his bodybuilder thighs squeezed into the dwarfed chair: a white tank-top shirt stretches impossibly over bulging muscles, even the baggy gray sweatpants are sculpted by hidden muscles. Roof lights reflect from his shaved head, gold rings gleam from black earlobes. Monk recognizes him, that iron-pumping jailbird from the aqueducts, from Highbeam's Rollin' 60s concrete lair, and, under that taut cotton shirt, inked into the hills and ridges of his muscled back, a tattoo of the city, a promise of escape.

"Standard," Asmodeous nods to the giant, motions Monk to take an empty seat.

"Here I am," Standard grins, "in the back of the bus as usual." Asmodeous sets his notebook on the polished ebony as he sits at the head of the gleaming table. Standard glances around at Monk, the gangsters, the two women, no indication that he remembers Monk, then he shakes his bald head and laughs. "Y'all one set of crazy-lookin' *wiggers*."

"San Quentin good?" Asmodeous asks.

"Oh yeah." Standard grins. "You just keep that cash and kush comin', double green, my man."

Asmodeous opens a recessed panel in the padded wall, pulls out an attaché case, hands it to Standard. Asmodeous extracts a reefer from the drawer, sparks its twisted tip with an onyx lighter.

The white punk with the transistor radio pushes Monk into a chair. Monk feels the bus sway left, gears grinding far away. He looks around the table, at these faces that seem evil, hard with a drugged depravity, like masks waiting for the spark of violence to animate them. Monk feels the bus accelerate: he's running out of time. *Find a way out now before it's too late!* He controls his panicked thoughts, trying to measure Asmodeous's face: *Why would he let me go?*

Brakes squeak, the smoky, silvery-lit cabin lurches, bodies lean forward as if hunched in Asmodeous's spell. "At last, excuse me for a moment." Asmodeous rises, his scarab eyes glitter. "Albion," to the gangster in black, "dope and drink all around, a toast, our moment is at hand."

Asmodeous stands at the pneumatic doors, bus idling to a stop. Air tubes hiss and the mirrored panels shunt open.

"Angels, honored guests," Asmodeous announces toward his infernal conference, Standard, Monk, everyone peering up through wafts of smoke. "El Tirili."

Monk staggers to his feet, astonished: El Tirili . . . the impossible masterpiece on the hidden canvas of an abandoned ghetto house . . . a riddle of space and time . . . and a sign, a key to his notebook.

The old Mexican radiates before them: ancient gold and silver sombrero, peaked like a straw wizard's cap; black eyes squint under the tattered brim, the old man's copper face wrinkled and pocked, desiccated with years of desert and mountain ranges, smiling down at the revelers, two tobacco-stained teeth and a gleaming gold cap; a blue, crimson, and silver serape drapes from his stooped shoulders, cotton weaved in interlocking geometric rings and pyramids and checkered plains that seem to shimmer in three dimensions; a long-sleeve Sir Guy lime-and-cobalt plaid shirt, black baggy cholo pants tied with a belt of silver-dyed hemp rope . . . and Florsheim Imperial shoes.

Monk studies him as if he's an apparition: El Tirili, the Reefer Man. Every tagger, bomber, graffitist, banger in the city has heard the wild stories, the rumors, the ancient Mexican in shimmering, rainbow clothes, never glimpsed, only his legendary bombs, murals, *placasos* illumine the city's disenfranchised fringes to amaze every angry or inspired fist that clutches a spray can. No one knows how old the great *pintor* is. Young paint guns swear he was the first to use a city for his infinite canvas, never having to *lambiche* or kiss ass to any gang or territorial boundaries. Crews haunt the city in night pilgrimages to see the sacred icons of his pieces and *pintadas*, whispering of the impossible age of each masterpiece, dumbstruck by each unique *eye-gasm*: bombs on the Pasadena Freeway from the '40s, iridescent tags on City Hall from back in '28, cloudy chiaroscuros on the Arcade Building documented since '24; puffy abstracts on certain Venice canals dating back to '05 . . . an outlaw impasto on the Pico House noted with horror in the local paper back in 1892 . . . Victorian houses in Angelino Heights deflowered by his rebel brush in the 1880s. A ghost, acolytes say he's an immortal imp, a living link back to the days when the first graffitists created ghostly works on ceilings using only the smoke from guttering candles. They say he made his own brushes and rollers from animal and even human hair; hammered and hand-rolled sheets of tin and steel to forge the first spray cans, using a secret mixture of ethyl-chloride propellant, carving valves and nozzles from wood, ivory, bone . . . mixed paints and washes in secret caves and cellars, bewitched colors no palette had ever seen before; conjured pigments and glazes in crucibles that cloaked his works with a patina that neither time nor man could destroy.

The ring of debauched angels nod in deference to the old master. Albion extends the smoldering nub of reefer to El Tirili.

The Reefer Man shakes his sombrero, extracts the biggest joint Monk's every seen, fat as a Cuban cigar. Monk studies the ancient brown hands, dyed a miasma of strange colors from decades of paint and spray: hands that never had to touch a *cuete* or gun.

El Tirili removes his sombrero, revealing perfectly greased-back black hair. His rainbow-hued hands untie the serape and neatly fold it over the sombrero like a metallic flag woven with geometric symbols. The Reefer Man glares at Standard with mad-dog, bloodshot eyes.

Standard rises, peels off the white shirt clinging to his great muscles, pulling it free like a shred of gossamer veil. El Tirili unbuttons his Sir Guy plaid, tosses it on ebony onyx: now both men turn, stand side by side.

"Behold," Asmodeous spreads his arms, "the prophecy fulfilled, the unholy united, the End-Time. The Demon red, who burnt towards America . . . the treaty . . ."

Monk stares at the map tattooed on both men: Standard's broad, ebony map of Watts he'd glimpsed in Highbeam's storm drains, the northern cribs inked in deep blue, a crimson tattooed route snaking south, Naomi Avenue paralleling Central Avenue, Sixty-seventh Street, Compton Avenue, then Seventieth east to Miramonte, meandering down toward Florence; but now, the scarlet trail continues south, on the sienna canvas of El Tirili's back . . . the blood line zigzagging from Compton Avenue to Defiance Avenue, snaking past Ninety-fifth, toward Ninety-ninth . . . south on Compton again . . . then 102nd, crooking west . . . and points south, turf of the Sombras, Vice Kings, Boyle Street Boys, 190th Locos, and more.

"The covenant is born." Asmodeous takes a tumbler of whiskey from Tyger. "A toast to all the dark envoys here. We are now an army, a rainbow of destruction. Rollin' 60s and the niggers . . . Las Sombras and the spics . . . Yin and the 880s, Yow Yees, all the ABCs—American-born Chinese gangs, all of Tong's angry children . . . and your humble servant," bows, drinks, his eyes twinkling, "the Slausons and every wigger OG in the city. A sea of black, brown, yellow, white, a reign of fury no force can stop!"

Everyone's out of their chairs, chinking glasses as Monk tries to shrink into his upholstered cushions: "Burn, baby, burn!"

Near El Tirili's olive waist Monk glimpses a spidery red line dropping south and the words *Success Ave*: he tries to follow the crimson tattooed trail but the Reefer Man's buttoning his Sir Guy plaid and lacing his shimmering serape, a dignified ancient graffiti gaucho, gold tooth gleaming as he grins across to Monk, the tattoo cartograph gone.

"This is where you disembark." Asmodeous smiles at Monk. Tyger, the transistor radio pressed against his ear, grabs Monk's arm in an iron vise and shoves him through the smoke as the brakes hiss to a stop. Monk's blood pounds in his face as he fights a rising panic; Tyger almost pulls him, Asmodeous and El Tirili flank tightly around him.

"Your notebook is your pass to freedom." Asmodeous and El Tirili block the closed silver panels of the bus door. "Two holy books, double is the power to he who unlocks both volumes." Tyger's radio has disappeared: Monk hears a click and Tyger's pressing a switchblade against his throat. "You and I are alike, but you are afraid to release your darker angel. Every day on these streets, you pass, neither black nor white, but which are you? You're both, white as an angel is the English child, but I am black, as if bereaved of light."

Monk stares into the madness of Asmodeous's cobalt-and-ebony-webbed eyes. Monk slowly slips his hand into the back of his shirt, extracts the frayed, sweat-sopped blue notebook bound with its rubber band, hands it to Asmodeous. Tyger's lips twist cruelly as he gently presses the switchblade into Monk's throat: a drop of blood glistens from the silver blade tip as Monk's eyes lock into El Tirili's old eyes, which seem to twinkle with a bemused patience that urges Monk to wait.

"Put away your claws, Tyger," Asmodeous says.

Tyger frowns and clips the switchblade closed. Monk's fore-head is beaded with sweat.

"Mr. Monk, it would be foolish, or at least premature, to elim-inate such an authority on signs and wonders. We may call on your expertise again. And this way, I can look forward to reading your next book of miracles." The bus doors hiss, panels unfold open, warm summer blackness beyond the silver step and curb.

"You've probably read it all before." Monk swabs his sweaty forehead with a palm, then rubs a trickle of blood from his throat. He steps down into the night, El Tirili behind him.

Pneumatic brakes hiss and the bus shutters, pivots away from the two men. Monk sees a flash of motion as the Reefer Man slips two spray cans under his serape: silver and gold iridescent letters, blocked like Aztec ruins—*El T*—shimmer on the metal side of the bus as it lurches down the street. El Tirili salutes Monk with a tug of his ancient, paint-spangled fist around the shining sombrero's straw rim, then the old *pintor* walks down the street, sparkling, jeweled Florsheims winking into the night.

Legs still wobbly with fear, Monk sprints into a dark alley, away from the fading, distant chug of the diesel bus. He turns down a street, no time to get his bearings. Another alley swallows him. After a few minutes he slows, his hand squeezing the coverless notebook tucked in his pants, *his* notebook. "Like I said, mother-fucker," Monk panting, "you've probably read it all before." The de-ception took less than thirty seconds: Asmodeous left the table to bring in El Tirili. Standard and Yin were distracted with the two women. Tyger had his eyes closed, nodding along with the transis-tor radio pressed against his ear, the other white thug standing, watching as Asmodeous appeared with the legendary graffitist. Monk grabbed the gangster's notebook, and, under the table, slipped the tattered, detached blue covers of his own notebook over the green cardboard covers of Asmodeous's book, and stretched Jax's rubber band over the covers. "Fuck." Now he's thinking about the terror, the perspiration on his forehead when Tyger pricked that knife to his throat. The sweat, the panic as Asmodeous held the notebook . . . Monk stared into those insane eyes, dreading any second that the frayed rubber band around the covers would suddenly snap . . .

25

I am a brother to dragons, and a companion to owls. My skin is
black upon me, and my bones are burned with heat.   —Job

Monk emerges from the alley, pulls out the ragged, coverless
notebook from under his shirt and scribbles on a back page: *Defi-*
ance Avenue, 99th . . . Compton. Already the inked maze of El
Tirili's map is fading from his memory. "Shit!" He stuffs the notebook under his belt, walks south, scattered headlights stabbing
through the darkness. Monk trudges across an intersection, head
tipped slightly forward like a ship against the current, a journey
south again, perhaps forever in some kind of fiery limbo: he'll skirt
down Watts, try to follow El Tirili's secret route, treaty, or trap
until he wears himself down into the oil and blood of these warm
streets themselves, or somehow finds harbor and home. Across
the street now, he shivers in the hot summer night, a palpable
dread infused with each intersection, as if these great asphalt
crosses gouged into the city are crossroads that vibrate with a
mystic nexus of violence and despair.

  South, near Ninety-sixth Street. White Mexican candles sputter on sidewalks, each azure flame burning for the souls of the

disappeared. Knots of men roam down the avenue and crisscross between light traffic. Every few minutes police cruisers punctuate the summer's heat with sirens as they swerve past cars. Monk passes a gutted taco stand, shop windows smashed or boarded up, an alley blocked and glowing with a flaming car. Up ahead, three men scurry from a building, throw boxes in an idling car, speed away into darkness.

Monk walks south on Compton Avenue to Ninety-seventh. The intersection is darker, quieter than Ninety-second—gritty shops on corners followed by rows of iron-barred bungalows and vacant lots. Walking under a burned-out traffic signal: a dead *white* rooster hangs from the signal's iron arch, a string noose furrowed in its neck, a gris-gris omen any white trespassers fail to heed at their own peril. A liquor store, two black men with shotguns standing guard outside its pulverized windows; a pawnshop, fire gutted, muddy shelves and debris and clothes scorched and soaked in black water, its iron grilles warped and scissored open across the sidewalk. Monk shakes his head: this is the paradigm of the ghetto—liquor to numb the soul and mind, pawnshops to feed the thief, the desperate, the addict; gas stations' neon winking illusory promises of mobility, flight, escape. Don't think about escape, you're not on the lazy nigger time measured out by bigots but ghetto time, fractured, torn away from white man's time and history: here, in this squalid inferno, a minute, an hour, a night has no reckoning, only an endless movement through darkness between points of flaming terror—perhaps only hours, only a few nights have passed in actual white time; there is still hope, he has to believe that maybe it is only the sixth night—this has all been a kind of reverse, dark echo of the creation, and the seventh day will dawn with some kind of light and peace.

On the corner, a couple of brothers are doing business out of the opened trunks of their two parked cars, hawking Afro wigs—for safe passage—get 'em while they last, a buck ninety-nine.

A telephone rings in the distance. Past a couple of parked cars and a boarded-up store: a graffiti-tagged phone booth, glass panels shattered. A working phone booth in the ghetto, its line not yet cut by tonight's clashing forces, a miracle here for Asmodeous's book of wonders. Monk lifts the receiver. "Hello!" The booth reeks of urine. "Hello! Tyrone! Tiresias—"

"I see yer ass, all right," a gravelly, ancient man's whisper crackles over static. "Head on down to East Ninety-ninth."

"Why? Who the fuck are you?"

"Boy, you got to dance with the dead 'fore you can return to the land of the livin'."

He drops the phone, dial tone bleating as the receiver swings on its metal wire. He staggers from the booth.

Monk heads south down Compton. Each street seems darker, narrowing toward the black clouds and charnel glow of the horizon. Cars trickle by, mostly black young men, interior lights on so brother won't open fire on brother; some backseats and trunks are heaped with tonight's plunder: whiskey and birdcages, shovels and sunglass racks, clocks and cigarette boxes, purses and mattresses, melting frozen dinners and bicycles. Angry voices howl from the street and passing cars, chanting, "No shame! No shame!"

Monk's carrying his coverless notebook, gripping its wad of loose and jammed pages. "I got my loot too," fist squeezing the notebook: he'd looted and pillaged the city too, sacked it like some kind of fabled, mythic city of old . . . plundered a treasure beneath all their noses, a treasure beyond price, the signs and secrets and voices in the notebook . . . It has to be a key, an insane, dizzying key . . . what lock is it all meant to open? A car passes, Monk watching a young white woman's face panicked, gazing out the window of its dark interior. The rear window's been smashed. The car turns, engine gunning, lost, looking for any freeway ramp, police line, some kind of escape, and disappears.

Ninety-ninth Street. *Tiresias.* Monk stops, looks around, nods: *This is the way . . . El Tirili's map.* A turquoise-and-cream

two-tone '61 Brookwood slowly idles, approaching from the opposite direction, no headlights. "Asmodeous," Monk whispers,
turns, runs. He hurls himself against a darkened doorway, pushes
open the metal grate, and slips inside the brick building.

A long concrete stairway leads down into darkness, a dim,
flickering light somewhere below. Monk walks down the steps,
scuffing his Keds in slow motion.

It's cold down here, not enough to make his breath mist, but
jacket-cold, like industrial air-conditioning. He's in a hallway
that turns right, where the sputtering light comes from. Folding
his arms over his chest for warmth, Monk heads toward the
shifting glow.

A large, windowless cinder-block room. Stainless-steel gur-
neys draped with sheets like layers of snow. Monk opens the
notebook, fans through waterlogged, torn, smeared yet still intact pages, finds the drawing of Standard's map he's sketched.
He slowly draws a crooked black ink line, continuing Standard's
route. Now he draws El Tirili's streets, quickly before he forgets:
Compton Avenue, Defiance Avenue, Ninety-ninth. *Fuck!* What's
next—he can't remember. Someone with a flashlight—the flickering light Monk saw from the stairwell—turns, the light beam
stabbing Monk's face as he shields his eyes with his hand.

"Nothing to loot here."

"I'm no looter. I got kind of chased in here by a gangster. I'll
head back now, don't want any trouble."

"Gangster, huh?" The flashlight plays over Monk's ragged
notebook in his fist. "Well, there's a back door if you wanna go out
to the alley." The figure walks closer, the flashlight illuminating
the floor and a gurney draped with three mounds of white sheets,
a shape that Monk with a shock realizes is the head, stomach,
and feet of a cadaver. "Long as you're not looting. I'm just closing
up. Come on, I'll show you the way."

Now Monk can see a middle-aged woman with dark, striking
eyes, her short, jet-black hair swept back beneath a plastic blue

visor. "There's nothing to loot here anyway, unless you're after the embalming fluid. They tell me the kids dip cigarettes in it, charge two bucks a smoke. Call 'em wets or greens for the color they turn. Oh, it'll get you high, but that formaldehyde and chemicals," shakes her head. "It'll kill you after a spell." She's smiling at Monk, her face pale, almost chalky; she's wearing a white long smock, its hem fluttering ghostly above black shoes.

"This is the morgue?"

"Overflow. Los Angeles Coroner's Department. Fire's knocked out the power here about an hour ago, they'll go to backup generators if they don't get it back on line soon. My name's Karen," holding out a pale hand.

"Americo Monk," shaking hands: hers is like leathery ice.

"You some kind of reporter, maybe for one of those Negro papers?" The flashlight shines down on Monk's notebook.

"Huh? This? No, just a writer."

"Too bad. I could show you some things. I know, I talk a lot. Well, I've been doing this job for twenty-one years, and there's no one to talk to." She laughs as they stop at one of the draped cadavers on its gurney. "'Course, I must admit, I do talk to 'em, had some nice conversations." Monk stares at the woman, who grins. "Don't be alarmed, just nice conversations in my imagination, they don't talk back—yet." She laughs. "You sure you're not a Negro reporter? All that madness up there, fire and death, I could tell you a few things. Take this."

Karen shines her flashlight at the corpse and slowly pulls down the sheet. Monk gasps: a black male, looks like twenty years old, large Afro, eyes closed as if asleep. "This is Willie Ludlow." She pulls a cardboard file from a shelf under the gurney, opens the folder, the flashlight illuminating a black-and-white police photo of Ludlow's chest: it's as if some beast ripped out his lungs in a gaping cavity of blood and bluish intestines. Monk turns away. "Sorry, but look, this is what I wanted to show you." Karen holds another photograph in the flashlight beam, a six-pack of Hamm's beer bottles on the curb. "This is what Mr. Ludlow was killed for." She covers the young man's sleeping face.

The woman leads Monk to another draped gurney. "This is Darrell Posey." She gently unveils the sheet from the face: a heavyset black man, short-cropped Afro, cheeks still puffy with baby fat. "I don't have to look in their dossiers, I know 'em all, talk to 'em every night. Darrell was shot seven times for stealing a radio."

Karen's at the third gurney and pulls back the sheet: a young black male, eyes closed, but his jaw is fractured and purple, caked blood still under the large, flat nose. "This is Michael Adams. Twelve years old. Shot three times. Didn't steal anything, just throwing rocks at the police."

Monk stares at her dark eyes shimmering beneath their blue visor: what did that old hoodoo say about shades? "There's plenty more. Ellis, stole a box of diapers. Shortridge ran from the police. There's Owens, drunk and belligerent. Flores, in the wrong place at the wrong time. Elliot, Jones, Whitmore. All he did was stomp on a police car hood. Must be about half a hundred now, they'll be a hundred more unless this madness stops pretty damn soon."

The flashlight illumines a clipboard with a sheaf of papers hanging by a chain near the metal doors. "You have to keep a record," her blue-tinted eyes seem to penetrate him, "otherwise all their pain and passing is for nothing."

They pass through two heavy swinging doors, this room as dark as the first, but Monk feels a slight warming temperature. "This is the autopsy lab. Don't worry, nothing to see, everyone's put away for the night. Watch your step as we cross our little river here, follow me." The flashlight angles down at the floor, a stainless-steel gutter runs across the threshold, water gently sluicing through the channel. Monk steps over the water, following her. The sting of formaldehyde and bleach burns his nose and Monk frowns. "Smells, huh? I'm used to it." Now Monk can see the long metallic autopsy tables, and the sinks and spigots and pipes that drain into the metal channels that bisect the tile floor. "Getting warmer, isn't it? Good."

Karen unlatches a heavy steel door and they step into the next room; Monk can feel the warmth inside. The woman shines the flashlight around: a large cinder-block gray room, windowless like the others. Two heavy, blackened iron carts on wheels in the corner; long iron hooks and poles standing in another corner; a row of heavy silver steel buckets lining a wall, and in the center of the room, a cement-block housing about the size of a car, with a clamped iron hatchway. "This is the cremation station."

"They all get cremated?"

"No, but quite a few. All the John and Jane Does end up here. Folks have six months to identify 'em, or into the flames they go. Most of my friends out there," she points to the rooms they've passed, "their folks won't be able to afford a funeral, so the city will cremate their loved ones and return the remains. We do offer a few reasonable coffins, nothing fancy. They're in the next room." She shakes her head. "Fire up there, and fire below, huh? Ashes to ashes."

Karen unlatches another heavy, heat-resistant door, and leads Monk into the next room. The flashlight beam sweeps over stacked rows of caskets. Urns of different sizes and colors and shapes line wooden shelves against the walls. "We call this one the 'Little Angel,'" patting a stack of white coffins, each casket about three feet long. "Can't keep 'em in stock with all these new-fangled drive-by shootings." She shakes her visored head. "Back in the forties and fifties, we'd get gangster stiffs in here, but they only shot their own. These days, damn kids spraying bullets from cars, not aiming, too lazy to even get out of the damn car, get some exercise, aim for God's sake, take some pride. Just unprofessional.

"Well, here's the office and the back door." She opens a gray-painted door with white frosted glass. The flashlight beam illuminates metal shelving with stacks of neatly folded and taped small brown paper bags, hundreds of them, each affixed with a typed white label. "Those are the ashes, I should say the remains. We keep 'em here one year, then if they're not claimed, they all get buried in one big grave over on some county land out near Alameda." The flashlight glows over a desk with a newspaper, thermos, coffee cup, small bottle of whiskey, and a shot glass. Karen smiles as she watches Monk stare at the paper sack on the desk. "Don't be alarmed, that's just my lunch bag," chuckling. "Would you like a shot of whiskey for the road, honey?"

"No thanks."

"Sure? You may need some strong spirits with you out there tonight. Well, be careful. They're burning down the town. No offense, but sometimes I wonder if it isn't a Negro cultural thing, all this burning, I mean. I read in *Life* magazine, I do a lot of reading down here when I'm not talking to Willie and Michael and my other friends that pass through the office. Well anyway, I read that every hundred years, you know, they torch everything in Africa, burn all the fields, raze the homelands, villages, everything, trying to strip away history, maybe that's what's going on out in the streets, Negroes burning away a history that hasn't been too kind to them, can't say I entirely blame them, white men do the same, don't they? With their bulldozers and money? Well, I warned you I talk too much, just a lonely old bat with my quiet friends. You read the paper?" Karen picks the newspaper from the desk, her flashlight shining on the front page. Monk shakes his head. "Today's *Herald Examiner*. Says five international scientific teams just discovered the age of the universe. Fourteen billion years. Now they know when the big bang banged. I'm afraid if they know when the universe began, you see, then soon they're going to figure out when the universe is going to end. All that fire and death outside in the streets, maybe that's the beginning of the end. Here's the back door. You sure you want to go out there?"

"It's the way home. I have a kind of . . . human map . . . but some of the pieces are missing."

"Human map, huh? Well, you must've come here for a reason. Only the dead pass through my door and you're not dead." She unlatches the iron lock, slides a steel bar, and opens the heavy steel door: outside is a rectangle of starlight, a parked black van stenciled LOS ANGELES COUNTY CORONER, a barbed-wire fenced alley that angles back toward Compton Avenue. "Be careful out there. Pleasure to meet you, Mr. Monk."

"You too, Karen." Monk shakes her still icy hand, Karen's ebony eyes twinkling beneath the visor's blue plastic, then she disappears behind the closing door, a last wisp of white smock fluttering like a trailing ghost, gone, a heavy bolt snapping closed.

26

Nobody dared fight the flames. Attempts to do so were prevented by menacing gangs. —Tacitus, the Annals, the Burning of Rome

National Guard battalions and police detour cars north, south, east, and west, away from the riots; the city's been garrisoned, sealed off . . . Parker and the Guard have designated the Los Angeles River and other concrete bifurcations as firebreaks once the holocaust begins . . . Contingency plans, on the governor's orders, are set in place: a vast swath of fires that might rage for miles west to Crenshaw Boulevard, north to Manchester Avenue, and south to Imperial, until the inner city is ruins and ashes . . .

Police cruisers block Compton Avenue. Cops siphon away a trickle of cars with flashlights below a hand-painted sign propped against a patrol car: TURN LEFT OR GET SHOT. A phalanx of cops in riot gear marches down the avenue. Monk slinks along the shadow line of brick walls: the cityscape to the west glows with infernal heat, a great shroud of black smoke and ash glowers above rooftops, blotting out the night.

Monk's rushed, swallowed by sweating bodies, a sea of angry shouting faces, raised pipes and bottles and bricks, wielding signposts torn from concrete like metal flags emblazoned STOP, YIELD, ONE WAY. He's pushing against the mob. He can't remember the name of the street, the last route he'd glimpsed on El Tirili's secret arteries south toward the harbor and Karmann: now the wall of bodies sweeps him back into 103rd.

This is the edge of the world. This is Charcoal Alley.

Darkness, visibility is only a few yards ahead in swirling ashes and banks of smoke. Every rooftop and store facade burned black; flames whip from doors, windows, parapets. Ahead, the only light is probing flashlight beams, or searchlight cones sweeping from helicopters above. Screams and shouts as men bump past Monk: he's pressed against baking brick walls: the asphalt beneath his soles is hot, melting. Down the street, black-and-white police helmets shimmer. Arcs of foaming tear-gas canisters sail through smoke, ping and roll between rioters. The crowd surges and he's pushed across the street.

Monk pulls up his wet shirt, presses it against his choking mouth, a billy club whooshing past his face as he springs away and into the shadows between two windows churning black smoke. An iron fire escape has peeled away, unmoored from its burning wall, angled across the avenue like a glowing skeleton. The great mob seems to slow, mired in darkness. Beyond the rioters, guardsmen and riot police hold their positions in massed rows, shoulder to shoulder across the burning avenue.

Copters scud above, searchlight-knifing ruby-glowing tunnels into crowds below as the officers and guardsmen hold the line. No one's moving beneath the circling helicopters' light beams and the rooftop flames above. Charcoal Alley glows before Monk, a hellish corridor of flames and smoke: more than the heat and terror, he can feel it, like some kind of force that's drawn him to this American ground zero.

Beyond the rooftops, burning palm trees glow like giant torches. Monk staggers along sidewalks that are invisible, carpeted by smoke. A news van lies on its side, flames roaring from its engine and wheel wells. He shakes his head: *The cops aren't after rioters, they're using the Guard to burn down the city with tear-gas bombs . . . my city, my graffiti, the signs and secret language . . . silencing voices in flames.*

A phalanx of riot police is pressed back as rioters boil forward. *Get out of here! Back to Defiance Street,* Monk's thinking, when gunshots and screams erupt near him: a cop, visor torn, face bloody with bits of twinkling broken glass, lurches past. Monk bolts past the charred hulk of a car and looks down in horror: a naked woman, cheek pressed into hot asphalt, pink taffeta dress burned away, only a singed hem fused to her belly, palm twisted around in terrible contortion, pale, ash-flecked thighs spread as if in some vain supplication . . . no, Christ, it's just a mannequin. Monk gazes across the street: a department store, gutted; burning mannequins watch the flames from shattered display windows. A white mannequin spills from the broken window, arms sprawled on the sidewalk as if to escape; its upturned male face stares at Monk, auburn wig burning, lips melting down into a toxic frown, his scorched eyes riveted on his companion smoldering at Monk's feet, perhaps a flash of anger or only flame's light in his dripping cobalt eyes: *I told you not to go out there.*

Monk pushes past three men kicking an officer, baton clattering over the curb. In the distance, rioters hold sputtering flares like crimson torches. Waves of heat refract the night, wavering everything into ghost lines. Monk's neck stings in agony and he looks up: a burning telephone pole, its creosote dripping in fiery black gobs from its crossbeams, melted wires spooled over the pavement, arcing in electric-blue bursts around the mob.

National Guard 1st Reconnaissance Squadron and riot police march south through the smoke of Graham Avenue, which ends at Charcoal Alley. Above in darkness, helicopters buoy, invisible, mining their searchlights through smoke and tear gas below. A gas bomb bursts. Monk is knocked to the pavement, men scattering over him. Shoes grind down on his thigh and smash his hand.

Police and guardsmen stand in phalanxes five men deep, an armored blockade across Graham Avenue, cutting off any escape south. Rifle barrels, face masks, black-and-white helmets glimmer with reflected flames. Around Monk, crowds lob bricks down the street, toward the gathering forces behind them. Across the avenue, the rear of a two-story brick-front collapses in a rushing flume of cloud and ash.

From the south, Beach Street ends at Charcoal Alley. Convoys from the 18th Armored Cavalry and the 40th Armored Division line both sides of the avenue. Guard jeep headlights illuminate rioters pushing through Beach Street, skirmishing in a relentless fury that unbalances cops and Guard.

Somewhere in the darkness, echoing down from flaming storefronts, invisible loudspeakers blare up and down the cindered street: *Burn, baby, burn . . .*

A volley of gunfire, then screams. The mob crests forward, fists and weapons raised, into officers and guardsmen huddled in flanks. Police grapple and pound nightsticks into crowds as Monk tries to skirt past. He sees a flash of white helmet and a blurring nightstick as he's clubbed across the face and crumples on the sidewalk. Monk's world is the baton as it rises over his face, poised to whip down and crush his brain—no more fantasies now: no more enchantresses, poet-gangsters, muses, fortune-cookie spies, hoodoo seers, monstrous chimeras . . . Hands grab the baton as rioters pull the cop to the ground, guard mask and uniform disappearing under kicking boots and smoke. A wall of men shout and surge forward, bricks, bottles hailing into police shields, pushing cops back. Monk's up, agonizing pain in his mouth as he spits blood, *Fuck, I'm gonna die here—*

Where the fuck is Beach Street? Monk limps down the sidewalk overflowing with darting men. A street sign droops, melted and warped into the pavement like an iron serpent. The Guard and police push rioters east into the burning vice of 103rd. Men fan past him. "Three for one! Three for one!" they chant, fists raised.

Monk's reached Beach Street North as it ends in the mael-strom of Charcoal Alley. The 106th Infantry and police troop down Beach Street, pushing into 103rd Street. Cops and the 18th Armored Cavalry march east through Charcoal Alley, pushing Monk and the rioters back. Choppers rake searchlights behind the gathering forces. In the distance, the clanking iron treads of tanks gnaw through heated asphalt as their terrible turrets roll closer.

Sir Soul's deep DJ voice, dark as tonight's moonless holocaust, still echoes between the sirens and shouts: *Burn, baby, burn.*

"Fuckin' nigger!" A cop smashes his shield into Monk's face, jabs his nightstick into his ribs as Monk collapses. The cop turns, flailing his baton into the crowd. Panicked legs and boots kick and trample past Monk.

"Get the fuck off me!" Monk's screaming as he blindly kicks and punches the rushing bodies above him. "I don't want to die!" He claws a black face, elbows someone's chest in panic, finally pulling himself up the baked concrete steps of a burned storefront. He staggers to his feet: Levi's ripped in shreds, knees covered in ash-caked blood. There is no light east for him, only the screaming, dark faces of the rioters who flee into their terrible, gathering fates. Down North Beach Street, then east and west like an armored, seething crucifix, battalions of police and National Guard march beneath the pyres of Charcoal Alley.

Monk squints up into the burning vault of night: only orange cinders and white ash escape, floating into starless copper skies: then the towering wall and roof frame of the gutted Beach Street Liquor Store, flames whipping from buckling trusses and joists, groans as bricks topple in flamy arcs; a blazing wave shudders and collapses down toward Monk. *Should've known the city would get me herself*—Monk covers his face with his bleeding arms as the rubble inferno buries him beneath its flaming tomb, only a great black cloud of smoke sparkling with incandescent embers roils into the glowering pall over Charcoal Alley.

27

The morning sunshine warms his gaunt face: it feels like God's hand caressing his cheeks, as if some kind of benediction finally flows over him and the destroyed city, after so many nights of fire, blood, hopelessness, incarceration. The rioters have vanished.

He walks along 119th Street, the sun's rays slanting in pillars between the shabby tenements and apartment houses. All the fire trucks, police cruisers, National Guard jeeps and trucks are only a few blocks away. To the east, a pillar of smoke rises into the morning sky, a churning obelisk to mark the past six days of fire. He shakes his head: *And on the seventh day He rested.*

The facade of the stucco apartment building is riddled with bullet holes, chips of plaster crunching under his pointy brown Florsheims. The two windows above the double doors are shattered, the shards of glass in the panes glinting in the sunlight. Four huge black men guard the doors above the steps, rifles ready in their hands: their black suits and bow ties starkly contrast with their purple fezzes with crescents and stars.

The Fruit of Islam glare down at him as he drags his weary feet up the stairs still littered with blasted chunks of stucco and concrete. Now two of the giants grin. "Welcome, brother." Shifting the rifles in their huge arms, they open the bullet-pocked doors and he steps inside.

He stands in a great lobby. Black men in black suits and bow ties work at long tables cluttered with telephones, piles of paper, pamphlets. There are blue-lit wall sconces, purple doors, bronze tapestries, but the lobby has been strafed with gunfire: walls, tapestries, doors are splintered and gouged with bullet holes; dust, bits of plaster and wood, copies of *Muhammad Speaks* stamped with boot prints are scattered across the scarred wooden floorboards.

"Welcome to the temple of Islam, my son." Two men approach him. A hunched old man in a black suit, but, unlike everyone else, a bright blue bow tie, gazes up at him; his milky chocolate eyes look like they're a thousand years old. A tall, rail-thin man stands at his side, his hand propping the old man's elbow for balance.

"Man, they shot the hell out of this place."

"The police, the white man is always at war with the temple of Islam," the old man speaks softly, "but they cannot destroy the temple, any more than they can stop the Negro's destiny toward Islam and unshackled freedom."

"Yeah, well, I know all about the goddamn cops and the white man, excuse my language, sir."

"Allah has brought you to us today. Why do you think you are here now, my son?"

"I wanna," he licks his lips nervously, looking around the shattered temple, the powerful, proud black men with rifles, "I wanna join, be like you, a Muslim or what you call it—"

"A fruit of Islam." The old man beams, extends his shriveled hand. "I am Elijah Muhammad." They shake hands. "Allah be praised, He has guided another brother from the darkness to the light of the Prophet. What is your name, my son?"

He licks his lips as if unsure of his name; there's a nervous anxiety in his thin body, as if he's always controlling an instinct toward flight. "Marquette Bonds."

The tall man leans over, whispers something in Muhammad's ear. The old man's wizened eyes flare open as he nods. The two men stare at him for a moment; now they can see something more than nerves and restlessness in the young man's thin, worn face: it is a sad intensity that radiates from him, the haunted gravity of those who have been swept into forces beyond their control. "You are the one . . . the young man whose fate sparked this holy uprising against our white oppressors. Allah has sent you, my son! Allah has marked you like the prophets of old, to bear the torch of truth!" Muhammad nods, squeezes Bonds's bony shoulders. "We welcome you to the fold, to the holy love of Islam, to the sanctuary of our temple. Mr. Shabazz here will direct you to Miss Nefertiti, and your new life shall begin. Praise Allah!"

"Thank you, Mr. Muhammad." Shabazz leads Marquette Bonds past a guard and up a shadowy staircase. A few steps down a narrow hallway washed with sunlight through a blown-out window, then Shabazz opens a white, bullet-riddled door.

Inside the room is a printing press in the corner, bookshelves, piles and stacks of newspapers and *Muhammad Speaks* pamphlets. A statuesque, beautiful black woman glides in her black Muslim abaya gown toward Bonds as the door closes behind him.

"I am Laylah Nefertiti." Her green eyes, framed by the long, tight braids of her black hair, seem to shine like gems.

"Marquette Bonds." He licks his lips, gazing around the room. Beyond the broken windows, he can see a wedge of the gray tenement across the street, and he realizes these are the windows above the main entrance of the temple that he'd gazed up at, minutes ago out in the street.

"Welcome to the temple of Islam, Mr. Bonds." She holds a book in her hands. "This is the Quran."

"The what?"

"The Quran, the Holy Bible. This is yours, to keep." Nefertiti presses the book into his hands. "You must read the first verse, called a *sura*. It will reveal how Allah has guided you to His holy path. Please sit down," as she indicates a chair against the other bullet-gouged wall. "You will read the first *sura* to me out loud, then we shall talk, and I will show you how to pray."

Marquette nods, squinting down at the strange book in his hands, and walks toward the chair near the printing press.

Laylah Nefertiti turns, glides to the shattered window, and gazes out. Below, 119th Street lies in shadows and slanted sunlight. To the east, two columns of black smoke taper into the August skies. Down on the corner, the signals are still not working. A cop car, lights flashing red, barrels through the intersection and disappears. She listens as Marquette Bonds reads the Quran, slowly mumbling, sounding out some of the strange words. Beyond the window, a diesel engine, perhaps a bus, rumbles faintly as it accelerates somewhere down 119th. Watching the tower of smoke rising into the eastern morning, she suddenly remembers that other young black man, Monk. Was he still out there in the rubble and police barricades, or—Laylah closes her eyes, silently prays not to Allah but to God—had he finally made it back home?

28

The black void of night burns into a red wall of flames: now a crimson membrane of light flutters, blinking to daylight as he opens his eyes. An olive-green canvas tarp stretches over the day, masking sunlight beyond. He props himself up on an elbow, wincing in pain, rubs his stinging eyes, looks around: a long tent, a row of cots filled with mostly young black men. Two or three plastic bags of plasma hang from wires hooked in the tent's cover, IV tubes like red vines coiling down into black forearms dangling from cots. He slowly twists, one shoe on the ground as he pushes himself into a seated position, his body racked in pain. His hand brushes sticky, clotting blood from his wild hair. Now he can see, down the rows of cots, one old man with both arms in slings mumbling to himself, and, near the tent's drawn-open triangular flap door, a young black man, his torso taped with bloody bandages. Even the ceiling's bleeding, two great scars of red slashed above— no, his eyes focusing, it's a cross, a red cross.

"My notebook," Monk whispers, his hand clutching at his stomach: it's there, his fingers rubbing the metal spirals, now he can feel it under his filthy, ragged shirt. He looks up. A National Guardsman stands there, a pistol in his hip holster.

"Sit tight. You'll be transferred to a hospital soon."

"No," Monk rasps, "I have to go home."

"You don't look too good. Maybe a concussion. Should have a doctor look at you."

Monk concentrates, his head throbbing in agony, trying to remember. "Where am I? One hundred and third Street?"

"Wilmington and Willowbrook."

"Bus . . . are the buses running?"

"Just some of the main lines."

"Imperial?"

"Yeah."

Monk staggers to his feet. "I know the way."

"Well, you ain't under arrest, but you look pretty clobbered to me."

Concentrating on his red Keds, Monk limps toward the flap of daylight past the rows of cots. Near the exit, a young black man, his face and jaw swaddled in bloody bandages, only his swollen eyes visible, glares up at him, fixing him, accusing him in silence, rage, and despair.

Emerging from the tent, Monk squints into the daylight. Ahead is Wilmington: only a few blocks south, then he'll reach Imperial. He staggers past guard jeeps and police cars. Two cops, shotguns balanced on their thighs, watch him as he hobbles toward the intersection.

•

The bus, its canary-yellow RTD Freeway Flyer paint and grimy silver skin gleaming in the sun, rumbles west on Imperial. The seats are empty, only five or six people in the last few rows. Monk slouches alone in the last seat, the notebook gripped in his fists, gazing out the dusty window: a patina of ash seems baked on the glass, tinting Imperial and the passing side streets into a gray netherworld. A silent, eerie panorama of visions through the window, like bombed-out ruins: charred, fire-gutted stores; scorched framing and wall shards like steps that ascend in vain from the streets; piles of rubble and debris.

In the late-afternoon light, each passing signal blinks red, Imperial a gauntlet of intersections barricaded by cop cars and National Guard jeeps. *The cops couldn't stop the riot*, Monk's thinking. *They needed the fucking Guard. Parker and the police . . . they're gonna lie about all this, a big fucking whitewash to cover the professor's failure.*

Past Compton Avenue, the bus lurches to the curb and stops, its hydraulic doors sighing open. An old black woman, hunched in a green, filthy shawl, steps inside and sits behind the driver. A waft of hot air and decaying stench fills the bus as the doors fold closed and the driver pulls away. Through the gray window, Monk can see a dead dog in the gutter as National Guard bulldozers scrape and claw piles of debris through the street.

He's thinking of the Reefer Man's mural on the abandoned house on Seventieth, the masterpiece that someone, or some force, wanted him to see, perhaps compelled him by the sign or spell scrawled in his notebook. The great *pintura* of cities past and future, of graffiti bound by time: its stories, its history and dreams are shaped—and shape—each generation of the city's people . . . and the papyrus, the word, that is bound by space: once written it cannot be unwritten; the word migrates from city to city, civilization to civilization, creating new worlds.

A street sign passes: Success Avenue. "Fuck," Monk whispers to himself: the street he remembers now, the secret passage on El Tirili's back. He opens the notebook, finds Standard's and El Tirili's conjoined maps, and draws out the routes: Compton Avenue south, 102nd west, Success Avenue—suddenly he remembers it all, the pen scratching deftly: Mary, Zamora, 107th east, the alley down to Hooper and beyond. Monk's fist squeezes the metal spirals of his notebook: somehow it's all inside now, a book of graffiti and signs, secret grids of the city . . . the stories of the voiceless, the dreams hidden in shadows . . . somehow he has to make the world see it, read it, so the truth behind the darkness and destruction won't be lost forever.

The hot bus is filled with the cloying, rancid stench of decay and death; Monk grimaces and breathes out of his mouth. The bus grinds past Central Avenue, barricaded by Guard jeeps: blocks north are the jazz clubs. *Strange meeting Mr. Hurricane at the Congo Club.* All those memories of his father . . . *Mr. Cool . . . fuck that, the father ain't the son . . . to be cool while your city burns is to play the fool* . . . there has to be a way to get them to see what he sees in the notebook.

Stanford Avenue rumbles past; just a few more blocks west to the Harbor Freeway, then south to home, to Karmann and the baby—their baby. The bus veers to the shoulder as an ambulance screams past, then the driver accelerates back into his lane. Monk can see the face of the white driver in his long mirror, his eyes glancing warily back at his handful of riders in the rear shadows. The reek of rot and death, the sticky vinyl seats and hot, stifling air make him dizzy; he tries to open the gray window but it's locked. He closes his eyes and remembers the morgue, the coroner lady, the cool, silent rooms and the smell of antiseptic chemicals and formaldehyde . . . the sheets slowly pulled from the cadavers . . . all those black and brown faces . . . men, women . . . boys . . . like sleepers that would never wake . . . *the notebook . . . make the living listen, or all this death is meaningless.*

The bus stops at San Pedro as a black man, a few rows up from Monk, tinkles nickels into the glass machine next to the driver and steps down to the curb. The doors fold closed and Monk braces as the warm, stinking air seeps inside. Beyond the window, Monk watches as young black men, shirtless in the late-afternoon heat, carry bricks from the burned-out rubble of storefronts. They lug the bricks, stacked heavily in their sinewy, sweating arms, to piles on the street corners as National Guardsmen, rifles in hand, watch over them. The bus lurches away, Monk's thoughts dark: black men working like slaves as the Guard, like masters, look on; they'd get a penny a brick, make these Negroes clean up their own mess . . . nothing will change.

Monk watches Main Street glide past the dying light filtering through his ash-streaked window. One more block and the bus will weave onto the Harbor Freeway and rumble south toward the water and Karmann. Monk turns away from the window, exhausted, tired of it all, and shuts his burning eyes. *Yeah, nothing will change.* If you rebuild the city, raze the ghettos for decent houses and parks, Parker and the white power structure will cry, "Crime pays! Don't reward these violent Negroes for riot and pillage!" Monk grins cynically: rebellion is in the eye of the beholder. The only real change will be more fear. The cops, the TV news, the gangs: they'd all seize on this fire and death, brand it with their own propaganda; somehow he must make them see the real rebellion, the secret history of brutality and injustice bannered on the walls and testified in his notebook . . . the flames might shine a light on the people in the shadows, on the stories written on the skin of the city's own walls . . . or his city will be only the first spark in a conflagration across the land . . . open their eyes, make them see the writing on the walls.

•

Monk hears brakes squeaking and opens his eyes. *Must've dozed off.* The bus lurches to the curb at a bus stop at the corner of Signal Street. Monk squints out the window: Harbor Boulevard.

Monk limps painfully down the aisle of the bus. His cheek and neck are smeared with ashes. His T-shirt and Levi's are torn and filthy: dark, dried blood is caked on his elbow and knee beneath the ripped jeans; dust and ashes fleck his kinky, long hair, his red Keds sneakers crusted with mud and plaster, dragging singed laces. He digs through his pockets, fishes out folded notes and papers: Jax and Sofia's registration and her driver's license. And a strange dollar bill that he hands to the white driver: reddish paper, *One Skrill* printed in blurred script, an oval portrait of a silhouetted man with a huge Afro. The driver looks at the bill, squints up at Monk. "Heard of these, never saw one before. My supervisor thinks they're rumors." The driver folds the bill into his shirt pocket and swivels the hydraulic steel shaft next to the steering wheel: the doors fold open with a sigh.

"Thanks, man." Monk steps down and onto the sidewalk, tucking the license and registration into his pocket, like spells that will one day conjure them up again. Sofia and Jax will find him; he's almost sure he gave them the pier's number back in their loft. They saved his ass at least a couple of times, and maybe he had stopped the cops from identifying the VW bug. Monk grins, picturing Sofia's eyes full of mischief behind the steering wheel, waving her cigarette as she railed against the system, like an unhinged Latin revolutionary turned getaway driver . . .

The notebook feels heavy in his hand, spiral wires snapped and sprung, pages wet, ripped, falling out, but most of his notes and crabbed ink words are still legible. Monk staggers south on Signal Street. His knee and elbow throb in agony. To his left and right, the concrete estuary of East Channel and the railroad tracks are soothing, deserted barriers: no cops, rioters, buildings in flames. A few blocks ahead, looming past Signal Street, the tin rooftops of the Crescent Warehouse Company shine in the setting sunlight: he can already see some of the rusted iron cranes and masts of the shipyards. Soon he'll smell the salted sea breezes. Exhausted, he walks closer to the harbor, to Slip Thirteen, to home and Karmann.

•

Near the end of the dock, Monk looks down, steps past one of Karmann's green rent-party invitation cards, stamped with a muddy boot print. He pulls his aching body up the gangplank, leaning on the railing; below, the blue Pacific scintillates and sloshes against the pylons of the pier, echoing from the iron containers of Boxville—home—that loom above him in rusted stacks and blocks. Midway up the plank he stops; his ribs ache but then he feels his face flush with blood: his mind races with clashing, jangled emotions—exhilaration, pride, devotion, scraped and battered to his soul but electric with the joy of being alive. He stands inside the open hatchway of a Matson container, a room off the lower decks, away from port side, west toward the infinite Pacific below.

The room is lit in halos from blue and yellow bulbs strung along the welded roof. On the upholstered car seat bench under the blowtorched window, a black girl he doesn't know sleeps, curled into a crumpled ball. He shakes her shoulder and her eyes pop open in startled alarm. "Go home. Time to go." She bolts up, staggers through empty beer bottles gleaming on the floor. Monk sees someone curled up in the corner on a mattress, half covered in an army blanket and a jacket, snoring. Monk kicks a shoe dangling off the mattress. The blanket stirs, the jacket slips down as Cooky rubs his palms against his face and blinks his bleary, bloodshot eyes, shaking his thin face at the figure looming above him under a blue bulb of light.

"What the fuck?" Cooky sits up, trying to focus his eyes.

"Time to go home, Cooky."

"Monk, is that you?" He stands, wobbly, still dressed in wrinkled pants and shirt. "Shit, what happened to you?"

"Go home. Get your fix before you get sick." Monk turns, ducks through a hatchway, and trudges up a steel stairwell; his knee explodes in pain as he limps to the top step.

He steps into the double-wide Sea-Land container. A string of yellow bulbs wash the room in a lemon glow. On the old couch, Marcus stares into the Zenith TV. The volume's turned off, silent black-and-white images in flickering static: shots of burned-out stores, fire-gutted buildings, National Guard jeeps and trucks on the streets. Marcus scratches his woolly beard and gazes up as Monk steps closer.

"Party's over, Marcus."

"Monk? Man, I didn't recognize you." Marcus sighs, pushes up from the couch. "Fuck, what happened to you?"

"Where's Dalynne?"

"Shit, she gone, been back and forth couple of times, but the bitch been gone for a while now. You been caught up in this shit?" Marcus points to the TV.

"Go home to Dalynne."

"We was only waitin' around to see you get home safe, nigger." Marcus scowls, scratches his wild beard as Monk turns away. "All right, I'm leavin', fuck it," Marcus mumbles as he grabs a half-full bottle of Monk's Courvoisier cognac.

Monk limps through the iron chambers like a stranger, a re-animated corpse in torn clothes, ash-and-blood-smeared skin under the garish strings of rainbow bulbs. On a red hammock strung from the riveted walls between two portholes, someone's lumped in its folds, snoring under a baseball cap. As Monk lifts the cap, a thin young black man he's never seen before stares up at him. "Get out." Monk can hear the Pacific lapping beyond the windows. Empty beer bottles and cans and plastic cups litter the floors and throw pillows and small tables. Monk stares at the black telephone mounted on the iron wall, its receiver suspended on its uncoiled line like a strange, dead pendulum clock: he resets the receiver in its plastic cradle.

In the WestCon container room, Monk kicks two bodies snoring, covered in blankets on the floor. Near the corner, in the light of a torched window, Slim-Bone and Felonius are hunched over a card table, still drinking cans of Brew 102, concentrating on their game of Ghetto Monopoly, a board game Monk made for a project before dropping out of his first year at Los Angeles Junior College. They slide their game markers—a tiny boom-box radio and a six-pack of beer—along the squares of blighted, condemned real estate: Grape Street, Jordan Downs, Willowbrook, trying to avoid the frequent Go to Jail squares when you must draw from the stack of orange cards that reveal no Get out of Jail Free cards, only further calamities and setbacks.

They look up from the game board. "Shit, here comes trouble," Slim-Bone rasps as Monk hovers like a specter over the table.

"Man, you fucked-up." Felonius shakes his head. "What happened to you?" His gold tooth gleams in the dusty slant of sunlight through the iron window.

"You okay, Monk?" Slim-Bone grins. "Man, we was worried about you, brother."

"You have to go, Felonius," Monk says. Then, in a softer tone: "You too, Slim-Bone."

"We ain't finished with our game." Felonius sips his beer.

Monk grabs the can and throws it against an iron wall.

"Shit," Felonius stands, "who the fuck do you—"

"Come on, le's go," Slim-Bone interrupts, grabbing his beer and wobbling to his feet.

"Yeah, fuck you, nigger." They swagger past Monk and disappear through a hatchway.

Monk steps from the ribbed walls of the WestCon box onto the open deck of a lower container's roof. He makes his way painfully up the welded boat ramp toward the rusted roof of an Atlas Maritime container. The sound of a high-pitched motor revs and whines above him in the sunlight.

Lil' Davey's on his red Vespa scooter, burning rubber, whipping the scooter in circles of black rubber tracks around the axis of his extended booted leg. The Vespa screeches, brakes, stops as Monk limps up. "Jesus, what happened to your ass?" Lil' Davey says over the whine of the scooter engine.

"Get out of here."

"I'll split in a while. I'm meetin' this chick down at the pier later."

"Get the fuck out."

Lil' Davey stands, all six foot six of him, glaring. There is something different, a hard edge in Monk's dark eyes. Lil' Davey shrugs, revs the throttle. "You *slay* me, man," grinning as the Vespa peels away, whines and clatters down the steel ramp toward the docks below.

Monk walks slowly toward the southern edge of the Atlas container's rooflines and crosses a plank that angles up to the corrugated summit of another container. He stands atop the apex of Boxville, the southern Matson container with its rooftop observation deck.

The sunset burnishes the observation deck in copper light. A plaintive saxophone, soft, scratchy jazz music, floats up from somewhere below. Monk stares down at the white plastic table with its overflowing ashtrays of Karmann's Kents, smiling at her red lipstick still traced and glistening on the filters. At the welded iron rail, he looks down into the Pacific lapping below. A few ships, freighters, and cargo tankers loom beyond the harbor, under a luminous sky, heavy and torpid in the water, stacked with containers like floating castles.

He gazes into the setting sun, into the infinite glow that bathes the Pacific in a crimson incandescence, fusing the sky and sea into a molten plain. Beyond San Pedro, tapers of black smoke still worm into the skies above the fire-raked city.

Monk walks across the deck toward the saxophone's soft call and the deep throbs of bass. Pausing at the metal steps, he gazes at the patchwork of thin pipes for handrails and stairs that descend diagonally, welded against the iron wall. He grips the notebook tightly in his fist, its spirals digging into his palm, as his other hand finds the cool rail. Below, through an open hatchway, the music fades away, now only the muted scratching of the needle as the vinyl circles below, her final record spinning closer to the center, like an invisible thread that gently draws him down to her, down to Karmann.

ACKNOWLEDGMENTS

Graffiti Palace would literally not exist, except as phantom bits of memory in my computer and my mind, if it weren't for my agent and friend, Bonnie Nadell. This was a much shaggier and longer manuscript, but she worked hard with me to shape and create my vision. Mentor, advocate, and dispenser of tough love to corral word-drunk writers; thank you, Bonnie. I'm also tremendously grateful to Sean McDonald, publisher of MCD / Farrar, Straus and Giroux. Sean has been tireless and fearless in his love of and belief in my novel. There are many publishing houses that would shy away from controversial and different books like *Graffiti Palace*, but Sean is dedicated to fostering new voices in writing. Sean's contributions to editing went way beyond prose; he helped me creatively with several key ideas and themes, watching over every step: from punctuation to fact-checking Los Angeles streets, from razor-sharp character and plot tweaks to book cover, and so much more; thanks, Sean. I'd also like to thank Alison Strauss, who was the first to see something in my writing and plucked my chapter from the submissions pile for Bonnie to read. James Draney and Daniel Mehrian were wonderful helpers, reading, noting, and discussing drafts of the book with Bonnie and me. At

FSG, Rob Sternitzky and Jackson Howard worked very hard on editing the drafts. Maya Binyam was great guiding me through the editing process. To Brian Gittis in the publicity department, and Jonathan Lippincott for the book's design: thank you.